FROM "SPRING'S PROMISE"

"You wouldn't . . . do anything . . . you're just trying to teach me a lesson," Felicia declared.

"Yes, a lesson. Many of them," Lord Neville agreed, and lowered his head and held her until she stopped struggling against his warm, sweet, moving mouth.

"That was the first one," he said. "By dawn, we'll have gotten to many more."

"You wouldn't," she breathed.

"Why?" he mused. "Because you'll blacken my name? Horrors. Or your father will challenge me to a duel? I'm an excellent shot and swordsman, from practice with so many irate fathers. No. I doubt you'll say a word. Your pride will not allow it. And I've no honor."

"Why?" she asked.

"Because that's the way I am," he answered.

And in Lord Nshe was about to d

D0949071

A LOVE FOR ALL SEASONS

Five stories by

Edith Layton

Ø

A SIGNET BOOK

SIGNET
Published by the Penguin Group
Penguin Books USA Inc., 375 Hudson Street,
New York, New York 10014, U.S.A.
Penguin Books Ltd, 27 Wrights Lane,
London W8 5TZ, England
Penguin Books Australia Ltd, Ringwood,
Victoria, Australia
Penguin Books Canada Ltd, 10 Alcorn Avenue,
Toronto, Ontario, Canada M4V 3B2
Penguin Books (N.Z.) Ltd, 182–190 Wairau Road,
Auckland 10, New Zealand

Penguin Books Ltd, Registered Offices:
Harmondsworth, Middlesex, England

First published by Signet, an imprint of New American Library,
a division of Penguin Books USA Inc.

First Printing, May, 1992
10 9 8 7 6 5 4 3 2 1

 REGISTERED TRADEMARK—MARCA REGISTRADA

Printed in the United States of America

"*Love, all alike, no season knows, nor clime,
Nor hours, days, months, which are the rags
of time . . .*"

—John Donne

Rough winds do shake the darling buds of May . . .

—William Shakespeare

SPRING'S PROMISE

It was a time for coming out and going forth in both the world of nature and man. After a long dismal winter, it seemed that everything was emerging, and it was a delightful thing to see. The buds, the unfurled leaves—newsprung green was in every leafy thing from the hedgerows to the meadows, where all the newborn sheep and foals rejoiced on the fresh lush green pastures.

And so it was more than odd, it was almost a crime against nature that such a lovely young thing as Miss Felicia Carstairs was returning in such a season— and so soon after she'd left, too. But so she did, coming straight back from London before her Season there was to have ended. She went from her coach to her house, and then the door shut behind her firmly. Everyone deemed it a shame. Because the squire's daughter was bright and beautiful, clever as she could hold together, and altogether one of the most winsome young pusses anyone had ever seen. Everyone in the village had assumed she'd go directly from her first Season in London to St. George's and then off on her newfound husband's arm—whoever that lucky chap might be—straight to his mansion somewhere else, so it might be years until they saw her again. Not that they saw her now.

She came home abruptly, in the midst of society's Little Season—and the countryside's most promising one, as well. Once there, there she stayed, not so much as sticking her adorably upturned nose out the door to watch the lilacs blooming. And anyone who knew her knew that in itself was almost as astonishing as her precipitous return.

Still, whatever her concerned neighbors might have feared, Miss Carstairs was not grieving. Or sulking. Or weeping. She was raging. That might have made them feel better had they known it. For that, at least, was much more like her.

"She doesn't say a thing about it, not a word," Mrs. Carstairs complained to her husband, three days after their daughter's precipitous return, "but if I mention his name, she goes rather white."

Her husband abruptly turned his head from the book he'd been trying to read. The polite, patently false, interested expression he'd put on while he'd half listened to his wife's constant verbal worrying at the subject of their daughter's behavior had vanished. His brown eyes were blazing.

"I had no notion!" he said angrily, tossing his book down and rising from their bed at once. "He was always so damned correct—at least when he was with us. Almost supernaturally so, now that I think on it, for he was a handsome enough rogue. I'd no idea he was as facile as he was handsome—or as untrustworthy, either. Well then, we shall just see about that, shall we, eh?"

"Not in the middle of the night," his wife said on a patient sigh, because for all her husband was seriously grieved, and doubtless capable of some violence, he looked very foolish pacing the bedchamber in agitation, looking for his boots, his pistol, or vengeance, with his nightshirt flapping about his knees. "And not because of anything the fellow did. That, I'm convinced of. Oh, do get back into bed, Hugh. It's because he didn't do anything improper that she's so chagrined—or so at least I suspect."

Her husband stopped in his tracks and gazed at her narrowly, a mixture of incomprehension and suspicion both writ large on his face.

Mrs. Carstairs sighed again.

"She fancied him, and he did seem to be courting her. Everyone thought it was a settled thing," she said. "Remember? And why shouldn't they? She could have had anyone, anyone. She was marked an Incomparable. And she chose him right off. Who could have guessed? I told you we'd be buying orange blossoms before long, and so I honestly thought we'd be," she said hollowly. "I even teased her about it, and we planned for the future—the reception and such," she confessed in a soft voice, as she plucked at the lace on her nightdress, gazing down, avoiding his eyes. "But I'm certain he never did a dishonorable thing, for if he had, he'd have asked for her hand. He is terribly correct, you know," she added, looking up at him earnestly. "Which was the problem," she went on glumly, "for I don't doubt that minx compromised him in some fashion—else why would he have offered for her, and so suddenly, too—when everyone knew he'd his eye on Felicia?"

"His eye, and not his hand?" her husband asked as he stood irresolute at the side of their bed.

"Oh, I'm quite sure of that," she answered before she breathed. "More's the pity."

"Oh, aye," he agreed as he clambered into bed again, now as crestfallen as she was, "for then I'd have marched him to the vicar double-quick, you can be sure. Not that I'm not tempted to do it anyway, mind," he added, taking up his book again.

"You can buy her anything she wants, Hugh," his wife said sadly, "and have done, always, now I think on it. Which may be part of the present difficulty, too, you know. But you can't buy her out of a broken heart."

"Aye, true," he grumbled, "but you've always been harsh with her, I suppose."

She flushed a little and looked away before she said softly, "But now I'm afraid of what she'll do. She's always had her way, and she wanted him so very much."

"Afraid?" he asked, a faint note of worry in his voice.

"Well, aren't you?" she asked.

"Oh. No, nonsense," he said a little too quickly. "She's reasonable, there's nothing she can do now, the deed's done. He'll be wed within weeks. The notice of the engagement's been in the *Times*, the invitations have gone out. She'll get over it, what else can she do?" he asked, avoiding her eye now as he pretended to read again.

She lay back and pretended to sleep, as they both thought of their darling daughter, Felicia, and what form her inevitable revenge—on the world—would take.

Felicia stopped staring into the looking glass. The answer wasn't there. She suspected the question never had been either. No, all she ever saw was the same thing: an oval of a face, ornamented with a pair of golden brown eyes, distinguished by a saucy nose, and framed by a great deal of brown hair to match her eyes. The matter of upturned lashes covering supposed mysteries in said eyes, shining tresses usually celebrated as silken, the promising lips, faintly blushing cheeks contrasting with porcelain white skin, and determined yet dimpled chin, she left to her admirers and fervently wished they'd leave it out of their poetry to her, too. Because most of them were bad poets, and her face, when all was said, was something she couldn't appreciate so much herself, since, she reasoned, she so seldom saw it. At least, she thought, glancing into the glass one last time, until recently, when she'd passed hours searching it for an answer.

But whether she only looked at her face or stood far enough away to see all of herself, and the bounty the abominable poets of her acquaintance appreciated mightily, but couldn't bring themselves to celebrate in verse because of her upbringing and theirs, she still couldn't see the answer. No matter, she thought impatiently, rising from a seat at her dressing table, she was done with looking for answers. There obviously were none that she could see.

He had danced courtesies on her, he'd spoken of the future—after he'd done presenting his past for her to approve and querying about hers. He'd danced with her at balls and sat with her at suppers, chatted with her at the theater and decorated the drawing room of her parents' rented town house all Season. And then he'd turned his coat and broad, well-tailored back on her, to offer for Miss Probisher. Plain, ineffectual, shy, and inane little Miss Probisher. Miss Probisher, the girl that appeared every spring Season, with the regularity, if not the glad welcome, of crocuses in the garden. Miss Probisher, such a fixture at every house party and ball that she went unnoticed as the background music played at them. Miss Probisher, who had gazed at Lord Jeremy Wallace, as if at the Annunciation, every time she'd seen him. Miss Probisher, who for reasons known only to himself and his Creator, would be his wife in a matter of days. Instead of herself, the much-feted, always celebrated, pretty, clever Miss Carstairs. Whom he'd said he loved. Well, Felicia admitted as she marched down the stairs, whom he had *as much* as said he'd loved.

It was unendurable.

But she was done with sulking and worrying, wondering at what it was in her that might have done it. She'd done with unworthy, spiteful reasonings as to how the unexpectedly sly Miss Probisher, or her father, had got him to do it. She was through with insane and fanciful imaginings as to why he'd done it, too. She tossed her head and straightened her slender shoulders as she went to join her parents for breakfast for the first time since she'd come home. She'd eighteen years in her cup, after all, it was time to be mature, to stop hiding and dwelling on what had happened.

Her father was very right in what he always said, she thought: She was a reasonable girl. No, as she was done with her first Season, however ignobly it had come to an end, it was time to use some of the worldly wisdom she'd acquired during it. It was time then, to show the entire world that none of it mattered a whit to her; she couldn't care less, it was too amusing to think she'd been affected in any way at

all, as if such a trifling thing could overset her. It
was time to have a marvelous time. A magnificent
time. It was time, as the young bucks said when they
thought she couldn't hear them, to go to Hell in a
handcart with herself. To show just how little she
cared what anyone thought, of course.

Her cheeks were flushed and her eyes were sparkling as she came into the breakfast room.

"You look wonderful, my love!" her mother cried
in glad surprise when she saw her.

"Just like your old self, puss," her father said
approvingly, rising to take her hand, as though he
were her gallant.

"Yes, I feel marvelous, too," she said, beaming at
the footman as he presented her with a dish of eggs.
"Wonderful," she added gaily as she took a helping.
"Excellent," she went on, with a glowing smile that
caused the footman to color up with pleasure, as she
helped herself to porridge, which she'd always detested. "Ah, it's good to be home again," she said.

Her mother sighed and her father repressed a
shiver of unease as they looked at each other anx-
iously, before they both began immediately chatting
about the morning and the latest local gossip.

They'd got past the fine day and through the tale
of the vicar's wife's tooth-drawing, had related the
story of John Richmond's new house built after last
year's fire, and were halfway through the details of
freckled and fortyish Glenna Blake's coming wedding
to the apothecary, when they saw the look that came
over their daughter's face. Mrs. Carstairs bit her lip
and exchanged worried glances with her husband.
They ought never to have mentioned a happy wedding. And so they hurried on to speak of any other
thing, seeing how Felicia had grown so suddenly still

and thoughtful, sitting with her egg-laden fork arrested in midair.

But Felicia scarcely attended to them, she was too involved with trying not to fall prey to despair again. Not because of Glenna's upcoming wedding. Or at least, not for the reasons they thought. But listening to her parents review the local past and chat about the program for the coming weeks had given her distasteful food for thought. It occurred to her that she couldn't go back to London so soon, nor could she bear to wait until autumn to astonish the world of the *ton* with her lightheartedness. But she could hardly dazzle them with her unconcern and insouciance even if tales of her merriment at the church picnic, annual strawberry fair, and Glenna Blake's rural wedding came to their ears.

Perhaps she could convince her parents to take her through Europe. But there was a war on. And, sophisticated as she tried to be, she was nevertheless a child of wartime and distrusted foreigners. Besides that, she'd a suspicion that it wouldn't impress anyone even if she had an uproarious time in Europe, anyone could be a mad success there, just look at that ghastly Princess Caroline. She frowned. Her mother kept chattering nervously, scarcely hearing what she was saying until Felicia looked up out of her dark study and said, "What?" Because she'd just heard a word that might lighten her sentence of exile.

"Ah—I said young Robert Grant came down with the mumps, and as there's ten children in the family, they're sure to have their hands full," her confused parent said, wondering at the new excitement in Felicia's face.

"No, before that," Felicia said, "when you were talking about his sister."

"Oh," her mother said, flushing, for in her rush of words, she realized she'd said a few uncharitable and rather warm things, "I just said that if young Meg doesn't watch her step, she'll be starting her own string of Grants—because Lord Neville's back in residence at Wildwood Court."

"I'd recommend she minds watching her skirts, not her feet, if she don't want to fall," Squire Carstairs said on a rich laugh, winking at his daughter, for he'd not raised her to be missish. "But she's little to fear—or in her case—anticipate from Neville. He's a rare rip, all right. But not in the way of seducing young village chits. No, his taste is more for London birds of paradise and other high flyers. I hear he's importing a brace of them for his hunting this summer. A little domestic chick like Meg has to watch her step near hayseeds and haystacks, my love, not lordly gents like Neville."

"Why has he come back?" Felicia asked slowly.

"Where else is he to go?" her mother said on a shrug. "He's been just about everywhere since he's been a boy. And he never much cared for the London Season. Wildwood *is* his home, however much he scandalizes it."

"Don't trouble yourself with thoughts of him," Squire Carstairs said, as he attacked his breakfast beefsteak again, "any more than he does with thoughts of us. Say this much for him, he is to the manner born. He knows his place. He lives apart from us and always has. He'll come, he'll have everyone's tongues wagging with the tales of his wild living, but that's just it—they'll be tales, come from gossips and snoops—like us." As he grinned at his wife's expression, he added, "And then he'll move on, having enriched the local merchants and enlivened the local social teas with stories of his doings. And as usual, he'll be three weeks gone before we know he's left. And a year gone before we miss him."

"You speak as if you were a blacksmith and he a grand duke," his wife said in some annoyance, forgetting the gossip in order to defend her family. "And yet you come from just as noble a family and are in line for equal honors yourself."

"Indeed?" he asked with great enthusiasm, "then you mean I can look forward to inviting a parcel of demireps here to amuse myself and my friends someday?"

While she protested that was not what she meant, and he saw that she was getting truly annoyed and so told her that no number of demireps could please him as much as she did—and then laughed, to spoil it—Felicia sat quietly and thought. If her parents hadn't been so involved in their usual teasing, they'd have noticed and worried, even though it was clear she was entertaining pleasant thoughts for a change. Because knowing their daughter as they did, they'd have noticed they were clearly *too* pleasant.

It was hard to pine for the rites of spring in London when there was such a celebration going on here, Felicia thought. She sat her horse in the midst of a meadow and let herself renew her love of the countryside, even as she tried to forget the love of her life for a moment. She might miss him, but no, nothing else of London, not now, she decided. How could she? For how might teas, balls, ridottos, and routs compare to robins and roses? What opera or theater could rival the hilarity of fields of riotously blooming

mustard and rapeseed, or the sight of brave, bright
laburnum weeping over every other garden wall? The
bird song, the freshness in the air—and the smell of
it! She inhaled deeply. A nose was a positive hin-
drance to pleasure in London, but here, in spring, it
was ecstacy to simply breathe.

She discovered herself astonished at her simple
joy, she hadn't realized how badly she'd missed all of
this. But then she recalled herself, and looked up and
about herself at more than the flowers and fields. For
however unexpected a treat she'd found, she hadn't
ridden out so far simply to enjoy rural pleasures,
after all. She'd carefully dressed in her best riding
clothes—a habit as green as the spring day, one a bit
loose in the bodice as well. Some girls might consider
tight clothing seductive, but being both cleverer than
most and of a certain innate sensual nature, she knew
that looser garments sometimes caught the eye much
more nicely, not only because they seemed more
ladylike, but because they allowed the imagination—
and other things, more play. Then she'd set a matching hat just so on the curls over one ear, and rode
out on a cream-colored horse to see if she could
attract her prey. Because that was how she considered the matter of attracting her notorious neighbor,
Lord Neville.

No more than her father did she think him any sort
of a threat to her. No, she reasoned she'd nothing to
lose but a dull morning as she waited for a glimpse
of him. But she'd everything to gain.

She'd heard about him, it seemed, since her cradle
days. Stories about Lord Neville, the rakish care-for-
nothing, had been the stuff of her childhood fables;
the tales of his endless exploits with the fairer sex
had been heard right along with the tales of giant

killers and other sorts of enchanters. Well, she
thought fairly, "eavesdropped" and "heard" were all
the same to a child, after all.

All she needed was for him to take notice of her
and pass some time with her—in public. And if, she
thought defiantly, as she had in the nights when the
secret shame of longings for far more than a certain
perfidious lord's hand in marriage tormented her, it
transpired that she eventually passed some private
time with the lady-killer, too, well, what of it then,
it would serve them all right, and wouldn't Jeremy
be sorry? But she wouldn't be. She'd triumph even
if she fell from grace. For whatever happened, she'd
stagger them all, she'd shock the world, and then
she'd sail back to town with a secret smile on her
lips . . . Still, in all, she admitted, on a sudden nervous restless pang, it would be probably best if her
wickedness remained where it had always been, in
her mind. And as she'd always been deft, if not successful, she reminded herself sadly that in her deal-
ings with gentlemen, she believed it would.

Then she'd dance back to London, triumphant. If
she couldn't have a dozen hearts on a string after her
absence from the social world, at least they'd think
she'd one notable one, and so then, she'd have the
pleasure of showing them she was not to be mocked
or pitied. As well as having the exquisite joy of
watching a certain lord expire of jealousy, or regret
. . . But, of course, it needed that she meet Lord
Neville, in order to get any sort of gossip started.

She stared into the mid-distance. A rider was coming along the narrow road beside the meadow where
she waited, her horse cropping the sweet spring
grass—the road so near to the boundaries of Wildwood Court, the one she'd learned her neighbor often

rode out along in the mornings. She'd left nothing to
chance but that which she couldn't control or try to.
She only hoped she'd recognize him. She could
scarcely think anyone she knew, knowing him, would
have been willing to give her an introduction, and
was far too wily to ask to have him pointed out to
her. What if, for some reason, he paid no attention
to her at all? She'd had enough of whispered laughter
and pity, thank you, to risk being seen to be rejected
by a man who they said accepted almost every female
since Eve.

She'd seen him in her youth from afar, and vaguely
remembered a tall, dark-haired, unremarkable-
looking gentleman. But time wasn't kind to those
who lived immoderately, just as the scriptures said.
By now, the wild young man the village spoke of
could have become so transparently loathsome or
comical that she wouldn't be able to bear so much
as an hour in his company trying to scrape up an
acquaintance that could lead to productive gossip.
She tensed and almost forgot herself so much as to
crane her neck up so as to get a better look at the
fellow who came riding by. But her first glance made
her shoulders slump in dejection. This couldn't be
him; this rider, even though he'd slowed his horse to
stare at her as she could not at him, was not the
stuff of delicious maidenly dreams and terrors.

He was more the material for a physician than a
governess's cautions, Felicia decided glumly. Because
he was terribly thin, and being tall, seemed gaunt
and gangly. His face was bony, his nose too long, and
he'd common brown hair under his high beaver hat.
Perhaps the sort of fellow that females might be the
ruin of, but not the sort to be the ruin of any. But
he was a stranger to her, and his clothes were a

gentleman's and fit perfectly over his lanky frame. His boots had a high gloss, and his horse was of impeccable breeding, so he might be a visitor to the vile seducer's lair, which made Felicia slide him another glance from beneath her lashes. There were more ways to angle for an introduction to the wicked gentleman of her choice than waiting all morning in a sunlit meadow for chance to strike like lightning from the cloudless sky, after all.

"Good morning!" he called, bringing his mount to a halt.

An unremarkable greeting made in a pleasant baritone, but it sounded like opportunity calling to Felicia.

"Good morning, sir," she said in a lilting voice, glancing up, then down, as a decent young lady should, as she drew in a deep breath so as to inflate her chest, as any lady shouldn't.

"A beautiful morning, being made more beautiful by the minute," he said with laughter in his voice.

She looked up sharply at that, being especially sensitive to laughter these days. And saw his eyes. And knew, in that moment, that it was the notorious Lord Neville himself she was looking at.

Because his eyes were dark blue, clear, and knowing, amused and amused at knowing it. They dominated his gaunt face and seemed to see everything about her all at a glance. His gaze traveled over her, obviously admiring the way her bosom had swelled, as well as noting everything about her face. She'd never felt so completely assessed and fully approved as a female before. Her mouth felt dry, she didn't know whether to be angry or flattered by his notice, much less which to pretend to be. As he watched her, she suddenly realized that his lean and hungry

look was real, in many several ways, most of which
she didn't know as yet. For once she dropped her
own gaze first, for reasons other than coquetry. And
then immediately raised it again, for she refused to
be afraid of anyone, and besides, she needed him.

"I am your neighbor, Felicia Carstairs," she said,
since that was the only thing she was sure of any
longer.

"Ah. And so then I am fortunate beyond my desserts," he said with such ardor that she had to laugh.

"You are Lord Neville," she said on a helpless giggle. "You have to be."

He inclined his head to the side and a slow smile
appeared on his thin lips.

"Alas. You've heard of me," he said.

"I'm not deaf," she answered, and then stopped
laughing, for it was possible, since he didn't exactly
laugh back with her, that she'd misread the rueful
grin and insulted him. She couldn't imagine rakehells
having such a sense of humor, come to think on it;
they couldn't and still carry on as they did, after
all. She was instantly sorry for giving offense, and
strangely enough, not just because she might have
whistled her chance at revenge down the wind.
Because he looked almost truly grieved.

"But you've struck me blind," he sighed, "because
the last time I saw you, your father introduced you
as 'Muffin' and then called you his 'sweet' and 'clever
puss.' You were, indeed, a charming child. But now
not only do I discover that your name is neither
sweetmeat nor pet, but 'Felicia,' and that you're
grown enough to have stopped me in my traces.
Where has your youth—and mine—gone, do you suppose?" he asked so seriously she almost believed him.

Until she looked at him closely and realized he was

far too young to be the wicked Lord Neville, and so then, likely jesting with her in everything. Which, though it might have delighted her so much as weeks before her abrupt departure from London, now set her back up. She was done with amusing people at her own expense. She gave him a frosty look.

"I beg your pardon, I did mistake you. Of course, you cannot be my neighbor, Lord Neville. I hope I haven't offended you, good day," she said icily.

"No, you've flattered me enormously," he said, ". . . I think. Because," he said musingly, "on the one hand, I ought to be pleased, I suppose, that you didn't think I looked wicked enough to be the depraved Lord Neville. On the other hand, since I am the depraved Lord Neville, I wonder if I ought to be furious, instead. What do you think?" he asked with every evidence of sincerity.

"You're far too young," she said at once, and then bit her lip at saying such a thing.

"But old in sin. Just ask anyone," he said reasonably. "And too, I started young."

She did hasty addition in her head and then began subtraction, for she was never very good at sums. But if she'd heard of him when she'd been six or seven, it might be that he could have been only sixteen when he'd begun his wild career, though that might be too young, how was she to know at what age a man could . . .

"I have blighted this poor earth for seven and twenty years," he said dolefully, though his eyes belied his somber tones. As her eyes widened, he added, "Yes, I did begin my wickedness at an early age. Although, I hasten to add, it was my intentions and never my achievements that first won me my bad name. It was the miller's daughter who first cried 'Wolf!' if you have the story right," he added helpfully, "although I was rather more of a cub at the time. Do you think your father will come after me with a whip for engaging you in this conversation, by the by?" he asked, as she sat staring at him. "And is that why we are having it, do you think?" he added pleasantly.

He was far too clever for her and much too experienced, she thought. But then again, she was never stupid and always respected wit, for she believed she had some, not to mention honesty—which virtue she didn't care to consider too closely right now, as he sat observing her even more closely. She decided she'd wronged him as badly as she'd been wronged; and it wouldn't be the first time for him. He likely met up with a great many silly girls and angry fathers just because of his reputation, and she supposed that was hardly fair. She felt she owed him some honesty.

"Perhaps that's so," she admitted on a rueful smile, "because I've been feeling very no-account since I've come home from London, and wanted to do something startling, that's true. But now I see you've better manners than most of the gentlemen I met there, and twice as much perception, as well as morality, and so see I was wrong. I don't doubt my father would shake my hand for engaging you in conversation, sir."

"He'd more likely shake his riding crop at another part of your anatomy," Lord Neville said gently, "and be right in doing it, too. I'm glad I gave you some enjoyment this morning, my dear, and sorry that I like your father so well, or I'd pursue our acquaintance. I give you good day."

"Well, and it's no wonder that you've such a reputation," Felicia said, swelling with outrage as he tipped his hat and began to nudge his mount along. "You do everything you can to foster it. I wonder you don't wear a great sign on your back, saying: Beware of rakeshame! Lock up your daughters!"

He stopped and looked back to her.

She glared at him, even as she drew in her breath at her effrontery.

And then he threw back his head and laughed. "My dear Miss Felicia," he said, when he could, "I should be honored if you'd ride along with me and tell me why you didn't meet up with any gentlemen of wit and perception whilst you were in London, although I can easily see why it was difficult for you to meet any with morality. But no more on that head," he said, shaking his own. "In fact, as I shall keep to safe language and topics, as well as to my horse, and you to yours, only the most bizarrely fanciful creatures will find anything improper in our meeting this morning. I'm just as wicked as they suppose, you see, and that's not merely bragging, whether you choose to believe it or not." He added with a smile, "But even they must admit that *that* creative, not to say, athletic, I am not."

She smiled back at him, although she wasn't sure she entirely understood his jest. But it was an invitation to friendship as well as a jest, and so she nodded as she nudged her horse forward, content. She stifled a pang of conscience, reasoning it wasn't precisely dishonest not to tell him she hadn't changed her mind about the reasons for wanting to continue her acquaintance with him. No, she refused to feel guilty, for from the look he wore as she rode forward, she imagined he hadn't been entirely honest with her either—if not saying everything that was obviously in one's mind was being dishonest, that was to say.

Now what the devil was Miss Felicia Carstairs up to? Lord Nigel Hayes Neville wondered as he rode back home alone an hour later. She wasn't trying to seduce him, although a less experienced man might have thought so, noting all her constant, silent enticements. She flashed her lovely light gold eyes, turned in her saddle so he could see how delightfully her riding habit didn't quite fit, and tossed her head as she laughed at his jests so he could see how her silky curls could shimmer in the sunlight. And bit her plump lower lip every now and again when she appeared bemused, so he could imagine how delicious it might be if he did the same. And none of it, he was convinced, was unintentional. Just as none of it, he reminded himself sharply, was intentional in the way he wished it to be or possible for him to follow up on.

It never failed to astonish him that young ladies of quality, as well as trollops, were trained to make gestures and motions that put their bodily attributes on display. Ah, well, he thought languorously, it was true that ladies didn't bend over to show quite so much bosom, twitch their hips, or lick their lips as they stared at a fellow, the way a delightfully wicked wench might do to show her interest. No, ladies were subtle. But just as blatant, if a fellow read the signs right, and he, he admitted on an interior laugh, certainly always had. They fluttered their eyelashes if they'd long ones, drew in their breath if they'd lovely breasts, and pouted to show pretty lips. But, as he knew too well, one class of female was usually only after money or sport. The other always wanted either sport or matrimony. He was always willing to engage in sport; the only cost that was always too high for him was matrimony. And too, there were females from either sphere who were simply incapable of reacting to a male with anything but flirtation, whether it was meant or not.

But Miss Carstairs hadn't been casting out lures strictly from force of habit. She was neither interested in the games he adored nor looking for matrimony—of that, he was certain. He knew how a female looked if she desired him, either for love play or for a possible husband. Miss Felicia hadn't looked remotely like that. In fact, remembering her laughter, her ready wit, and the lovely form they were within, he felt a pang of regret for it; although he knew her station in life, her family, and her youth made anything she had as unacceptable for him to partake of, as it would be for her to give to him. Still, she was definitely looking for something from him.

She was too intelligent to simply be seeking excitement, he mused as he rode on, too clever to flirt so close to danger, and had too generous a spirit to be making mock of him. Or so he believed, and he believed he knew his fellow man and woman well. To his regret. After all, he knew just how to shock them, and tease them as well as please them, although he'd grown bored with doing so, and now lived, he thought, solely for his own pleasures.

It was no bitter youthful love affair, no cruel mother or faithless father that had made him what he was. Orphaned young, yet with wealth and title, and good friends and relatives to see him through, he supposed he could have grown up to be as unexceptionable as they all had been and were. But it hadn't happened. He wasn't quite sure what had. Because the years had fled, and he found that the world saw him as a libertine—on reflection he supposed that he was. He thought, when he thought about it, that it was because he'd not fallen in love with the right woman at the right time. Instead, he'd fallen in love with what he could have with all the wrong ones, and somehow in so doing, one day woke to discover he'd cast himself forever beyond the pale of those females society deemed right.

It seldom bothered him. For it was only true. Oh, how he enjoyed that which he found with females, often, variously, and in constant variety. Although it made him an outcast in some circles, it included him in others, since intelligent men chose their friends for other reasons than their titles: those they were born with, or those they had been given. He was no rapist or seducer; he'd be bewildered at the idea of ever using force to obtain such sweet pleasure, and thought his angular looks such a drawback that he could only seduce blind women if that had been his bent. If it had been, he thought wryly, he'd have a very lonely bed. But he seldom did.

Because he paid well to see it never happened. All he did, had ever done, was to purchase what pleased him. He was in no way perverse that he could see. In fact, it usually amused him to be considered a rakeshame, when he thought about it. But to be honest, he thought as he neared his ancestral home, he usually tried not to see very far. He made no apologies to anyone, least of all himself. He shook his head, and his long, thin hands closed hard on his reins, as he realized he was doing just what he most disliked now.

Miss Carstairs had engaged him on several levels, and he wasn't at all sure he liked it, but he was sure he liked her. And was intrigued by her. He knew that he oughtn't to see her again, so much as he wished to. She was a mystery and a challenge, and her open friendliness was something altogether new to his experience. Because he didn't know what she wanted, but was beguiled by the faintest stirring of hope that it was nothing more than friendship.

Still, he knew he wasn't the right company for someone as lovely and bright as she was painfully young and innocent. And was diverted by the thought that he was truly tempted to horsewhip himself for his behavior—he paused at his gatekeeper's lodge to smile over that.

Yet he was an adult and a man with control, both in and out of bed, he thought wryly. He could entertain himself with a young lady in proper fashion, however improper society considered him. If he could not, he thought on a sudden start, his eyes turning a darker blue with distress, then he had certainly gone beyond libertine to a thing he didn't wish to contemplate. And if he had done, then he didn't wish to live with himself.

No, he thought, looking out at the bright springtime morning, he wouldn't condemn himself as the world had done, he couldn't. He rode down the lane to his home, and as he did, on impulse he reached up and snatched at a low hanging bough of pink and white cherry blossom, broke off a bit of it, and then absently brought it to his nose. Springtime, he thought: surely it wasn't wrong for a man to try to observe it from close quarters, just one more time. And surely not, if he vowed to merely appreciate it in its brief season, not to tamper with it, but to leave everything as he found it when he'd enjoyed it enough.

Lord Nigel Hayes Neville tucked the bit of blossom carefully into his buttonhole, and rode on.

*   *   *

He didn't have butter-soft blond hair that drifted over a high white forehead, she thought, or speaking brown eyes, and his lips were thin, mobile, and not carefully sculpted works of art, like a certain gentleman she knew—she'd known—Felicia silently corrected herself. And his chin was square, but his face was so long one scarcely cared that it was finished off so neatly, she noted narrowly as she stole a glance at his profile . . . Oh! but his profile didn't bear speaking of. Lord Neville's face could certainly not compare to a certain absent gentleman's she couldn't forget—except for most of the time when she was in Lord Neville's company, oddly enough.   •

In fact, the most one could say for that face, Felicia decided, even after one got used to it and actually looked forward to seeing it—as she did each morning before they met, as if by chance, when they went riding—was that it resembled that of a kindly horse. But it was he himself who had said that, in fact, he boasted of it on a laugh that showed even white teeth. That was before he added that it was a mercy fashion called for gentlemen to wear such high white neck cloths, because at least it spared the world the sight of his Adam's apple, which, he claimed, as if with pride, was prodigious.

Nor was his form a manly ideal. He'd not the willowy, languishing frame of a dandy, or the neat, compact muscular body of a Corinthian, or even the thick, full-bodied swaggering shape of a hearty country sportsman. He was as gangly as a colt, and moved with the same oddly-fitting gawky grace. But all equine comparisons faded when he spoke, for his voice was dulcet. Or when his eyes were noted, for they were too wise even for a man. A singular-looking gentleman, Felicia thought, puzzled yet again by his odd attractiveness in spite of all his defects. And never one anyone would take for a voluptuary. But so he was called, and so he admittedly was.

It was difficult to see how he'd gotten such a reputation, but it might be, as he'd said, that the sight of good gold was far more enticing to certain females than good looks. That must have been the case, because he never did or said anything in the least . . . No, Felicia admitted, thinking back on his behavior toward her, he might not have done anything, but he always said irregular, shocking things a gentleman ought not to say to a young lady. But they were always outrageously funny and never failed to make her laugh, except when she didn't understand them, and then it was he who grew grave and changed the subject, as she supposed, she ought to have done. And those weren't the only outrageous things he spoke about with her. No, he dared discuss all manner of things a gentleman rarely did with a well-bred girl: literature, the arts, philosophy, and politics. But really, she thought, she'd never known how much fun it could be to scandalize oneself. Or to try to scandalize oneself, she amended.

Because for all that she left a trail behind her that a blind man could follow, and never left in the mornings without making a great show of it and the fact that she'd dressed for her ride with as much care as for a coronation, no one seemed to have noted. And so though they'd met for over a week's worth of clement mornings, no one but their horses had seen their meetings, and they certainly couldn't comment on it over tea. She'd have to consider how to hasten the matter of discovery. Or teach horses to gossip.

"I haven't even begun chatting," he remarked as

they came to the part of the road where they could ride side by side, "and you're already smiling. Oh, I see, you finally understand my jest of yesterday."

"Beast," she said conversationally, "I always understand your jests, it's just that I am often too much of a lady to let you know it."

He grinned. "You see," he continued as if she hadn't spoken, "I'm quite out of the practice of speaking to pure young maidens, but I've made a remarkable discovery now that I've begun to. I ought to publish my findings, I think," he said, eyeing her merrily, "for I've found a thing that should put fond parents' minds at rest. You can say the most lascivious, improper things to a truly innocent young female, and she'll never have a clue. I think the reason more of you aren't corrupted," he said with an air of great discovery, "is that most of the time you don't realize someone's trying to corrupt you."

"Have you been trying?" she asked.

His face became solemn. "No, Felicia, I have not, and well you know it," he said quietly.

"Why not?" she asked, greatly daring, because she could look down at her horse's ears instead of at him as she did.

"You know very well why not," he said with a trace of anger. "Coloring up or looking down won't save you, my friend. And you also know that if I thought you expected anything of the sort, I'd ride off and leave you this moment."

"You don't think I'm handsome enough," she said in a small voice, looking at him with the most deeply hurt expression she could manage, enjoying herself very much now.

"Of course you're handsome enough," he snapped, and then stared hard at her. His expression changed from alarm to resignation, though his eyes sparkled. "If I didn't think it would be misconstrued if it were seen, and so end with me having to marry you, I'd haul you off that saddle and put you over my knee," he said at last.

"No," she said a little sadly, "no one would want to marry me, of course."

"Cut line, my dear, it won't wash . . ." he began, and then saw something in her eyes that made him lower his voice and say, "Most men would want that very much, you know. The fellow must have been in debt to his ears, blind as a bat, or monstrously stupid to have passed you over for another."

"He was neither stupid or in debt," Felicia flashed back at him, deeply sorry she'd ever mentioned Jeremy at all, even if only in passing as she'd done the day before, since Lord Neville had immediately guessed the whole of the half she'd hinted at.

"Only you," he said on a half smile, "would defend a fellow who'd kicked you in the sensibilities. You know, my dear, you ought to shake the dust of the countryside from your little feet and place them squarely back in London town again, just to show him that you don't care a fig. I'd take you back and squire you at all the *ton* parties if I could, I think. But if I so much as acknowledged you in the street, you'd be ruined. In fact," he said in a different tone of voice than she'd ever heard from him, "I'm beginning to think that even these little morning rides, however pleasant, are too dangerous for your reputation. My stable men are mute as mice on the subject of my doings, that's why they work for me at such good wages, but they seem to be looking at me a bit oddly these days. You haven't told anyone, have you?"

"Heavens, no!" she said, and felt virtuous enough to say it wide-eyed, for hinting was never saying.

"There you are," he said, unfamiliar seriousness making him stern-looking. "You ought not to be meeting up with anyone you have to keep quiet about."

"I don't mind," she said airily, and was discomforted when he gazed down at her and said with every evidence of sincerity, "But I do, my dear, be sure I do."

Lord Neville measured the carpet in his study to the window, and then turned to pace it down to the other side again. The thing couldn't go on as it was. There was too much danger for her. And none for him. For he, he thought, stopping in his pacing to run one long hand through his hair, he was already slain.

It had been going on for three weeks now, and every morning had become more important than the previous one, every afternoon more dreary, and every night more unbearably lonely than the one before, as he waited out the long hours until morning again. The most incredible thing was that it seemed to him it was the same for her. There was that light in her eyes now when they met, there was that droop to her lovely lips when they parted, and she never kept still when they were riding. Of course, it could only be that she was so young and trusting, and needed a friend. It might only be that she was still languishing for that fool she'd fancied in London. But he could—he did—make her forget when he tried to, didn't he?

Yes, all true, he thought, resuming his pacing, but if he were her father, he'd never let her wed such as he. And if you were her father, Idiot, he told himself savagely as he swung about to pace the length of his room again, you wouldn't think of marrying her, would you? His syntax might be as tangled as his thoughts were, but that corrupt he was not, although now he thought the entire notion of marrying her perverse, considering who and what he was. And he dropped to a chair and dropped his aching head into his hands, considering just that.

He scarcely recognized himself, he was so astonished at his own thoughts. He'd never been impetuous except in matters of his appetites, and that occupied only his body and a few hours of his time. This encompassed his whole life, heart, and future. Surely a few weeks was far too little time to know his mind. But now he saw it had not happened all at once, it had been a slow process for all its relative brevity. So it was with springtime itself. Flowers didn't burst forth from the earth at the first touch of warmth, it took a gradual lengthening of daylight; it was the constant, steady, almost imperceptible lightening of the hours that brought what seemed to be instantaneous change. And so it had been with him. She had come to him like springtime, and he'd basked in her warmth all unknowing, until this love had blossomed. He acknowledged it on a stifled groan: he loved her, Felicia Carstairs. He, Lord Nigel Hayes Neville, the corrupt Lord Neville, the renowned rakeshame shunned by polite society—and rightly so, he thought—and famous libertine lover of light ladies. He was in love with springtime herself, and what was he to do now?

If he continued to meet her and was seen at it, he'd ruin her name to the point that any subsequent offer of his would seem like a concession to society when it was made; and not the concession to his humanity, loneliness, and love that it would be. It was necessary that she know exactly what his offer meant and was. And so then it would have to be made soon. But how could he aspire to her? But if he didn't continue to see her, he'd certainly run mad.

It was a wonderment. She'd come to mean so much in such a little while, and he'd never so much as touched her! Although he yearned to. He marveled at that. As well as at his intuitive knowledge that if he won her, he'd never want another. For the thought of having the body of a woman whose soul he loved was so staggering a notion, promising such bliss, that the idea of ever having a mere body to toy with again seemed infantile to him now.

Thinking of that, he rose in alarm, remembering he'd have to hasten to send out notes to cancel that mad and carnal May Day frolic he'd planned for himself months ago, in that drear winter of his life before he'd met her. And then he had her father to call on, respectfully, hat in hand. How did one go about that? he wondered with excited anxiety, astonished at his eagerness to invite insult. He was certainly no prize, but he made her laugh, surely he could make her care, if he had not already. There must be a way he could tell her father that, he was glib . . . but this was not, he realized, a time for glibness.

He reviewed his assets as seriously as he had his liabilities. He was not very young, but neither was he very old. He'd sown his wild oats—plantations of them; he was, he thought as he stood still and contemplated it, if no better than most, at least preferable to some. He had a title, funds and land, relative youth, and for a wonder no diseases or infirmities—and none of the spirit either since he'd met her. As for his past—it was precisely that. As for his name, what was in it he'd change as drastically as he hoped to change hers, until it stood for honor, not license. He'd devote his life to her, he'd never have a better occupation, she'd not be sorry— he'd vow it. Carstairs seemed a decent fellow, he should be able to convince him of that, and how much he could do for her, and how much he needed her . . .

He needed her, he thought with incredulous joy. And rose to his feet to pace, plot, and plan again.

But first he would speak with her. That wasn't how most gentlemen would go about it, but he was not like most gentlemen. He had to be sure before he addressed her father. She'd had enough embarrassment at the hands of clownish suitors. She must know his exact intent before the world did. If his suit distressed her, it would never be known to another living being. Of course, he thought on a slight smile as he eyed her now, if it distressed her, he wasn't sure he'd leave this interview precisely as a living being either.

He wondered if they were already so attuned to each other that they communicated without words now. For today she seemed nervous, too. She avoided his eyes, fussed with her skirts, and fairly hummed with tension he could almost feel. But then too, today was, after all, the first day they'd sat side by side, and not on the backs of adjacent horses.

They sat on a stile near to a meadow, and their silence was profound enough to make the sheep seem to be bellowing. It was unusual for them to pass three minutes together without talking, and so their silence was as unsettling as it was becoming awkward. He broke it.

He cleared his throat. "I've been thinking . . ." he began.

"So have I!" she said eagerly, swinging her head to face him. There was a hectic flush on her pale cheeks, and though she looked at him, she seemed to not be seeing him as she went on excitedly, "May Day's coming. Everyone's been invited to the Carrols' for dancing, but no one of any account will be there above an hour. Everyone's going to the wood for the bonfire and dancing. Will you come with me?"

He literally couldn't answer for a moment. It required a great shifting and turning in his mind before he could. He'd been about to take out his heart and offer it into her hands, and had been so preoccupied with the way he would do it that her prattling about May Day took him aback. He was almost angry at her for it. But then he gazed at her vivid face and named himself a fool. How should she know? And at that thought, and what it might auger for him, he grew still, and she took his silence for an answer and pouted.

"The Carrols', of course, are fusty antiques," she said. "They think there's something scandalous about the old rites, so they're giving their tame frolic to lure us all away from the revels. But it won't do. Well, perhaps it will for their daughter Elizabeth and her sort, but I promise it won't for me. Oh, it should be such fun, I've never gone, but always heard. Now I'm old enough, and I hear one must have an escort, oh, come with me, do, please," she said, grasping his hand, touching him for the first time.

But they both wore gloves, so that alone wasn't what kept him to silence for another space. She sounded so young, so ingenuous, and so she was, and so his heart sank, thinking of it, and what he'd been about to say to her. He felt very old as he answered, patting her hand as would her most elderly uncle as he did.

"But it's not fusty of the Carrols, only wise of them. And of course, you'd need an escort if you went to the wood, preferably one with a suit of armor to protect you as well as himself, because the doings on the eve of May Day *are* scandalous," he explained. "Perhaps not for the village girls—for that's how many of them catch husbands, if not even more intimate souvenirs of the festivities—but certainly for a girl of good birth. No, you oughtn't to go, and I wouldn't take you. And as I haven't been invited to the proper party, of course, I believe we'll have to let the evening pass—if, that is to say," he said haltingly, with somewhat less than his usual assurance and a good deal less humor, "you think my alternate proposal isn't better, because, you see, my dear—"

"But *you're* scandalous, so why should it matter to you?" she said impatiently, cutting him off in order to press her point, for it had seemed the very thing when she'd dreamed it up in the night. It was the perfect way to let the world see this blossoming friendship and all that it was, as well as how little the other they thought had affected her had actually meant.

His dark blue eyes grew darker.

"I *am* scandalous," he said evenly, "but not lost to what is not. You oughtn't to be seen with me, anywhere, and most certainly, not there. Felicia," he said more gently, seeing her lips tighten, "to put it bluntly, it was a celebration of rites of fertility in olden times, and it's still a night for mating. Sometimes for life, and sometimes"—he shrugged his wide-winged shoulders—"simply for pleasure."

"But you'd be there with me," she persisted.

"You trust me so much then?" he asked, as pleased as he was dismayed by the thought, and confused by it.

"Well, of course," she said with a bright smile, "we're friends, aren't we? Or so you always say we are."

A terrible thought came to him, and being only human, he pushed it away. But being who he was, he remained aware of it, crouching in the foreground.

"Yes, but as a friend I can scarcely subject you to such gossip," he explained. "And too, even if I'd protect you from the other revelers, how can you be sure I'd save you from myself?" he asked with a failed attempt at a leer.

"Piffle," she said on a rich laugh. "What a poor excuse for not coming with me. You've never been seen anywhere with me," she wheedled. "I begin to think it is you who are ashamed of being seen with me," she teased.

The thought he'd banished hunkered down at the edge of his consciousness, waiting. There were so many things he could do now, he thought with despair: he could get on with his proposal, he could take her up on her flirtatious challenge, pull her into his arms, and kiss those lips he'd been craving since they'd met, and then he'd have to come out with his proposal; he could ignore his passions and change the subject. Instead, wincing inwardly, before he could stop himself, he dragged the thought from the borders of his mind out into the light.

"Unless, of course," he said, "you want to be seen with me, and anywhere, for whatever reasons I am now persuaded you have. For it just might be," he said thoughtfully, "that you'd think it a fine thing if

our friendship were discovered, and perhaps misconstrued, just to let the world—or a certain six-foot-
tall part of it, for example—know you've not
returned home to pine about things that cannot be."

She stared at him, and felt a tremendous surge of
relief and gratitude. Because the thought of deceiving him in any way hadn't set too well with her of
late. The more she'd gotten to know him, the more
she liked him. And the more she liked him, the less
she liked the idea of engaging his love for her venge-
ful purposes. Although she also thought it improbable
she could. Because it wasn't just his gold that had
attracted females, she'd swear to that now. He was
an expert at dalliance. But he'd never tried to take
any liberties with her. She felt a bit insulted as well
as wistful whenever she thought about it, which she
had with increasing frequency of late. Yet per-
versely, the thought of physical love with him was
so startling that she shied away from it every time
she dared imagine it. She didn't know why that was;
she'd doted on daydreaming about Jeremy's kisses.
But the unlikely and increasingly present thought of
Nigel, Lord Neville's mouth touching hers always
caused her mind to skitter away, and her body to
shiver.

Now her lips curved up into a sly smile to match
his own. He was always so clever, she rejoiced at
how he always understood.

"Yes. Just so," she said contentedly, before she
frankly grinned at him. "I could do with just a wee
hint of scandal, you know."

He stared at her for a long moment, and in that
moment she couldn't look away, although she wished
she might. For something very like hate and near to

fury blazed in his eyes, before something in them
died. And then he arose.

"Ho hum, so that was what this little courtship
was all about all along, wasn't it?" he said in a deadened voice. "You risked a great deal for a little vengeance, love," he said, looking at her as he never had
done, his eyes raking up and down her with amused
contempt. "What if I had been a conscienceless de-
spoiler, after all? Would the loss of your virtue have
been worth a few seconds of pity from your lover?
Why is it?" he asked no one in particular, "that the
young are always so sure their ruin or death will
serve to hurt their faithless lovers? People bury
nasty thoughts, love, along with their dead. No one
suffers like the sufferer, you see. But I suppose you'll
have to learn that. I wonder if I ought to tender you
yet another lesson?" he asked, putting his long hand
beneath her chin and tipping her worried face to his.

He lowered his head to hers and stared at her
mouth while she caught her breath, but then his own
lips curled in a smirk.

"I think not," he said, dropping his hand and drawing
back, "for if someone saw us, I'd have to wed you for
it, and that, I could not bear. Good day, my dear, and
happy May Day eve. It's just your sort of festival, I
think, after all. I wish you luck with whomever, or
whatever, you do manage to snare in the wood."

And then he walked away. He mounted his horse,
and after one last comprehensive look at her where
she still sat dazed, silent, and staring back at him,
he rode off.

The frock was perfect. Light and gauzy as a spring
breeze, green over a white underskirt, with a yellow
trim; her father said she looked like a blooming daffo-

dil, and they all laughed over that. She'd got very good at laughing over things she didn't find very amusing these past days. Why, just look at the way she'd simpered at all the trite things gentlemen had said to her at the Carrols' tedious dance party tonight, Felicia thought. Anyone would think she was having a delightful time, when it was only that she was imagining the better time she'd be having soon, when she managed to slip away to where she was really bound this moon-drenched night.

Then she'd got the excruciating headache she'd been planning, and then Mama said that of course she could return home. And after only one doubtful pause, then agreed that she could go with her maid Betsy, so that her parent's social evening wouldn't be ruined as well, as Felicia had thoughtfully requested. Then Betsy, after all her refusals and all her good reasons and arguments, nevertheless told Mrs. Finch, the housekeeper, that she was sleeping. And after Felicia tossed a paisley shawl patterned like dappled shade over her shoulders, she slipped away from the house to the wood, with Betsy stifling gasps of laughter and fear at her heels, as they stole like shadows across the lawns in the soft spring moonlight. Just as she'd planned.

For who could deny her anything? None but two men ever had, one of whom she'd loved, and the other, she hated. And if she felt dreadful after deceiving her parents, she felt a burning sense of glory at how she was not doing what either gentleman expected: she was not at home, repining. She was not out trying to snare anything but fun, either. "Only the sufferer suffers," he'd said. Well, and she certainly wasn't going to suffer. She was done with that. She was going to dance, sing, and drink wine, and do who knows what else with whomever asked her sweetly enough, for she was tired of suffering, that was the whole point of her defiance.

The bonfire was deep in a clearing in the wood. If Betsy hadn't led the way, guided by secret paths, Felicia would never have found it. It was in among the tallest trees and tangled brush, so that even the bright blaze of it was obscured until the observer stole into the clearing where it roared and sprang in its confines, like some great, exotic orange beast caged in a circle of tree trunks. When they first arrived, all Felicia could do was to stand and stare and get her breath back, as she watched the shapes of revelers feeding it sticks, boughs, and occasional bottles to crunch and pop.

"There's the maypole, up there—aye, high up on that hill," Betsy breathed on a chirruping giggle.

Felicia looked up to see the tall, thick branchless tree implanted on the hilltop, outlined against the starry night, and was surprised to find herself shivering at such a simple sight.

"We'll swag it with hawthorn blossoms, and every other kind we can find, and dance about as the sun comes up," Betsy said in an excited undertone. "At least those of us who can stand, will," she said, and laughed her new, breathless laugh, before she whispered, "Ah, there's Tom Slade, the prentice farrier. He'll give us a swig to keep off the night, and see that I've grown up some since last May Day eve just as well, he will," she added as if to herself. "I'll be right back. Mind, never move from this spot, Miss Felicia," she said, suddenly stern, suddenly acting much older than her own seventeen years, suddenly a stranger in this weird night, "like you promised, mind, or I'll tell your dad, I will, never doubt it.

Don't move," she said on another gasping laugh, and slid away into the dark, and then into the leaping orange glare of the bonfire.

Felicia saw her move from the darkness and approach a tall, slender man, and took in her breath in shock as the fellow put his arms around Betsy, and drew her into his arms until there was but one wavering shadow to be seen of them both. But, no, she thought with relief, that wasn't Betsy. The girl coming up out of the dark to tap that thick-bodied fellow on the shoulder—the one who then swung around and raised her high in his arms before he lumbered off with her into deeper shadows, as everyone laughed, that was she. Even as Felicia looked about in dismay, she saw she was wrong, for there was Betsy, arm in arm with a man, strolling away from the fire . . . And then she realized that she didn't know where Betsy had got to at all, but wherever it was, it couldn't be a proper place, because most of the women and men were joining or were already joined in improper ways, all in silhouette against the brightly blooming night.

She turned to go at once, for whatever was to be done here would be her undoing, whatever else she did not, that much, at least, she knew now. And walked into a pair of arms.

"Oh, lass," the burly shape said. "Now we be two, I've been lookin' for such a one as you."

Panic gave her the wild force needed to surprise him enough to loose her. She swung away and bounded back, backed into the wood, and fled. She ran until her breath caught, and then crouched, gasping, her heart beating so loud she couldn't hear the hoofbeats. And so she was totally unprepared when he slid from off the horse's back, gathered her up, and leaped back up into the saddle with her struggling in his long, strong arms.

"Be still!" he said, and she was. For she recognized his voice at once. She lay against his breast, striving for air.

"Fool," Lord Neville said conversationally as he walked his horse on through the wood. "I thought you'd be here, and here you are. How predictable," he sounded disappointed.

And he was. But he would have been more upset if he hadn't found her. He'd left his guests as the moon rose, as soon as he'd got word of how she'd left the Carrols' party early. His name might ensure his not getting invitations to proper affairs, he thought with bitter triumph, but his money could buy him information about anything he chose. But he hadn't exactly chosen to see what she'd done this night, he simply couldn't help worrying, any more than he could stop thinking about her since their last encounter. Well, he'd challenged her, hadn't he? he thought, as he felt her breath coming more slowly and evenly against his chest at last.

She raised her head from the sanctuary and prison of his warm, hard chest.

"And so you rescued me. Hurrah," she said coldly, trying to gather her wits, wondering why she felt so marvelously good suddenly, though she was so deeply ashamed.

He laughed. "Certainly not," he said. "You weren't in great danger—none, in fact, if no one recognized you. They're none of them rapists. They're all local lads, neighbors, and friends. If they'd seen you clearly, they'd have shunned you. No fellow there wants the squire down on his neck."

"Then why did you come for me?" she asked in a

little cracked voice, a sudden hope and terror rising in her breast.

His face was lighter than flesh could be in the bleached light of the moon, and his smile colder than the moon itself.

"To do your will," he said. "You wanted to scandalize didn't you? So then be my guest, literally. I've a charming house party with some special friends coming tonight. Far, far more suitable to your purposes than a rural May Day revel. Those fellows you've just left would never take advantage where none was given. They act from joy of life and lust. They were simple, harmless buffoons. I am not."

She'd got her breath back only to lose it again. His set face told her more than his words had.

"I don't believe you," she said bravely, though she very much feared she did.

"Then don't," he said, shrugging, "It makes no matter."

But now she'd got her tongue and her wits back.

"You certainly wouldn't . . . do anything . . . to me, that is. You're just trying to teach me a lesson," she said smugly, for this was the Lord Neville she knew, after all, and so never the man of legend she'd thought she'd get to know.

"Yes, a lesson. Many of them," he agreed, and lowered his head and brought his mouth to hers, and held her when she began to struggle. And held her as she stopped struggling and lost her breath entirely again against his warm, sweet moving mouth.

"That," he managed to say when he was done, and he thought he'd never be done, not really, as he raised his head, for he was amazed to find himself as shaken as she was, "was the first one. By dawn, we'll have gotten to many more."

"You wouldn't," she breathed, "b-because, you'd have to m-marry me, and you said you couldn't bear that."

"Shall I have to? Shall I just?" he mused. "And why, I wonder? Because you'll blacken my name? Horrors. Or your father will challenge me to a duel? I'm an excellent shot and swordsman, from practice with so many irate fathers, you understand. No. I doubt you'll say a word, my dear. Whether you like my lessons or not, though I believe you'll like them very well. But I think you'll never say a syllable to anyone about them or where you actually were tonight, if they even discover you've been gone. For you'll be back by dawn. Because those theatrics are caused by pride and honor. Your pride will not allow it. And I've no honor."

"Why?" she asked.

"Because that's the way I am," he answered easily.

"No, why are you doing this, trying to frighten me," she said.

"Because it's what you wanted."

"You know better," she said softly.

"Of course, that's why I'm doing it, too. And also because," he said so quietly she knew it would be truth she'd hear, "you're not the only one to seek vengeance. I want revenge, too."

And then she was very still.

The house at the old Court was aglow with light and laughter, and should have been a welcoming sight. But she was chilled, even coming into the warmth from out of a cool spring night. She was ashamed, and very sorry she'd hurt him, far more than she was afraid she'd be hurt herself. Because she still couldn't believe he'd harm her. But the one glance she got at his guests told her that they might.

Not that they looked anything but distinguished to her confused stare. The several gentlemen were dressed in the highest fashion, the sort of evening clothes she'd seen at the most expensive entertainments in London. But their expressions were not like anything she'd seen before. It might have been their avid curiosity, as they saw their host carrying a woman in his arms as he strode into his great hall; or the amount of wine they'd doubtless drunk this night; or it could even have been the inconstant, flickering candlelight that painted their faces with emotions that caused her dread. But he'd been right, these weren't faces lit by simple joy of life and lust. They were countenances suffused by something born of lust and mated with boredom, and there was nothing simple or joyful about them. She hid her face in his neck, although she scarcely had to, he held her so that they could see nothing of her but her general shape, and that caused them as much merriment as chagrin.

As he mounted the stair, they called after him.

"What sort of host is this? You're supposed to share with your company, Neville!"

"Aye, that's so! A good host sacrifices the very best for his guests, and if you went out especially to get her, she must be special."

"Perhaps he means to bring her down last, as dessert."

She heard their laughter even above the pounding of her heart, and then she heard it no more. For it seemed to have stopped with her own pulse, as he carried her into a room and then abruptly dropped her onto a bed. She scuttled to a corner of it, and peered up at him from under a quantity of hair that had been loosed from it's careful pinnings.

His face was expressionless.

"Do not move," he said angrily. "You may not know what awaits you here, but you've seen what's outside. Far worse, I promise you, than anything that will happen here. Stay where you are," he commanded.

His hand went to his hair to absently straighten it, and then to his waistcoat, where he loosed a button. She caught her breath, and it may have been that he heard it in the quiet room, for he seemed to see her again. He smiled a smile with nothing humorous in it, turned on his heel, and went out, closing the door behind him.

She was off the bed before the door closed. He was strong, far stronger than his lanky frame suggested, and so he'd have no difficulty returning her to the massive bed she'd fled. But she felt safer on her feet. She went to the door immediately. Only to drop her hand from the knob as she touched it, because she still believed him. Whatever was out there was likely to be far worse than whatever would transpire in here.

It was a lovely room, she thought, glancing around herself, majestically furnished, all in tones of crimson and brown. If it weren't for the fact that it was so blatantly a man's bedchamber, doubtless, she thought, huddling by a wall near to the window, she'd be quite comfortable here. The window, she saw when she pulled the heavy draperies back, was high above the ground, and the long sloping lawns looked cold and hard as snowbanks in the blanched and eerie moonlight. So here was decidedly better than there, she thought, as she chewed at the skin at the base of a thumbnail, just as he'd said. And he had been a friend, and she refused to believe . . . but then the door slowly cracked open.

The woman was beautiful. The one that stood behind her was even more so, and the third lovely face that peeked into the room was so filled with light and merriment that Felicia felt her pent-up breath all come out in a sigh of relief.

"Coo! Wot 'ave we 'ere? A damsel in distress?" the merry lady said on a low chuckle, as she and the others stepped into the room. "Or just 'nother sister 'ere to 'elp us out t'night?"

The first woman shook her blond head. "Nah, don't think so. She's private stock. You the lord's goods?" she asked Felicia curiously, as she stepped about the room, running her fingers over the surfaces of the chairs and fabrics, as though pricing them.

"I have been abducted," Felicia said at once. "And wish nothing more than to go home."

"G'wan!" the second woman said, her huge blue eyes widening. "Never say so! It's better'n a melo-dramer," she remarked to her friends, before she took Felicia's cold hand and patted it, saying, "Poor thing."

"Can you help me escape?" Felicia asked eagerly.

"Shouldn't think so," the blond woman said from the bedside, where she was running her hands against the silken coverlet. "We can't do anything but what we came here to do, and if you're for his lordship, we can't even do that for him."

"Don't know why yer complainin' 'bout that, Dilly," the merry lady said jauntily. "There's 'nuff work to keep you on yer back 'til dawn as 'tis."

"At least I won't have sore knees like some I can mention," the blond woman retorted.

"We're here to work the party, you see," Felicia's

blue-eyed comforter said gravely. "Satisfy the gents, and all. Us and some others, we came down from Lunnon for it. And so we can't do anything for you, poor girl. And I must say I'm that surprised. Because Neville's a rare dog, but an honest one, or so I thought."

"Nothing with a prick is honest," the blond woman remarked from where she was standing back, evaluating a landscape on the far wall. "Except for my grandda, and that's because he's been dead a dozen years."

"But please," Felicia said urgently, "there must be something you can do, I must leave here now."

"We ortn't to even be in here," the blue-eyed woman said sympathetically. "We just heard the fuss and came to take a peek. You're smashing, and a real lady, that I can tell, because you haven't a drop of paint—though you could use a bit, you're awfully pale, and do you know, your lashes would stand out even more if you put a dash of bootblacking on them. And wouldn't she look a treat with a bit of charcoal over her eyes, they're that striking even so, don't you think, Pearl?"

The merry lady nodded, but before she could speak, Felicia cried, "You don't understand, I must leave here. I don't want to be here."

" 'Course we unnerstan'," the merry lady said impatiently, " 'Tis you that don't. We can't do nuffink. 'Cept what we're paid to do, which is ter service the gennelmen 'til they drop—or droop," she said on a giggle to the blue-eyed woman, who was watching Felicia with a tender expression.

"Higher than a kite, before you even start work," the blond woman remarked in disgust as she picked up a gold-handled magnifying glass from a writing table, measured it against the size of the tiny reticule she carried, sighed, and then put it down again.

" 'Tis the only way I ken start work," the merry lady said, her voice so sad that Felicia finally noted, with a start, that it was only paint that kept the sweet face still smiling radiantly.

"I'm sure he'll be kind," the blue-eyed woman told Felicia. "And even if he's not, he'll likely pay well. Generous gentleman, I'm sure. Ah, don't fret. I was only twelve when I started, you're all grown."

"Try eight, fer me," the merry lady said dolefully.

"Try eight at one time for you, you mean," the blond woman said absently, as she turned over a snuffbox and squinted at its trademark.

"You great cow," the merry lady said furiously, "I never done more'n three at a time, an' you know it."

"You would if you could find another place to put one," the blond woman countered.

"Yes, well, but think of the money she'd make, and how fast she'd get it all over with, too, if she could," the blue-eyed woman said consideringly.

"Don't be more idiotish than you can help, Irene," the blond woman snapped.

"I was only trying to make peace," Irene protested in hurt tones, as Felicia stared at her in dismay, her own eyes wider than Irene's great blue ones now.

"Don't bother," the blond lady said. "We'll have to get to work in a trice, and they'll be no time for fighting for anything but breathing space then."

"Ladies," a deep voice said harshly, and they all turned around to see Lord Neville standing in the doorway, his long bony face very grim and white, "I believe it's time for you to descend the stair—if you still wish to."

"We knowed we ortn't to 'ave come in here," Irene

said nervously. "We only wanted to cheer the lady up a bit."

"Here's something to cheer you a bit more," he said wearily, holding out a bank note to her. "For your word you've forgotten you were ever in here."

"Done!" she said, and the note was whisked from his hand as she scurried past him through the doorway.

"Done," and "Done!" said the other two as they followed and snatched up the other two he proffered, and were gone down the hall, leaving nothing behind them but a last blue-eyed wink and the flowery remnants of their overwhelming scents.

"And done," he said softly, looking at Felicia, his hands now empty and in white-knuckled fists. He opened them, turned them palm up, and held them out to his sides. "I am so sorry," he said with infinite weariness. "This never was what I meant. I'm not at all sure now precisely what I meant," he admitted on a dusty chuckle. "Never this of course. Revenge in the shape of a good fright, but never this . . . dishonor."

"You dishonor yourself more by employing those poor creatures," Felicia said, squaring her shoulders, although her lips trembled.

"Oh, yes. True, true," he said, "that's very true. But there's nothing new in it. This was, however, a new low, even for me. Ah, don't. Please, my dear, do not."

"I'm trying not to," Felicia complained, as the tears slid down her cheeks, and then she was trying even harder not to weep as he held her gently against his chest, and with cold and ineffectually shaking hands, trying to straighten her mussed hair and wipe her tears, before he jerked away and took a step back from her.

"There's a back stair, we'll take it," he said, holding out one long hand. "They'll never know we're gone, just as they'll never know you were here. Come along," he said, as though to a dull child, as she simply stared at him. "I'm taking you home."

They rode in silence all the way. She'd stopped weeping, but not inwardly. He said not a word as his horse paced along the moon-whitened roads, until they came to the wooded track that abutted the kitchen gardens at the back entrance of her house. He stopped the horse and sat silent, watching her downcast head, as she struggled for the words to say half the things she felt.

"I'm sorry, sorry, sorrier than you know," he finally sighed. "Believe that. I never thought you'd see them, much less hear them. I'm not in the way of corrupting youth in the normal way of things, you know."

"But you are in the way of corrupting those poor women you hired, aren't you?" she said, raising her head and glaring at him.

He gave a short cough of a laugh and looked at her with fond exasperation. "Trust you," he said, "to champion them. I doubt there's much left to corrupt. I employed them, that is all. And paid them very well."

"But they don't like the work they do!" she said angrily. "Or, at least some of them don't," she added, for it was hard to feel much sympathy for the blond woman, even now.

"Oh, child," he said sadly, "no bawd ever meant to be one, or so at least they say. Just as no caged criminal is ever guilty, and no beggar can ever find work. I didn't create the problem," he said more slowly, "although, I grant, perhaps I've abetted it. That much, I give you. And this, too," he added, "I've done you a great wrong and will try, somehow, to make it right. If you like, I'll offer for you—ah, don't wince—no? Then I'll simply say that if word of this gets out in any way, be sure I'll admit all and marry you out of hand, however you feel about me at the moment. The world's opinion will be a harsher fate to face than I could ever be if I didn't, I promise you. I'm sorry, but I won't let you suffer for my mistake."

"Only the sufferer suffers," she said bravely, and saw him wince now. "No thank you. Anyway," she added honestly, "my parents aren't home yet, and I can be within my room in a matter of minutes. We have a back stair, too. No one will know, if the . . . women don't talk."

"They won't, even if they knew what to say," he said.

She should really jump down now and be gone, she thought. Or else he ought to help her down, but he only sat gazing at her, his eyes deep in moon shadow, unreadable to her as his set face was. Then he passed a hand over his face.

"What else can I say?" he asked in subdued tones. "Forgive me, please."

"Oh, for heaven's sake," she said, surprised to discover herself more irritated with him now than she was ever frightened of him, or so it seemed, for she couldn't bear to see him so stricken, however much he deserved to be. "Do stop it! You may have almost ruined me, but you didn't. And you certainly didn't kill me."

"Did I not?" he asked in a curious voice. "Perhaps

not precisely. Perhaps I only killed a bit of your youth—and innocence. Which may be the same . . . Felicia," he said in a voice deep as the night. "Whatever memories you take from this, please know that what you learned at Wildwood tonight has nothing to do with life as you will live it, and less to do with love between men and women—however the mealymouthed might term such acts as were discussed. Whatever the women said—what goes forth between them and the men who buy their services is not at all like an act of love—or so, at least, I've been told, and do devoutly believe."

"Well, of course," she said stoutly, although she could only pray he was right. "I knew that before you did—if you're only just discovering it now."

He laughed, swung down from the horse's back, and lifted her down to the earth. Before he let her go, he spoke again.

"You'll do," he said tenderly. "That's precisely what drew me to you, and got me angry with you as well, and none of it is due to any fault in you. You're youth itself, Felicia, that's your charm, and that's your right, and I'd no right to expect anything more from you. Like this very season," he mused, looking over her head out into the night. "Like Spring itself. Beautiful and beguiling, but always taking us unaware. Such a cool and clement night, isn't it? And yet yesterday it was blustery; tomorrow it may be hot as Hades, or then again, it might even snow. It's the nature of the season, and part of its allure, the wild capriciousness, the sudden storms, the shining days, nothing young is ever stable. Or ought to be."

He saw her head cocked to the side, as if in confusion, touched the tip of her nose with one gloved finger, and smiled a crooked smile.

"Good-bye, my dear, and forgive me when you will, if you will. Now, get gone," he said abruptly, "before this night grows a second older."

She gave him a last look, and gathered up handfuls of skirt so her hem wouldn't drag on the dewy grasses, then fairly flew across the gardens. She dared to look back when she was entirely safe in her room with the door locked behind her. She was panting for breath when she finally drew back the corner of the curtain from her window to look out again. He was still there, at the edge of the lawns. Or perhaps it was only a thin shifting shadow, for when she looked again, he was gone.

She didn't have to plead a headache in the morning, for she'd a monstrous one, as well as fear, to keep her to her bed. But she hadn't been discovered. Betsy hadn't noted she was gone until long after she'd left the bonfire, and all she commented when Felicia said she'd gone back home because she'd got bored was "Good thing, that" before she smiled her new secret smile again. In the two days that followed, there wasn't a word about Lord Neville's wicked house party. Waiting for one was part of the reason her head ached so.

And so it wasn't at all surprising that when Squire Carstairs looked up from his breakfast three days later and announced, "Neville's gone," Felicia dropped her cup of chocolate.

After the mess had been cleared, the cloth changed, and Felicia had a new cup of chocolate in a grip that even death would not have deprived her of, her father spoke again.

"Daresay you heard some shocking stories, eh? The truth is, insofar as anyone can get to the truth about the fellow, that he had one of his usual parties

snugged in at Wildwood, but they'd hardly got settled in—or in their case, unsettled in," he said on a
grin, "when he routed them up and out, and closed
down the house again."

"Gone?" Felicia said.

"All over but the shouting," he said merrily. "And
the only one repining is the wine merchant."

She nodded. So it was over. And then she shook
her head. For it was not.

"Have you the headache again, dear?" her mother
asked, seeing her pallor.

"Not again," she answered in such a troubled voice
they didn't believe her. ". . . Still," she said.

"We'll get you a cold compress and some chamo-
mile tea, soothing for the nerves," her mother said
comfortingly.

Felicia nodded, although it hurt to do so. Because
she could scarcely ask for a specific to stop her from
constantly thinking so hard it made her head ache.
And moreover, knew that it was more, not less,
thinking that she had to do.

"It's a very handsome invitation," Mrs. Carstairs
said hesitantly.

"Exceedingly proper, too," her husband agreed.
"Must be some truth to the rumors. Although who
would have guessed it? Neville a pattern card of
behavior? But they say he's mended fences everywhere in London, renewed his credit with his up-
standing and noble cousins, from the Leeds to the
Newleys. Aye, he's done his time at teas and musi-
cales, sat with all the proper dowagers, swapped gossip with every old campaigner, and been bored to
bits by every pillar of society in his clubs. Now, he's
back at Wildwood, without his usual wild life," he

chuckled, "and opening it to the *ton* for this house party. And here we are, invited to it. Quite the do, I hear. Got young Miller and Dearborne, Lords Fabian and Leith, Austell himself, even the young Earl of Connaught coming, and a few score more. All top of the trees. Daresay we won't have to twist your arm to get you to go, eh, puss?" he asked his daughter.

Felicia gave him a quick sunny smile as she looked up from the book she'd been reading when her father had come in with the post. He nodded; she looked wonderfully again, had looked better every day these past days, too. Clear-eyed and clearheaded, the unusually warm, dry summer might have had something to do with it. She said it was all the rest she'd gotten, for she'd passed a great deal of time walking and reading, not racketing about as she used to do. But she'd not been sulking. In fact, she'd been a delight. He privately thought that forgetting that bounder, Jeremy Wallace, might have had more to contribute. Whatever the cause, it was wonderful to have his saucy little puss back, however much it was true that she wasn't quite the same as she'd been before her fateful Season. She was completely recovered, but something was gone or had been added. She shone now, the squire thought fondly as he stared at his only child, rather than sparkled—that was it.

"I would like to go, yes," Felicia said softly.

"It's a wonder he's asked so many male eligibles, you'd think a fellow who looks like he does would want to keep them far, especially now—not that he's bad on the eye, but so many of them are handsome as they can stare," the squire commented idly.

His wife and daughter's looks of inquiry were enough to make him go on.

"Rumor has it that he has, or is about to offer for his cousin, Lady Newley. Bit long in the tooth, but all the crack. Handsome woman, and with a head on her shoulders, too. They were seen everywhere together in London. Imagine it, Rake Neville with a bluestocking like that. Ah, well, I suppose we all have to grow up sometime. I say, are you feeling quite the thing, puss?" he asked, because his lovely daughter had grown very white.

"No . . . yes," she said, "I suppose you're right, about growing up, I mean."

"Now, now, if you don't want to go, say the word, your mother and I don't give a rap. Thought it would just give you a head start on the new Season. Not that you need one."

"Indeed, you do not," her mother said at once. "If you don't care to go, there's an end to it. Although," she added wistfully, "you would be the prettiest girl there."

"No . . . yes," Felicia said, smiling weakly. "I mean I do want to go, I must. You're quite right."

And before her parents could start worrying over her again, she began to quiz her mother about which gown to wear for the occasion, so that they'd put her moment of distress down to her week of the month or the thought of her Season, instead of the season of her heart—which was suddenly dead winter.

There had never been a summer like it on the whole green earth. The world beyond the artificial world that had been made in the ballroom of Lord Neville's stately home might be steeped in high summer, but the summer he'd had created here was the

stuff of *A Midsummer Night's Dream:* half fantasy,
half theater, far too beautiful to be anything but
unreality.

Tiny candles winked like fireflies among the myriad
fresh flowers blooming over the high doors, and
among the vines swagged high, and then looped down
low from the gilded ceilings. Fountains spilled blue-
perfumed waters to cool the pots of palms and ferns
that created instant forest dells nearby to the orches-
tra that played Mr. Handel's music before the dancing began. Stone and metallic trees of rare design
bloomed with rarer flowers that had never grown on
trees, all about the great ballroom, so that every man
felt like a satyr as he peered out from behind alabas-
ter tree trunks, at every lady who felt like a nymph
in the enchanted glade.

"Cost a pretty penny, I daresay," Squire Carstairs
told his host, as they stood surveying the company;
the elder man in some sense the host of his host,
since his was the district the house was in.

"Yes, but well worth it, I think," Lord Neville
replied.

"The ladies are certainly enchanted," the squire
agreed, smiling at his wife and daughter.

"Ah, but your ladies were before they came to my
poor home," Lord Neville answered softly, gazing at
Miss Felicia Carstairs as she held her head high and
avoided his eye.

She was magnificent, he thought, watching her.
But different. Or was it only his weeks in London
that had dulled his eyes? Because for all she was
changed, he couldn't say what it was that was different about her from the constant image he held in his
mind's eye. She wore a gown of gold net over deep
rose silk, and her light brown hair was dressed high;

she glowed like her topaz eyes, and he'd never beheld anything more beautiful. Except perhaps, for the frightened green girl he'd seen trying to hold her chin equally high the night he'd brought her to his bedchamber here. For all the pain it caused him, Lord Neville looked away then, before he turned to greet a late arrival.

He looked no different, respectability might have been a heavy burden for him, or his soul might have been lightened by his repentance, it was impossible to say. He looked as he had always done, Felicia thought. His tall, bony frame was correctly dressed in black evening dress that contrasted with a shirt and neck cloth white as the moonlight had been that last night she'd seen him. His long face was animated by polite conversation, but even from afar she knew his dark blue eyes were filled with secret humor. Just as he had always been—except for the night he'd brought her home past midnight, when the world had sat on his high shoulders and weighed his spirit down. Not handsome, no, she thought, smiling at the ridiculous thought of anyone finding him handsome. Lady Newley must have a discerning eye. For he was, Felicia thought, before she turned away to take compliments from her suitors like a proper young lady should, only wildly attractive, not at all handsome.

It wasn't until the schottische was done, the third polka played, and the guests beginning to scent dinner on the breeze caused by the servants carrying trays to the dining tables, that she managed to slip away. Felicia told her throng of gentlemen she'd a seam to repair, her mother that she was off to the withdrawing room, a friend she met at the door that she'd just come from there, and only in that way could she make good her escape. She'd never forgotten the back door.

But neither did she ever forget her host. So she was only mildly surprised when she heard his voice compete with the pulsing drone of crickets as she stood in a patch of moonlight on the terrace in back of the Court.

"I fill the house with blooms of rare and wondrous design, and find you out here admiring ivy," he said solemnly. "Can I never get anything right in your case, my dear?"

"You've done it all very right, and well you know it," she answered on a smile. "You even managed to make your bow and take an introduction to me without so much as a blink. I was impressed."

"No difficulty at all. Rakes," he explained, as he came up beside her, "are most accomplished at deceit."

"I'd heard you've given that up," she said.

It was a moment before he answered. He was overwhelmed to discover her scent, at least, was the same, a combination of lily and lilac, he thought. But her calm aplomb was new. It worried as much as surprised him. Something had happened while he was gone, he thought, involuntarily tightening his stomach muscles, trying to arm himself in some fashion against whatever he might discover that had transformed the delightfully flighty girl he remembered to this newly composed, magnificently serene one.

"Ah, but the skills remain. Let me see," he said thoughtfully. "I can still climb rose trellises in the dark of the night, hoodwink husbands without a misstep, and ah, yes, the graceful way I deliver my secret summons to hidden assignations are yet a delight to behold."

She giggled. Thank God, he thought, she still giggles.

"Your guests," she said, sobering, "will be seeking you."

"My guests," he said, leaning against the stones of the terrace wall and staring at her, "are stuffing themselves. No one misses anyone when one is feeding. That's a prime rule of nature. You've become more beautiful, I think, that's it, that's the change I see in you. How do you like your party?" he asked when she didn't answer his compliment, having, he realized with a flicker of annoyance at himself, no good answer to such an obvious thing, of course.

"My party?" she asked, her eyes opening wide, and pleasing him very much with her surprise.

"Part of my atonement," he said. "I invited every eligible gent in London here to please you. I would have hauled that fool you liked so well here as well, but not only is he wedded, but he really is a dead bore, my dear. I cultivated him for your sake, but not even for you would I endure him another moment. He talks horses. Incessantly. And he says 'I see' as regularly as a tic when you say anything about anything else, even when he clearly does not. Whatever did you see in him, I wonder? . . . Besides his face—which is not that magnificent, really, although I certainly have no right to point my bony finger at anyone else's face."

"I was very young," she said softly.

"Just so," he began, smiling—but she cut him off abruptly and said, "Please let me be the first to offer you my congratulations."

"For what?" he asked, genuinely alarmed, wondering if it were sarcasm, wondering what he'd done to offend her now.

"I hear you're about to announce your engagement. To Lady Newley," she was forced to add when he stared at her.

"Do you? Hear that, I mean," he asked. Then recovered enough to say with some emotion, "Please, I pray you, don't say a word to her about it . . ."

"I understand," she said softly.

"I doubt it," he said. "I don't think she's faint-hearted enough to actually die of fright, and doubt she's cruel enough to expire laughing, but I shouldn't want to tempt fate."

"I'm so sorry," she said quickly, and put her hand on his sleeve in sudden sympathy.

"Are you?" he asked curiously. "Why? Neither of us wants the other in matrimony. She was kind enough to reestablish me, but she enjoys that sort of thing, and I could only bear it by thinking of the result, not the whole dreary process. Becoming a rakeshame is the easiest thing in nature, if not so very much fun once you've established yourself as such. But becoming respectable is a hellish chore, and if it weren't for the fact that once so, one remains so unless one takes to tweaking the vicar's wife's . . . Oh dear," he said with much mock distress. "You see how easy it is to fall from grace?"

"Then why bother?" she asked him, as genuinely confused as suddenly elated.

"For you, of course," he said, and then hastily added, "Of course, I know you are very young, and have no reason to trust me, and I'd understand if you'd another fellow in your eye, or wanted one. But for all I know how vastly unworthy I am, I don't think I could live with myself unless I made some effort to win you. I mightn't have a chance, and know it, but I did want to make the attempt. And not just because I can't forget your kiss. Although, I'll admit that's a very strong point to an ex-rake, of course. But then there's your conversation, that must be what appeals to my new correct sensibility. I'm healthy, wealthy, and if not necessarily wise, at least you can see I don't eat much. I'd make an economical husband, there's also that. Ah, well," he said too airily. "If not, of course, I've invited every acceptable male in the kingdom that was free this weekend, as well, for your perusal."

"I see. You want forgiveness," she said.

"I want you," he said. "Or at least, yes, your forgiveness," he added quickly when she was still. "At least, can you forgive me, Felicia?"

"Only," she said at last, "if you forgive me."

"Good God! For what?" he asked, his night blue eyes wide.

"For being so very young. I blush to remember it now," she said, shaking her head. "You gave me unclouded friendship. I gave you nothing in return. Worse, I tried to use you," she said, repeating now what she had worked out all through the long weeks of summer, "in just the way I accused you of using those poor women—oh, not carnally—but still only for my own fell purposes, without a care for your feelings in the matter. Only it was worse, because I was a friend. What a jest," she said wonderingly, "I was supposed to be the innocent, and you the unprincipled one."

"But I hurt you," he protested.

"Less than I hurt you, I think," she said, "because it made me grow up, and all it made you was respectable."

"A poor exchange, true," he said, daring to smile now as he added, as he felt he must, "But in a sense,

I took your innocence—not in a good way, not in the way that would have made us both happy."

"Piffle," she said, and he grinned. "It was time. You said I reminded you of spring, and it's a lovely compliment—a belated thank you, by the by. But you forgot the most important thing about spring. It's changeable because it *is* a state of change. It turns to summer. It must. There can't be an eternal spring, who'd want one?"

"Me, if it was you," he said. "I'm hopeless. Whatever you decide to be, will be fine with me. Although I think now I see the change I was wondering about. You decided to be a woman, didn't you? I'll miss the girl, but oh! the woman. Felicia Carstairs, could you be happy with a stodgy fellow who'd never stray from your hearth except to put out the cat? If not, I'd try to be rakish again, but I'd rather not, if you please. Or if you don't—for pity's sake, say something, don't just look at me with those glowing eyes."

But she never answered in words, though he didn't mind at all, because her mouth spoke silent volumes against his.

"Oh dear," he finally said, tasting tears, and drawing back to look down at her face where she'd hid it in his neck cloth. "Is this a no? Or a happy yes? Or is it only spring showers?"

"Piffle," she sniffled. "Yes, of course. And it's nothing but a summer storm."

He couldn't kiss her for laughing. But then he couldn't laugh for her kissing him.

And the fruits will outdo what the flowers have promised . . .

—Francois De Malherbe

SUMMER'S
FRUIT

Lady Adela Clermont, Viscountess Clifford, smoothed her hair back from her fair face with one small gloved and trembling hand. She wet her lips and gazed at her reflection in the glass. Her dark eyes were so bright with apprehension that they fairly shone, and her face was without blemish. She stared at herself in her new blue walking dress, and saw that it fit as well as the modiste had promised, and that meant exactly as the latest fashion decreed. She looked for a long, considering moment, trying to envision herself hastening down the pier to meet her husband, after all these long and lonely months. Then she sat down abruptly and stared into the looking glass, without seeing a thing. It wouldn't do. It could never serve, no, not even if she were only simple Mrs. Clermont again.

No cosmetic would improve matters. There was no need for a touch of rouge, for the thought of seeing him again, and so soon, sent healthy color flying to her cheeks. Her lustrous inky tresses had been

curled and set about her small head in the highest
style. Her face would look as he remembered it, just
as he always wrote that he dreamed of it in all his
beloved, loving letters. He'd be pleased, except of
course, for the fact that she'd also changed out of all
recognition. And there simply wasn't time enough
for her to change back. His ship was due this very
afternoon.

She hadn't expected him back so soon, he'd been
promised to Wellington for the duration, but then his
uncle had died, and he'd come into the title, and as
the last of his line, there was no thought of him being
allowed to stay anywhere near the front lines. Wellington was firm about such things. Adela sighed. For
all she'd longed for Euan until it was literally painful,
finding even her body ached for him, finding that life
without him was a void that no amount of food or
drink could fill, still now she wished his uncle had
held on to life for just another month or two. A person could achieve a great deal even in such a little
time. She'd waited so long, a little longer would have
been all she'd have needed. A person could go without, and fast and exercise . . . but he was here, or
almost so, and so there was no point in thinking of
what could have been.

She drew in a deep breath and held it hard, and
gave herself one last look in the mirror before she
let it all out again. It hardly mattered, the image
scarcely changed. Her fashionable frock was belted
high under the breasts, and let to drift over her
stomach down to her little toes. Fashion this decade
was cruel to ladies of her present conformation.
There was no hope of escape in yards of material
either, for her frock was light and gauzy because of
the summer heat. Perhaps, she thought, on a glint

of humor, he wouldn't recognize her. Lord knew, she
scarcely did. She felt ill to her sizable stomach at the
thought.

"The ladies is here, ma'am," her maid said in a
little voice from the door, because she saw that her
mistress was near to weeping again. And knew that
the thought of her company might make her cry
harder. She was wrong. It only made everything
about Adela dry up with fright: eyes, mouth, and
heart's blood.

Adela went down the long stairs of her town house
with regal dignity, because, she thought with bitter
self-knowledge, she'd look a fool and a half if she
tried to hurry. Her smile froze fast to her lips when
she saw, from the look her mama-in-law shot to her
daughter, that she looked that way even so. That,
she could scarcely help, she thought resignedly. In
truth, the elder Mrs. Clermont would think that of
her if she were slim as a nymph and graceful as a
gazelle—as she had so lately been. That memory
firmed her voice, as well as her resolve as she
greeted her in-laws. Euan was coming home, and he
loved her, or had done, and they had never cared for
that at all, and so it was.

"Mama-in-law!" Adela said, as she offered her
cheek to her.

"My dear," Mother Clermont said, as she kissed
the air near to Adela's proffered cheek. "Have I not
begged you to refer to me as 'Mama'? "

"So you have," Adela agreed. "Do forgive my
wretched memory."

But not my dearest memories, Adela thought, as
she offered her cheek to be similarly bypassed by her
sister-in-law. For 'Mama' is a word that signifies love
to me, and that, my dear lady, you neither want, nor

have for me; nor then shall you ever have that name from me.

"Such a sultry day! You cannot mean to wear a shawl, my dear!" Mother Clermont exclaimed, as Adela's maid covered her shoulders with the shawl she'd requested.

"I am susceptible to chills, and we shall be near the river," Adela said, grateful that her mama-in-law hadn't named her wrap a tablecloth, for it was near to that in size. All to no avail, she thought on a sigh, for a glance at the pier glass in the hall showed it hid nothing, no more than a drop cloth covered a pianoforte from view.

"Indeed," Mother Clermont said, exchanging a knowing look with her daughter. "Ah well. Come along, the carriage is waiting, and we don't want to keep poor Euan waiting for us, not after we've waited for him so long, do we?"

It was more than sultry, the high ceilings of the town house had kept in some of the previous night's cool, so the hot, humid air in the street was a distinct and unpleasant shock to Adela as she stepped out to the pavement. London felt like the Ivory Coast today. Those fashionables who had taken to the air for surcease from the unreasonable heat found their mistake immediately, and discovered that the mere act of walking tripled their distress. Gentlemen of fashion strolled by languidly, their high white neck cloths wilting; sunstruck ladies twirled parasols and plied their fans with an energy that nothing else about them equaled.

Adela pulled her wrap tightly around herself, and taking the footman's hand, managed, after some embarrassing maneuvering, to wedge herself into the traveling carriage. As she sank to the padded squabs of the seat and tried to arrange herself against them, she felt the leather stick to her damp, overheated arms and legs in an unpleasant, insinuating way, and when she tried to adjust herself comfortably, it responded with nasty sucking sounds. She sat upright, clinging to the hanging handhold, and resolved to endure. She'd only been a viscountess for a matter of weeks, but she'd been raised to be a lady.

"We'll just sit together here, facing you," Mother Clermont said. "No need to move, my dear, or crowd in on you. There's plenty of room for Frances and I to sit side by side here, we don't take up much space—oh! That is to say, we're quite comfortable, aren't we, Frances?" she asked her daughter as Adela inwardly cringed and outwardly smiled at the reference to her bulk. "And so we'll have a chance to chat as we go on."

But they mostly chattered to each other, Adela thought with relief, for she hadn't a word to say to them. She preferred to look at them rather than speaking to them anyway. They resembled Euan so nearly it gave her a pang to see them so close. They'd his brown hair, although his was always sun-touched to bronze streaks, and his dark complexion, although his was usually tanned to dark honey, not camellia-toned, his light hazel eyes, and, unfortunately for them, his strong features, as well. But neither had his charm, his wit, or his slow and gentle smile; nor his muscular form.

It was only a mercy that neither his mother nor sister had his height and body mass. For he was slightly above average in height, and had a strong, compact and muscular form that Adela still missed by her side in their bed at night, even though she'd only rejoiced in sharing it with him for a brief two and a half weeks. Mother Clermont was of medium height and wiry configuration, and her daughter Frances, a confirmed spinster at six and thirty, was generally the same size and shape. They were not half so physically attractive as women as he was as a man. In fact, Adela wondered idly if they loved Euan so ardently because he showed the world how well they might have looked if they'd been born male, before she discarded that thought as unworthy and possibly unlucky.

In truth, she didn't know them well at all. They lived in the southeast, and seldom came to London. In the seven and a half months since she'd been wed, Adela had only met with them on a few occasions: for her engagement, at her wedding festivities, before Euan's departure for Spain, and now again for his return. Mother Clermont was so devoted to her son, it might be, Adela thought fairly, difficult for her to accept any female who'd caught his eye and then his heart; and not just the one who'd no living parents, and so had a love for her husband so strong it wouldn't brook competition, even his mother's. And Frances was so shy, it well might be that she'd a lively terror of a girl who'd been the toast of the town in her brief Season.

Now, gazing at them, seeing how nearly they resembled what she so longed to see, Adela felt a rush of warmth for them, wondering if she'd misjudged them, taking their timorousness for lack of heart and their shyness for coldness. She found herself leaning closer, as if she could catch his scent and feel his warmth after all these cold months by simple proximity to something near to his image.

Mother Clermont noticed Adela's concentration.

She paused with a bonbon halfway to her mouth. She looked to it, and then at Adela.

"Oh!" she said consciously, "I hadn't thought—would you care for one, my dear? I didn't offer because . . ." she hesitated, pointedly avoiding a glance at her daughter-in-law's considerable bulk, ". . . that is to say, you did say you were slimming . . . but they are refreshing, and it's such a hot day, should you like one?"

Adela's mouth was parched as a desert, and her body steaming, but not so hot as her rage, though she held it in. It was a peppermint, she could smell it from where she was, and she thought she'd have given anything for it and the cool illusion of ice and water that it would bring.

"No thank you, Mrs. Clermont," she said sweetly. "You're quite right, I'm slimming." Rag-mannered, cruel, boorish, and spiteful old harridan, Adela thought, as she added on a rippling laugh, "Though of course, one can scarcely tell, can one?"

"But I'm not at all sure that's wise, my dear," Mother Clermont said, her bonbon forgotten. "As I said yesterday, and I'm sure Euan will agree . . ."

"It is far too hot," Adela said in bored tones, "as it is, the motion of the carriage is making me ill. I shouldn't want to try my constitution further."

"Oh, heavens! Of course not," her mother-in-law cried with the same horror at the thought of illness manifested in such tight quarters that her daughter's face showed.

"Should you like us to stop the coach for a bit . . . until you feel more the thing?" Frances asked nervously.

And then tell Euan it was I who made you late?

Never! Adela thought as she said, "Oh, certainly not. We're so close now, after all, I can endure."

But she wondered about that. For thinking of it—of how near she was to seeing him again after seven months; of how, having said good-bye to him in January's snow, she was actually about to see him again now, this very, airless August afternoon—she felt, for the first time, really ill.

She was late, no, he was early; he wished she'd come early, and then was ashamed that he actually resented her not having arrived at dawn to wait for his ship to arrive. As he would have done, Euan thought, with a bemused grin, if it were she he were awaiting. But as he'd never have guessed himself capable of such thoughts, much less behavior, he doubted she'd know of how he burned to see her . . . to touch her . . . to hold her close again. He gave himself a mental shake, and took to watching the wharf again, surprised and a little ashamed at his strong surge of lust at the mere thought of his wife. And pleased by it, as well, of course.

Not many men could say they'd wed the lady of their most secret, lustful dreams as well as of their higher heart and mind. And then, moreover, discovered that their lady was of like mind, heart, and body. But he had. It had never been a matter of matching fortunes, families, titles, or interests. He'd been a mere Major Clermont then, with the army behind him and before him as far as he could see. For his uncle had been a relatively young man, and so while he'd known of the succession, he'd never seriously considered it a possibility. He'd a good family and adequate funds, and if he'd thought of wed-

lock at all, it was a thing for the distant "then."
"Now" had held enough diversion for any fellow.

He was fortunate in his career, he loved it—or
had—before he'd experienced the brutalities of war,
and fortunate in his appearance as well—or at least,
enough so that he always found young women, if not
young ladies precisely, who were willing to indulge
him in his pleasures as a pastime. He privately
thought the uniform helped a great deal. But he'd
never considered himself even remotely a lady's man.
At five and twenty years, he'd known a few warm
relationships, too few for his liking, too many for his
pocketbook. And as an army man, a few far more
brief encounters, of course. None had ever involved
any region remotely near his heart. He'd never
expected to be leveled at the first sight of an Imcom-
parable of the London Season. And had never imagined she might be similarly struck by him. But so it
had been.

"Struck," he decided, was the exact word.

He'd almost dropped his cup of punch when he'd
seen her. He'd been standing among friends at a ball,
and had been counting the moments until he could
gracefully take his leave. A moment later he knew
there weren't enough hours in the night for what he
hoped to accomplish. She'd hair the color of jet and
eyes dark as midnight but soft as sleep, and pale
white skin with just a touch of wine for her lips and
her high cheekbones. And a straight little nose and
wine-colored lips, and long lashes and high breasts,
and she moved like the sighs a man might utter in
his most erotic dreams. And she'd lips very nearly
the color of Beaujolais.

She'd stared back at him when she'd seen him,

and had seemed to forget what she was saying to whomever it was she was talking to just then, too.

They danced a measure of a country dance, and then the waltz. And her skin burned through to his palms through her gown and his gloves. He took her in to dinner, and then as soon as he could, to the theater, the opera, and to whatever soirees he'd got invitations to. It never failed to astound him that she accepted him every time, and yet he never found enough time alone with her for more than a stolen embrace that brought him equal parts of frustration and heady delight. Because she was always chaperoned, always correct, and always looking at him with every incorrect thing he hoped to see deep in her sparkling dark eyes.

Even if his time hadn't been measured out for him by his obligations, he wouldn't have had enough time to court her. She might have had anyone she wanted, and it nearly killed him that he knew it. Each time he managed to hold her close, to feel her body so yielding to his own, he knew he'd never find another like her, and that he ought to leave off courting her, for it was certain madness. But every time he didn't hold her, he knew he couldn't stop himself from trying for her again. It wasn't long before he had to ask for her hand, not only because he was impelled by his desires, but because he'd received his orders to march, and he couldn't bear the thought of going— perhaps to his death—without ever knowing if she'd really wanted him, too.

She'd said yes. He couldn't quite believe it when he arranged for their special license, or when he told his friends and introduced her to his family, or even when he made arrangements for their brief honeymoon. For she'd refused to let him go without mar-

rying first, she'd wanted him exactly as he'd wanted
her: soon and forever, no matter what Fate decreed.
She'd trustees for her fortune and a concerned cousin
for her guardian; they'd investigated him and to his
utter astonishment, they'd allowed the union. He
believed that if she'd still her parents, they'd never
have permitted it. His own doting mama and adoring
sister had tried to discourage him—for aiming too
high, he was sure, because there was no other reason
they could have not wanted her for him. For aside
from her legacy and her loveliness, she was only just
eighteen. And he knew she could have had anyone.

Nor had he believed it even that first time, when
he'd the right to hold her in his arms alone, and in
his bed at last. Nor even later, when he'd irrevocably
made her his own. Because even then, a moment
after his fulfillment, he'd wanted her again. Not only
so that he could bring her the pleasure they'd strived
for that nature had prevented her from attaining her
first time. But because he'd begun to understand that
he might never have enough of her; that the scant
moments nature allowed them to actually be one
were nothing like the hours he required.

They'd had hours. Long, sweet hours together in
the day and in the nights. He learned her body, and
she, his, and by the second week of their marriage,
she'd learned to take her pleasure, thereby increasing his. There'd never been such a woman. She
turned to him as many times as he to her, and had
been as eager to love as he; it was as if he were
making love to his own desires. There actually came
a time when he scarcely knew whose pleasure it was,
and whose cry it was that greeted it when it came.
They'd truly become one. Even now, thinking of her
curving, heated, lissome body as it moved against

his, seeking, he yearned for her to the point that
he had to tear his mind from her lest he embarrass
himself.

And so it had been for every minute of all these
lonely months without her. It had sustained him
through much, on and off the battlefield, and kept
him celibate without so much as a moment's struggle
with his morals, for he found he'd no desire for anyone but her. Her letters pained and comforted him,
because she felt the same. Now, he was within seconds of seeing her again, and he could scarcely con-
tain his glee and despair. Because, doubtless, he
thought with a frown, he'd have to greet his mama
and his sister as well, and it might be hours until he
could bid them good-bye and take her in his arms in
their bed again.

Still, as much as he anticipated the moment, it was
hard to look forward to pleasure when there was so
much pain about him. He looked around and not
seeing her, saw what was obviously there before him
at last. This was a shipment of those men, or, as in
some cases, those surviving parts of them, that had
managed to return, breathing, from the war. He'd
been so involved with thoughts of life and lust, he'd
ignored the plaints of those who'd only just barely
escaped, however temporarily, from death.

He recollected himself, and as if in atonement, left
his post by the rail where he'd been waiting for a
glimpse of her. He began to help some of his com-
rades from the ship. They filed down the gangway
lame, halt, and blind; lacking limbs or senses—or
minds. And for all he knew there was no avoiding it,
he felt guilty again for leaving the cause simply
because he'd a title, an estate, and other new responsibilities to claim. So it was that he was preoccupied

with working and walking a poor lad to shore on his new crutches, when he heard the glad and familiar cry: "Euan! Haloo!"

"There he is!" his mama cried, and he was lucky he could hand the boy off to his family before she cast herself into his arms, weeping and laughing at once.

Then Frances wrapped herself around him. He was genuinely glad to see them and hold them. But seconds passed and he still didn't see her. A cold dread seized at his heart. So many things might have gone wrong. He was no longer a stranger to death and disaster, his face was grim and grave when he finally was allowed to step back from his glad welcome.

It was on his lips to ask, when he saw her. And he sighed, forgetting everything but the blessed sight of her. Her eyes were wide, dark, and filled with pain that bordered on delight, a look he so well remembered from other, more intimate times. Her lips were parted and trembling. She stood apart from him, waiting. He held out his arms. But she did not rush into them. She hesitated.

Puzzled and hurt, he finally really looked at her. And lost his smile and foundered, thinking of what to do or say.

Now she stepped forward. There were tears in her eyes.

"Euan," she breathed, and then she saw his expression clearly. And flinched. She took a breath and said in falsely light tones, "What a look of amaze. You knew I was carrying your child, Euan."

"Yes. Of course," he blurted, "But not how much you were carrying!"

The silence in the carriage during the ride home was earsplitting. His mama chattered on about all

the things she'd already written about in her letters
to him, and even shy Frances had two or three dozen
comments to add. But Adela said nothing, and it was
that which Euan heard so loudly that his head ached
almost as much as his heart did whenever he looked
at her. Because he'd compounded his difficulties the
moment after he'd first spoken, when, at a loss for
further words, he'd relied on his body to communi-
cate with her, as it had always done.

He'd taken her in his arms a scant second after his
awkward mis-saying. And tried to hold her close.

Well, and what did he know of pregnant females?
He was the only son of a widowed mother and an
older spinster sister, he'd scarcely ever seen an
expectant female, or at least one that he particularly
remembered. He must have seen many, of course, he
realized; it was just that ladies seldom appeared in
public in such a condition, and when he'd seen women
in similar cases who weren't ladies, he'd scarcely
thought about them, even if he'd noted them. Why
should he, after all? So how was he to know that it
would feel so strange to hug one? So humorous, actually? As if she'd wedged a thundering, great, hard
melon up under her skirts? One that separated them
as effectively as a real child standing between them
might have done? He'd been shocked as he'd been
disoriented, and it was only the devil's own hand in
it that he'd tried so hard not to laugh that he'd
frowned. And then stepped back from her to say,
"Well, well, well."

Wonderfully well said, he thought miserably, frowning even more now and looking at her again. She sat
beside him, gazing out the window, looking out past
his very nose, as if he weren't there at all beside her,
as he'd longed to be for so long, it seemed like a bad

and distant dream now to him. Her profile was the same; there was the same straight little nose he loved to kiss, the same longlashed eyes, the same—no, he thought sadly, he never remembered those full and tempting lips being held in such a hard, straight line.

"And so we wondered if you'd like us to stay on with you instead?" his mother said now.

He hadn't heard a word that preceded the offer. In fact, he only noted it at all because he'd been studying his wife's expression when it was said, and he couldn't help but note the infinitesimally small reaction to it that she registered before she could compose her face again. Her lips had parted on a small gasp of distress, and then they'd drooped before they tightened once again.

He turned a polite, questioning face to his mama.

"Of course, we can go home, there are a thousand things to do. But since dear Adela is so . . . indisposed, we wondered if you should like us to stay on with you? Actually," his mother said, pointedly looking out the window with a noble expression as she went on, "we're staying at a hotel just now, because we didn't want to discommode poor Adela unduly for only a few night's stay, but since she is . . . if you'd like us to move in, and stay on to help until the blessed moment arrives, why then, there's no discussion necessary, we shall. In fact, we've offered."

"But," Frances said in a tiny voice as no one answered, "Adela hasn't asked us to."

"The 'blessed moment,'" Adela said in a tight voice, "shall not be until summer is over. It's to be in late September. It is now early August."

"How very good of you, Mama," Euan said smoothly, "but I'm a selfish beast, remember? I'm home now, and intend to take care of matters entirely. It's time

I got on with being a husband before I begin to be a father. We've only ever had two weeks alone, you know."

Adela looked at him then. She flashed him a look of pure relief and gratitude.

"Of course, we only wished to help, we never intended to put ourselves forward," his mother began in suffering but falsely bright accents, in the exact tone of voice she'd always used whenever he'd resisted anything she wanted him to do. The tone of voice, he remembered, that had spurred him on to enlisting as much as the world-conquering ambitions of the little corporal had done.

"Kind of you," Euan said gently, "but there's no need to put yourself out, and I've a great need to. I need to get to know my wife again, before my son or daughter takes up all her time."

Adela turned to smile at him, so radiantly that he suddenly remembered the other expectant ladies he had seen: Renaissance oils of the Madonna at the Annunciation. Thinking of that, he grinned.

"Because if the little wretch takes up her time," he added, smiling as he gazed pointedly at that which occupied his wife's lap, "to the extent that he already has her person, I doubt she'll have so much as a second to spare for me until he's of an age to go to school."

And so the remainder of the carriage ride was deafeningly silent. At least so it seemed to the Viscount Clifford, formerly Major Euan Clermont, even though he kept up a steady line of talk about his speakable war experiences the whole while. For he never heard a word he was saying. And though he'd been cited for bravery many times, he never said a word to or about his wife, for the lively fear that she might slay him if he did.

"I'm sorry," he finally said when they'd dropped off his mother and sister at the hotel, and they'd gotten back to the town house, and he'd done with greeting the servants, and they were alone in the hallway together, at last.

He hadn't addressed a private word to Adela since they'd been in the coach, but she didn't misunderstand what he was referring to.

"Well, I thought it was amusing," he said when she didn't answer at once.

"*You*," she said with tears in her eyes, "would!"

The evening of his homecoming went downward from there.

They ate dinner between uneasy sporadic silences. Once they'd discussed the menu and the weather, conversation foundered. At least he ate dinner, for he noted she only nibbled at her food, since she'd likely no place to put it, he thought gloomily. He knew it was a damnable thing, but he couldn't stop looking at her abdomen and thinking how uncomfortable it must be for her, even more so than it was for him. Her sweet uplifted breasts had grown fuller, and now almost rested on the enormous new prominence—he'd felt how hard it was and it astonished him that her slim frame could bear it. He brooded about it when he wasn't thinking about how changed she was in every way.

When she'd been slim and lithe, her personality had been just as sweetly flexible. Now there was a heaviness about her, a ponderous weight seemed to sit on her tongue as well as her body, and for the life of him he didn't know how to lighten it. He'd been the one to make her that way, after all. He found his bouts of guilt actually preferable to the other new and nasty thought that kept intruding. For the first time since they'd been made man and wife, he wondered if all his love for her hadn't been so intimately involved with their intimacies, that now that they were no longer possible, love wasn't either.

He declined sherry and escorted her to the small salon, as if she were a visiting aunt. When she'd settled in a chair, a process that made him wince, she arranged the shawl, which she'd never removed, citing a chill even in the overheated dining room, about herself and stared at him moodily.

He hadn't changed, she thought with joy and hate. Oh, his tan was deeper, his hair was worn shorter and had many more sun streaks, and he was definitely slimmer, but that made him even more attractive. He'd only sown the seed, the process of impending fatherhood wasn't visible anywhere on his person; she wondered if it were anywhere in his heart. He hadn't asked much about the baby except for a few courteous questions as to her health. And when he wasn't looking in astonishment at her belly, he was quickly looking away from it, as if he were embarrassed at being caught staring. But not as embarrassed as she was.

"I've not gained that much weight," she said suddenly, causing him to look up at her face in surprise. "It only appears that way. These fashions aren't as kind as in our mothers' days; stiff sweeping skirts would have hidden much. As it is, the doctor said that ladies of my . . . configurations," she took a deep breath and blurted, "tend to exaggerate matters. A woman's—attributes normally increase at this time. As I began with more," she said, smoothing the shawl over the shelflike projection of her bosom, with mingled pride and cold humor, "I now have a great deal more. He says," she said, losing her air of calm for a moment and looking at him with huge worried eyes, "that it will all return to normal afterward."

"I should certainly hope so!" he said, laughing. "But I'm only joking," he explained quickly, as he saw his poor attempt at lightening her mood only darken it further. "I meant to say that of course I know it's only temporary . . ."

"How selfish I am," she announced in a brittle voice. "Here you are, newly come from the wars, and all I talk about is myself. Tell me, how was it?"

Since he had told her in innumerable letters all that he felt suitable for a lady's ears, and since he found he didn't want to tell this hostile, matronly stranger anything else, he only shrugged.

"Do you think it could wait?" he asked. "It's late, I've been traveling for weeks, all I really want is my bed . . ." he paused, and before he could think about what he was saying, asked, ". . . It is still *our* bed, isn't it?"

"Oh," she said, her face growing pale, "I didn't think, would you be more comfortable alone? I can always move into the blue bedchamber . . ."

"I hadn't thought, either. Would it harm you if I shared a bed with you . . . to sleep, I mean," he said, horribly embarrassed, wondering whether she thought he wanted more from her, wondering if she'd thought he were some sort of perverse creature that would force his hungers on a woman in her condition.

"Oh no," she said, equally quickly, "there'd be no harm. I only wondered if you'd feel uncomfortable with me."

Of course he would, but he couldn't say so, and not only to spare her feelings. But because he discovered he didn't want to be alone tonight. He'd known how it was with her, had celebrated it for months, in fact, comforted by the idea that if he should perish, in some way he'd live on. But he hadn't known the reality of it, or perhaps he'd only not wanted to. The thought of having her in his bed tonight in a different way had sustained him through so much—his voice was filled with that and other longings he didn't dare contemplate as he answered her.

"If you wouldn't mind, I am weary of sleeping alone," he said.

It was all she could do not to weep as she sank into the feathers of their bed at last. She'd waited until he came out of his dressing room and extinguished the lamps before she ventured forth from her dressing room. And then she settled into her side of the bed. It was a rich man's bed, a huge bed, and the feathers so soft that once she'd picked her place and settled into it, she might as well be sleeping alone. In the old days, during those two wonderful weeks, they'd joked about it. They'd made a nest together, and laughed in the mornings when they'd risen to see that they'd left only a single deep furrow in the center of the bed.

Now she lay alone and saw in the dim glow of a starry night, that there was, at last, another body sharing the mattress with her. It was clear he didn't wish to see her any more than she wished him to see what he'd made of her. But she'd dreamed—after all, the doctor had said they could have marital relations until the end of this month. She'd been counting the days since he'd set sail for home with the same concentrated fear and anticipation with which she'd counted them after he'd sailed away, and she'd begun to wonder if he'd left her with an unexpected farewell gift. Because for all she'd changed, she still longed for his touch, and hoped it might ease her doubts as it surely would her other longings.

This was nothing like any homecoming she'd imagined. He'd been a lusty man, delighting in her body, and that in itself had set her to worrying. As the curves he'd taken such pleasure in became more swollen, she'd dared hope he'd rejoice at seeing the proof of their love, as she could not when envisioning his reaction. As her body changed beyond her wildest expectations, she'd anticipated everything from his being smug, to his being revolted, but never his being a disinterested stranger. He'd not even attempted to touch her. Not even so much as to caress a blameless white shoulder.

Still, once he'd been her lover. And he was home at last, and whole. Though she might almost hate him now, she could not but rejoice for that.

"I'm glad you're home, Euan," she managed to say in soft, unemotional tones, repressing tears, speaking into the empty night.

He wanted to hold her, he needed to kiss her, he wished he knew what to say to her. But she was as changed as she was obviously hostile, and he feared her rejection as much as discovering the truth of who this woman was that he'd married. It was a moment before he could answer.

"I'm glad to be here," he said. And wished it were entirely true.

Breakfast was easier. She'd risen first, called her maid to the dressing room, and gotten bathed and dressed before he'd awakened. And so she'd been at the breakfast table waiting for him with all the ammunition she needed. She had all sorts of fodder for conversation at her disposal.

First, there were the plans for his acquiring a valet to be discussed. Of course, as an army man he could do for himself, but he no longer had so much as a batman, and he was a viscount, not merely a major now. When that was resolved, there was the stack of invitations that had been delivered with regularity since the word of his return had gotten out. And if all else failed, she'd the *Times* to open and peruse and ask his opinions about.

Her heart leapt up when he entered the room and smiled at her as he used to do. She grinned back at him. With the heat of the day still muted by morning and the sunlight all around them, it was as if the events of last night had been all part of some hazy bad dream brought on by heat and exhaustion. He abandoned the head of the table to come sit near to her, and with the lower portion of her body hidden by the cloth, it was, for that brief time, as though nothing had changed—except there had been no glorious night more recent than that last one last winter for them to remember as they gazed at each other.

He exclaimed over the excellent quality of the food, so welcome after army rations, and was delighted to see his Adela, his well-remembered, beloved wife, smiling back at him at last. He ate his breakfast and listened to her talk, feeling that the awkward pair of last night had vanished with the morning light. He agreed to the idea of a valet immediately, and asked her to see to acquiring one for him. As she read off a few of the invitations to London's social whirl, he nodded, his mood lightening even further, watching her lips, if not her words, his world slowly returning to normal.

"And then Lord and Lady Leith are in town for a space, and request our presence at an informal supper tonight. I thought you'd like to go," she said comfortably. "You were once a friend of his, as well as of her late father's, I recall."

"I hope I'm still Leith's friend," he said. "Yes, it'll be good to see him again. I hear she's grown to be a beauty, too, against all odds. I'll let you know if it's true."

"Maternity has changed my figure, Euan, not my eyes," she laughed. "I hope I can see for myself."

He put down his coffee cup, and looked at her with a slight frown.

"You can't mean to go," he said. "It'll be hot and crowded, if I remember anything of London 'dos."

"I'll survive," she said airily. "Town's scarce of company now because it's summer, so it shouldn't be too dreadful a crush. It will be a rare treat for me. Yes, isn't that a change? I'm thrilled to attend any sort of evening social. I haven't been anywhere at all, since I . . . that is to say, without you."

But his frown remained.

"I know you stayed in London to await my return," he said, "and appreciate it. But surely you'll want to be quit of it now. It's beastly hot here, and dirty. Don't you want to stay home and rest tonight, until we can leave?"

"Leave?" she asked confusedly.

"Yes," he said, "I've got some business to take care of, and some friends I'd like to see. But the sooner I can get you back to the country and the good, fresh air, the better it'll be for both of you, surely."

"My doctor is here," she said, stiffening.

"Well, he ought not to be," he said, frowning deeply. "I thought you'd have one at home by now."

"Which home?" she said coolly. "I've never lived in Sussex with your mama and sister. That's their home, certainly not mine without you. I left Eaton Hall to my factor and tenants when I married you. I've stayed here in London and never set foot in the viscount's estate in Kent, for I wouldn't, you know, without you. No, *we*," she said too sweetly, "have lived here in London since you married me and left *us*," she concluded through tightly closed teeth.

Because it was altogether possible he didn't wish to be seen with her, she thought. And in the ordinary way of things, she wouldn't, couldn't accompany him, not in her condition. It just wasn't done. That was why she'd had to refuse all invitations since she'd begun to inflate so alarmingly. But the invitation was to an informal get-together with old friends, the sort of casual thing she might attend without shocking anyone, without shaming herself or him. But then, too, she thought, her jaw tightening, it was possible he simply didn't want to be seen with her there—or have her see him leave afterward. He'd complained of an empty bed. If that were so, he'd been chaste for seven and a half months and two days, as she knew all too well. It was entirely possible that now that he'd seen her, he wished to share his bed with livelier company.

He saw the set of her chin. What did he know of her condition, after all? Peasant women tended the fields until the moment of birth, or so they said. Perhaps ladies could see to their social obligations until the last minute as well. For although she'd said they'd a month and a fortnight wait, it looked, to his

anxious eyes, as though he might become a father if
she sneezed too hard.

"Well, excellent," he said. "If you don't think it
will be uncomfortable for you, I'd love to have your
company."

But as she couldn't bear the thought of the heat of
the day, she retired to the cool precincts of the salon
to read, and as he had a dozen errands to run, he
left the house soon after. And so for all they'd been
apart for exactly two hundred and twelve days, as
each of them knew to the precise hour, they didn't
see each other again until evening, and both of them
were enormously relieved by that, although they earnestly wished they were not.

The pink silk was obscene; that color and material
was never meant to grace the shape she saw in the
glass. And when the great pink silk-covered expanse
that dominated her view surged to the side, as it was
wont to do, the effect was terrifying, even to herself.
The heat made the silk hard to peel off, and disquali-
fied a dozen other dresses as well. The sheer blue
was for daytime, the black, only suitable for mourning, and white was entirely out of the question,
unless she wanted to look like an unshorn sheep or
a cloud, Adela decided.

It was too hot for sleeves, and her arms looked
quite well without them; they were her most superior
asset now, she thought glumly, staring into the glass.
But she'd nothing to match them, and no frock that
didn't make her look absurd. But what could a creature whose navel was suddenly discovered to be
turned inside out expect? she thought in despair and
self-loathing.

She almost gave up, until her clever maid produced

a patterned muslin with every seam let out, one with
fluttery lilac ribbons, to match the intricate chinoise-
rie design. She would be in highest style, if not
grace, Adela decided moodily, seeing how ill she
suited the lovely fabric, even if it did suit her as best
she could hope.

The patter of sudden rain on the windows cheered
her. It might be that she could keep her oilskin on
throughout dinner. Or that a nice, dismal, damp, and
cool English summer would finally commence, so that
she could wrap herself to her ears and look well. It
was only her luck that this singular summer of her
fecundity was the hottest one she could remember.
She could do with a frost, she thought, until she saw
Euan when she emerged from her dressing room,
and felt warmth rush to her heart as well as her
cheeks as she gazed at him. For though he was
immaculately dressed in his evening garb, and the
tight-fitting fashion flattered his muscular form, it
made her wish she could see how truly slender,
strong, and graceful he appeared without his garments again, as she used to have delight in doing
before she took to dressing in secret and going to
bed in the dark.

"You look lovely," he said, holding out his hands
and catching hers, as he leaned his head back to see
her.

"What a lovely lie," she said bitterly, "for the only
way you can see me is to step back, and yet if you
lean any farther back, you'll fall."

"I'm sorry," he said awkwardly, dropping her
hands. "Do you detest it so much?"

"Don't you?" she asked.

Before he could think of how to answer, she cut

him off, "Yes, yes, I know, and there's no other way to get heirs, is there? Shall we go?"

"You really do look wonderfully well," he said, sorry he was a plainspoken army man and not a glib fellow used to dealing with ladies. He was sorrier still that he wasn't used to dealing with this new wife of his. "Your face is even lovelier than I remember," he said, speaking only the truth as he saw it.

But it seemed he'd finally said the right thing, because her eyes lit up and she took his arm, and didn't complain once as he assisted her in making her difficult way down the long stairs.

Lady Leith was a redhead, which was not at all the fashion. But she was beautiful even so, and so would always be in her own fashion. She was charming, almost boyishly candid, and as enthusiastic about life as she seemed to be about her new and doting husband. Adela would have liked her very well if it weren't for the fact that for all her feminine lush curves, she was almost boyishly slender as well. Once she herself had had such a supple waist, hadn't she? Adela thought as they greeted their host and hostess. And only a hand span had separated one hipbone from the other, she remembered, and so Euan used to demonstrate, with pleasure, to her. And she could waltz gracefully, sit comfortably, and the gentlemen would eye her just as appreciatively as they now did their hostess, hadn't they?

And the ladies would ask her about other things than breeding.

"Oh yes, quite comfortable, thank you," Adela said to her hostess's kind inquiry.

"Next month," she said to Lady Nugent.

"Yes, my first," she told Miss Hancock.

"A boy or a girl, so long as it is healthy, but I think Euan would prefer a boy," she told Mrs. Hathaway.

The gentlemen used to speak with her about more than the past and her husband, she recalled.

"Oh yes, very proud of him," she said to her host. "But of course I remember, it was the waltz at the Adamses' house just before I was wed last December," she informed Lord Knight. And, "Dreadfully, I missed him dreadfully," she told Peregrine Wallace. And, "Yes, and so I haven't gone about much of late, it certainly has been a frightful summer," she agreed with the Baron Stafford.

And then they all, for a mercy, let her be.

The ladies were kind, but too curious, for they none of them had any children yet, and she didn't know how to play at being the enchanted expectant mother. All she wanted to do was hide, from them and the gentlemen. Because Lord Knight had once vowed he'd slay himself since she wouldn't have him, albeit with a twinkle in his eyes, and Peregrine Wallace had sent her flowers, and Baron Stafford had been a delightful flirt. They'd all been part of her court, but she ought to have remembered that they'd all been Euan's friends, too, for then she'd never have come to let them see her now.

She scarcely did even now. She sat silent, avoiding their eyes. And so the gentlemen privately thought she'd made the wrong choice in Euan—wouldn't have thought so, charming fellow, but one never knew, poor girl. The ladies thought her sullen, disagreeable, or simply overset by the profundity of her obvious condition. And she wished the night was over almost as much as she wished it had never begun. So it was as altogether wrong for Euan to ask her what the matter was when they got back home, as it would have been for him not to.

She tossed her gloves on the dressing table, and spun around to face him. This was the first time they'd been alone and obviously wide-awake in their bedchamber since he'd returned the day before.

"Wrong?" she asked shrilly, "Wrong? It's a lucky thing you weren't in the infantry, Euan, if you can't see what's wrong. Your horse probably had to lead you to the fray. Or else you listened for the cannon. What's wrong is that I am ridiculous. What's wrong is that I am swollen like a bladder, and I waddle, yes, I waddle when I walk, and your mother thinks it's charming, but then she never cared for me and doubtless suspects I deserve such misery; I am fat as a stoat, though I can't eat a thing, nothing looks well on me, gentlemen pity me rather than flirt with me, and I have a navel that has turned inside out! That," she said, taking a breath, "is what is wrong."

He knew everything she said was so, and felt as bad about it as she did. But his pride in approaching fatherhood had been fanned to life by all his friends congratulating him for it, and he felt guilty for his pleasure, both now and at the time he'd started her condition. And she did look a fright. But he had been getting used to it, had begun to find it almost as endearing as it was becoming interesting, and had been nerving himself to ask if he might touch her, to get the literal feel of the transformation that was occurring. But the mention of her navel stopped him short in every way. He'd seen a great many things on various battlefields and beds, but what she claimed bemused him as much as it amused him.

Pity stirred him, remembered love searched for

the right words, but before he could find them, pride and guilt spoke up for him.

"It's what happens when a man and a woman make love, Adela, I'd think someone might have told you," he said angrily. "I'm sorry that you find bearing my child such an ugly experience, but even sorrier that you think all a woman has to do in life is flirt and wear fashionable clothes."

He was entirely right, and that made it worse. It was petty of her, and she was as ashamed of herself as she was unsure of his love. But she'd never let him know it.

"It's very easy for a fellow to sow and then let someone else reap for him," she said with a sneer.

"Is it?" he asked, his lips white. "Odd. I find it most difficult."

He turned on his heel and strode to the door.

"Good night," he said as he touched the doorknob, for even in a rage he couldn't help but be polite. "You needn't worry about me disturbing you tonight. When I return, I'll take the blue bedchamber."

He left her, wishing he hadn't even as he did, and left her wishing she could run after him and run him through, with words or a rapier.

She passed the night wondering, as usual, who it was that was romping so busily beneath her spread hand, as it lay upon her abdomen. And, as unusual, who it was that Euan was romping with in a different bed all night.

He went to an inn where no one knew him, and drank a deal more than was good for him, for he'd a hard head that allowed him to overindulge. Even if he were the sort of fellow to become wild and merry in his cups, the thought of her face as he'd left kept sobering him. And the thought of her body, as it had been and as it was now, kept his mind far from the females that occasionally approached him.

In the morning, he'd nothing to show for his unhappiness but circles beneath his eyes and an aching head. But she'd a resolve. She met him at the breakfast table with her plans.

"You were quite right," she said, and his eyes softened as he gazed at her. "London doesn't suit me now. I shall do as you suggested. I'm going home."

It was a measure of his hurt and confusion that he didn't think to ask her which one until he could no longer see her traveling coach after it turned the corner and trundled down the street.

"But how ghastly!" Charlotte Murray breathed. "And in all this heat! What an odd welcome that must have been for you after all those long and lonely months, poor lad," she added on a low chuckle.

Euan stiffened. Such a double entendre would be barely tolerable if it had been made by an old friend, but coming from a lady who was the widow of an old friend, there was nothing he could do but smile and hope he'd misinterpreted it. Actually, he mused, he was so bedeviled by such thoughts these days, it was possible that was the case.

"It was a surprise, yes" was all he said before he drank down the rest of the champagne in his glass.

She smiled up at him, a knowing little twist of a smile that sat well on her dark, exotic face.

"What a farewell that must have been, to have produced such a bountiful welcome," she chuckled. "Arthur always said you were a thorough fellow."

"Arthur," Euan said with a smile of his own, remembering his old comrade-in-arms and realizing that was just the sort of thing he might have said, "would have made a cake out of me and a party out of it; he loved a jest. Good Gods—I do miss him, still. It must be difficult for you."

She shrugged, a pretty gesture that made the web of brilliants hung at her smooth breast tremble and wink. "One gets used to such things, when one must. It's been two years, after all. He wouldn't have wanted me to mourn forever. He, of all men, would have known how hard it is to warm oneself with memories."

Too late, Euan remembered his old army friend's casual promiscuity that had always shocked him so much he'd always ignored and tried to discount it.

"But you, of all men, must know that for yourself now," Charlotte said on another rich and low chuckle. And in case he tried to misinterpret her again, she leaned, ever so slightly, against him. But not so slightly that he didn't feel the tightly knitted nubs of her breasts, through her thin gown, nudge him into just such memories. The current fashions might be cruel to his wife, but they suited Charlotte very well. And him ill, he thought.

They stood at the sidelines of the dancing at the Vauxhall Gardens. It had been such a warm, long night, after such cold, long months, that he'd thought to hunt up some old friends and stray breezes this oppressive, lonely night. It was only natural that they ask old Arthur's widow along as well—as well as several other ladies and women who were friends of his friends. That had reassured him as to the innocence of his night's desires, for he knew how easy it would be to hunt up other sorts of stray females at the gardens, and had resisted the thought, if not the urge. And now this, from a lady he'd considered safe . . . or had he ever? he wondered, as he looked down into her amused eyes.

She was small, her dark head reached just to the top of his shoulder, and so her breasts were currently burning small holes in his side, near to his heart. Although that wasn't involved in this at all, he thought, and held hard to that thought as she grinned wider, continuing to stare up at him. She fit very well in his arms, they'd already shared a few polkas and waltzes, and he knew very well the other recreation they could pair off nicely at. It would only be for a few hours out of a long life, and the relief would be even more welcome than the pleasure she offered. He needed her, Lord knew that was true, and as she hinted and was now saying in bold silent ways, she needed him. How long should a man stay celibate, after all? And Adela would never know, if she'd even care. She obviously didn't want him. It had been a week since she'd left him, months since he'd had her. He didn't even know where she was now, after all.

But he knew how she was. He sighed and stepped away from Charlotte's invitation. Even if Adela never knew, he would. And it simply wasn't fair. He might be many things, and capable of more, but he was always fair, or so his men had always said. Adela couldn't attract anyone's attentions but a midwife's now, that was part of her anger with him. If she yearned as he did, he could understand some of her rage. Not all of it, of course. What the rest might be—whether just the chagrin of a trivial girl who found herself suddenly unattractive, or the fury of a woman who didn't wish to bear his child, or something else unthinkable—was a subject he avoided entirely, since such thinking was so filled with hurt and disappointment with her. But the obvious, at least, was his fault. He couldn't make it worse. Anyway, Charlotte knew all his friends, and who knew who might talk?

"So faithful?" Charlotte breathed. "But Arthur's gone, never to return, and your wife's gone and you're at loose ends. I thought you'd like to pass an interesting night."

"Too interesting, I'm afraid. I'm a dull dog," Euan apologized, "and like the Arabian who scorns a sip of wine, afraid to acquire more exotic tastes."

"Nicely said!" Charlotte applauded literally, clapping two small gloved hands in glee.

He bowed, she laughed. He was very grateful for his old friend's morals now, for it seemed his widow was equally casual about both lust and loss. For as soon as the music stopped, and Alfred Pettigrew, late of His Majesty's Light Hussars, stepped out of his partner's embrace, Charlotte begged a dance of him. One raised eyebrow served as Alfred's silent query, a slight smile and nod was Euan's answer, and he was surprised to find himself equally relieved and chagrined as he watched the two whirl away together.

"Alfred's all elbows and knees," Miss Stinson, his deserted and flushed partner complained. "A regular Jack of legs, and we've known each other a dog's age. I never thought I'd have a chance to dance with you, though," she said, eyeing his muscular frame with an equal show of hunger and coyness.

Dancing with Miss Stinson was far more difficult for Euan than standing at the sidelines with Charlotte had been. She was a tall, exceedingly well-developed young female, and for all he knew she was dim, ill-bred, and overly aggressive, still, he soon found himself in a positive agony of desire. The dance was a waltz that she chose to execute with just the sort of abandon that moralists had cautioned about when the waltz was first introduced into society. It was a singular lesson as well as a weird sort of relief for Euan to realize that it was only the proximity of soft skin, breasts, and undulating hips that had drawn him to Charlotte, after all. For if he could desire such a clodpoll as Miss Stinson with even more urgency, he realized, he was far more in need than was sane or safe.

She was staggered when he bowed and left her after the dance, since his body had all too obviously told her how enthusiastic his response had been to her. It must be that he was transmitting some sort of silent signal to females now, he brooded as he strode off into dark gardens, the way a stag in rut does. Because it was painfully ironic that he was now more successful with women than he'd ever dreamed of being when he'd first dreamed of being successful with them. And he wasn't even in uniform any longer. But Miss Stinson was out of the question, whatever his body had pleaded. She'd definitely talk, she'd never stopped all the while they were dancing, after all.

There were anonymous females plying their ancient trade everywhere to be seen in the dim glow of the gaslight in the gardens. Some were young, and some were quite lovely. They couldn't talk to anyone who knew him about anything more than the color of his coins if he chose to have one of them give him surcease. For they'd know little else of him except for his quick anonymous coupling in the dark. The thought stirred even as it disturbed him, and he slowed his steps to stare at a blond young woman, who stared back at him with equal interest.

She was blond, and Adela was dark, and so he'd not even think of her as he . . . lovely, he thought with rueful merriment, as he picked up his pace and strode out of the gardens, yes, excellent reasoning, Major; it's a good thing you're a civilian now, and it was only a lady of the streets you faced and not the possibility of a more permanent death than the little one you were considering, he told himself angrily.

Yes, certainly, he continued to jeer at himself; imagine you won't think of her during, even though you can't stop thinking of her before. Yes, of course, he told himself as he reached the entryway and raised his hand for a hackney coach, and so why not buy a twopenny whore and have her under London Bridge as a drunken officer he'd once known had done. And then moan and lament about the miseries of your clap for months afterward, as he'd done, too? Euan had known enough gentlemen and soldiers who suffered from love's complaint to know the folly of that course. But he also knew it was his conscience that would burn far more.

No, he thought wearily, laying back against the squabs of the hackney coach, exhausted with unspent desire, it was time to go home. Wherever that was.

This summer of her ripening, this interminable season of growth, had been a rich one for nature as well, Adela mused as she strolled through the garden. Dragged and panted through the West garden, she corrected herself. Because that was the only way she could walk in the heat with her present bulk. And as yesterday afternoon had been passed in the Rose garden, the morning in the South garden, and she'd already admired the Knot garden, drowsed in the Herb garden, and daydreamed by the banks of the Water garden, this must then be the West garden. She imagined if she stayed up all night, the helpful staff of her husband's recently inherited home would be pleased to show her the Dusk, Midnight, and Dawn gardens, because she supposed Great Pollard Court had those, too. It had everything else. Except for its master in residence.

She couldn't help thinking of him here, where he was supposed to be, although he'd not set foot here since his accession to the title. But where else was she to go? Certainly not to his mother. Her own home was let out. Her cousin would be almost as appalled as she was at her not being with her husband at this crucial time. And she would not stay in London to see him dishonor her by making love to others, or pretend to not see him doing it, as so many other *tonnish* wives did.

She'd never thought to have this sort of marriage. It had been one of the reasons why she'd married him so out of hand; he'd seemed as sincerely drawn to her as she to him. And as sincere about love as she was, too. So it had been in those first and only days of their true union. Those early days had been filled with love and longing instantly met with carefully taught repletion. She'd been genuinely glad to discover herself carrying his heir when he'd left her so alone. At first. But then she'd discovered she'd no one to share the strange and wonderful changes that were taking place in her. An orphan and product of an elite girl's school, her old friends were wed and with their own families, and everywhere else in England. And her best friend was gone. But she could scarcely write:

"Dear Euan,
    You'll be happy to know that I've stopped casting up my accounts every morning. Now I merely feel bilious.

It's odd how my breasts have become numb and yet tingle as they continue to swell, and even more curious how like a rock the bulge in my abdomen is. How are you, my dear? . . ."

No. She could scarcely even imagine herself saying it to him—but she might have whispered it to him during long shared nights. To make matters worse as the process went on, for once her lavish configurations served her ill—she was alarmed to discover how very *enceinte* she appeared. She had to give up excursions to the theater long before other women might have, and as for grand social affairs, they were out of the question for a lady in her condition with no husband to accompany her. That might have been when the resentment began. It might have grown through the lonely months as she realized she'd only known him for six months, all told. Had only lived with him for a fortnight and a day before he'd left her. And perhaps had never really known him at all.

Then he returned, changed outwardly only by an increase in his attractiveness, but changed otherwise even more than she had. Because she'd only changed her appearance.

But he'd been staggered at the sight of the change in her, had stolen furtive glances at her when he wasn't gaping at her abdomen outright, spoke to her in stilted ways while he ogled her, and then stayed strictly to his side of the bed, before he stayed out all night. And never touched her. She didn't know if she was more disappointed and wounded by his attitude or by her own foolish misreading of his character.

Well, but a melancholy mother made for a dismal child, she told herself now as she sniffed back an omnipresent tear, and tried to appreciate the lavish spread nature had put before her.

The roses, marigolds, lavender; the pots, vines, and bushes full of other myriad blooms had full-blown blossoms, and the bees were celebratory as they thronged the gardens, too busy, too drunk on this lavish summer to pay any attention to humankind. It was too much to take in all at once for them and for her. Adela started back to the house. The huge drawing room here at Great Pollard Court was gilded and frescoed, as full of light and color as the gardens, but a deal cooler at the height of day.

She did have a sumptuous home, she told herself, a devoted staff, and a new and kindly doctor who seemed to know what he was about, and only a month to go now, after all. But she stopped tallying her remaining blessings when she caught sight of the coach laden with baggage that was being unloaded in the front drive. She recognized his bags, the same one's she'd packed up with him that winter's night a thousand years ago when they'd loved each other, and her heart rose high. Until she realized it must only be that he'd decided there'd be talk if he weren't with her now. For he hadn't written or communicated with her in any way during the whole nine and a half days she'd been gone from him.

Well, and so she guessed she could always go back to London again, she thought sadly. Before she got hold of herself and realized with considerable relief and despair that the Court was such a huge place that she might live here with him and not see him for weeks at a time.

"My dear," he greeted her as she came into the drawing room, "a magnificent place, isn't it? Do you think you'll be happy here?"

The servants were watching with pleased little smiles upon their faces.

"How could one not be, my dear?" she answered.

"How did you know I'd be here?" she demanded as soon as they were alone.

She paced their enormous bedchamber, refusing to meet his eyes, wishing he wouldn't watch her so closely.

"You weren't at my mama's," he said in a flat voice, from where he sat by a window, at his ease. "You'd hardly go to your cousin, and I saw that your tenants were ignorant of anything but my kind attention to your property. I'd done enough traveling by the time I decided to come here, and besides, where else should you be? Except with me."

"Except," she said, "that you didn't seem to want me."

"Or you, me," he answered.

"Well, then . . ." she said, and stopped. For she didn't know how to go on; and for all she'd been about to demand a separation, the rapid beating of her heart echoed that in her lower body, and she suddenly remembered that she had more to speak for than herself now. If she went on, she might lose control, and she certainly wouldn't allow herself to weep before this stranger who'd given her the burdens she now carried.

He rose and went to look out the windows at the long lawns.

"So long as we remain here together," he said in that new, flattened voice, "I think we ought to share a bedchamber. We've caused enough talk with our sudden separation after our long one as it is, I think. Even my mama had heard of it."

"I'd think she would have," Adela said, and swallowed the question that sprang to her mind: having to do with how many cheers his dear mama had given on hearing the news.

"I won't disturb you," he added, "in any fashion. I can sleep in the dressing room with none the wiser."

"Or cling to your side of the bed as you did in town, if you wish," she said lightly, for really, she'd this awful urge to laugh or cry.

"Whatever," he said with an abrupt wave of his hand, as if it made no matter, as if all of this didn't make him feel as cruelly used as much as it made him feel a monster. "I shan't bother you."

"No," she said with absolute honesty, turning away, "I rather thought you wouldn't."

They maintained an uneasy truce for two days. There were the servants and their duties for the new viscountess to continue to acquaint herself with, as well as the state of the household stores: linens, silver, china, and all else necessary for a grand manor house in the country. The weather continued its un-British clemency; each day dawned soft and warm, and ripened to heat, before it cooled to a fair star-struck evening. But Adela could feel the atmosphere thickening, as before a summer storm. She arose after her husband in the mornings, avoided him adroitly until their silent luncheons, went her separate way until their mute dinner, and then retired to her bed, leaving him to his books, his sherry, or whatever he found to solace his solitary nights. But she felt familiar stirrings of rage and insult whenever she found herself noting his trim form, his narrow hips and waist, his broad chest, or caught so much as a glance from his disinterested, lovely hazel eyes.

He'd known this feeling before, Euan thought, this prickling at the base of the neck, this sudden bitter taste on the tongue, and tightening of the gut. He remembered it from the last seconds before battles he'd faced; and experienced it whenever he met her. He saw her in passing, and passed her as often as he could in his daily routine. There were fields to see and tenants to meet, workers to get to know and papers to go over. A factor could do only so much, a landowner must know his own territory as surely as a soldier did. He found the work engrossing, more so when he realized it kept his mind from that which otherwise never left it. She was still lovely.

That was the damnable part of it. Once his eye had adjusted to her new contours, she was as lovely as before, perhaps, in a new way, more so. Perverse as it might be, in light of her lack of love for him as much as her current state, he desired her. Which made him furious and frightened.

On the third night of their shared residence at Great Pollard Court, they dressed to go out for the evening.

"I don't know if this is a good idea for you," Euan said, as he came in from the dressing room and found her studying herself in the glass.

"I believe it is," she said smoothly, adjusting a tiny shivering diamond flower of an earring. "I've been invited to go, I know I ought to go, and I shall go. Do you think I will disgrace you?" she asked, rising and facing him directly.

She wore a light, gauzy frock of light blue with an intricate embroidery of darker blue upon it. A fringed shawl in similar colors laced with gold was draped about her shoulders, and she looked, he thought, both imperial, and young and fragile, for all her obvious state. He stared at her for a long moment.

"Disgrace me? No, not at all," he said quietly.

"Thank you," she said coldly, "but beware, such flattery will certainly go to my head."

"I only wondered if it was safe for you to go out tonight," he said as coldly.

"Oho!" she said on a brittle laugh. "So you fear I'll be stolen away by some impetuous youth!"

"I wondered if a coach ride was wise at this stage of events," he said in bored tones, busying himself by readjusting his perfectly formed neck cloth in the glass, so that he wouldn't either strangle or embrace her.

"If," she said through her teeth, "you remembered the day this began, if not the one on which it's supposed to end, you'd know I've another three weeks, at the least, to go. They are our neighbors, and I ought to get to know them so that I've someone to talk with. For all I don't know her or her family, I did know him, or at least of him, in London. Everyone in the district will be there—oh!" she said, breaking off and eyeing him sidewise, noting his tight-fitted buckskin pantaloons and his intricately patterned waistcoat. "But perhaps it's not whom I might meet that troubles you, but who you may not be able to meet with me by your side?"

"If I'd wanted that," he said icily, "I would have remained in London."

"And you did not?" she asked with bitter humor.

"Perhaps I did—too much. Perhaps that's why I left," he said.

Her dark eyes flew wide. He felt as stricken as she clearly was, but before he could think of what to say to heal what he'd said, her head went up and she spoke again.

"I could have had anyone," she said, her eyes glistening with tears. "Anyone. Lord, what a fool I was."

And because he thought so, too, had always thought so and worried about when she'd realize it during all those long months of their separation, he spoke up immediately, reflexively, as he would parry any saber thrust to his heart.

"Indeed, there's the root of it, isn't it? You've never thought of anything else but your beauty and your availability, have you? No wonder you despise your condition, and the man who made you so."

She stood still as stone and let the silence fill up the room before she spoke again. She stared at him, hoping for at least his compassion, for she didn't think she could go on with the conversation without breaking, and yet didn't know how to break it off now.

"I carry your child, Euan," she finally said, hating herself for having to say so.

"Ah, but you never wanted to," he said, staring back at her.

"We cannot go on like this," she said, turning from him, lowering her head and shaking it back and forth, holding her grief by concentrating on the feeling of the cold earrings swinging against her cheeks. "Indeed, we cannot."

"No, we cannot," he agreed in a dry, dead voice. "We must discuss it. An annulment, of course, is out of the question. Perhaps a permanent divorce is, too—unless you're willing to brave society and the law courts. I'd be willing to testify to any sort of misrepresentation you wish to accuse me of. It makes no matter now, I'm out of the military. But if you like, we can attempt merely a physical separation at first, and see how that suits."

She nodded.

"Yes. Well, I expect we'd better send our regrets," he said heavily, turning to the bellpull.

"Indeed not!" she said, pulling herself erect. "Now more than ever, I suppose, I shall need to know my neighbors—oh—or shall they be yours? It hardly matters, I could do with some gay company tonight, I've been alone far, far too long."

"As have I," he agreed, and offered her his arm.

"We'll discuss this later," he promised as she put her hand lightly on his arm, and she walked, regal as a queen, and he, dignified as an executioner, and they left the scene of battle.

The noise, the sheer exuberant cacophony of many people talking at once above the sound of music, was as loud as it was welcome to the ears of the Viscount and Viscountess Clifford when they were admitted to their neighbor, the squire's, house. Their carriage ride had been, after all, silent except for the sounds of the creaking coach and the laboring horses. And though they'd each separately thought nothing could lighten their private and heavy hearts, the sound of human merriment washed over them, and washed away the invisible blood they'd drawn from each other. Now they could, at least, stand side by side and pretend to be a couple, and not two distinctly unhappy souls.

"Lovely, lovely," Squire Carstairs said, as he surveyed the viscountess, after he'd greeted her. "My lady, you grace our home, welcome."

Since this was positively loquacious coming from the squire, his wife stared at him. The viscountess was charming, but the squire's idea of a compliment was usually a "You look splendid," and to a strange lady, much more likely to be only a nod or a grin. Then she smiled; it was probably just the punch and his overflowing heart speaking. That and perhaps, she thought merrily, the recent exposure to his soon to be son-in-law, Lord Neville. For the young man had a facile tongue in a clever head; how else, she often wondered, had such a lean long-shanks got himself the name "Rake Neville"? Her dear daughter, however, Mrs. Carstairs thought smugly, had put an end to that, for the fellow was as devoted as a day-old duckling and twice as silly over his fianceé. That was the coup that caused this party tonight. That, as well as being yet another way to continue to show the countryside that Rake Neville had met his match at last.

But her hostess's second of startlement at her husband's praise made Adelà flinch. She held her head higher; it was a thing she'd have to get used to, it was a thing that was temporary, and it was too late to turn tail and return to the Court now anyway, she thought.

"Lo!" a tall, thin, long-jawed young gentleman said with wonderment as the viscount and his lady entered the ballroom. "Comes a hero! And a heartbreaker."

He put one hand over his heart and sighed audibly, much to the delight of the guests who stood in a crowd around him. "My lord," he said to Euan, his great show of humility ruined only by his mobile mouth's increasing grin, "you return to us after fighting the French, and capture yourself a Greek goddess to bring to us, as well. How did you manage it? Well-done!"

But now Adela was sure she was being mocked. And so before Euan could answer, she spoke up.

"Because the goddess obviously couldn't run very far," she said sweetly, and as the guests wondered if they ought to show their smiles at her wit, or ignore it out of courtesy because of its veracity, she added, "and so I doubt such a one ever existed. Certainly I've never seen her. I doubt there was enough marble in all of Greece to sculpt such a goddess, sir."

"Oh," the tall gentleman answered, his blue eyes registering what seemed to be real dismay, "but I have. My lady, I didn't jest about that. I referred to Demeter, the great goddess of all fruit and flowering, the patroness of increase. She's no nymph or dryad, true. Her beauty lies precisely in her lush abundance, and so she is always portrayed, and so she was worshiped. For not only did they always have a word for it, but the Greeks had respect for life and the great gift that it is. I never meant to mock, my lady," he said earnestly, taking her hand, "only to praise you. And salute your husband for having the wit to have found you. It's doubtless the only clever thing he's ever done," he added, grinning at Euan.

"What? Only a moment ago I was a hero!" Euan complained.

"So you are still," the tall gentleman said, "but who ever said they had to be clever?"

"Right again," Euan laughed. "Nigel, I'd cross swords with you any day, but never wits. I concede," and he held his hands out in supplication, before the gentleman clapped him hard on the shoulder, and laughing said, "It's good to see you, my lad—Oh, I'd forgot: it's 'my lord' now. Felicia, love," he said to the honey-haired young woman who stood close to him, "here's a brave and honest soldier for you to meet, and his lovely lady as well. And my lord, my lady: I present to you Miss Felicia Carstairs, the

woman who defeated me as soundly as our hero viscount trounced the enemy. The difference is: never was
a victory more earnestly desired by the conquered."

Having said that, he gazed at the smiling young
woman at his side, and in that moment honestly
seemed to forget there was anyone else in his
vicinity.

"There it is," Euan said with feigned exasperation,
breaking the charming, but awkward moment. "If
we'd sent him to talk to Napoleon, Adela, I might
have been saved the trouble of going to fight."

"You've acquired wit along with a beautiful wife
and a title; I hope matrimony suits me half so well,"
Lord Neville laughed.

"These two were obviously schoolmates," Felicia
Carstairs said, taking Adela's hand and taking her
aside. "I'd have known it even if Nigel hadn't told
me of it when he said how anxious he was to see you
two. Only old schoolmates can be so dreadful to each
other. How sorry I am that I don't have an assort-
ment of females to insult each time I see them, but
I was taught at home." And when Adela had stopped
laughing, she added, "And how lovely to have you as
my neighbor, welcome, my lady."

"Oh, 'Adela,' please," Adela protested, "for I was
simply Mrs. Clermont until only the other month,
and if you call me 'my lady,' I shall pass the evening
looking over my shoulder to see whom you're addressing. Unless, of course," she said as she was struck
by the sudden thought, "you wish me to call you 'my
lady' too, when you're wed."

"We'd be so busily 'ladying' each other, we'd never
get any good gossip told," Felicia said on a laugh.
"How lovely that I've a new friend as uncomfortable
with a new title as I shall be. I hope we'll remain

friends for many years, for my new home, Wildwood, is as far from here as the Court is, in the opposite direction."

Adela's spirits rose. She and her candid, merry new neighbor weren't that different in age or temperament. It would be beyond wonderful to have such a friend, one she had so much in common with.

"And when shall you acquire that new title?" she asked.

"In early spring," Felicia said dreamily. "Oh how I wish the winter were past, it cannot be soon enough! I know its unfashionable to admit it, but how I envy you! To be wed to the one you love, and to be—as you are!"

And then Adela knew how little in common she had with her new neighbor, after all.

When Lord Neville noted his fianceé's absence, he came to claim her and relinquished Euan. Then Euan and Adela made the rounds of the room, meeting so many neighbors and townsfolk that Adela knew she'd never remember half their names. But as the time passed, she also realized she'd never been held in such esteem before either. The title, of course, accounted for much of it; the fact that so many of her new neighbors were farmers and stockmen, no doubt, also accounted for her popularity in her present fertile state, she though sardonically. But it was nevertheless an unnerving experience. Living in London and having gone to a select school with many classmates from the nobility, she'd never seen or experienced the outsize respect a title netted one among country folk. Euan, as an officer, hardly noted it. It just gave him a warm feeling of return and belonging—that vanished, of course, whenever he looked at his lovely, polite, and entirely otherwise occupied lady.

They didn't dance, of course. She thought she could, if no one were there to look at her, but as that was absurd, and her husband didn't ask, naturally the matter never arose. The lucky thing, both the viscount and his lady often thought to themselves as the evening went on, was that there were so many people to speak with, the fact that they exchanged not one private word with each other was not noted: perhaps, each thought, not even by the other.

The dinner was hearty and delicious. Everyone ate as though they expected a famine, very much as they did in London, although there, there was far less speculation about recipes. Squire Carstairs raised many a toast, and many a toast was returned, and as the evening wore on, the merriment grew louder, and the resultant noise was far less noticed. The viscount and his lady passed as much time as they could with the engaged couple, for when Lord Neville and Felicia weren't transfixed by the fact of each other, they were jubilant because generous fortune had also cast them such perfect neighbors. Whenever Euan and Adela remembered the truth of their situation, they were as grateful for Lord Neville and Felicia's presence as they felt guilty and saddened by their true circumstances.

But nighttime festivities in the country ended far sooner than they did in town. At about the time late arrivals would still be filtering into a grand ball in London, the squire's guests began to bow themselves out. And so it was at a far earlier hour than Adela had expected that she was assisted into the coach again. Used to London entertainments and hours, she wasn't at all tired, even in her present state.

Which was as well, for the sudden quiet inside the carriage reminded her of what she and Euan must discuss when they returned, and that itself would have banished any thought of rest or sleep.

But Euan, after a rare evening of talking and jesting, drinking and enjoying himself with good company, forgot himself so much as to muse aloud as they drove home.

"Imagine! Rake Neville tamed. And by such a dewy-eyed chit! Who would have thought it? But there's no mistaking, I've never seen him happier, lucky fellow," he said wistfully, and smiled, until he heard what he'd said, and could have bitten his tongue off for it. But Adela didn't reply. He wondered if the party he'd so enjoyed had only increased her wrath with him. She hadn't danced or flirted, after all, he thought resignedly. And so she was likely well armed now for their promised talk, he decided, and only musing on how much she would rail at him for.

She *was* thinking of their coming talk, but a rut in the road caused the carriage to jolt, and she felt a sudden pang in her abdomen. Only that. But it caused her to shiver in fear, and not for her physical safety. Because it reminded her of all the things the women had chatted about with her tonight. For the first time, she allowed herself to think of what she was actually about to do, what she would do after he left her, and what it would mean to them—all three of them.

Now she no longer pretended there wasn't another besides Euan to consider. It pleased her to think of it as "him," and a "him" with hazel eyes, for she could think of nothing more beautiful, and Euan would certainly return now and then to pass time with a son,

however far afield he went. But it could as easily be
"her," and two women alone would be harder in this
hard world, she thought, biting her lips as the carriage dipped and bucked again.

"Damned roads! Are you all right?" he asked, holding out a hand to steady her.

"Yes, yes," she said, although she was not.

He sat back and bit back whatever ineffectual
thing he thought to say, and wished with a fervor
he'd not felt for the supernatural since he'd been a
boy that he were as glib and good with words as
his friend Nigel was, just for one night, so he could
somehow put things right. Or at least put them so
that he could understand them.

She sat still, vainly wishing she were as fresh and
unjaded as Felicia. But because she'd lost her faith
and worn out all her wishes over the last months,
she soon stopped and asked for no more than a hope
that she could be a fraction as unafraid of the future,
as well.

They were quiet as mourners as they stepped into
their hall, and as slow as pallbearers to reach their
bedchamber. He dismissed his valet as soon as he
could, and she sent her maid away with a trembling
hand. And they met at midnight at the foot of their
bed, to finish off the sick thing that was their marriage, so they could bury it as properly as they were
able.

He wore a dressing gown, and she a nightrail with
a robe over it, and he'd a moment to remember when
they'd have considered themselves overdressed as
such. She sat at her dressing table with her head
averted, her long dark hair shadowing her expression
as she waited for him to speak. And as he was the
man, and as he'd made the promise, he realized he

must. He cleared his throat, and wished he'd words worth saying, words he didn't dread hearing.

But he noticed she was weeping before he could speak.

"Don't, don't," he said at once, dropping to a knee before her. "We can talk about this some other time. Please don't."

"I don't want to," she insisted pettishly. "I don't mean to. It doesn't signify, it doesn't mean anything," she lied. "My condition makes me foolish. Pray disregard it. Go on, go on, you were about to say?" she asked with eerie dignity as tears streamed down her face.

"How can I?" he asked, running his hand through his hair in exasperation, "with you leaking like a wash bucket?"

"Oh! Do spare me such sympathy!" she cried.

"You asked me to," he said in vexation. "What in God's name do you want then?"

"Not your sympathy," she said.

"Then what?" he said, his light-filled eyes so filled with torment that she had to look away because she couldn't see them clearly for the tears in her own. "Good Lord, what do you want, Adela? I wish I knew," he said fervently. "I wish I'd the words Nigel does, or the address, or the wit. Just what is it you want of me? I don't know. In all honesty I do not. I never understood women very well except for you, and you not at all anymore, you're so changed. But by God, I wish you were not, and that I could talk to you as we used to do."

"But we did not Euan," she sobbed, "never. We touched, and we made love, but we never talked, don't you remember?"

"Lord, yes," he said, holding her hand, trying to

touch her cheek, "but that was enough, we spoke that way, didn't we?"

"Yes," she said on a watery, broken laugh, "but all we said was. 'good' and 'better' and 'yes, do that' and 'oh, my love,' and we can't do that anymore."

"Stop crying and I'll say 'good,' " he said desperately. "Yes, there, you're smiling, 'better,' " he said. As she looked at him and smiled a little more, he said, "Yes, do that." And when he saw how successful his jest had been, he forgot it for the look in her eyes, the one he'd not seen in so long he'd begun to think it had only been a happy dream he'd once had, and said, all unknowing that he was crowning his jest, "Oh, my love."

She came into his arms, as he wanted her to, and he discovered she fit there, if not so comfortably as before, then even better in other ways. He stroked her hair and murmured, "Tell me, please. What have we done? What are we to do? I can't bear this. I'd rather face an entire division of infantry unarmed, than one of your tears. I'm so sorry, my love, for whatever it was that I did, for whatever it was, I couldn't help it, I don't think. Tell me."

"I don't want your sympathy," she said into his neck.

"What do you want?" he begged her.

"Your love," she whispered.

"But you've always had it," he said in such honest confusion that she knew it was so.

"You stared at me as though I were a mon-monster when you fir-first saw me," she said, beginning to hiccup.

"Well, you did surprise me. I know, I know," he said at once. "I oughtn't to have been surprised, but I held a picture of you as I'd last seen you, and didn't expect what I saw. It didn't mean I didn't like it. I just didn't expect it. Hold you breath and count to ten," he said, feeling her body continuing to lurch spasmodically.

"You did-didn't touch me," she said.

"Well, of course not. I was afraid to. What do I know of such things? I was an idiot. Old Samuel Tonkins got enough wine in him tonight to tell me a thing or two about that. He's got fourteen children. And never missed a night in his dear Sal's arms until a full moon before each new Tonkin arrived, to his and Sal's delight, he bragged. Of course, it was vulgar and improper, and his dear Sal would have murdered him had she heard him, and I only pretended to be amused by him. But I was ashamed—of myself. And angry with myself, too. Think of what I missed!"

"Too-too late," she cried, beginning to weep again, "it was too late to do that anymore as of last Sunday!"

"You were counting . . . !" he said slowly, with wonder and tenderness, before he said with even more concern, "Perhaps a glass of water? If you hold your nose and drink, that should do it. I fear you'll shake something loose," he said, and was rewarded with a reluctant grin, before she hiccuped again as answer.

And then he discovered the perfect cure for her problem, and his. When he raised his lips from hers, he spoke again, and with absolute honesty.

"I love you very much, and have got to like the way you look so much this way that I fear I'll be put off if you return to your previous shape too quickly. I don't want to leave you. And I don't want to hurt you. And I'm ashamed at having been so afraid of you and for you," he said.

"That's the only thing I wanted to hear," she said, leaning her forehead against his. "Why couldn't you say that when we first met again?"

"I didn't know it," he answered truthfully, and then added more gently, "and why didn't you ever tell me that?"

"I didn't know how," she said.

And then, for all that they were keeping country hours, they sat up through the night, talking, and holding each other, and talking some more, until cock's crow told them they'd passed the whole of their first real night of love together.

They'd gotten into the habit of reading poetry at each other to pass the last of the long summer afternoons. "*To* each other," as Euan said, would not be strictly true, since she made such a fuss whenever he read Mr. Wordsworth, and he guffawed at her favorite passages of Byron.

"Very well then," she said, putting down her book, and sitting back on her cushions in the shady gazebo, "your turn."

"I thought you'd never ask," he said, and plucking a grape from the bowl before them, popped it into her mouth. "Be still, so that you can hear and appreciate the beauty of the poem," he commanded, before he raised his volume, cleared his throat, and read:

Shall I compare thee to a summer's day?
Thou art more lovely and more temperate . . .

She sighed with pleasure, he'd never read her a sonnet,

"Rough winds do shake the darling buds of May,"

he read on, "And summer's lease hath all too short
a date . . ."

She groaned so loud he stopped abruptly and
looked at her in alarm. She began laughing at what
he'd been thinking, to judge from his face. And then
laughed the more at her jest and placed a hand on
her abdomen as she subsided to giggles.

"It was the line," she explained, " 'All too short a
lease,' indeed!" she said with mock indignity, groan-
ing again, "it seems forever. Don't you wish it were
done?"

"Oddly, no," he said, suddenly serious, moving
closer to her and placing his hand over hers to feel
what was leaping beneath it. "These last weeks have
been a wonderful time for us. A time we'd not have
had else. How many people can say they've had the
chance to really get to know the one they love? We've
been lucky, I think, that we loved, and then had to
learn to love anew."

"This poetry has been very good for you," she said
equally seriously. Then looking down at their hands,
she said on a joyous laugh, "I agree. And I truly
don't mind either, anymore. Why, it even doesn't
look so large under your hand as it did alone."

"Nothing looks so large as it does when you're
alone," he said with hard-won soldier's and lover's
wisdom.

She gave him such a tremulous smile, he almost
blushed. And feeling as ridiculous as he did grand
about that, he smiled back at her, picked up the book
again, and read:

Sometimes too hot the eye of heaven shines,
And often is his fair complexion dimmed . . .

He read on, but she only half attended to his words, she was so intently watching his face and adoring the sight of it, until he read:

But thy eternal summer shall not fade,
Nor lose possession of that fair thou owest . . .

Then she sighed so heavily that his hand, which had remained on her abdomen, rose and fell. He left off, closed the book, and looked his query at her.

"My 'eternal summer' shall not fade, nor shall I lose possession of that I own?" she repeated in a tone filled with mock woe.

"Perhaps not eternal," he admitted, "and perhaps that's not really bad, there may be too much of a good thing. But surely, there's a little more time for this special joy, is there not? After all," he said thoughtfully, as his hand moved over the tight expanse it rested upon, "it's not *entirely* inside out yet, is it?"

It was wholly due to his superb army training, he was to insist for many years after, that he was able to subdue her wrath so that his firstborn didn't suffer the indignity of having to greet the world from a gazebo. For he did pacify her in a classically peaceful way and very nicely, too. And so the returned hero, Major Clermont, Viscount Clifford, bravely saved the day, postponed the hour of his son's birth, and not insignificantly, saved his own head and preserved his favorite volume of poetry, too.

. . . The leaves dead are driven, like ghosts from an enchanter fleeing . . .

—Percy Bysshe Shelley

AUTUMN
LEAVES

Although the nursery was snug enough this autumn night, and the fire in the hearth chuckled over warm and secret jests, now and again it was interrupted by the sound of a thin cutting wind keening at the windows and whining at the eaves, as though the night were complaining about its banishment. They were in the heart of London town, one of the most modern populous towns on the wide earth, but the sound of the wind and the words of the tale the children were listening to made them draw into a closer circle and glance, now and then, to the far corners of the room, as if they feared seeing more than the dim outlines of the hobbyhorse, dollhouse, and wardrobe there.

"And so young Tamlane disappeared," the soft voice read, "and nowhere on earth could he be found, for though his beloved Ellen searched for him, she saw no sign of him, nor did she hear a word. It was as though he'd never been, for all they'd been in love, and plighted their troth, and set the day of their

133

marrying. It came and went, and Tamlane was nowhere to be found."

The children, five in all, sat still and expectant, save for the youngest dozing in Nurse's arms. Nurse smiled the smile of an old woman hearing a familiar tale. But when the other children happened to glance to her, the shadowy firelight transformed the seamed face they'd known forever, so that old became alien. The flickering light played over her wrinkled face so that she'd seem to be sneering now, and then to be suffused with some dread, unholy mirth, as Miss Penny read the promised Halloween story in a low and thrilling voice.

"Poor Ellen lived alone thereafter, and thereafter always sought Tamlane," Miss Penny read. "But neither tinkers nor their crones, nor gypsies in the meadow did more than tremble when she spoke his name. Still, never did she believe she'd lost his love, for she'd had it and knew his heart, if not the direction of his wandering soul."

Young Thomas, who'd have been the first to mock any mention of something so ridiculous as love on any other day or night, sat wide-eyed, as though his seven years were halved. And his siblings, Mary, Elizabeth, and Timothy, fought both sleep and terror valiantly as the hour and the tale went on.

" 'Ah, Tamlane,' she would sigh," Miss Penny read with a sigh in her soft voice as well, " 'Ah Tamlane, my love, my love, where are you and where have you been? Tamlane, Tamlane, my love.'

"But one day, one dim autumn day . . . much like today," Miss Penny said, looking up from her book, for she'd been adding to the story for effect, and as a natural storyteller, the effect on her readers had made her invent more each moment, "Ellen was wan-

dering in the dark wood far from home, and she
found a bush of broom. She plucked a sprig from it,
and held it to her nose, for the scent of it, faint and
frostbitten though it was, reminded her of spring and
her days with Tamlane. She took another and another,
trying to recapture the moments, but when she'd
plucked the third, she gasped! And dropped it in
amaze."

Her audience seemed to have stopped breathing.
Even Timothy, who presently detested his sister
Elizabeth to the point of mania for her recent theft
of his favorite toy soldier—held in ransom for the rag
doll he'd teased her by taking—drew closer to her
side, though he was already so close, he might have
been riveted there.

"It was none other than Tamlane himself she saw
before her!" Miss Penny read, and the collective sigh
of relief that greeted this was louder than that of the
last log collapsing in the fireplace. "He was dressed
in gold and green, like a prince of fairyland, and
stood tall and straight. He seemed twice as comely
as he'd ever been. For his fair hair glowed, and his
blue eyes were fiercely bright. But they were lit with
a strange and desperate sorrow, Ellen saw.

" 'Ah, Tamlane, my love, where have you been?
Where have you come from, my love, Tamlane?'
Ellen cried.

" 'From Elfland, my love,' Tamlane said in a voice
of great sorrow, 'For the Queen of the Faeries hath
taken me for her lover, her consort, and her squire.'

" 'But why did you go with her?' cried Ellen.

" 'I went hunting one bright autumn day, my love,
after a fine white hart I'd spied. But once in the
forest I spied her no more, though I rode and rode
down the long day. At last, weary, I feel to sleep on

the green grass at the side of a gentle hill. I was
awakened by the light of the moon with a kiss, like
none I'd ever known. Not so tender as my mother's,
or so sweet as yours, my love, but unlike any I've
ever known. I opened my eyes to find myself with
the Queen of the Faeries, in Elfland.

" 'Oh fair!' Tamlane sighed. 'Oh fair is she! How
fair is that land, my love! With silver streams and
golden apples hung upon jade trees; the music is like
laughter and there are no tears, and I've never
known such joy. I'd stay there forever were it not
for the memory of you—and the knowing of one other
thing . . .' "

Miss Penny paused, and gazed without seeming to
see at her rapt audience.

"What? What?" cried the children severally.

"That," Miss Penny said firmly, albeit with a little
smile as she closed the book, "you shall hear tomorrow night . . . if you're good."

There was a chorus of disapproval, and a few half-
hearted pleas for a less impossible payment for their
story. Still, they soon subsided, because kind and fair
as their governess was, she was a governess, and a
good one, too. Their bedtime had arrived, they knew
it, and were consoled only by the thought of the con-
tinuation to come. If they were good. Which didn't
seem too promising a likelihood, since Timothy immediately pinched Elizabeth, saying in a threatening
voice, "You be good, hear? Or we won't get to hear
the rest." And in between tearful choruses of "He
pinched me, the little beast pinched me," Elizabeth
gave back as good as she'd got, causing Thomas to
stand up for his little brother so nobly that Mary was
left with no choice except to box his ears.

"Eh. Looks like you'll be tellin' no tales tomorrow

night, lass," Nurse said on a chuckle, as she shifted her beloved burden and rose with him still sleeping in her arms.

"There are other nights, many, many nights to come before All Hallow's Eve," the governess, Miss Bronwen Penny said simply, causing the grieved combatant's tears to subside long enough for the nursery maid to get them to bed, so Miss Penny could hear their prayers. Which, this night, had all to do with hearing the rest of the tale of Tamlane.

"I'm not at all sure that it was the sort of story you ought to have told before bedtime," Miss Mayhew said repressively.

Bronwen sighed, pulled her cape about her shoulders, and looked about the park before she gazed down at her gloved hands in her lap. She was instantly sorry—not that she'd told the story to the children, but that she'd told Miss Mayhew of the telling of it.

"They wanted ghosts," she explained as patiently as if she were addressing her youngest charge and not another governess. "They begged for ghosts, phantoms, headless coachmen, and dismembered limbs that crept in the night. Halloween is coming, you know. I gave them faeries and lost love instead, which suited them as well."

"As well it should," Miss Mayhew said on a sniff. "But still, my dear Miss Penny, I fear the Faerie Queen in 'Tamlane' is evil and cruel as any monster. And, I might add, there's a certain amount of . . . uh," Miss Mayhew's pale face grew red, and not from the wind for she sat with her back to it, ". . . sensuality, shall we say? in her nature and the content of the tale, which is inappropriate for infants."

"Well, so it may be, but so I should never say to
the children, believe me," Bronwen said indignantly.
She'd been about to say *she'd* always loved the tale,
but Miss Mayhew's pinched nostrils warned her from
that course. And who was to say Miss Mayhew
wasn't right, after all? she thought as she shifted
uneasily on the hard park bench. Miss Mayhew, after
all, had been trained and bred to the position of governess, as Bronwen herself had not been.

Miss Mayhew was six years her senior, and at one
and thirty, had been out as a governess since she'd
been one and twenty. Bronwen's position as governess to the Baron Rhodes's family was her first one.
Miss Mayhew was tall and thin, and wore spectacles
that frosted over when she went from a heated room
to a cool one, or when she and Bronwen went from
a cool subject to a heated one, as now. For now Bronwen couldn't see her friend's small blue eyes, her
spectacles had become so misted over. Bronwen fid-
geted, she very much disliked disconcerting her
friend, and not only because she was so grateful to
have her to call "friend." But because she'd so much
to learn from her.

For Miss Mayhew knew how to dress with style
while being just out of style, how to speak in company so that no company but her charges would hear
her, and how to appear in public without being seen,
as any good governess should. It was true that the
colorless Miss Mayhew had a natural proclivity for
such. But she also knew how to teach without shouting, how to curtsy without groveling, how to be a
lady in the unladylike position of complete depen-
dence on her employers, who might not be her bet-
ters. In short, she knew how to act as a servant,
which she was, while behaving as a lady, which she

also was, a task that Bronwen was still trying to
perfect.

For she tended to speak her mind, and do as she
thought best, and the only reason she escaped cen-
sure, she was sure, was because she so seldom had
anything to do with any adults in her new household.
The baron and his lady produced infants with great
regularity, but seemed to think that was the extent
of their involvement with them, apart from having
them clothed, fed, and educated. And that was precisely how that was done, too—for their nursery was
far apart from the rest of their London town house
in every way.

If Bronwen hadn't met Miss Mayhew at Hatchards
bookshop on her day of rest, she might have no adult,
apart from Nurse, to speak with at all. For the
housekeeper knew her place, as did every other servant, and Bronwen was only just learning hers.
Among other things. She'd already learned that the
only daughter of a widowed country gentleman had
to earn her own way when that gentleman suddenly
passed to his own reward and left not one to her—
but only mortgages and unpaid debts. She'd learned
that her lack of dowry combined with only commonplace good looks left her a choice of enduring insulting
offers from certain men, or more respectable ones
from far from choice others, or earning her own way.
She'd chosen her own path.

She'd gotten a position and made a living wage.
But she'd yet to learn how to give up her hopes and
dreams. Still, she'd only been at her trade for a year,
and she'd many more years to look forward to, to
learn it in. *If* she stayed at her trade, she realized,
and remembered again how much she needed a men-
tor like Miss Mayhew. Because it seemed she still

hadn't gotten it right. Miss Mayhew disapproved of her choice of colors for her wardrobe. Bronwen had chosen deep browns, dark russets, and subdued greens for her governessing garb instead of having her frocks and shawls made up, as they'd previously been, in the pastel colors of youth. For as she was small, and had mud brown hair and eyes, surely, Bronwen had thought, she'd now have natural concealment, and so sink from view.

But Miss Mayhew disapproved. She saw at once how the deep, rich earth tones complemented her young friend's thick brown hair and huge, tilted eyes, and only served to point up her clear, faintly gold-blushed skin, making her look like some lovely woodland creature, and not a staid governess. She never told Bronwen that, of course, for that wouldn't do. She only suggested that when Bronwen could get the money together, she outfit herself in invisible gray, black, and bleak brown, the colors of servitude in the *ton*, as other governesses did.

But now she'd disapproved of Bronwen's teaching, and that would never do.

"After all," Bronwen argued, "one might say that nursery poems are in themselves violent. Why, think of the wretched gory mess there must have been with those three mice when they lost their tails, and as for sensuality—why that new rhyme about 'Georgie, Porgie' is clearly about a royal . . ."

"Just so!" Miss Mayhew said triumphantly, "and precisely why you ought to stay with Bible verses and improving tracts!"

Useless to say she knew she should, but she abhorred them as much as the children would, Bronwen thought sadly, her brief verbal rebellion ended by such sane reasoning.

"A lovely day," Miss Mayhew observed as a peace offering, after they'd sat in silence for a while.

"Yes, beautiful," Bronwen said sorrowfully, looking at the brown-leaved trees about them, "but not so beautiful as home."

And though she'd lived half a kingdom away from where Bronwen had, and they both knew it well, Miss Mayhew nodded in agreement. "Nothing," she said in a small, stark voice, "is so beautiful as home."

It wasn't the usual stoic sort of answer Miss Mayhew gave when her younger friend suffered from loneliness and doubt in her new position, but it was an honest one. Who better than she knew how hard it was to call one's employer's home "home," after all? She'd cheer Bronwen when she could, but just as she so often instructed her young charges, the far better path was to accept the truths one could not change, rather than to hope for impossible things. Still, it was autumn, a time for drawing in, a time for seeking warm and safe refuges, and so both women remained quiet for a long while, despite the growing lateness of the hour, remembering lost and hopeless causes.

Miss Mayhew thought of a fond mama, a parlor crowded with personal things, and the lost joys of having her very own cat drowsing by the hearth of an autumn night. And Bronwen thought of sharing hot chestnuts and tart, windfall apples with friends, of pulling hot buttery taffy with them and having it fall to the floor—to be saved from the dog at the last minute, shrieks of laughter accompanying the rescue—and of roaming through the wild woods seeking nuts and the last late bramble berries with a friend at her side.

All her friends: there'd been Alicia, long wed to

John Trumbell now, with two children of their own; and Mary, betrothed to her Samuel for years until he'd come home from the sea to take her away with him; and Joan, gone to live in Scotland with her Joseph; and Nick, dear Nick, gone to adulthood and vanished forever into the unknowable world of titled young gentlemen. He'd have grown up and on beyond her in any case, someday. For even if Papa had kept his fortunes intact, it wouldn't have been a pin to what Nick was in line for. But before Papa had gone, Nick had, to his inherited rewards, and then he'd never come to stay with his cousin, her neighbor, James, of a summertime day again. And James had wed Miss Corcoran long since, and moved to Ireland to manage her estates.

Her childhood, Bronwen thought resignedly, was vanished as completely as poor Tamlane had been. And her life was not a faerie story.

She was thinking of Tamlane then, to keep from thinking of what could not be in reality, and working out how to tell the children the rest of it without compromising the tale, or herself, when she saw the elegant company riding down the bridle path before them. And in that one instant, they seemed like a vision from the tale she'd been thinking of. For they appeared with the setting sun, and their coming was heralded by the sound of their jingling spurs and lilting laughter. They were a richly caparisoned company, and not only far more handsome than even the most elegant riders who usually frequented this park and the row, but singular in that they were most of them gentlemen, vying for a position beside their obvious queen. And she was as lovely, regal, imperious, and fascinating as any Faerie Queen.

She was young and yet old enough to seem sophis-

ticated. And beyond beautiful, of course. She rode a
magnificent white horse, and wore a green velvet
habit, and had a charming velvet hat with streaming
veils atop her long and shining midnight hair. Her
smooth face glowed dark and light as moonlight in
the setting sunlight, and she'd eyes as gray and deep
as the coming twilight. They tilted up with amusement when she sounded her bell-like laughter as her
gentlemen continued to vie for her attention.

A tall, lean, elegant fellow rode at her side, so
saturnine and amused at the other gentlemen's efforts,
so languid, cool, and superior to them, that Bronwen
had no difficulty placing him as the Faerie King: willing to let his lady stray because he knew her needs
so well, but full of secret wrath, tricks, and deceit—
for the revenge he always took on those who wandered with her. The other men were young and
comely, almost mythically so, or so they seemed to
a cold and lonely, fanciful governess who'd stayed out
too long in the windy park, Bronwen thought, with
sudden insight. She'd a moment to laugh at herself
and her own wild fancies.

And then she saw Tamlane.

He was slender and lithe, and his hair, beneath his
high beaver hat, was as yellow as buttercups and as
fine as flax, and his profile, as he turned to jest with
his lady, was that of a classic statue's. He was, in
all, as manly—yet fragile—and heartbreakingly
handsome as any hero of any stirring tale. Or so she
thought until he turned to look at her, as though her
admiring stare had itself called out to him. Then she
saw his bright eyes were as cruelly malicious as his
wide and mocking smile was, as he looked at the
pitiful pair of no-longer youthful governesses sitting
in their drabbery on a park bench, lusting after the

truly alive, young, and beautiful people as they rode by. Or so, she imagined that brilliantly scathing glance said clear as spoken words as he gazed at them.

She felt herself shrink, but she could not, would not let herself drop her gaze or look away, as any proper governess ought. For she was, in her hidden heart, no less than they, and so her defiantly proud look said, even as the young gentleman made some remark about her, and they all of them, as if on some secret command, looked her way. And laughed, of course.

The lady laughed loudest, although it might only have been that her melodic laughter sounded clear as a hunting horn over the naturally lower bass notes of the gentlemen's merriment. They all of them laughed, except, Bronwen noted, for the man she'd designated the Faerie King. She noted it as her eyes desperately sought some human kindness, some reassuring nod or smile, so as to assure her that their monstrous jest was about something, someone, anything else but herself. But though he was not amused, his face held no comfort for her. Nor did it show pity. Something else was living there.

He looked full at her, and Bronwen at last lost her composure and gasped. For she saw his eyes clearly in a glance of last true light then. And in that instant caught a glimpse of something desperate and filled with pain in those strange, shocking eyes. Men who'd looked out over limitless seas, endless spaces, or into the heart of desolation itself might have such eyes. Their color was as wild and unforgettable as their expression. They were lightning blue, a clear electric blue that contrasted with his tanned face; a blinding blue she'd seen flash in the heart of certain opals, or

in the wide summer skies. And in Nick's dear face,
as well. But his had been alive with more human
emotions, of course.

Another moment, and the expression was gone.
She could catch her breath again and lower her own
gaze. She knew when she'd been defeated. Let the
gay company ride by, let them have their joke, it
made no matter to her anyway. And so she was more
than amazed; she was, in those seconds, genuinely
frightened when she heard the slight jingling sound,
the halting half steps of hooves drawing near, and
the snort of a horse exhaling close by. In that mad
moment, she wondered if one of them had decided to
ride over her body, to show such worthless beings
what might happen if they'd the effrontery to try to
face them down.

"Bronwen?" the deep, clear voice asked in puzzled
tones, "Bronwen Penny, is it you?"

She looked up to see Nick gazing down at her in
perplexity, his now adult face handsome as boyhood
had promised, his eyes no longer distressed with
unthinkable concerns; only mildly troubled, as a
man's might be if he found himself awakening in a
strange place.

"Nick?" she asked, though she knew him now, and
realizing that, said on a sudden smile, all fantasies
forgotten, "Nicodemus?"

"At your service," he said, laughing now, now
much more the boy she'd known. "But what are you
about to be sitting here at dusk—and in such clothes?
Fie! Halloween night is weeks away, what masquerade are you at, you madcap girl?"

"None, Nick—or rather, my Lord," she corrected
herself at once, as the truth she was about to reveal
about her position in life took control of her enjoy-

ment of life once again. "I am a governess now. Ah.
May I present my friend and co-professional, Miss
Mayhew? Miss Mayhew, this is Nicodemus Brand,
now Earl of Fairlie, an old friend, from happier
days."

He frowned and sketched a perfunctory bow from
his saddle, never taking his eyes from Bronwen.

"How's this?" he asked, "a governess? But your
Papa . . ."

"Father passed on some while ago, and left me
obligations," she said with the small smile she'd
learned to wear at the thought so nicely, neatly
expressed, "which I now fulfill by being a governess."

"But Mary, and Alicia—little Joan, and James," he
asked, his confusion plain to see, "your friends—our
friends—could they not help you?"

"They've grown and gone to their own lives now,"
she said. "Haven't you heard? Why, little Joan has
little ones of her own, and James crossed the Irish
Sea without looking back some four years past. And
I've no need of help, not really, for I'm five and
twenty now, remember, and quite able to take care
of myself."

"Five and twenty and unwed! And such a beauty!
Why here's a mystery," the yellow-haired young gentleman said from close by. But his smile was a sneer
and his tone of voice made the compliment an insult,
and his leering look of appraisal was even more of an
insult than his secret amusement was. Bronwen
raised her chin and looked to Nick.

"Yes, a mystery, but not yours, Rowan," Nick said
in a hard voice.

Then he turned his attention to Bronwen again and
said, still frowning as if with concentration, "But five
and twenty! It scarcely seems possible. It was just

yesterday when last we met and you were a lass, and I a lad, looking forward to . . ."

"Nick!" the lady called, and he broke off speaking to look to her. She guided her horse into mincing steps as she came abreast of him, and glancing down at Bronwen as though she were even lower than she appeared from the vantage point of horseback, studied her curiously.

"Lady," Nick said, "Here is Bronwen Penny, a friend from early days, a girl I knew at home. And her friend. Ladies, I give you the Lady Blythe, a good friend of my latter days."

"What a lot of friends!" the lady said on a tinkling laugh. "How happy we should be! But come, Nicodemus, our time is short, our evening awaits."

He hesitated a moment, gazing down at Bronwen, his dark head to the side, and his lady said again, "Nicodemus . . .?"

Then he looked at her, and then Bronwen had to look away. She hoped Miss Mayhew had, too, for if she'd thought "Tamlane" a sensuous tale, the look Nick gave to his lady made it seem a Bible tract by comparison. She'd never seen such a look, she could almost feel the longing and tension sparkling between them, and it humbled even as it irrationally angered her. Nick must have looked away at last, for Bronwen heard the horses on the move again. Only then could she look up to see him by his lady's side once more, in the midst of the merry company.

At the very last, he remembered her. It seemed to surprise Lady Blythe as well as Bronwen when he raised his hand and called, "Good-bye, dear little Bronwen. God keep you," before he turned and rode away. For the lady glanced back once as they moved on, regarding Bronwen narrowly. Then the yellow-haired young fellow Nick had called Rowan said something, and they all laughed.

Bronwen and Miss Mayhew sat silently until the last sounds of their musical laughter had died away.

"It's grown late and cold. What were we about to stay so long? Come, we've no business lingering here," Miss Mayhew said abruptly.

But Bronwen could only nod as she arose and let Miss Mayhew lead her away from the dark onrushing night.

" 'Oh fair is that land, my love,' Tamlane sighed, 'but fairer still my lady Queen.'

"Ellen sighed as well, to hear her love speak so, and her heart was sore for it, but grew even more sore afraid when next he spoke.

" 'Every seven years her due is paid, for every seven years it comes due. But I've no coin of Elfland in my fine silk purse, nor does such coin rest within my velvet pockets. Neither do they expect one of me. I fear my soul is the price I must offer up. Oh love, I fear it is my soul that is coming due,' Tamlane said.

"Ellen shuddered at the look upon his fair face, and in that moment, knew that this was true," Bronwen read.

She drew her breath to read on, and there was an earsplitting screech.

"He hit me! He hit me!". Mary shrieked, even as she threw herself upon her brother with the obvious intention, and very near success, of snatching him bald.

"Did not! Did not!" cried Timothy, in transports of furious pain.

When she, Nurse, and the nursery maid had finally

gotten them sorted out, it became apparent that
Mary had been hit by a flying hot cinder from the
snapping fire in the hearth, and schooled to such
abuse, had immediately fixed the blame on her
brother. But by then, it was too late to mend matters
easily. Timothy was in hysterics, Elizabeth, having
taken up the cudgels for Mary, had inflicted scratches
upon Thomas, and even the baby had been frightened
into hiccuping fits. All their plaints were intensified
when they heard they were to hear no more of Tamlane for seven entire nights, for their several parts
in the night's bad business.

But Miss Penny was adamant. If she felt a bit of
a beast because she knew she was taking advantage
of a situation that had suddenly turned in her favor,
she didn't show it until she was at last alone. Then
she sank to her knees as she gathered up her book,
and remained there, staring into the villainous fire.
She didn't think she could bear another page of
"Tamlane," had neatly avoided it, but to judge from
the deprived audience's wails of complaint, didn't
think she'd be able to escape it once the week was
up. She held full sway in these rooms, but the baron
and his lady hated to see their children's unhappiness
almost as much as they hated to see them at any
length. But they'd surely hear of their offsprings' distress if Tamlane's exile went on for an hour over the
stated week. Beyond that, Bronwen admitted, she
was, after all, doomed to be fair by nature—if not by
her employer's decree—even though at times such
as now, she despaired for it as well as for her own
fancifulness.

Because there wasn't a doubt in her mind that she
was getting too overwrought over the matter. That
Nick and his lady reminded her of "Tamlane" because

she'd been thinking of it when she'd met them in
eerily similar circumstances was no more than an
amusing coincidence that she doubtless would laugh
at and forget if she led a normal life. But hours alone,
and more hours with children, simple Nurse, and a
credulous, uneducated nursery maid were taking
their toll on her, and too well she knew it. One day
a week with Miss Mayhew was scarcely a remedy for
it. If anything, Bronwen thought sadly, her friend's
cold rationality sent her fleeing further into fantasy.

She and Nick had been dear friends as children,
and might have been lovers in her newly maturing
mind then, but only there and then. Now Nicodemus
was lost to her, and no faerie tale was needed to
explain it. The look he'd exchanged with his lady had
done it very nicely. As to where he'd been? In her
position, Bronwen heard about the nobility, but
because of her position, never dared ask all about it,
and had never heard his name mentioned in London
gossip. As to why he'd seemed genuinely tormented?
For all she'd known him as a boy, what did she know
of men? Or his circumstances? Perhaps a man who'd
been a gallant, honest, forthright boy would resent
the sensual thrall his love obviously held him in.
What did she know of such things? Bronwen thought,
blushing as ruddily as Miss Mayhew ever had. Perhaps it was because Lady Blythe *was* unfaithful to
him, as she'd musingly imagined the Faerie Queen
would be to her consort. What did she know of Lady
Blythe, after all?

But at that, Bronwen sat up as suddenly and
straight as if she'd just been struck by a blazing cinder herself. For that was a thing—the only thing in
all of this—that she might discover. Seeking out gossip about an exotic lady new to town, although a

lowering objective for a proper, well-brought-up
lady, was a far healthier exercise for a lonely governess than dreaming of elves and enchantments could
ever be, wasn't it? She gazed into the fire, seeing an
escape from fear, if not madness itself, in her plans.

But Bronwen was doing a different sort of research
on a late afternoon some days later. She was seeking
another version of "Tamlane" in Mr. Scott's *Min-
strelsy* at Hatchards, when a shadow fell across the
pages. She was not so surprised as she should have
been when she looked up to see Nick gazing down at
her. There was something rightly mystical about his
appearing as she studied the tale that had returned
him to her. She closed the book, swallowed hard, and
turned to face him, as she supposed most of London
wished they could do. Because she'd completed her
other research days ago, having discovered that he
and his lady had set London as agog as she'd been
at the sight of them.

Lady Blythe and her coterie had arrived in town
with the shock of a thunderbolt coming from a clear
blue autumn sky. All that was known so far, so far
as the most knowing gossips of all—the maids, footmen, and understaffs of the *ton*—knew, was that the
lady was obviously clearly superior to most females
in wealth and experience as well as beauty and
haughtiness. That was enough to make her adored
by all. She'd come from afar, and more would be
known about her as soon as she and her companions
took up some of the dozens of invitations they were
being issued. And, oh yes, the handsome lord who
was always at her white shoulder was the expatriate
Earl of Fairlie, and he obviously was as enraptured

with her as all the rest of London was—although it was clear he knew her far, far more intimately.

Just now, however, he was smiling down at Bronwen, as though he could read her mind.

"No magic," he said to her unspoken question, "I asked the most knowledgeable—the servants—to discover where you lived, and where I might find you. This is your day off, therefore: Hatchards."

She blushed at his discovery as well as at how neatly he'd paralleled her own inquiries and wondered if he'd discovered them, too.

"You look the same, surely you've been telling tales," he teased as she blushed redder, "about your years."

"I've twenty-five of them," she said on a sudden smile of pleasure, "and you have changed, for you didn't used to be such a flatterer."

"No, I was more usually chasing you with spiders, and daring you to cross streams in my wake, wasn't I? When you smile," he said, suddenly serious, "the years fall away."

She couldn't say the same for him. Close up, like this, she could see the bleakness never left his startling eyes, for all his lips might say or do. Realizing what she did wish they might do, frightened her. For she'd no claim on him but an old acquaintance, and no way to further even that acquaintance.

"Why have you not wed?" he asked abruptly.

Once, when they were young, he might have asked such a question, once he might have had the right to, but now she was as affronted as perplexed by his lack of art. For surely nothing less than an artful man could have won the Lady Blythe for so much as an evening.

"That's hardly a question you can expect me to answer—fairly or honestly, my lord," she said coolly.

He seemed as confused as chagrined, and made a sound of exasperation. "Blast it, Bronwen, you know me better than that," he said.

"Do I?" she asked.

He looked at her for a long moment and then sighed. "No, no, I expect you could not. How many years has it been? No, I believe you do not. But we could remedy that, couldn't we? We could go somewhere and sit and chat . . . where's your maid?" he demanded on one of the frowns that had once been so rare, but now frequently flitted like shadows over his lean, dark face.

"A governess doesn't have a maid," she said softly, fearing for his wits, suddenly wondering whether Lady Blythe's company wasn't three parts compassion.

"I'd forgotten," he said on a grimace. "All of it, your position, and mine, and all that. But where's the harm in sharing a glass or two of cider or a cup of chocolate, at that charming tea parlor just down the street?"

She was about to jest, to ask how many children he had now, since that was the only reason the polite world could understand if they discovered an earl sipping his chocolate with a governess in a public tearoom. But the words caught in her throat as she wondered if he'd any, after all. She stared up into his light eyes, noting again his long, thick eyelashes—unfair that a boy should have them, she'd thought then, cruel that such a man should have them, she thought now.

"Oho!" a light, silky voice interposed, "the master and the maiden, all secluded in a glade of books. What's this?" the slight young man Nick had called

Rowan jested, taking the volume from Bronwen's nerveless fingers, "a book of folktales? Are you a man of legend now, Nicodemus?"

"Has evening fallen so soon then," Nick said harshly, wheeling to confront the young man, "that you're already so desperately in search of amusement?"

Bronwen looked out the window to see that the shadows had, indeed, lengthened, and was shocked at the lateness of the hour as well as her chagrin at seeing it. She might have talked herself into going off with Nick were the sun still high, but there was no way she could excuse herself so far as to accompany him into the night. For there was no way that society would, and she needed her position as much as she needed his friendship. She could survive without one, for only one was a real necessity, no matter how badly she wanted the other.

"I must go," she told Nick. "Good day," she nodded to Rowan, and then snatching her book back from his hand, she made for the stair.

"Ah, the mistress shall be vexed," Rowan commented with pleasure.

"Shall she?" Nicodemus asked wearily, before he saw the last of Bronwen's dark skirts disappear down the stair. Then he added in colder tones, "Shall she, indeed, be vexed that I met and spoke to an old friend? Or is it the bearer of the tale she'll be vexed with, do you think?"

"You've learned a great deal in your time with us, haven't you?" Rowan asked, with something that might have been respect.

"Not enough," Nicodemus said in a voice low as a whisper.

"Oh no, of course not!" Rowan replied with a shout of real laughter.

* * *

She never expected to meet him again, but then, Bronwen thought, how should she? She never went anywhere that a fine gentleman might, or rather, anywhere that a fine gentleman might without his looking like a fool. Her sole excursions during the six days of her working week were with the children, and to such enthralling places as their bootmakers, their friends' houses, and the park. And when they were in company, it was usually in the midst of a company of other children. So that *if* any nobleman were mad enough to be inclined to stop to chat with a governess, he'd be delighted to find himself surrounded by children, several other curious governesses, and nursemaids.

At such times, she'd laugh at the folly of ever expecting to see him again. Then she'd mock herself for even supposing she might. Which was eminently sensible and most clearheaded of her, except for the fact that she did meet him, again and again, in the next week. Always by accident, and always for only a moment.

He'd bow to her in the park, comment on the weather, and give her good day as she went down the street to the merchants she must visit, and once, told her how well she was looking and remarked on the book she was reading as she was sitting in the park and telling herself she'd never see him again. He was always alone and on his way to somewhere else. But it was remarkable how many times their paths crossed, and even more regrettable that it fed her fancies and set her practical doubts to rout.

When Bronwen's next day out came, she dressed with exceptional care, and wore a russet walking dress, with a shawl from her happier days, of intri-

cate design and bright autumnal hue. She pulled her
heavy brown hair up at the top of her head as usual,
but released the back of it from it's neat bundle, letting it fall to her shoulders in its natural curling
waves. Having no cosmetic but her expectations, she
nevertheless looked at herself in the glass and
thought that she looked almost young again. She
intended to go walking to the park with a book to
while away the autumn hours, in case he did not
appear.

But she thought he might. That gave her step an
unusual skip as she went to the great front hall, and
set her lips to smiling. In those few moments if she
were not the girl she'd been, she was far lovelier,
because she'd grown into a more serene beauty, and
her joy would have made even a plain girl glow. The
butler and the footmen thought they knew the reason
for her exalted state. They shook their heads and
thought privately, and after she'd gone, publically—
in the servant's hall—that it took all kinds, didn't it?
Because they knew what she'd forgot.

For when she got to the hall, she found Miss
Mayhew and Mr. Edwards awaiting her. And only
then did she remember she'd an appointment to walk
out with them this day, just as she had on so many
other Wednesdays, whenever she'd nowhere to go
and nothing else to do. Which was often.

"You look very well," Mr. Edwards said approvingly, bowing his neatly combed, glossily pomaded
head, before carefully putting his gray hat back on
it. But so he said every Wednesday. Miss Mayhew
nodded. He offered the women each an arm and said,
"Shall we?" as he did every Wednesday when they'd
met. They left the house to go for a stroll, Miss
Mayhew on his one side and Bronwen on the other,

as they always promenaded every Wednesday that
the weather permitted.

Sometimes Bronwen went only with Miss Mayhew,
but increasingly of late with Mr. Edwards as well.
At seven and twenty, he was looking for a wife, and
it was doubtful, Miss Mayhew said, that it was she
he was looking at with such intentions. Bronwen
thought it best to ignore both the comment and the
intentions. But she could not ignore the opportunity
to walk out with him. After weeks of being solely in
female company, and half of that, infants', it was so
pleasant simply to have an adult male's companion-
ship that she endured Miss Mayhew's speculations so
that she could have such a simple pleasure as merely
hearing a masculine voice addressed to herself.

Whatever his other intentions, Mr. Edwards was
always only too happy to fulfill that need.

Today, as ever, he spoke about his difficulties at
work, and the neat way he'd resolved them for his
employer, the dean at the small boys school where
he taught Latin, when he wasn't performing his
duties as personal assistant to Mr. Proctor, Dean of
St. Simon's, himself. He'd ambitions to be dean himself someday. But as Mr. Proctor was only in his
sixth decade of life and the prime of health, he could
only hope to perhaps be recommended for another
such exalted position if one came available elsewhere,
as he often said . . . or for Mr. Proctor to drop from
a sudden apoplexy or a bad clam, as Bronwen often
thought irreverently.

For she never jested with him, not the way she
might with another friend. He hadn't the capacity for
much levity, nor a playful sort of intellect. But neither was he too toplofty, and this was uncommon
in a world where most men believed themselves so

infinitely superior to women as to be almost a separate breed; and any man with a decent income believed himself to be worlds above a woman who had to toil at being a paltry governess. And he was kind, not stupid, and well enough looking, if one didn't go in for dash. For he was a smallish man, with small even features and brown eyes that didn't need spectacles except to read, and he'd all his teeth and most of his dark hair. His hair was his pride, and he polished it with macassar oil as lovingly as any housekeeper would an antique table, to the point that one could see one's reflection in it.

But Bronwen wasn't tall enough to see if the sparsely leaved trees above the long park path they walked along now were reflected in Mr. Edwards's glossy locks; she only came up to his shoulder, and this, among many other things, greatly pleased him about her. She was quite beautiful in her modest way, he thought, and very intelligent, yet this didn't put him off, frighten him away, or make him question his presumption as it might in another female. Because she was also orphaned, indigent, alone, and poorly recompensed for her hard work. In short, she'd make an excellent wife. And she'd hardly get a better offer—for matrimony, at least—he thought, frowning, because he spied a cavalcade of fine young gentlemen riding near, and they all seemed to be staring at her.

He could scarcely blame them for that, but it was the *way* they stared that alarmed him, and made his palms grow so sweaty his gloves grew tight even in the brisk autumn air. For he was only one man, and not a very fierce one, and they were prime bloods and heartless ones, from the look in their eyes and his knowledge of their breed.

He oughtn't to have walked the women so far afield, he thought nervously, he never should have kept them out so late; London was never so safe by dusk as it was by day. But his pleasure in Miss Penny's company had made him rash enough to suggest one more stroll to settle their constitutions after they'd taken their usual tea. He blamed himself for his selfish excess, and only hoped the Lord would protect the women, for he was sure he couldn't.

Then he saw the lady riding up to join the halting party, and let out all his breath in a relieved sigh. They'd not get up to much with a lady among them, and certainly not with such a lady: superbly mounted on a white horse, exquisitely dressed, both youthful and beautiful, and clearly of good birth. She rode through the mass of them to the front of the party, and they parted ranks for her as though by silent command. She was obviously their leader and their inspiration, and the way they looked to her made it clear she'd only fallen behind because she'd been chatting with her own especial cavalier, who rode abreast of her.

Now she stared at Mr. Edwards and his two companions, and then she laughed in a singularly beautiful and oddly frightening way. Or so Mr. Edwards heard it, the way the fox might hear the clear clarion call of a hunter's horn and the belling of the hounds. If he was no longer afraid for his skin, there were other fears raised beneath it, deep within his secret, anxious heart. But then he was a timorous fellow, and always aware of his inferiority to the wealthy and privileged class he admired, which this magnificent lady so clearly personified.

"What's to do, my lads? Why do you tarry?" she asked. "Ah. Why, it is your Miss Penny, is it not, my dear?" the lady on the white horse asked the lean, dark, and saturnine fellow mounted on a fine chestnut beside her.

"Indeed," the dark gentleman agreed in bored tones, and then eyeing the silent trio standing looking up at the mounted company, he added reluctantly, as though his sense of what was proper outweighed his idea of what was pleasant, "I give you good evening, Bronwen. Why are you abroad so late? The park holds danger after dark."

"Ah yes," a bright-eyed and yellow-haired youth near to the lady sang out. "But do see, Nick, she's got a brave gallant to protect her! Who should she fear then?"

"All that shun the sunlight," Nick said in the same deadened laconic tones, although he stared hard at the young fellow. "All who only dare creep out from under the rocks at dark, Rowan."

The blond fellow looked astounded and whistled, low, long, and almost soundlessly, though his long green eyes sparkled with humor as he slewed them around to look at the lady on the white horse. Her lovely face grew still.

"And darkness falls fast," the lady said through clenched teeth. "Come, Miss Penny, do the pretty and the correct; pray end our curiosity as to your escort. Introduce us please, so that we may be able to leave you."

"Lady Blythe, my lord," Bronwen said at once, wishing she were anywhere but where she was, disliking Nick's silence, the lady's impudence, Rowan's amusement, and the many hard and shining eyes she faced as much as the fearful looks Mr. Edwards darted at them. "You remember my friend, Miss Mayhew. May I also present another friend: Mr.

Edwards. Mr. Edwards: the Lady Blythe, from abroad, and Nicodemus Brand, the Earl of Fairlie, from another time and place, and . . . their various friends."

She'd somehow managed to make the introduction sound as civil as it was absurd, and Bronwen was proud of herself, until the lady spoke again.

"Mr. Edwards, of . . .?" the lady prompted delicately.

"St. Simon's School, I am personal assistant to Mr. Proctor, the dean," Mr. Edwards replied promptly, bowing low and bobbling up, looking both proud and humble at once, a trick he'd picked up from watching Mr. Proctor with the parents, and one he felt he had down rather well.

"Oooh," the lady said with what Mr. Edwards took to be interest and respect, and Bronwen knew to be vast amusement. "Why, fie on your dire speculations, Nick," she said, turning in her saddle to look at her companion, "for see what a lot of educators one finds in Green Park after dark!"

Nick nodded, though his expression grew even more bored, and Bronwen wished the night would pour over her like ink so she could no longer be seen.

"And in whose employ are you, Miss Penny?" the lady asked, and Bronwen could feel as well as hear the restlessness of the waiting party and the casual malice of the question so clearly that for a moment she almost dared not answer.

"I am employed by the Baron Rhodes and his lady," she answered, raising her head.

"Why, how wonderful!" the lady said with glee. "We've been invited to a soiree at your house not two nights hence! I do hope he's asked you, Miss Mayhew and you, Mr. Edwards, as well," she added, as though it were not utter nonsense. "E'en so, if he does not," she said with as much threat as laughter in her silver voice, "we shall certainly meet again, Miss Penny. For I'll be sure to ask the baron to allow you to be present. 'Til then, Miss Penny, adieu!"

The company roused itself, bowed, and waved, their horses jangled and snorted, and they rode off into the night. At the last, Bronwen saw one face look back to her.

"Lady," Rowan murmured in a voice like the sighing night wind as he rode up as close to Lady Blythe as her sleeve, seeing Nick glance back at the forlorn trio they'd left in the growing dark, "My lady, have a care. She holds a last piece of his heart, which he may not be able to live without, like the earth and the changing seasons. She may have no family left, or money has she none, but she's of an old and good family, is our little brown maid; older than yours or mine, I think. Autumn itself is her friend. Look more closely and see for yourself, she's no ordinary maid. Tiny and wise, bright-eyed and nut-brown, look at her pretty proportion, size, and general comeliness, and note that she's all the colors of the growing earth."

"And I am moonlight and stardust, and I slide through his mind like water, and fit to his body like his second breath, have you never heard him praise me?" Lady Blythe laughed. "What have I to fear from a little brown maid?" she said, and looked with smug delight at her dark companion on his great horse . . .

. . . Only to see him look back and call into the deepening night, "God keep you Bronwen, until we meet again!"

*   *   *

" 'Ah Tamlane, my love, my love Tamlane, is there nothing I can do to save you?' poor Ellen cried.

" 'On only one night in the mortal year can I be saved, my love, only on that night can a brave soul save mine.' Tamlane said. 'For on that night, on Halloween night, I ride with the faerie court through Scotland and England. If you would save me it must be then.'

" 'Tell me how I should, and I shall do it,' Ellen declared.

" 'But there's danger for you, my love,' Tamlane sighed, 'On the one night I may be freed, there is the most danger for you, I fear.'

" 'I fear nothing if I may free you, only tell me how I should, and I shall. For love knows no fear, as fear knows not love, and I have nought but love for you, Tamlane,' she swore, and it was true," Bronwen read, and turned the page.

But, "Miss Penny, 'tis time," an excited maid called from the doorway, and Bronwen put down her book, knowing more than her storytelling time was lost. The children didn't leap up and run to the door, as they would on any other night for such a treat as being allowed downstairs to meet the company. Such was their fascination with the story that they lingered, still half caught in the tale, so that Bronwen and Nurse were able to check their finery for last minute corrections.

But Mary's hair was still neatly plaited, and Elizabeth's ringlets free of jam, and Thomas's shirt was white as it had come from the laundress still, and Timothy had only a burr to remove from his thatch of hair, and a shirttail to tuck into his nankeens. Baby was wiped so clean of his dinner his plump face shone red, and Nurse wore her best cap, its ribbons

so full of starch and tied beneath her jowls so tightly,
that a quick turn of her head might well sever it from
her neck entirely.

Bronwen wore a woolen frock, unfashionably high
at the neck, of a brown color deep as earth and as
dark as roots, the same color as her troubled eyes.
Tonight the lady would make mock of her, she was
sure, and surely so would her gay company. Perhaps
it would influence the baron and his lady enough to
make them decide to let her go, for they abhorred
the unfashionable in furnishings or people. But that
wasn't what had made Bronwen unable to eat her
dinner this night. Or what made her heart sink when
she'd heard the faint but joyous sounds of company
arriving downstairs for their dinner earlier. It was
the thought of Nick thinking ill of her because of the
lady's spite; it was the thought of how ill she'd think
of Nick if he allowed it, much less was influenced by
it.

She went down the stair in the wake of the children, and told herself as she did, over and again,
that she was a governess and they were the children
of the house, and so they were the ones the company
wished to see, and she, only a shadow at their backs,
as it should be. And so she thought and prayed. And
so it transpired that it was to be. And so it was, in
a way, even worse than spite might have been.

The room was so full of fine guests that all Bronwen could see at first was their number and their
finery. The room swam with their rich perfumes, and
the peculiar overheated aroma of too many persons
packed into a space too small to accommodate them,
which meant that the baron was having a truly successful soiree. The gentlemen were all in black and
white; their evening dress allowed for lavish color

only in their waistcoats. But the ladies were like blossoms of radiant and tropical hues, and their jewelry: their faceted rings, bracelets, amulets, necklaces, and earrings sparkled in the gaslight and firelight like so many swarming, twinkling insects busy at the exquisite blooms.

"Ah, the beautiful children!" cried a glad voice, and looking in the direction of the overly enthusiastic cry, Bronwen saw them, all of them at once, all together as they always were, and wondered why she'd ever thought the other guests sparkling and beautiful.

This time there were many ladies among Lady Blythe's company, and one was more wonderously lovely than the other, and none so rare as the lady herself. The other ladies wore white, pink, or powdery pale yellows and blues, matching their escort's waistcoats in their hues, as well as in their bodily attractiveness. The lady herself wore a thin silver gown that sparkled when she breathed, and showed her high breasts, lean flanks, and long white neck to perfection, for she, her ink black tresses let down to flow like the darkness at the edge of the moon, was perfection itself. It was unfashionable for a lady to wear her hair down, and however daring the styles were these days, still not at all the thing for one to wear a gown so close to the skin. None of that mattered, she was her own fashion, style, and creation. And Nick, at her side, wore a waistcoat of silver and black tapestry, and was handsome as he was unapproachable, for he didn't so much as look at Bronwen where she stood behind the children.

As why should he? she thought, with fairness and sorrow.

The company cooed over the children, made them recite bits of rhymes and lessons, applauded their cleverness far more than it was worth, and generally made a great show of adoring them in the few minutes they'd have to put up with them, as was always the case with the children of the *ton*.

"And what story are you currently reading?" asked Lady Blythe as the baron and his lady beamed at their accomplishment of having offspring to entertain their guests with.

"We are hearing the story of 'Tamlane,' my lady, for Halloween," Thomas said.

The overheated room grew cold and still in that second, or so Bronwen thought and then felt a frisson of true fear for the first time. But it was only for the despairing thought of how her odd life was making her odd, and prey to foolish fancies.

"Indeed?" the lady said coldly, her eyes arrowing to Bronwen, seeing her, instantly separating her out from the shadows. "How clever, Miss Penny, how daring, too. But is it wise?" she asked. "That is to say, is it not a tale to give children night terrors?"

"Oh," said Nick languidly, his hand going to touch the back of the lady's neck lightly, to stroke beneath the flow of long and silky hair there, "I'd think not. I was raised on it, and I've no fears—of anything but your wrath, my dear lady, that is to say."

"It's a tale to do with the redemptive quality of love, not the triumph of terror my lady," Bronwen said before she could stop from saying what the sight of Nick's hand upon his lady's skin made her wish to.

"Oh, well then, see?" Nick said on a throaty laugh, as his lady stretched out her long neck like a cat at his exploring touch, "How little I learned from it entirely. So then how should it influence these children badly? Which of us mortals learn from our les-

sons, after all? And how much pleasure should we
have if we did?" he whispered, low enough for his
lady's ear, loud enough for them all to hear.

They all laughed then, and the lady's set the loudest, it seemed. But when they'd done, the baron
seemed puzzled.

"How comes it that you know our governess, my
lady?" he asked. "Have you children?"

"Or plans for any?" Rowan called. "—From the
way Fairlie is stroking away, I did but wonder," he
added with such false contrition that he set all the
company aroar.

"No and no!" the lady cried in mock horror, making
a show of smacking Nick's hand with her fan. "The
earl knew Miss Penny a long while ago, in childhood,
it seems."

"A long, long while ago," Nick agreed, gazing at
Lady Blythe and smiling at her, before his gaze
dropped to her lips.

"I think the children ought to go before they learn
too many lessons," Rowan commented, and amidst
renewed laughter, Bronwen and Nurse made their
curtsies with the children, and herded them up the
stairs again. Bronwen did not look back. Which was
as well. For if she had seen him looking after her
with sorrow and regret, she'd have been just as upset
as she'd have been if she'd not seen him looking anywhere but at his lady's ripe, smiling mouth.

Of course the party took its toll. Timothy had to
be practically plucked from the ceiling to get him
into bed, Mary kept babbling about the pretty ladies,
Thomas worried whether his answers had been
clever enough to please his father, and Elizabeth

began casting up the contents of her stomach as soon as she'd got into bed.

"Wormwood," Nurse said wisely, nodding her head. "Aye, and feverfew," she muttered, before waddling away to her rooms for the medicaments she needed.

"So much for your nut brown maid," the Lady Blythe told Rowan in a laughing whisper when they left the baron's house as the stars wheeled over their heads.

"I think not," he answered soft as the night breeze's caress on their cheeks. "No more than night truly ever vanquishes day, for hers is the power of sunlight."

"And of what use is that to her," the lady laughed, "for conquering those who live and love by night?"

Nick, awaiting her at the bottom of the short stair leading from the town house, turned, inclining his dark head as he tried to catch their light whispers. She floated down the steps like streaming moonlight, and caught his arm and laughed up at him.

"Rowan thinks you might rise early tomorrow. He doesn't know you'll be as weary at noon as you will be at dawn," she laughed.

One dark brow rose as he looked down to her face, which glowed luminous as the growing moon's, "Are we promised elsewhere this night?" he asked, puzzled.

"Only to our bed," she answered, raising her lips to his. "Is that not enough?"

He made no answer that could be heard as she stopped his breath with her mouth.

*   *   *

"Aye, wormwood have I in plenty," Nurse said worriedly, "but not a speck of feverfew left. One's good, but two's the sure cure."

"Can't you send a footman to rouse the apothecary?" Bronwen asked, looking worriedly at Elizabeth's pale green-hued face.

"Any other night," Nurse said, "they're all at cleaning up after company now though. You know how mistress is; if there be speck on the floor by dawn, it'll be their posts to pay for it."

"But if you tell her Elizabeth's ill . . ." Bronwen began, and then remembered that the lady of the house had gone to bed, and nothing but fire or her noontime chocolate would rouse her until then. That was the rule, and none dared break it, especially not for anything as paltry as something to do with the children.

"I'll go," Bronwen sighed, seeking her cloak in the wardrobe. She put up one hand before Nurse could speak, "Beth's afraid of her shadow, much less the night," she said, and shamefaced, but relieved, the little nursery maid nodded violent agreement. "It's only a short walk," Bronwen went on. "Who'll look to molest a small brown shadow? For that's what I shall appear to be," she said, putting her cloak on and drawing the hood over her hair. "And who else is there to go?" she added sadly before Nurse could speak.

As there was no answer to that, she simply nodded at the silence and left the nursery, to slip, like a shadow, down the back stair.

The night was not as dark as she would have liked. Bronwen wasn't accustomed to the night, nor did she find any affinity with it as poets did, moonlit or not. Velvety dark would have suited her purposes and

quelled her fears far better than the odd half-light of
the moon did. For the moon lit her way in a curious
manner, bleaching the pavements and blanching the
life from familiar objects, making hobgoblins of trash
bins and poor stunted sidewalk trees. It was flat
green light, much like that on poor Elizabeth's face,
she thought, hurrying along the silent streets, hoping
to amuse herself out of her sudden night terrors, glad
of her slippers, which skimmed over the cobbles like
bat's wings—and then was sorry she'd ever made
that comparison in her mind. And so it was only natural that she should shriek when she saw the dark
shadow loom up out of the darker ones to come to
her side.

"Good God, Bronwen. It *is* you. Whatever are you
doing out so late, and alone, in the night?" Nick's
voice demanded.

But her heart was still beating so fast it dragged
all the breath from her lungs.

"The apothecary's," she managed to say at last,
holding her hands before her as though she were
praying, as if only by holding them so tightly could
she steady herself, "Elizabeth's ill. She needs feverfew, and no one else could go."

His face was in shadow and shadowy moonlight,
the flat light that cast doubt on everything, and she
couldn't read anything she trusted in his expression.

"The apothecary's not far. I . . . I was just going
to waken him and get a paper of feverfew for Elizabeth's potion," she explained. "It's the very thing—
with wormwood—for such complaints . . ."

"Do you know the danger?" he asked angrily. "Is
a paper of feverfew worth your life, or honor? What
sort of a life have you found for yourself? Is there no
one to look after you?"

Perhaps because she thought he might have offered her more than advice; perhaps because the sight of him so soon after his defection from her this night was too sudden, she recovered herself. Anger drove out fear, as always.

"I'm safe enough," she said defiantly. "I'm well cloaked and covered, and even without, I'm only a poor brown little thing, a governess, with no money or jewels and so of no account to footpads, and with no great beauty to interest mischief makers. It is your ladies, Nicodemus, who have something to fear on moonlit nights, not I. And . . . and the child needs her medicine," she added.

He stood gazing down at her, and she took no comfort from the fact that his expression seemed to soften, for it might only be the weariness of the hour, or the vagaries of the strange light. But his voice, when he spoke, was gentle and sad, and older than his had ever been.

"Of course, the child. How like you, Bronwen. So good and so true, you bring back that part of myself I'd thought I'd left in the mists of memory. Once I wasn't so different from you, was I?" He shook his head. "Bronwen, dear little Bronwen, you are so wrong. Few ladies have so much to lose as you, for few have half as much to start with. Come, I'll go with you, you ought not to be alone."

She walked on with him after pausing to ask, as it suddenly occurred to her, "Why are you here now?"

"My quizzing glass," he said softly. "I left it, and came to retrieve it. It was a lucky thing, wasn't it? Come, I've not much time left."

The apothecary woke and then worked faster to the tune of a gentleman's summons than he might have to a woman servant's gentle pleas, and so Bronwen had the paper of feverfew in short order. The gratuity he received for his troubles might even have made the apothecary as glad of his interrupted sleep as he assured the fine gentleman that he was.

They hastened back to the baron's town house, but now that danger was past, Bronwen suddenly found the blank light almost attractive, and heady with lack of sleep, almost wished they could hold hands as they had once, so long ago, and stroll for a while through the strange night. But they were back before she could begin to formulate a means to let him know he'd inadvertently dealt her pain earlier in the night, or even begin to think of a way to tell him she'd already forgiven him for it. She paused at the front steps as she readied herself to leave him, but before she could speak, he did.

"When I'm with you," he said slowly, hesitantly, his dark face unreadable, for all his voice held pain and wonder, "I'm young again, and the moonlight pales before the thought of the sunlight we shared. You make me think all kinds of renewal possible. But it is not," he said abruptly. "And no illusion can change that, or the fact that I've changed beyond reclamation. I wish I could help you, Bronwen, but my help would be to your harm. That I know. The best I can do for you is to leave you as I found you, but I do so wish I didn't have to . . ."

He studied her face intently, and leaning toward her, touched her lips with his own. She felt a tingling, and a tenderness, and a warmth in her heart as well as her lips, then felt like crying as much as she did like pulling his head closer and letting him draw her closer, as he began to do. But a merry voice calling out from the dark called her back to herself, as he raised his head and quickly stepped away.

"Ho! Nick! I have it. No need to disturb the good baron and his lady," Rowan said as he walked out of a shadow and into the pale moonlight. "Yes, the glass, the glass you'd said you'd left here. But I remembered, not two minutes after you'd left us, that I'd seen you put it back into your inner jacket pocket, where you never carry it. No wonder you thought you'd left it behind," he said happily.

Nick absently slipped his long fingers into his inner pocket as he stared at Rowan, and nodded. "Yes," he said flatly, "So I did. Clever Rowan, so observant."

"Ah but never doubt I'm not the only one," Rowan said pleasantly. "Hello! Who is that? Why, it's Miss Penny! But isn't it a bad penny that's always supposed to show up, not a good one? Which you surely are. But then what are you doing out so late, my dear? Did our wicked earl convince you he'd dropped his glass upon the pavement and beg you out to help him hunt for it? Beware, my dear, that's the oldest trick in Londontown."

The moonlight flattered Rowan, his yellow hair became silver, his green eyes sparkled in it, and yet he looked no handsomer to Bronwen. She thought him false in any light, and disliked his pointed remarks. But she noted Nick made no defense of her or himself, nor offered any excuse to Rowan any more than he did to her. So she told Rowan briefly of her errand, thanked Nick coolly for his escort, bade them both good night, and then turned to the house while she could still see it through her blurring eyes.

But Nick stopped her as she set foot upon the steps. Rowan stood back a pace, too discreetly waiting for his friend, as Nick took her hand in a brief clasp.

"Rowan's right," Nick said with a forced grin. "I'm not a good fellow any longer, Bronwen, not at all the one you remember. I run with a mad set, live a wild life, and cannot think of what will ever save . . . turn me from it," he corrected himself quickly with a crooked smile. "For all you remind me of the good things of my youth, I'm not the man I used to be. You, you are lovelier than even I guessed you might become," he said more softly, gazing at her. "But then," he shrugged his wide shoulders, "I'm far too fond of loveliness now, too . . . or what the world considers loveliness," he added quietly.

"The best thing I can tell you is to forget me. But I will not, cannot, shall not forget you," he said with sudden passion, before he dropped her hand and said wearily, "Much good that will do me. But it might just, just a little, as a single candle in a window dispels the dark. Go with God, Bronwen, and think of me no more. Good night, good-bye."

She turned to see him stride toward Rowan, as the younger man said with amused sympathy, "Too right, my lord, too right."

Nurse mixed the paper of herbs with her own stores, and together she and Bronwen, sweetening the mixture with a little sugar and wine, got Elizabeth to drink it all down. And there it stayed, as though it really were a magical potion. But long after Elizabeth's stomach had been settled, and the last wakeful child's excitement had dwindled to sleep, Bronwen sat awake in her bed, watching the moonlight-made shadows making their silvery circuits across her bed, over her single chair, and down the carpet to dawn.

* * *

" 'If you would save me,' Tamlane said, 'you must stand at the crossroads betwixt the stroke of midnight and one of the new day, with holy water in your hand, and wait for the party to come riding by on Halloween night. For all the wild party from Elfland, dressed in their finest for their great holiday, will come pounding by the crossroads at that darkest hour of the night, my love.'

" 'But if it is Halloween night, and all in their finery and masked for the rites, how shall I know you, Tamlane, my love?' Ellen asked.

" 'I shall ride with the finest court of them all, by the side of the Faerie Queen on her milk white steed, and I shall wear her sign at my breast. Look to my hands, the left shall be gloved, but my good right hand, which you now hold, will be bare of all but the memory of your sweet touch, my love.'

" 'Ah, so I shall know you, but how shall I save you?' Ellen asked.

" 'You must take your courage in your two hands and leap at me, and I shall fall to the ground as if you dragged me from my mount. Then seize me and hold me, whatever transpires, hold me, for they have great magic and will turn me into every loathsome thing I have been with them, and more. But hold me till they turn me to a white-hot iron, then cast the holy water over me, and I shall turn again into a man. Then cast your mantle over me, and I shall be yours forever, in and of the world again,' Tamlane said. 'But it is a hard thing, and a dire danger, and if you shall not, I shall understand, my love.'

" 'I shall do it,' Ellen said," Bronwen read, and then closed the book.

There was an immediate outcry, which she hushed

by raising her hand and saying, "I've saved the best for last, for tomorrow *is* Halloween night, and you shall have the end of it then. It's only fitting," she added, and they all grudgingly admitted it.

"Now, my dears, you must excuse me, for your mama is taking you to see your aunt this afternoon, and as there's no room in the coach for me, I've a half day off—which I shall pass in buying you some Halloween treats—if you behave well today, that is to say. I shall see you at dinner," she said, and left them to the care of Nurse, so that she could take advantage of her rare holiday.

"It is not my place to tell you, but someone must, because Mr. Edwards is a good man, and a sensitive one, if not, as I gather, the one of your dreams," Miss Mayhew said in neutral tones, avoiding Bronwen's eyes, as they sat upon a park bench in the weak autumn afternoon light.

"Indeed, I've broken my word by telling you this," she went on, "for he most especially requested I should not tell you of his plans after he apprised me of his intentions, and asked only if I'd kindly refrain from accompanying you this coming Wednesday afternoon. No, no," she said at once, as Bronwen tried to speak, "I was not insulted, and am not. How else can the poor man ask for your hand? As I know you," she said more forcefully, "I felt that in fairness you ought to have time to think it over. That is why I requested the hour off to see you today, and sent to you to meet me. If he'd asked all at once, I am persuaded you'd refuse him, for you're a romantical sort of a young woman. But I felt it my duty to remind you, you're no longer precisely a young woman. And that he offers an escape from what surely must be an intolerable life for you, for you weren't raised to it, as some were. And even they find it difficult, I assure you.

"He's not handsome or clever, to be sure. But he is kind, and tolerably well-off, with expectations. And so far as I can see, and I do hope you can clear your eyes of fairy tales long enough to see it, too, there's no other who can—or more properly stated perhaps—who *will*," she said shrewdly, "save you from a life of penury and servitude."

But, Bronwen wanted to cry out, perhaps there's someone I may be able to save from a life of some sort of servitude to something he detests in his heart, I know he does, for so his eyes told me, and so his lips said when they were silent against my own.

"I don't know," she said softly instead, "I don't know what to say or do."

"So I suspected," Miss Mayhew said comfortably, rising and shaking out her skirts. "But I'm persuaded you'll think of the proper course—for yourself, and Mr. Edwards. You may be a dreamer, indeed, who can blame you for not wishing to relinquish the dream of the security and ease you once had? But I know you're a sensible woman at heart."

Bronwen arose and faced her friend and said with sudden passion, "But I'm not, after all, for all I can think is that it's not right to take a man as husband to escape a life of servitude and tedium, and only that."

Miss Mayhew looked amused. "Had you been governess to as many families as I have, my dear," she said smugly, "you'd see that it is possibly the most common reason for young women to enter wedlock. For while marriage itself is servitude, the recompense is better than any other employment, and the position is permanent."

"But I've not really lived yet, nor done anything I wished to do," Bronwen said, as though to herself.

"No, how should you have done?" Miss Mayhew said sympathetically. "You're no longer a young lady with fortune and family behind you. But that is where you must put those dreams. The Earl of Fairlie is a friend of those days, I know," she said softly as Bronwen avoided her knowing eyes. "Yet see how he aids you. Be sensible, my dear. See the world as it is, not as you dream on it. He's fallen into the toils of a mysterious temptress, it is true. But she's no Faerie Queen, and he no innocent stolen or seduced into her service. She's just a beautiful, if vicious, noblewoman—as he is a dissolute and careless nobleman . . . whatever he may have been, be sure, so he is now."

Well, and had he not admitted just that to her himself? Bronwen thought as a tear appeared while she was trying to swallow down the hard lump of reality that caught in her throat. Miss Mayhew saw her chin trembling and produced a small lavender-scented handkerchief and handed it to Bronwen.

"It is not easy to be an adult," Miss Mayhew said in a thin voice as she rummaged in her purse seeking another handkerchief, which she may have intended to use for herself, since her own two small blue eyes had completely disappeared behind the sudden mist that arose on her spectacles. "Or rather I suppose it is once one becomes accustomed—but it's difficult to become accustomed. Some of us must, and some never have to, which is why, I imagine, there are so few true adults in this crowded world."

She looked away from Bronwen's downcast head and went on too brightly, seeking to divert her grieving friend, "Why see here," she said on a shaky

laugh, as she fished two folded strips of paper from
the recesses of her voluminous purse, "here's youth.
Here's what a careless young gentleman thought to
give me as a reward for a small favor. Young Lord
Malverne, a rackety young gentleman, elder brother
to my young charges: I translated a little note that
his 'friend'—whom I suspect is truly his inamorata—
left for him, in Spanish! And he gifted me with a pair
of tickets to a masquerade! As though a woman such
as myself could use them!" she laughed overmuch at
her little jest so that she'd an excuse to sniff away
her foolish, sympathetic tears.

"A masquerade?" Bronwen asked, looking up suddenly and staring at her friend.

"Why, yes," Miss Mayhew said, a little taken aback
by Bronwen's interest. She squinted at the tickets
she held. "At the opera house tomorrow night in
honor of Halloween, as if the sort of people who fre-
quent masquerades care a rap what they're to celebrate," she said on a last sniff.

"But that's just it!" Bronwen said excitedly, forgetting her present pain for a moment. "There are no
'sort of people' who attend them, everyone in London
goes. I've heard about them forever. Everyone gets
into costume, they drink, eat, dance, and sing, and
no one ever has to know who or what they really
are. Dukes go, they say, as do dustmen. It's most
democratic."

"Oh to be sure," Miss Mayhew said, "most democratic. Cyprians go, as do procurers, if you don't
mind my plain speaking, as well as all sorts of low
gentlemen and lowlier men." She held the tickets up
so that she could rend them into pieces, but before
she could, a small gloved hand came down upon hers.
And that little gloved hand shook.

"No," Bronwen said, "Please. Oh, Miss Mayhew. Just once," she said, and from the sudden light in her eyes, Miss Mayhew knew precisely what her friend was about to ask, and began to shake her head in denial.

"Just once," Bronwen persisted. "And what better night than tomorrow when all of London will be in disguise? And likely thoroughly disguised as well, what with all they'll be drinking at the various festivities?" she laughed at her pun and went on excitedly. "Dear Miss Mayhew. Youth is foolish, I know. But it's gone so soon. I'd like, just once, to do something foolish and youthful before I give all over to being old and sensible. You're right about so many things. I know Nick is lost to me, and that increasingly of late I live in the tales I tell the children. Do you think I don't know that? It worries me more than you can imagine. And yes, I know I must make a new secure life for myself, however unsatisfactory it may be to my romantic notions.

"But just once, I should like to be a fool. Wouldn't you? Especially if no one would ever be the wiser? Can you imagine Mr. Edwards ever going to a masquerade with me, even after we wed? No, nor can I. But if we were to dress in costumes, we two, who should ever see us? And if they did, know us? Two dreary little governesses out for a night at the opera, dressed as queens of ancient Egypt—or gypsies—milkmaids, Columbines, or goddesses? And yet to have that memory, so that we knew something no one else would ever suspect; why I suspect such a merry secret could lighten even our darkest years to come, don't you? Oh please, Miss Mayhew, tomorrow night, so there's no time to worry over it, and less to fret. Can we? Shall we?"

"Oh my dear," Miss Mayhew said with great and tender sympathy, as she slowly shook her head, "I understand. I do. But can you see me there? Me? Please, my dear. Can you think of any mask that could conceal my good sense? . . . My unfortunate, but unfortunately necessary good sense," she concluded on a sigh.

The room was still, so quiet the fire only mumbled beneath its red breath in the grate, as if it, too, were trying to hear the softly intoned words the young woman was reading from the book. The night, too, was still and cold, no wind wailed at the windows. And yet somehow this night, this moon-drenched, silent, silvery night, that was even eerier, for it was a perfectly apprehensive Halloween night.

"And so Ellen promised Tamlane, and so she was there the next night, Halloween night, at the very stroke of midnight: that dark and witching hour that is in no clock or calendar, that cursed and magical moment that is neither yesterday nor today. And at the very first stroke of midnight, she heard the hoofbeats coming out of the silent night. At the second, she heard horses whinnying and their trappings jingling. At the third, the sound of their rider's spurs jangling, and soon, betwixt the fourth and the fifth, she saw all the faerie court come riding up out of Elfland, on their wild revels. And then by the sixth stroke, they were riding so close by her, she could hear the crackle and sigh of the rider's stiff brocades and silken finery shifting, as they rose in their saddles to urge their wild mounts on.

"They were masked and dressed in costumes both rare and rich. She saw what seemed to be elves and faeries, as well as birds and animals, things with

horns where no living thing ever grew them, things
with more eyes than a peacock—and not just in their
tails—things with wings and feathers that never
flew—or that you would never wish to see fly—and
all of them, all the rare, rich company, came pounding past brave Ellen as the strokes of midnight
counted onward to the new day.

"And then she saw the Faerie Queen, indeed, how
could she miss her? For she wore silver and white,
so that she was almost one with the moonlight, and
her hair was the color of the space between the stars
in the night. She rode on her milk white steed, and
there was a small shining crescent moon held fast in
her streaming hair. By her side rode a lean man all
in black, from hair to boots, with a cape the color of
the deepest night flying out behind him, so that if
you did not look sharp, you'd have missed him, but
for the gleam of the crescent moon at his throat that
was his cape clasp, and the softer glow of his one
long white hand, which without a black gauntlet like
his other, clutched the reins of his madly racing
steed."

Bronwen sighed and turned the page, then lifted
her great brown eyes to her enraptured audience.
Even Nurse sat forward a little, and the baby in her
arms had his eyes wide, as though even he knew
what the storyteller was saying, her voice was so
thrilling to hear.

"Then she knew it was her own Tamlane," Bronwen said. "And as the seventh stroke was heard, she
took a grip on the bottle of holy water she carried,
and at the eighth, she waited for him to ride past
her, and at the ninth, she held her breath . . ."

"Oh! Time's wasting, hurry, hurry," called Mary,
and Thomas bounced in his chair. Elizabeth's fingers

were in her mouth and Timothy didn't so much as think of telling on her for it, for all children sat hunched and fearful.

"And on the stroke of midnight, Ellen leapt from behind the bush of broom and sprang at Tamlane's frothing horse!" Bronwen said all of a sudden. She waited for the exact count of twelve herself, and then went on.

"She seized at the reins, and pulled at the rider, and before you could say 'spit!' she had the rider down in the dust of the road."

This, strictly speaking, was not in the book, but Bronwen's audience was enchanted, and there was even a muted "hoorah" heard.

"As soon as she saw this, Ellen wrapped the black-draped rider around in her arms, so that he was covered by her mantle. 'Alas!' cried one of the faerie crew, for they'd halted their horses to see. 'She's won! She has Tamlane fast!'

" 'Not yet!' cried the Faerie Queen," Bronwen said, automatically changing her voice to the silvery sound of Lady Blythe's. " 'Come brothers, sisters, 'tis time for magic.'

"First they changed Tamlane to a block of ice, so cold it burned at Ellen's arms. Then they turned him to a raging column of fire, but she closed her eyes, gritted her teeth, and held onto him. Then the fire died, and she felt a loathsome squirming in her arms, and opened her eyes to see she held a great hissing venomous snake. She held on. Then the snake writhed and she felt a great hairy burden in her arms instead, and looked into the gnashing teeth of an enormous bear. But she held fast. To see that the bear had turned to a snapping weasel, which struggled so hard that she almost lost hold of him. But she did not," Bronwen said to a collective sigh of relief.

"Then what she held grew man-sized, and turned white-hot as an iron, and then, Ellen loosed the cap of the bottle in her hand with her chattering teeth, and cast it all over the white-hot thing in her arms. A great hiss of steam arose, and when it faded, she held her beloved Tamlane fast, exactly as she remembered him and as he'd always been.

"When he'd done kissing her . . . er, thanking her," Bronwen invented quickly, "they looked up to see the faerie court riding off and away. But before they vanished forever from view, they heard the sad and furious Faerie Queen singing:

'She that hath taken young Tamlane
Hath gotten a stately groom,
She's taken away my bonniest knight,
And left me nothing in his room.

But had I known, Tamlane, Tamlane,
Before we came from home,
I'd have taken out thy heart of flesh
And put in a heart of stone.' "

"And then they were wed?" Elizabeth asked.

"Yes, and so lived happily ever after," Bronwen said.

"The faeries never came back for him?" Timothy asked nervously.

"Never," Bronwen said firmly. "She'd won him back entirely, and broken the spell by all rules of our nature and their nature. So they no longer ever had power over him again. Because her love was true and brave, and though she was only a mortal woman, the power of those of the earth is always superior to that of those beneath it, as is the power of the day over that of the night. For though they must each in their turn surrender to the other, so as to share the twenty-four hours of the day, dark you know, can always be dispelled by a light, however little it may be. And yet there's no dark that is dark enough to put out all the light."

"Bravo Miss Penny!" Timothy cried.

After they'd given their three muted cheers, the children were allowed to have a secret tea with the little cakes she'd brought them. They went to bed without complaint and lay there eyeing the full moon riding so high above their nursery windows, unafraid, even if it were undoubtedly still high Halloween night; for now they'd the secret of dark versus light.

"Never fear," Nurse chuckled, helping Bronwen into her hastily contrived costume as soon as they'd put the children to bed and got back to Bronwen's small chamber. "Nary a word'll pass my lips. Neither footman nor maid'll say a word neither, you'll see. It's that good to see you being young for once't—as we all was—or wisht to be. I'll watch over the babes, and let you in by the back stair when you've had enough frolic. Eh, and so shall you. Now look at you!"

She could have dressed as a lady from another century, for Nurse knew of a great many discarded dresses in the trunks in the attic, and with the many clever hands of the household staff at her disposal, she could have masqueraded as a queen, a clown, or a Columbine, as she'd said to Miss Mayhew. But as it was spur of the moment, and she'd only a day to decide and cobble together a costume, Bronwen

decided to go in the first, simplest, and most comfortable guise she could think of.

Her gown was silk and copper brown, a favorite
one from her carefree days that she couldn't bring
herself to leave behind with them. Over it, she wore
a long brown-patterned shawl that came to her
knees, but it was entirely disguised by cutout fabric
leaves in all the various hues of autumn, so as she
moved, it seemed as though she were caught in a
flurry of leaf fall on an autumn day. Many of the
leaves had been culled from a costume made for a
child's entertainment in some long past generation;
the rest had been hastily and merrily contrived by
the children and many other helpful household hands.

On her brow and over her heavy brown hair, which
she'd loosed to fly with the autumn breeze, Bronwen
wore a wreath of golden leaves—or almost exactly
like gold—for they were made of heavy fabric and
hearty color, and complemented her costume as gold
always complements the earth from which it came.
And so she seemed an elemental spirit of the earth.
In sunlight she would have looked like a pagan repre-
sentation of autumn itself; in the night, in the subtle
moonlight, she was like the forest at midnight, as
much part of earth as the moon was of the sky. It
suited her, in color, form, and spirit, exactly.

"Yes," she said with pleasure, as she turned this
way and that to see the leaves rise and fall on her
breast and flutter over her body, "perfect. My Papa
was from Wales," she told Nurse, her eyes gleaming
as she inspected herself in the glass. "He was brown
and sturdy as a nut. He teased Mama, who was so
very English, by saying that his family was descended
from the little people: the Brownies themselves, who
fled England when humans came. And so he said

we'd always have fresh milk from our cows, well-cobbled shoes, and the blessings of the earth upon us. Tonight, just tonight, I do believe him," she laughed, as she drew a brown mask over her eyes, and let Nurse tie it in back.

Then she let Nurse carefully arrange her long brown cape over her costume, and after she'd given her helper a quick, spontaneous hug, she went to the door, looked both ways down the corridor, and hurried down the back stair.

There was a hackney waiting down the street, and a grinning footman helped her to it. When the door was opened, she gasped to see an enchantress waiting for her there: a female wizard, with stars, moons, and runic symbols emblazoned on her long cape, and a tall black hat covered with sparkling magical signs upon her head. Bronwen giggled as the door closed and she settled into the opposite seat.

"It *is* you, Miss Mayhew, is it not, oh mighty wizard?" she asked as the coach drew away with a little jolt, and she valiantly suppressed her laughter, for she could think of no other female wizard who'd wear spectacles over her mask.

"Indeed," Miss Mayhew said, and Bronwen was sure the small blue eyes were dancing with merriment. "A most excellent disguise, is it not? And you, my dear, look wonderfully."

"We both do," Bronwen said. "Oh, my dear lady, we shall have such fun this one Halloween night! Stolen treats are best, are they not?"

"Not at all the thing for a governess to say," Miss Mayhew countered, before she said comfortably, "but very true, my dear, very true."

They were silent as they left the hackney and entered the great opera house, not only because of fear of discovery, but from awe. There were hordes of people there, and all in costume: all glittering, laughing, and clothed in weird, fantastical, amusing, beautiful, or simply absurd costumes. They were all so busily eyeing each other that it was as though it were a parade where the participants and the onlookers were one and the same—endlessly moving and always watching each other. The stage of the opera was filled with merrymakers, long benches had been set up everywhere, and the audience, from the pit to the many tiers of the theater, were filled with people in such costumed array that they might have been performers themselves here on any other night.

There were Harlequins in plenty, cavorting and dancing, and Columbines and milkmaids by the score; a dozen Romeos romanced another dozen Juliets— and sometimes Romeos as well—while kings squired shepherdesses, and queens and princesses stood drinking and laughing with devils and chimney sweeps. Music was playing and some were dancing, and others talking and promenading, or simply showing off their costumes. Bronwen and the lady wizard merely stood and gaped, and got much pleasure from it.

"The dinner will come late," Miss Mayhew said. "This is quite spectacular. Thank you, my dear. You were quite right," she said, pushing her spectacles up on her nose, the better to see it all. "For I am not myself tonight, nor do I regret it. I'm a great and learned wizardess, as, I suspect, I've always wished to be. And in my wisdom, I do think, I truly do, that we ought to visit the punch bowl, seeing as our tickets—which are of the very highest caliber— provide us with the opportunity to do so as often as we wish. It would be uneconomical not to do so," she concluded.

"Not to mention ungrateful," Bronwen readily agreed.

The punch was an odd red color, but it tasted rich, warm, and fruity—luxuriously so—and so like all the things Bronwen had been without since she'd been without her family. She had a cup and then another, and when Miss Mayhew looked to her again, she never noticed how many Bronwen had drunk, for she'd her third cup in hand by then, and it might have been her first, she'd downed them so fast.

But Miss Mayhew had two cups herself. It made her so instantly merry that she laughed when they were approached by a demon, again when their hands were solicited for a dance by a pair of cavaliers, and she amazed herself and Bronwen when she accepted an invitation to the dance from another wizard. "For how often," she explained in a slightly slurred voice, "does one get to dance with a co-professional?"

Bronwen fended off would-be partners as she watched the pair narrowly. But when it appeared that the two wizards were talking more than dancing, and with great animation at that, she relaxed and took another cup. When the dance was done, and Bronwen had refused many more prospective escorts, Miss Mayhew was returned to her side.

"This is Mr. Jonathan Sumner," Miss Mayhew said, introducing Bronwen to the tall and bony wizard, whose wispy white hair beneath his high conical hat was very possibly his own. "He is a man at law, but even so, a most interesting gentleman."

And so he must have been, Bronwen thought generously, for Miss Mayhew's glasses were so misted over, she doubted her friend could see past her reddening nose. Bronwen gave her approval to the pair and left them to their excited conversation, which

was all to do with Norman versus Celtic law, and so
she decided it would be safe enough, even if Mr.
Sumner hadn't seemed as genuinely pleasant and
educated as he did.

Bronwen strolled and observed the company as she
sipped at her fourth cup. The punch had helped her
enjoyment at first, but now she felt a little melancholy, and attributed it to the fact that this swirling,
glittering company was very well, and very exciting,
but nothing like the Halloweens she loved and
remembered. London had no darkened hedgerows to
house bats, no moonlit country paths with a full,
witchful moon riding high over them, no jack-o'-lan-
terns gloating and swinging on high in the hands of
older children leading the way to unknown mischief.
There was nothing fearful here, Bronwen thought
with a sort of hazy, easy sentimentality, only that
which was fantastic. Never had she felt so far from
Tamlane, and the terrors of Halloween. She'd come
late, and now the hour grew later. Midnight
approached and she'd felt no fear save that of discovery, and that only for a moment when they'd first
arrived. She felt, in the midst of high fantasy, totally
bereft of it.

And then she saw them. It was them, it was unar-
guably them, for they were more fantastical than any
in the whole of the crowded Opera house, and would
have been, even without their mad disguises.

They stood in a group, as they always did. And
they gleamed and shone, and wore bells and bright
hanging jewels that shivered and sang at their every
movement. Tonight they were all dressed as animals,
or mad representations of them. They wore deer
heads, and vole muzzles; they were foxes and cats,
and winged things, goats and wild boars with white

tusks, and things that would have fled into a forest
if there'd been anything but a forest of costumed
Londoners hedging them in. They wore fur and skins
and feathers, sable and ermine, fox pelts and eider-
down. They were covered from crown to toes, but
behind their masks they'd the same glittering eyes,
and Bronwen knew them very well.

Bronwen stood to the side, in her trembling leaves,
and her eyes sought the one she knew would be there
among them. The Lady Blythe was in their midst,
and was unmistakable, for all she wore a silver mask.
She was all in silver again; with a great moon pin set
in her inky hair above her high white forehead, she
was the moon itself. And he was at her side. Had
Bronwen not looked for the lady, she'd never have
seen him. For he was all in black: black domino, and
sash, and breeches and boots—save for one gleam of
silver from the pin at his throat that clasped his black
cape closed, and the fact that one of his black gloved
hands was bare so he could hold his cup of punch the
better. And yet all in black, he was still the most
human of them.

Bronwen's head was throbbing. She was unaccustomed to the late hour, and less used to drinking
strong punch. She remembered, as if from afar, the
words to the old tale she'd told this very night. She
could almost hear the church bells of London tolling
this last hour of this weird night, and so with the
punch percolating in her veins and a pain in her heart
as she watched him bend his head to listen to the
lady as they promenaded, Bronwen stepped forward.
She walked forward, quiet and quick as a leaf blown
in the night, and put her free hand upon his ungloved
one.

"My lord," she said, "I give you a good night."

It seemed he stumbled, in his step as well as his conversation. He saw the little woman clad in her russet and brown autumn array, and stared at the gold at her forehead, and then into her deep brown eyes. He saw through her mask, and said not a word, though he knew very well who had spoken to him.

"What's this? Why see, it is Autumn herself who accosts him," cried Rowan's voice, through the mask of a golden fox.

"I see," said Lady Blythe. "What a strange place for a governess, what a dangerous place for a governess, what a folly for a governess to approach strangers in such a place on such a night is it not, my friends?"

Nicodemus Brand, Earl of Fairlie, stared down at Bronwen coldly, and his bright light eyes were the color of frost on the pane on a winter's morning. But she stood still, and kept her hand on his, and waited for him to speak to her.

"Indeed," he finally said, through clenched teeth, as though the words were forced from him through his towering fury, "she should not be here, not now."

But Bronwen only stood, with her hand on his, the leaves of her costume shivering from the force of her rapid breathing.

"Could it be," he hissed through his teeth, his bright eyes narrowing, "that she seeks more than her decent position can offer her? Perhaps she searches for others—more exotic ones, shall we say?"

The company laughed, and Bronwen's brown eyes widened, and her hand shook, but she did not move it from his, and she stayed at his side. Ice, she thought dazedly, and then fire, and now snake, she thought, yes, and then bear, was it not?

"Oh come, little squirrel," he said gruffly, as the

laughter abated, "should you not scurry home before you are eaten alive by the merrymakers here?"

Yes, bear, she thought, bemused, and raised her eyes to his, to wait for what would come next.

His hand writhed beneath hers, as he sought to pull it away, and he laughed, at last, when he saw how she still held fast to it.

"Really, my dear Bronwen," he said sweetly, archly, "I'm flattered, but surely you could have found a better time and place for such a proposition?"

Her eyes snapped open wider at the sound of her name. The punch she'd drunk cleared entirely from her dizzied brain in that instant, as they all of them laughed uproariously—those who weren't snickering— all the costumed animals from the lady's court, and all the others within hearing. Then she realized at last her foolish, stupid folly, her child's dream that had become such hideous reality. Because ice and fire, snake, bear, and weasel were in a faery tale, and this was real cruelty in a real and cruel world.

She looked into those hard eyes that stared down into hers, and without thinking, brought up her hand and dashed the cup of punch she'd held into his face. Without waiting to see it stream down his face, she turned and ran to the exit door. But somehow, she still had his hand in hers as she did.

He stopped her at the door and pulled her hand hard, swung her around to face him, then wrapped his arms around her and hugged her close. And for all she hated him, she threw her arms around him and held on tightly, too.

"Ah, Bronwen, my love," he breathed into her hair, after he'd done kissing her the first time. "Forgive me, it was not me that was speaking. Forgive me, it was never my will. This is, and I shall never

let you go now, never. Thank you, my love, for
remembering me and letting me remember who I
was, and see what I'd become through your eyes—
your innocent, honest eyes," he said as he buried his
face in her hair, and breathed deep of the real human
scent of woman and the perfume of the autumn night.
"Thank you for never letting me go, my love, my
love," he said in a broken whisper, and it wasn't the
punch she'd thrown that she felt dropping from his
eyes to mingle with her own tears on her cheeks.

They looked up once to see Lady Blythe leaving
with her company, and then were lost in each other's
arms again.

Miss Mayhew was lamentably shortsighted, and
she never denied it. But she was a superior governess by nature as well as training. She'd highly devel-
oped senses, strong protective instincts, and a firm
sense of what was right. So for all her absorption in
conversation with her fascinating escort, and with
all the odd canterings taking place within her most
singular, lonely, and private heart, still she sensed
something amiss. As though suddenly hearing a clarion call over the comments of her fellow wizard and
the din of the crowd, she looked up. And even with
the shifting light and the changing patterns of persons around her in their outrageous costumes, she
immediately saw her young friend Bronwen deep in
a gentleman's arms, and further saw she was not
struggling to be free. So she plunged into the crowd
with the alacrity of someone bent on saving a child
fallen into a raging torrent. But so she was trying to
save Bronwen from drowning in the gentleman's arms.

It was a blurred and dazzled Bronwen who emerged
from the earl's arms with a tear-drenched face and a

kiss-bruised mouth, but she never looked better or happier then she did at that moment.

"Ma'am," the earl said when he saw Miss Mayhew's frown. Recognizing the face of propriety and authority from his infant days, and struggling to banish raging desire and absolute delight from his own face so he could appear calm and bored as a gentleman ought, he said, "Please be the first to congratulate me. Bronwen is to marry me, and there is no happier man in all England or Scotland tonight."

Not for no reason was Miss Mayhew highly recommended. She ruthlessly quashed her unworthy jolt of surprised envy and rejoiced for Bronwen, even as she applied her considerable intellect to what must be done next.

"Ah, and so I do, for in that case you are a lucky gentleman, indeed, my lord," she replied. "But what of her being the least-talked-about young woman in all England and Scotland tomorrow night?"

They left the masquerade together, the two wizards, the autumn girl, and the dark gentleman, and as they strolled through the night streets of London, they discussed what was to be done for the sake of society, propriety, and good sense now. At least the elder wizards did. The younger couple held hands tightly and agreed to anything that would make it possible for them to hold far more of each other the sooner. Mr. Sumner, it transpired, had friends in higher courts than those of law, and he vowed to help make the union legal with all the speed that London was capable of, as Miss Mayhew, her mind working smoothly in the correct pathways it always did, aided him in arranging matters judicial and pastoral. That decided, they let the happy couple be, to walk side by side before them, murmuring secret foolishnesses any decent wizard would understand, and understandably stop listening in on.

The Lady Blythe and her company had ridden to the ball this night, and though they'd mounted in great speed as they'd left it, now they rode away from it in slow, silent, closed formation. They were impossible to miss, riding in stately procession surrounding their moon white and dark lady: the birds and the beasts, the toothed and the fanged, furred and feathered, so weirdly at home in the moonlit streets at the last of this fantastical night. And yet the earl and Bronwen seemed not to see them as they passed by. But the wizards noted them narrowly.

The Lady Blythe's slight shoulders drooped, and her dark head was bowed low as she murmured something to her fox-headed escort. Miss Mayhew, noting this, spoke up, low and solemnly, as though to herself. But Mr. Sumner, attending her closely, as he had from the first, heard each soft word of the old weird rhyme she intoned.

"She that hath taken my Tamlane
Hath gotten a stately groom,
She's taken away my bonniest love,
And left nothing in his room . . ."

Miss Mayhew grew still then, but as the steeple clocks all began to sound the last hours of the night, she heard a deep voice beside her continue on her theme, as Mr. Sumner recited the last of the ancient rhyme:

"Had I but the wit yesterday
That I have got today,

I'd have paid the Fiend seven times his due,
Ere I'd let him be won away."

Miss Mayhew looked at him in surprise.

"A lovely old tale," he commented, "and not the
least of your attractions, my dear, is your correct
application of it. The Lady Blythe is from fully as
wicked an old family as the Queen of the Faeries
herself, I fear. She's new in town, but her family
name comes up in my researches time and again, in
ancient as well as modern matters of disputed
estates, lost heritages, piracy, and all sorts of
infringed rights. And she appears to be cut from the
same cloth. No, her name is not so forgotten or
obscure as she pretends or might wish it to be, however far from home she's traveled, however far she
might wish she'd been from it tonight," he said. And
then added, "It's a great relief to see young Fairlie
disenchanted with her at last.

"As to that," Mr. Sumner paused, and deliberately
turned so that Miss Mayhew would have to turn as
well to continue speaking with him, for they'd
reached the house where Bronwen was employed,
and he'd seen that the earl was employing himself
completely in a lover's good night that Bronwen
seemed to be enjoying as much as he was, ". . . I can
see that young lovers might be moved to great haste
to wed, and it is not so unseemly as it is only wise,
I believe."

Miss Mayhew had seen what he had, and as wise
as he, never let on, but only moved on a few paces
with him as he continued to speak. "But older lovers
have an even greater reason for haste, I think," he
mused, "considering all the time they must make up
for. Do you agree, my dear Miss Mayhew, my dear,

dear Miss Mayhew?" he asked. "Or shall you make
me wait an eternity, now that I've discovered at last
who it is I'd wish to pass the rest of my share of it
with?"

Miss Mayhew closed her eyes to more than the
young lovers' good night then. And shed a quiet tear
and then grew a quavering smile before she answered
as she knew she must. But even so, she didn't take
very long in answering. Not for nothing was she clad
as a wise woman this night.

An early lamplighter, out to douse the beacons of
the night as day approached, saw the young couple
locked in an embrace near the stair to the Baron
Rhode's town house, and after a glance, disregarded
them. The fellow was masked, but there was no need
for alarm; he was no footpad or highwayman, but
only obviously a gentleman, and from what could be
seen of the lady—who seemed to be shedding leaves—
she was his very willing captive. Costumed or no,
such carryings-on were as nothing to the lamplighter,
who had seen all sorts of lovers in his long years in
London. Nor did he more than chuckle, when walking
on, he saw the remarkable sight of a pair of star-
spangled, high-hatted, fully gowned wizards embrac-
ing. It was a curious thing, but this was, after all,
the end of Halloween, London's most curious night.

But even he paused, when at the last, before the
sky began to shimmer with first true dawn light, he
came to the borders of the park and saw a fantastical
company of birds and beasts riding by. As he
watched in fascination, they began to wave farewell
to each other, as one by one, they left the procession,
melting into the diminishing night. At the last he
stood gaping at the only two left, for they were
worth staring at on any night: a golden fox riding

beside a lady as silver and magnificent as the waning
moon.

And then, as first light did pierce the gloom, the
lamplighter's vision blurred. He shook his head and
passed a hand over his eyes, for his work, so near to
flame and smoke, made his eyes watery and unreliable at times, and this, after all, was dawn's first
unreliable light. And yet when he looked up again,
he thought he saw the silver lady and her escort
simply vanish, with the last of the magical night.

*With thanks to the kindly spirit of Joseph Jacobs, and his beauti-
ful telling of the classic story of "Tamlane" in *More English Fairy
Tales*.

"... A man whose blood is very snow-broth; one who never feels the wanton stings and motions of the senses ..."

—William Shakespeare

SNOW
BROTH

"A ghastly day for a funeral," the young gentleman remarked in a whisper.

"You'd prefer a balmy day with green trees filled with joyous bird song? Curious. I think this the ideal weather for an interment," the young gentleman he'd addressed said softly. "In fact, were it mine, I should have liked a bit more wind and snow, with perhaps a dollop of sleet thrown in for good measure. I'd want my mourners to suffer somewhat, I'd think. Actually, in my case, I believe the weather would be the only thing to make anyone unhappy."

A "too right" and stifled laughter was his answer. As well as a sharp poke in the ribs from the parasol of the black-clad young woman on his right.

"Hush, Beau," the lady hissed. "And you, too, Creighton. Uncle deserves a bit more respect."

"So he did," the fair young gentleman she'd addressed as "Beau" answered readily. "And so he had it in full measure from me while he lived, and well you know it. But no one but the minister wants it now, and he's a prosy old bore. Even Uncle thought so."

"Lord, yes," the other gentleman agreed, "yet here he is, a fellow Uncle avoided at every turn, and he's naming him everything but a saint."

"Astonishing the virtue one accrues by passing on," Beau mused, brushing some snow from his greatcoat shoulder as they stood by the grave site.

"He was a good man," the young lady insisted.

"So he was," Beau agreed, "but he didn't make a profession of it."

The young woman was either about to argue with him or bid him to be silent again, but a sudden blast of cold wind sweeping across the bare burial grounds literally took her breath away, and she shuddered instead.

It was a cruelly cold winter, and it had only just begun. But still the birds were dropping, frozen, from the trees, and for once, the beggars in town looked as if they really would be pleased to do the same. The Thames was freezing over, and the snowdrifts piling up. The grave diggers would have to be paid double again, for even though they wouldn't actually drop the coffin until the ground relented somewhat, they'd toiled like oxen to dig even so far as they'd done in order to make the ceremony look respectable.

The many black coaches that stood waiting for the survivors of the burial party were so swathed in snow by the time the vicar had done saying his last prayers that they'd lost all their funereal splendor and looked as sparkling white as wedding coaches. And the cold high white domes they'd grown during the ceremony insured that the hot bricks and woolen blankets they held were tepid when the mourners were at last free to try to use them to comfort frozen fingers and toes.

"I should be pleased to help warm you," Beau offered when the lady complained at how cool the hot brick at her feet had become as she settled back in the coach. But when he made a motion to enfold her in his arms, she pulled away and grimaced.

"Faugh! You're all over snow and ice," she cried, shying away from him.

"But he's got a warm heart," Creighton protested.

"Much good that will do me," the lady grumbled. "Close the window! Whatever are you staring at?" she asked, noting how Beau was now looking out at the rapidly departing funeral goers.

"I wonder who the black-draped wench is, the one with all the veils?" he commented as he obeyed her and slid the window shut. "I've never seen her before."

"Aye, I wondered at it, too," Creighton said with some interest. "Nice-looking little bit, too."

"As if anyone could tell, she was draped in so much black, and veiled besides," the lady said, and then laughed. "Ah, I'd forgot who I was speaking to. You two can probably see through steel if it's a young female in question."

"Steel's a little more difficult," Beau said thoughtfully, as Creighton laughed. "For you, Coz, perhaps."

And then they all laughed with relief as well as at the jest as the coach pulled away from the graveyard.

It was as slow a journey back from the graveyard to the deceased's town house as it had been when the hearse departed from there, because the roads were treacherous now, and the snow continued to fall. By the time the carriage containing the two young gentlemen, the lady, and her maid was stopped, all

aboard were chilled through, although only the young
lady complained about it. Languid airs and graces
were fashionable for gentlemen, but Lord Beauford
and Creighton, Lord Pope, took fashion only so far.
They stepped from the carriage with grace and ease
even though it was so cold that when they smiled at
each other over the way the lady was grumbling,
their teeth hurt from exposure to the frigid air. As
they'd all known each other since they'd first gotten those very same teeth, the lady only muttered
something about "great oafs who lacked the wit to
feel cold," as they accompanied her up the stair.

The late fifth Earl of Compton's town house was
thronged with other half-frozen mourners, and so the
sixth Earl of Compton had all the fireplaces roaring,
and the servants serving hot punch and arrack, along
with other strong liquors and light refreshments. The
late earl had been a bachelor, and the new earl's
wife and three grown daughters were prowling the
various downstairs rooms, murmuring about "poor
Uncle's" deficient masculine tastes in home furnishings and planning renovations in fittingly solemn low
voices when they weren't being consoled for their
great loss by the other guests.

There were a great many mourners, as the late
earl had been a scholarly, but not a reclusive fellow.
But as the afternoon lengthened, one by one the
recently thawed guests bid their hosts farewell and
prepared to face the elements again. For it would
only get colder as the hour grew later, and so they
all said as they departed. They left in great numbers,
but they left a good number behind them, for the
earl's family was not of inconsiderable size. There
was no sense in making anyone take unnecessary
journeys in this weather, the new earl and his man-

at-law had agreed, and so the last will and testament was to be read to the family and those who had reason to expect bequests as soon as the casual visitors had all left.

"She's here, and she's staying here," Creighton, Lord Pope, informed his cousin in a low voice.

"Yes, so I noted," Lord Beauford said musingly.

"You would," the young woman who'd been in the carriage with them said, giving the fair young gentleman a significant look. "Although what you can see is beyond me. She's not spoken to anyone, and tries to fade away when anyone seems about to speak with her. In fact, she's been skulking about as though she were pricing the china. And she's not lifted that black veil once."

"Yes, she has," Beau replied absently, "when she sipped at her punch."

"And when she had some ham shavings on toast," Creighton added.

"But who on earth is she?" the Honorable Lavinia Peckingham asked. Then her blue eyes grew brighter and she asked, with a delighted and growing smile, "Never say Uncle had a familiar? But she looks so reserved and elegant, for all her clothes are absurd and out-of-date, very like a lady," she said with fascination as she stared at the mysterious black-clad woman.

"Who is to say she's not his daughter?" Beau asked lightly. And as the lady's eyes grew wider, his cousin Creighton grinned and added, "Or his wife?"

The lady gave an indelicate snort, and presented both young gentlemen with the back of her head as she marched into the library in order to obtain a good front seat for the highlight of the day: the reading of the will.

The nearest relatives took the seats closest to the man-at-law and the fireplace, distant relatives maintained their proper distance, and friends and neighbors sat on the fringes with the servants, as though the monies left were to be thrown in the air for the inheritors to catch. Thus the best deserving automatically chose the closest seats. The woman in black, the three young persons who had first remarked on her observed, stood at the back of the room. This caused the two gentlemen to raise their eyebrows at each other, and positively thrilled Miss Peckingham.

Scarcely anyone attended to the lawyer's first words. Everyone knew old Howard was getting most of the funds along with the earldom, the town house, and the manor as the entail specified. And too, the lawyer commenced speaking by droning on about "the late, and dearly loved earl" in a dry old cracking voice, seemingly intent on giving another funeral oration. It was true he'd known the old earl forever, as he'd said, but it did begin to seem as though he were going to talk exactly that long before he got down to business. The company was too polite to chat, but scarcely anyone attended to him. Until they heard a startled gasp and an indrawn moan coming from the back of the room.

The lawyer heard it, too, and so paused, adjusted his spectacles, and gazed out over his audience to where all the heads were turning. A small female, all in black, stood wavering, holding on to the back of a chair. She was veiled, but her face was turned to him, so the lawyer cleared his throat and repeated what he'd last said, for he was a careful man-at-law and never one to let an issue go misunderstood.

"Ah, as I said," he continued, "the late earl was a kindly man, and it was always a wonder to those of

us who knew him well that he never wed . . . Oh, I
say," the lawyer said and stopped talking.

For the woman in black had gasped once more,
swooned, and crumpled to the floor.

The first thing she saw was a fair, concerned face
bending over her. For one blurred minute, because
of his tender, bemused expression and the proximity
of his faintly parted lips, Marjorie wondered if she
were the dreaming princess about to be waked with
a kiss. And then all the curious faces behind his came
into sharp focus, and she gasped once more and tried
to sit up all at once.

"No, I shouldn't," he said in a soft, calm voice, as
he supported her head. "Just rest easy, my dear."

A dreadful scent teased at her nostrils and she
struggled in his hands as he spoke sharply to someone just out of her sight, "Oh, get those noisome
burnt feathers away. The only thing they'd wake is
the dead, and they make all others wish they were
so. Besides, Mrs. Huntington, she's already revived."

This time he gave in to her struggles, and helped
her to sit up. With her veil pushed back, she could
see her aide and captor was younger than she'd
thought he'd been when she'd seen him at the ceme-
tery, certainly somewhat closer to her own age of
eighteen than the eight and twenty she'd imagined
him to be. From so close she could see his eyes were
kind and of lightest blue, and they gave humor and
humanity to what from afar had been a thin, cold,
sharply defined face. His thick hair, worn a la Bru-
tus, and overlong at that, was more dulcet gold than
the bronze the harsh winter light had shown it to be.

His companion, at the grave side as well as here,
was of the same age, and in the gaslight his hair was

glowing chestnut, not rusty brown as it had been in the icy glare of day. But he was as handsome as she'd thought, and his ginger brown eyes just as merry. The young woman who'd accompanied them then, as now, was just as lovely a dark beauty as she'd thought, though not as calm and sophisticated as she'd first appeared. For now, at least, she gaped from over the shoulder of the chestnut-haired gentleman as though she were seeing a raree-show. Which reminded Marjorie of her present condition.

"I beg your pardon," Marjorie said at once, in a clear little voice, looking up at the assembled persons gazing down at her. "I never meant to cause a scene. I've been traveling all day and through two nights, hoping to get here before the end, but only arrived in time to be at the grave side—and at that, only at the very last minute. But what you just said, sir," she said, looking at the man-at-law, "quite took my breath away."

There was a profound silence; Marjorie could swear she actually heard the crowd about her licking their lips. She spoke up bravely, for if a thing had to be said, so she would say it, that was her way.

"For you see," she went on, her voice quavering just a little, "although I never expected a welcome, precisely, I never expected such utter denial. . . . And what you said, sir," she said, gazing at the lawyer with tears starting in her soft brown eyes, "about my grandfather . . ."

The in-drawing of breaths from two dozen throats at once made a sudden vacuum, she was sure, and explained why she felt dizzy once again, and she was grateful for the fair gentleman's warm hands that still held her shoulders firmly.

The old man-at-law spoke first, and his voice quivered with indignation.

"I knew the Earl of Compton for threescore years and ten, my dear young woman, and I can assure you, he never fathered a son or a daughter, within or without the marriage he never made!" he said with suppressed fury.

Marjorie swallowed hard. And shut her eyes, and wished they would all go away. Beau felt her slender shoulders wilting and held her more securely. But she only opened her eyes at the increased pressure of his touch, looked about, and spoke in confused and weary tones.

"The Earl of Compton?" she asked miserably. "But this is Regent Street, is it not?" As the assembled company nodded, like so many hand puppets, she thought confusedly, she went on, nodding herself, "So I thought. I told the coachman I was seeking the old earl, who was gravely ill, and he told me the sad news, then took me directly to the graveyard . . . Oh my!" she said, straightening and holding a trembling hand to her lips, "Oh heavens! Then my grandfather, the Earl of Chesham, is still alive?"

"Ah, no," Beau said gently, "I fear he passed on not two days ago. In fact, his funeral was at the other end of St. Michael's churchyard not an hour before ours was held."

"Not 'ours' precisely," the lawyer corrected him carefully, "the late Earl of Compton's. Oh dear, what a misapprehension. I daresay you missed Chesham's funeral because there was such a meager crowd there. Three in attendance, I believe," he said with a curious smugness in his voice.

"Four, if you count his cook," another gentleman put it.

"Six, including grave diggers," another added.

"Exactly so. A singular misfortune in many ways," the new earl said ponderously. "The *Times* put it very well, I think, when they said in most politic terms, that the two earls died as they lived, not a hundred yards apart, although as we are all aware, leagues apart in style and substance, I fear."

There was a general stir and muted agreement to that, and the company eyed Marjorie with sympathy and a certain unnerving interest as she finally stood up before them. She stepped free of the fair-haired gentleman's hands, and faced the strangers before her. They saw an uncommonly good-looking young woman, small and well formed, with a mass of pale hair and a fine-featured, fine-complexioned oval face. Somehow, the closer sight of her caused several onlookers to look at her with something other than sympathy and more than speculation, she thought nervously.

"Then if you'll pray excuse me, and accept my deepest sympathies, as well as my apologies for whatever distraction I've caused," she said far more bravely than she felt, "I shall go and present my credentials to my grandfather's man-at-law now."

"You need not hurry," the late Earl of Compton's man-at-law said dryly, "for I expect you'll have quite a wait until he can see you, my dear."

The mourners chuckled. Marjorie could see nothing but amusement upon their several faces. She turned her own inquiring gaze to the fair man who stood so near. He looked sympathetic, but he, too, smiled as he spoke.

"I believe the problem is that if you claim kinship with the late Earl of Chesham, you'll have to take a number and cool your heels, perhaps even until spring warms them again, before you are seen," he said softly.

"I hadn't guessed," she said in surprise. "Is his family so large then? But how can that be? I was told my father was his only son, and that the earl remained unwed after my grandmother died."

"So he did," the lawyer said, "and we were told his son died leaving no issue, just as he did . . . ah, legal issue, that is to say. But that, my dear, as you certainly know, is no deterrent to the many claims being laid at his doorstep now—as before. And not unjustly, I fear," he said on a gusty sigh, "as he was, a most singularly, ah, active gentleman, withal."

Marjorie had been raised to be civil to her elders, and having been born and raised in the countryside besides, had little experience before large groups of people. But rage made her forget where she'd been born as well as how she'd been bred. She reached into her heavy carpetbag, pulled out a roll of papers bound with ribbon, and brandished them at the aged lawyer, as a man might present his dueling sword. But instead of *"en garde!"* she simply said, through small, white, and tightly clenched teeth, "My papers, sir."

Bemused, the lawyer unrolled them, and as many of the company looked on over his shoulder, perused them. The young lords Beauford and Pope continued to gaze at Marjorie with slight smiles still on their faces. But the lawyer's aged face became whiter by degree, until it was whiter than the creamy yellow papers he held. He stared up at Marjorie in astonishment when he'd done, as those who'd read faster were already doing.

"By God!" he said, forgetting he was in the presence of ladies in his deep shock, " 'tis true!"

*   *   *

"You cannot go alone!" Creighton said firmly.

Marjorie sighed. The three young persons had introduced themselves to her as Lord Beauford, Lord Pope, and Miss Peckingham, and were now trying to see to her welfare. They were well-meaning and most kind, and so far as the gentlemen were concerned, perhaps even a bit more than that. But they were also strong-minded, not to say dictatorial, and used to having females obeying their commands. But she was not used to obeying. It wasn't that she was rebellious; she didn't think she'd ever done anything stubbornly willful, but she'd never had anyone ruling over her either. Papa had been fair and had trusted her good sense, and Aunt Winslow was incapable of ordering her own affairs with any skill, much less her niece's. She wasn't precisely bullheaded, Marjorie thought, but she did know her own mind. And so she told them.

"You may know your own mind, but clearly, you do not know London, its modes or its manners," Miss Peckingham said, and at Marjorie's suddenly conscious look on hearing this, the dark young woman threw a bright glance of triumph at the two gentlemen.

"Bravo, Livvy," Beau said with an amused grin.

The three young people had repaired to a small salon with Marjorie during the reading of the will, for as the lawyer said, their bequests were expected and none too startling—or valuable to any but themselves. Beau would receive the chess set with the mandarin figures he'd always admired; Creighton, the whale-tooth cribbage board and pegs he'd so liked as a boy; and Livvy, the porcelain clown that had always amused her when she'd visited as a child. Not great treasures, to be sure, as Livvy said, but then, as Creighton noted, they certainly didn't need any. Although, as Beau added, giving the lawyer a mockery of a hopeful stare, they certainly wouldn't have been averse to receiving some.

With Livvy's mama promising to let them know if there were any shocking inheritances to wonder over, they were free to entertain their unwitting, and now unwilling guest, Miss Marjorie Makepeace, long-lost and legal granddaughter to the late George Henry Abingdon Makepeace, Earl of Chesham.

"They'll eat you alive," Creighton said, as Marjorie stared at him, "if you go there alone. Do you know how many persons are clamoring to be let in, much less are in there badgering the lawyers already? Chesham left a fortune. He didn't run through it, much as he seemed to, because he was as mean with his money as he was with his fellow man—and woman, especially."

"He spent what he had to for his pleasures, and they were many and various," Beau explained. "And he spent as little as he had to as well. But as he didn't discriminate in his selection of wine, women, and songs, he didn't have to waste a great deal of money. Such pleasures come cheaply in London, I'm told."

This last, of course, said in innocent accents, made Livvy stare at him in humorous disgust, while Creighton laughed outright. Marjorie, however, didn't know him well enough to laugh, nor did she feel remotely humorous.

"I never did know him, of course," she said a little sadly, "nor did I wish to, to be honest."

"I doubt you could be otherwise, poor child, could you?" Beau asked quizzically.

"Oh, yes!" she said at once, her brown eyes wide,

"I could be. I intended to be, actually, had I arrived in time to find him still living. After all, I could scarcely be rude to a man who was mortally ill, no matter what dreadful things I'd heard about him. Well, actually," she said on a sigh, "Papa never said truly terrible things about him, which made me think Grandfather even worse. I couldn't imagine anyone vindictive enough to bar father forever simply because he married against his family's wishes. For there wasn't a more forgiving soul than he was; some might say he was weak-willed . . . Well, I suppose he was, in that he never had the energy to actively dislike anyone. He merely avoided those he didn't care for. Aunt said that was the nobleman in him."

"I doubt that," Creighton laughed. "*That* must have been the commoner in him, a true nobleman would have been chafing at the bit to run his enemies through."

"Or grind them underfoot," Beau said on a twisted smile.

Marjorie didn't smile back at them. She grew very still, and then arose from her chair in one graceful movement.

"I am a commoner," she said with quiet dignity, "or at least, by your lights, half of one. I think it's time I left. I thank you for your advice. Good evening."

"Good grief," Livvy said, "prickly, aren't you? Who cares, they're only jesting."

"I'm not," Beau said, "I'm fascinated. Which half is it that's the common one, my dear? Is the division vertical, or horizontal? Is it one you can show us here and now, or do we have to wait until you know us better?"

Marjorie bit back her laughter, but it made her

look like she was trying not to weep. In truth, she scarcely knew the difference herself now. It had been a long, harrowing day into night for her. She looked as weary as she was, and as confused as she felt; her face was milk white, her pale hair was coming loose from its ribbon, she brushed it back with one slender hand so she could better see the three young persons who were gazing at her. She looked very young, lost, alone, and lovely to them.

"Where are you staying tonight?" Livvy asked.

"I'd thought to stay with Grandfather . . ." Marjorie began.

"*Most* uncomfortable there," Beau remarked, as Creighton said, "I doubt the sexton would permit it."

"You'll stay with me," Livvy announced.

"But . . ." Marjorie began to protest, and was silenced as Livvy held up one hand.

"It would be absurd to go out in this frigid weather, seeking a hotel," she said. "Moreover, you have already made one mistake in coming here, as you admitted. And another, perhaps far worse, in going anywhere in London without a maid. However, how should you know, coming from the countryside as you do? Do not make a third error. Be guided by me. I am entirely respectable, as is my entire family. Be sure, in London, what we do is done. You shall stay with me tonight, Miss Makepeace. Tomorrow we shall see what else is to be done."

Marjorie nodded. She was entirely exhausted, and moreover, however strong-minded, wise enough to know when she'd met a superior force.

"Kind of Livvy to take the little one in," Creighton said on a yawn some hours later as he bade his cousin

good night, when they left the gaming house where
they'd passed most of the night.

"Not a bit," Beau replied, pulling on his gloves.
"She'd kill for the honor. This way, she doesn't miss
a thing."

Creighton chuckled, "Oh, true. Shall I see you at
Livvy's in the morning then?"

"Certainly. At first light," Beau said, signaling for
a hackney cab. "Only the ice prevents me from sleeping on her doorstep, actually. Do you think I wish to
miss a thing either?" he asked, and correctly took his
cousin's laughter as answer.

The quartet of fine young persons at the door
impressed the butler. Before he'd come into the late
Earl of Chesham's employ, he'd seen many such. He
might have become used to flyblown noblemen and
females he'd not have introduced to the kitchen cat
in his years with the earl, but he remembered persons of better breeding well enough. The two young
blades were arrogant, handsome, and monstrously
annoyed with him; the two ladies staggered at not
being immediately shown in. But there was only so
much room in the house, after all.

The salons had been filled each day since the earl's
illness, as was the drawing room and the hall, and
the lawyers had taken over the library. So he told
the young gentlepersons in genuinely grieved tones.
For one young lady was such an eye-catching little
handful of blond fluff that the late earl himself might
have been moved to part with an extra groat or even
a civil word in order to bear her company, and her
speaking brown eyes were swimming with tears. The
other young lady was so darkly handsome and imperious, the butler automatically pulled in his stomach

and stood straighter than he had in years. But facts were facts, and a guinea was fine, as he told the gentlemen sadly, moved to less than his usual studied eloquence by having to refuse what one of them was clearly reaching for in his waistcoat pocket, but there simply wasn't any more room.

"Not even for the late earl's legitimate grand-daughter?" the fair gentleman asked in astonishment.

Before the butler could begin to tell him how many with exactly the same claim was littering up the house and pacing the Aubussons at the moment, Beau produced a card, not a coin, from his vest pocket and said angrily, "Very well, here is my card. Miss Makepeace, the late viscount's daughter, will be staying with the Miss Peckingham. Have the earl's man-at-law contact her, before legal proceedings begin. Ah yes," he added, "and your name, my good man?"

"It's very crowded, indeed, do you think we ought to come back another time?" Marjorie asked softly after they'd been immediately granted entry and then bowed into the drawing room, having success-fully wended their way through the press of human-ity in the outer hall.

A great many of those in the hall had taken excep-tion to being bypassed, for it transpired that the hall was actually the waiting room for the salons, and they, in turn, had to be endured before the crowded precincts of the drawing room were available to them. But Livvy was too fascinated by watching and listening to the persons around her to do more than snap, "Don't be poor-spirited. Here we are, and here we shall stay until they see you."

Marjorie was too downcast to argue the point.

She'd begun to hear some of the conversation, too. A young woman with improbable bright red hair, wearing a frock that wouldn't be permitted on the stage in the town Marjorie had been raised in, was holding court nearby, proudly proclaiming herself to be "the only ackshul leegul Countess of Chesham, no matter what them drabs back there says."

There were at least three shabbily dressed young men claiming to be the earl's by-blows, and two other well-dressed ones who claimed the same thing pointedly ignoring them and each other. Too many infants and children to count were being shown by proud mama's of diverse stripe, all claiming the same heritage, though no two looked alike in anything but their boredom and bad behavior. Marjorie didn't want to know or guess what sort of relationships some of the others present were claiming.

"I've noticed she's quiet only when she's defeated," Creighton said too loudly to Lord Beauford, although he looked at her with merry mischief in his smile.

"Are you?" Lord Beauford asked her with a sympathetic, if quizzical grin.

"Do you think," Marjorie asked with absolute honesty, "that any of these persons might be in any way related to me, actually?"

He hesitated, losing his smile for only a moment as his cool blue eyes looked into hers. And then asked gently, "Would it matter?"

"Why should it?" Creighton told her. "You ought to see some of our relatives, and it never bothers us in the least."

"Rather, you oughtn't, you seem a delicate sort of female," Beau said. "But having unbearable relatives would put you right in style. Members of the *ton* are expert at distancing themselves from unwanted relations."

"Oh yes, all sorts of relations: those maternal, paternal . . . and infernal," Livvy quipped, arching a finely drawn brow and indicating, with a slight list to one shoulder, a buxom young female who was smiling at Beau with something more than passing familiarity.

For once the languid nobleman seemed at a loss, but then he only breathed, "Touché, Liv," and grinned, before he acknowledged the buxom female with a tilt of his fair head, then turned his back on her.

She scarcely seemed to mind, and why should she? Marjorie thought sadly, since she was, as she loudly proclaimed when the company began shouting and vying for attention as the butler came back into the room, "The earl's leegul get, an' I kin prove it, I kin."

But it was Marjorie and her company who were next admitted to the library. And the papers she produced caused the team of men-at-law to whistle as they read them.

"Seems right, and you've the look of the maternal side," one of the lawyers said at length, after asking her a few pertinent questions. Then he put his hands on the table and stared at Marjorie.

"The title, of course, goes to Hugh Carstairs, a country gent, and a nephew once removed," he said. "Unless one of that lot out there comes up with more than bribes and false papers," he added on a grim laugh. "And he gets most of the money besides. The old earl was careless of his time and place, but he'd a great sense of family. Aye, your father and you are mentioned in the bequest. He was to get nothing.

You . . . well, my lady, if all is proved, and I see no reason why it should not be, there may, indeed, be something for you eventually."

Marjorie rose from her chair. She drew herself up to her not very considerable height. But when she spoke, she seemed to grow inches.

"Odd," she said, "I really hadn't thought of that when I came flying from home to see him when I read that he'd been taken ill and was in danger of dying. I was more interested in finding family. For I've only my aunt now, and she's my mother's sister. I should like to meet the new earl and his family, as they must be mine as well. The inheritance, you see, is not of such great moment to me. I'm not wealthy, but my mother left me a competence, and I've enough to get by adequately, thank you. I doubt I should ever use the title anymore than my father thought it right to use his after his father disinherited him, but I'd like to have it acknowledged, if only for his sake. Please let me know what you decide. I should be back at North Haven House with my aunt, within the week."

"Miss Makepeace shall be staying with me," Livvy said.

"I shall be returning to Worcester," Marjorie said firmly.

"No, the lady's weary; disregard that. She'll be staying on with me," Livvy declared.

"I shall not," Marjorie said.

"Do contact me if you wish to speak to Miss Makepeace," Beau said, handing his card to the lawyers.

"Be in debtor's prison, you keep dropping those things like autumn leaves," Creighton told Beau as they ushered the arguing ladies out.

"I know," Beau sighed, "with the fine vellum and embossing, it comes to a pretty penny. Do hush, Livvy, she'll stay. I'll bind her, Creighton will gag her, and we'll stow her in the cellar if she keeps arguing."

From the look Marjorie shot him, it was entirely possible she believed he meant what he said. But then, from the look he returned to her, it was possible he did.

They walked as two couples would. It was only natural that they sort themselves out for their stroll through town, they couldn't walk four abreast even on London's wide pavements. And as ladies seldom walked arm in arm when there were gentlemen present unless they'd not met in a while and had much to speak about, and Marjorie and Livvy had passed much of the previous night in close conversation, it only made sense that they form two pairs of male and female now. Creighton escorted Livvy, Marjorie had her hand placed lightly upon Beau's arm. Literally. For when they'd stepped out of Livvy's town house, he himself had put it there, before proceeding down the street with her.

She didn't mind, although she felt so good about it, it made her feel bad. Because Lord Geraud Beauford was both handsome and charming, as delightfully attentive as he seemed to be attuned to her every nuance of mood. Which was, when she thought about it—which she had since she'd first seen him—only natural, after all. For there was no doubt in Marjorie's mind that Beau, as he begged her to call him, was a rattle, if not a downright rake; a fashionable young gentleman of wit and cleverness, style and panache, with no substance whatsoever, and very possibly, no heart.

She hadn't much chance to discuss the gentlemen with Livvy the previous night, even if she'd the temerity. Livvy had only kept questioning her until she'd learned enough to formulate her own plans— and of course, Marjorie's. Miss Peckingham was a very strong-minded young female, only three years Marjorie's senior, and yet leagues ahead in determination as well as sophistication. Perhaps, Marjorie had thought when she'd gazed at her insistent hostess in her nightclothes and had seen a young woman of lovely form as well as face, that was why she was as yet unwed at the great age of one and twenty— and even more startling, was not nagged by her parents to alter that unusual and unfashionable condition. Because the Viscount Woking and his Viscountess seemed as undisturbed by their daughter's single-mindedness as they were by her singular state. They accepted their daughter as they did her new houseguest, with breezy unconcern. Did no one in London, Marjorie wondered now, as she had begun to last night, care deeply for anything at all?

"Creighton was right, you grow very still when you're distressed," Beau observed, gazing down at her and slowing his steps. "Are you cold? We'd thought a brisk walk the best way to introduce you to London. This way, we'll have a perfect excuse for not stopping to chat with the fashionable and invariably tedious persons we're sure to meet. But if you're chilled, we'll ride instead and simply wave, like visiting potentates, at all the *ton*."

"No, no," Marjorie said. "It is cold, but bracing. The sun is out full, and besides, I'm used to far colder weather. It may be frigid today, but you've all these buildings to block the wind, as we've not in the countryside, you see."

"Yes, but I still don't see why you're so glum," he persisted.

"I just wondered . . ." she said, and paused. Seeing his amused face and cocked eyebrow, she decided to be as forthright as Livvy and so immediately voiced the thought that was disturbing her, "I wondered why all of you—you, Creighton, and Livvy, who are cousins, after all, and who all knew your late uncle and obviously liked him, are not grieving for him now."

"An excellent question," Beau said, much struck. He stopped to think about it. "I suppose it's because we liked him very well, but were never precisely close," he said musingly. "It's difficult to miss someone you only saw now and again. I expect I'll miss him more at Christmastime than I do now, for he was a familiar face at the dinnertable then. Our Miss Makepeace here," he explained to Creighton and Livvy when they stopped in their turn as they came up to them, "was wondering why we're all not grieving for Uncle. He's less than a week dead, after all. I suppose she's shocked at it. Come to think on, I suppose I may be, too."

"Don't be a flat, Coz," Creighton said. "Uncle was all very well, but he wasn't a warm man, except in pocket. He treated us well, but not with doting kisses and confidences. Though we did get gratifying bits of change now and again when he visited, didn't we? No, his books were his life, and now that he's lost that, we've his books to remember him by. Or rather, old Howard does. It seems fair enough. He collected old manuscripts," he explained to Marjorie.

"Yes. Just so," Livvy agreed, giving Marjorie an

indulgent smile. "Uncle had small use for children, and concealed it well enough to suit all of us. He never wed, nor cared to; the broken spine of a book might break his heart, no female's wiles ever would. But he was a good man, in all, and no one ever said an unkind word about him—save, perhaps, for your grandfather. They knew each other from school days, and your relative was heard to say that ours had ink in his veins, not good hot red blood."

"Which was true enough," Beau said. "And so, you see, my tenderhearted lady, we'd all look like idiots, and would be, in fact, if we pretended to be grieving for Uncle. For his sake or ours. I suspect the only earthly thing he's missing now is ink stains on his fingers. Ah, but what your grandfather is missing— now, that's a thing I can only discuss with you when I get to know you much, much better, so do let's get on with that," he said with great eagerness, as his cousins laughed, and he led Marjorie on down the street.

They met a great many fashionable persons for Marjorie to stare at: a gentleman dressed all in green, who always dressed in green, they said. Another who not only forgot her name a second after they were introduced, but forgot his own as well; another noble pair out walking with the wife of one of them, who was, the cousins told Marjorie when they were out of earshot, not quite sure—at least, from the way she behaved—whose wife she actually was. They met kind ladies and haughty ones, chatterboxes and reserved ones, the mistress of one lord, and the master of another—a legion of fine persons whose less than fine relationships staggered Marjorie, and made her feel a veritable country bumpkin. But her face showed nothing but polite interest. She may have been a country girl, but she'd been well brought up and had her own fine sense of dignity.

And so she was shocked as well as oddly gratified when Beau bade her good-bye at the end of the afternoon.

He looked into her eyes, and carelessly brushed a lock of her fine, long, pale hair back from her brow.

"You likely were the death of your nanny," he said affectionately, "because I'll wager for all you were a neat little person, your hair must have always looked like a gypsy's. An albino gypsy," he laughed. "But never mind. You impressed everyone today. You've a natural regal quality. And I, at least, was most impressed with how well you behaved. I never had to pick you up from the pavement once, although, I'll warrant, you nearly swooned several times over. Well-done, little one," he said gently, and took her hand and raised it to his lips, before he took his leave.

"A cavalier, is our Beau," Livvy said with a sour smile as soon as he'd gone.

"With that name, I'm not surprised" was all that Marjorie could say because she felt so much more.

They went to the theater, they went to the opera, they were seen at a musicale, a dinner party, a tea. And all in a week's time. By the time the second week began, the three cousins and the rediscovered heiress were an established phenomenon in the *ton*, and were as accepted and remarked upon as the green man and the forgetful lord.

Now and again, when she was changing her clothes, or about to fall asleep—the only times she was ever alone anymore—Marjorie would wonder how long she ought to stay on with Livvy. Because for all Aunt

Winslow sent word she was delighted with the arrangement, and it was a wonderful one, Marjorie knew very well it was an imposition, and a temporary one, at that. It was true that Livvy seemed as pleased with her guest as she was with the attention she received for harboring the late wicked earl's long-lost granddaughter. But Marjorie honestly didn't know if her hostess liked her for anything more than that.

She didn't know Miss Lavinia Peckingham very well, for all the time they passed together. Because when they were with the gentlemen, they spoke all together—when Marjorie wasn't speaking only with Beau. Which was as natural as it was gratifying. It seemed to Marjorie that Livvy found her naïveté astonishing; Creighton appeared to find it amusing, but Beau said he thought it refreshing. She believed him. He was never patronizing. They'd discussed a great many things and agreed on most. When they didn't, he found a way to laugh over it—with her, never at her. For all his facility with words and people, she never doubted that.

But when Marjorie was alone with Livvy, Livvy spoke only of what they'd done or what they'd do when they were together with the gentlemen again. She seemed no closer to Creighton than to Beau, or for that matter, to Marjorie herself. Livvy was, Marjorie thought one night as she lay in bed and her eyes were closing, a self-contained, cool sort of person. But then, she thought, weren't they all, after all? And not wishing to pursue that thought further, she allowed sleep to come and save her from it.

In the few weeks that she'd been with Livvy, Marjorie had been, by turn, amused, startled, and now and again puzzled by many of London's customs. But only one thing truly astonished her.

"Heavens! I could not, of course," she said.

"You fear I'll tread on your toes," Beau said mournfully.

"With good reason," Creighton said. "Never fear, my dear, I'll keep him from you at sword's point when the music begins."

"You misunderstand," Marjorie said worriedly, her brown eyes troubled as she gazed from cousin to cousin. "I'm in mourning, how can I attend a ball?"

"We're in mourning, too," Beau said, "and will be even more so if you don't come to the Swanson's ball with us. We'll carry on disgracefully, I warn you. Weeping, gnashing of teeth, tearing of hair, wailing and all that—the lot, I promise."

"We're well-known villains, at the worst they'll think we've corrupted you, puss," Creighton reasoned.

"Don't be absurd," Livvy snapped. "No one expects you to mourn Chesham. It would be hypocritical, would it not?"

"To be sure," Marjorie admitted in a small voice, for once unsure of her decision, "but certainly society expects one to be hypocritical, does it not?"

"Yes," Beau said thoughtfully, "very true. But just as certainly, we were sure you didn't give a rap for society. I suppose we were mistaken," he added, looking at her with what she was sure was new appraisal in his cool blue eyes.

"No, she's quite correct," Livvy said. "But you don't entirely comprehend," she advised Marjorie. "We're not precisely above society, no one is. But my cousins and I are in a sense, society itself here. No one believed us deeply attached to our uncle, and so we dare defy some fusty rules and society ignores it. Our families are well placed and well regarded, and they've no objection to our socializing now. I can't speak for Beau and Creighton's parents, as they reside in the countryside, but mine only paused their own entertainments for the duration of the funeral. Certainly," she said on a laugh, "no one in their right mind would expect anyone—most especially yourself, to put on the trappings of grief for a thoroughgoing villain like Chesham. Indeed, they'd think it very odd in you.

"But now I do wonder," Livvy said with a sudden chill in her voice, "as Beau does, at your demurral. For I can't for the life of me understand how you could so blithely agree to attend the theater, the opera, and other social functions, but balk at a ball? This is, indeed, a new sort of hypocrisy, even for London society. Is that how they go about things in Worcester?"

"No," Marjorie said, her face flaming. "It is not. I had not thought . . . I was so swept up . . ." she paused, realizing it wouldn't be fair to blame the cousins for sweeping her away in their various enthusiasms as they had, for she was, after all, responsible for her own mistakes, "I see. You're quite right," she admitted.

"You could, of course, wear lavender, which is half mourning," Livvy conceded. "That would be a rather nice touch," she said, thinking about it. "Yes. Charming. And so shall I."

"Cheer up. In for a penny, in for a waltz, my dear," Beau whispered to Marjorie. "And, of course, save two for me."

* * *

Although she'd performed it a dozen times before,
now as she danced, for the first time Marjorie began
to understand that the waltz *was* a wicked, sensuous,
daring, and altogether wonderful dance. But then,
she'd never danced with Beau before.

He held her no closer than absolutely necessary,
because they were on stage, as it were, before all
the *ton*. But he held her no further than he had to
either. She wore gloves, so his hands never actually
touched her own, although she could feel one warm
palm at her waist and the other against her own
palm. They didn't stand as close as they might in an
embrace, as all the dance's critics claimed, but close
enough so that she fancied she could almost feel his
strong and slender body against her own. But then,
she fancied quite a lot as she danced with him.

Marjorie had been instructed in the art of kissing
by James Golightly and John Langley, at home. Or
rather, in the shadows at a dance, and the anteroom
at a birthday party, at other persons' homes. She'd
thought it fascinating, but however delightful, had
curtailed her further enlightenment out of a lively
fear of having to become Mrs. Golightly or Mrs.
Langley if she hadn't a care. For James and John
were well enough as neighbors and friends, but not
half so fine as the dream husband she nightly
entertained.

She wasn't thinking of husbands now, but rather
of those few lessons—no, she admitted, forcing her
gaze from his eyes in pleased but panicked confusion
at what she thought she saw there—she'd been thinking of those well-shaped, slightly smiling lips and
what they might do. And wondering if they might do
as well with hers as he was doing with the waltz.
They moved together wonderfully well, so well, she

was almost glad when the music stopped. Because that had been the second waltz they'd danced together, and so the last they could in all propriety share tonight.

He bowed and led her to Creighton, who was only too pleased to take her into a quadrille with him. She'd danced so much this night with so many hopeful gentlemen, and yet, she thought, as she again covertly watched Beau step gracefully through another dance with another lady, she only remembered him. There were handsomer gentlemen, she was sure. But surely he was the most attractive, and he made her laugh, he smelled like ginger and soap, and his touch made her feel thrillingly foolish. And there was that about him that made her think he was thinking of that touch whenever they met.

She stood at the sidelines at last, pleading exhaustion, and sipped at her hot punch, for it was fiercely cold again outside tonight. Even in this crowded ballroom, the wind had found ways to stream through every chink of the house, causing the candles to flicker, the fires in the hearths to soar with each gust, and the ladies to shudder whenever they danced near a window, whether it was tightly closed or not.

Creighton took his ease by standing with her, amusing her with bits of gossip about the dancers as they watched them dip and slide past, and entertained himself with the way her eyes widened at each new scandalous tidbit she heard.

"Oh dear," she said, interrupting him, as the strains of the waltz struck up once again. "Oh my. Beau's leading Livvy into the waltz again."

He raised a graceful russet brow, "What's toward,

child? Shall you break my heart? Never say you're jealous."

Her color didn't rise at his teasing, nor did she give him a darkling look such as Livvy did when he was too ridiculous, nor did she even glance at him, though many other ladies did, for he was extremely handsome in his evening dress. Instead, she bit her lip, never taking her eyes from the waltzing couple.

"I mean to say, this is their third waltz together," she whispered. "They must have forgot. But it simply isn't done, no one can have more than two, Livvy told me that," she said, raising troubled eyes to him, as though she thought he might find a way to gracefully part his dancing cousins before they created a scandal.

"There'll be no trouble, puss. You aren't thinking. How much punch have you had?" he jested. "They're engaged, after all."

It seemed to her that the music stopped then, although it must have kept on because all the couples kept on dancing, as her thoughts went whirling. But just as Creighton had once observed, she went deathly still when she was truly upset, and so he never heard her say a word. As he was looking at his cousins just then, he never saw how all the color fled her face at his words. For when he looked to her again, she was smiling—at her own stupidity. And she was smiling so, he never thought to wonder at why she was so very still.

She knew she danced with others after that. And must have said the proper things, for many promised to pay her morning calls. Or so she thought they said. But she said nothing when Beau took his leave of her at Livvy's door at last, only looked disbe-

lievingly into his eyes, before she quickly looked
away, and never back again.

"Well, now then," Creighton said, when they'd left
the ladies behind their safely closed doors. "Where
to, Coz? The night's young, as are we, and bitter
cold, but methinks there's a warm lady or two we
might while away the rest of it with. You've got your
obliging, merry Maryanne snugly housed on Curzon
Street, but now I regret I bid my rapacious Jeanette
adieu just the other week. So I thought Maryanne
might have a friend . . . devil take you, am I talking
to the wind?"

Beau stood lost in thought, his expression grave,
his fair hair, beneath his high hat, blowing in the
wind. He turned bleak and wintry eyes to his cousin.

"What did you tell Marjorie about me, when I was
dancing with Liv?" he said quietly.

"Be damned to you," Creighton said in annoyance.
"How shall I remember? Why should I remember?"

"She grew white as snow, that's why," Beau said.

"Oh," Creighton said, his own expression growing
serious, "Oh be damned to you indeed, Beau. I told
you, you were playing with her overmuch. She's not
up to snuff, though she's a dear. And damned to Liv,
too. I suppose neither of you thought to tell her the
way things were, did you? At any rate, I'd wager
she didn't know, and I know she don't know the way
flirtation works in town. Now will you let her be?"

Beau only stood and looked out into the night.

"Good God, Coz, you've not let yourself become
involved, have you? That would be something rarely
wonderful, wouldn't it?" Creighton said, shaking his
head.

Beau recalled himself and turned his most charming smile on his cousin. "Have I ever?" he asked

lightly, "in all the years you've known me? For more than a passing hour, that is to say? Don't worry, child, I'll recover. I always do," he reminded his cousin with a slow and sadder smile. Then he said very softly, "Alas, don't I always?"

"True, too sadly true. But enough soul-searching, it's only two hours into the new day, my boy," Creighton said with forced merriment. "Now, shall we be off to see your so-convenient Maryanne and discover what toothsome friend she can summon to warm another cold lad as she will her own on a frosty night?"

"No," Beau said, "No, I think not. I am, surprisingly enough, weary. I think I'm off to home, alone. It may be I'm coming down with a cold. Some other frosty night, perhaps," he said, touching his hand to his hat before he left his cousin. "Because I think," he mused as he walked away, "they'll be many, many more of them before the spring."

Marjorie said little as Livvy's maid assisted her in taking off the finery she'd worn to the ball, and less as Livvy, sitting in a chair in the guest chamber, shared all the gossip she'd garnered this night. It was only when Livvy, complaining that she'd have had a better coze with a block of wood, was preparing to leave for her own room, that Marjorie spoke. By then, the maid had left them alone.

"Livvy," Marjorie said, as she blew out her lamp, so that her face would be in a dimmer light as she spoke, "why did you never tell me you and Beau were engaged to be wed?"

"Ho! As soon tell you the winter is cold. I assumed you knew, I expect, although now I realize I'd no real reason to. Except that everyone has known, forever. He asked for me when I came out, as our families expected. He was one and twenty to my eighteen then, and so they didn't mind that we never precisely named the day. Well, we both wanted to have some fun before we set up his nursery. I suppose we will have to name the day this winter sometime, so we can wed in the spring, before I turn two and twenty. It's just that neither of us thought to as yet. Why!" she said suddenly, staring at Marjorie. "Good Heavens! Have you formed a *tendre* for him? He's a monstrous flirt, but he'd be horrified and very much ashamed of himself if you had taken him seriously, I think. I've warned him in the past about the effect he has on young females," she said crossly. "But have you?" she asked with no malice, or regret, but only the liveliest curiosity.

"No," Marjorie said in a rich, warm chuckle, so full of honest amusement that Livvy laughed with her. She seldom lied so well, but then, Marjorie found it incredibly easy to laugh since she was really amused at her own gross idiocy now. "I just didn't know until tonight," she went on. "I suppose it explains why you're always biting his nose off, like a wife of many years."

"Yes, I suppose I do," Livvy said slowly, as she thought about it. "But that's the way it often is, isn't it? One sets a pattern of behavior with a person in the beginning, and so it stays. For the life of me, I can't change it now. I always bossed and badgered him about when we were children, I expect I'll be a terrible shrew once we're wed. Poor fellow," she said with as much relish as sorrow, making Marjorie laugh again.

They parted laughing. And Marjorie was still chuckling as she lay her head on her pillow, before

she started crying into it. At least, she thought with
the same bitter humor that had let her preserve her
face and her secret during the last terrible moments
with Livvy, now she knew just how temporary her
stay here was to be. For now she knew it was ended,
and that she must leave, at once.

The new Earl of Chesham was nothing like the old
one, and that was a blessing and a relief to his servants, and a cause for considerable speculation in the
ton. Hugh Carstairs had been a country squire before
his elevation to the nobility, but he was a good-looking man in the prime of life, with a pretty wife and
a lovely young daughter, who was, moreover,
engaged to be wed to a gentleman rake who'd been
tamed at the sight of her. Or so the gossip went. The
fact that Rake Neville's manor was a stone's throw
from the Carstairs' own house contributed much to
the course of events. Or so the lovely, laughing Felicia Carstairs told her newfound cousin Marjorie, as
the Viscount Neville protested it was never so: one
look, and he'd given his heart and then his black book
of addresses away.

They entertained Marjorie in the drawing room of
their new town house, and it seemed that their very
presence had already begun to drive the shadows
from it. That, and the fact that the servants had
labored like madmen to spruce the place up for the
new owners, and maintain their positions by so
doing. They need not have worried. It appeared that
the new earl was as aware of his duties to his title
as his predecessor hadn't been. Which was consider-
ably so. Because after he'd passed the obligatory half
hour with his new relative, and she arose to take her
leave, he immediately asked that she not go—ever.

"We're close relatives, are we not?" he asked. "The only closer, I understand, is your aunt. You've already given Worcester most of your life. Now's our turn."

"Do come stay with us, dear," the new countess urged. "This place has dozens of rooms. Stay at least until Felicia weds this spring, and then after, as well, if you can remain single yourself. For when she leaves us, we'll likely be dreadfully lonely."

"Oh, piffle!" Felicia laughed, "What a bouncer! They can't wait to hand me off to this dreadful fellow," she said, smiling lovingly at the lean nobleman at her side. "But please, Cousin, Come stay with me, at least until I wed. It'll be great fun, for I don't know London at all, and I can't live in this fellow's pocket every moment until then, no matter what he says."

"Her papa won't let her until we're wed," Lord Neville said gloomily. "How provincial, is it not? You've been in London for all of three weeks, so do tell him so, Miss Makepeace," he urged her.

When they'd done laughing, Livvy spoke up. She, Beau, and Creighton had come along to the new earl's town house this morning, just as they'd accompanied Marjorie everywhere since she'd come to town. Although Marjorie knew it was odd to have them with her for this first meeting with her new cousins, she also knew it would've been insulting to ask them to remain behind. And for all she was uneasy with them now, she'd been even more so at the thought of meeting new relatives, who might or might not want her acquaintance.

"Miss Makepeace has been most comfortable staying on with me," Livvy said complacently. "And after all, we don't live far. I don't doubt we'll see each other often," she assured Felicia, "as I'm to be wed to Beauford here in spring as well, and our gentlemen are acquainted."

"Oh, but I've never had a cousin my own age," Felicia said. "Can't you reconsider, please, Marjorie? Won't you stay? We're both country girls, after all."

It was prettily put, and the earl and his lady seemed as eager for Marjorie's acceptance as they waited for her to speak. They were warm and extremely polite. Still, Livvy, a lady who always had her way, looked serene, undisturbed at the possibility that her houseguest might desert her. Because it was obvious that the new earl and his lady were in the throes of putting a new household together, since the old bachelor earl's standards were not that of a family's. Moreover, they'd a fashionable wedding to arrange for the coming spring, and there wasn't a doubt in anyone's mind that Felicia Carstairs only needed the proximity of her lanky fiancé to make her world go around.

"Thank you," Marjorie said with great relief, "I will."

Although her newfound cousins repeatedly apologized for the state of the bedchamber Marjorie was given, she found nothing amiss with it. The furnishings were old and out of fashion, but it was clean and comfortable. The room was down the hall from Felicia's, and Felicia was as charming, merry, and eager for friendship as she'd appeared to be. But she was also very much in love with her tamed rake, and that meant that everything she said, did, and wanted to talk about eventually revolved around him. And though he was as facile a companion as any gentlemen Marjorie had ever met—which explained how he'd got his reputation, she reasoned, for he was lean and long-shanked, and in no way an Apollo—his every thought centered on his beloved Felicia, just as his every glance indicated how much he wanted to be alone with her.

Which meant that even if the gentleman had the graceful manners of a diplomat and the sweet tongue of a spy at a king's court—and he very nearly did—and the lady was as friendly as a child and yet as warm as a dear friend—which she clearly was—it wasn't great fun to be in their company. A fifth wheel, Marjorie soon discovered, would feel far more necessary than she did when she passed time with them. For at least even if it served no use, it would roll along, unnoticed, which she, of course, could not.

Despite her firmest resolve, because she really knew no others in London, she realized she eventually must take Livvy, Beau, and Creighton up on some of their many invitations. Or so, at least, she told herself. After all, she could scarcely avoid them, as they were everywhere to be seen in fashionable London. Or so she tried to convince herself. Nor could she be rude or cold to them when they did meet, for they certainly didn't deserve that. They'd never deliberately misled her. She, after all, was the one who'd misunderstood their ways. So she at last accepted. But they must never guess why she'd left Livvy and tried to estrange herself. And that she vowed to herself.

The winter set in hard. That meant terrible privation for many, and death for many more. But it also meant extravagant new forms of play for the idle and wealthy ladies and gentlemen of fashion. The ice and snow, like so many other rare and transient things, were beautiful, even if dangerous and occasionally lethal if not taken in moderation. That made it outrageously fashionable, of course.

Yet for once, as Felicia gleefully informed her cousin as they dressed to go out on an icy afternoon, country girls had the advantage over their citified hothouse cousins.

"You'll see," Felicia chortled, "I doubt one of those fine ladies who shine at Almack's and star at balls can so much as stand up on skates, and just try to imagine them in a snowball fight! Whereas we could circle a frozen pond before we could add to three, couldn't we? This time," she said gleefully, "we have them!"

"Perhaps, but why should you care?" Marjorie asked, smiling at her excited cousin. "Your Nigel wouldn't give any of them a glance even if they took to skating on their hands."

"Now, that would be something," Felicia agreed, laughing, before her piquant face grew somber and she said seriously. "True enough, and I'm very glad of it, but *I* know how no-account they think me because they're all the crack and in their estimate I'm little more than a lucky little country chit who was in the right place at the right time. I am, and I was, but how I should like to show them I'm far more."

"But you are," Marjorie insisted. "And your Nigel was clever enough to see it, and so I'm sure he'll be happy to tell you."

As he did, when he came to call for them.

"Of course, you can out-skate, out-think, and out-look any other female in the *ton*," he declared as they strolled to the park, "and out-kiss them, too," he added to his fiancée in a whisper, as Marjorie pretended outsized interest in the leafless trees.

He was entirely right—at least about the skating, Marjorie thought. But she had to grin at her cousin when they saw that once again the city girls knew how to take advantage, even of the fact that they had none. Because although Marjorie and Felicia could glide across the pond with grace, and look very lovely at it, too, the fashionable young ladies of the *ton* could make every use of the fact that they couldn't. And they did. They slipped and slid and gasped with terror and dismay at how their legs betrayed them to show daring glimpses of how well-turned they were. And they were coddled, petted, and reassured by their escorts. Then they could pretend to learn to skate by languishing deep in a gentleman's embrace, even in front of their chaperons. For how else could they negotiate the treacherous ice, if not held close in a strong fellow's arms?

Not that it made any difference to Felicia, Marjorie noted, for she and her lord skated off almost at once, hand in hand, thigh to thigh, eye to eye, graceful as a pair of swans, and about as interested in the other humans as a pair of them might be, as well.

The park was crowded, for the wind was still and a brilliant sun rode high in a blue sky. It gave little more than light to the scene though, for the temperature was frigid. The chaperons, companions, older ladies and gentlemen, timorous females and less hardy males, fops, servants, and other onlookers stood on the snow-covered frozen ground, hovering around small fires that had been lit to keep them from turning to ice, as anyone might if they didn't keep turning themselves this day.

And so most of those who were able were on the

ice, being pushed in one-seated sleighs by their gallants, or skating in pairs, trios, or even linked in twisting snakes with other laughing skaters. Marjorie skated for the joy of it, not just to keep warm, for aside from her stinging nose and cold-chafed cheeks, she was comfortable in her woolen frock and new cherry-colored woolen pelisse. The pelisse had a hood, and though the swansdown it was trimmed with didn't do a thing against the cold—except flutter in a most becoming way in the breeze—it matched the great muff she carried before her and warmed her whenever she thought of the luxury of it. The matched outfit had been Livvy's idea, of course, and Marjorie had never owned anything finer.

She skated along the perimeters of the pond, liking the feeling of freedom, for now she was, even in the midst of the others, very much on her own. Lord Neville and Felicia had been nearby, but now she saw them glide away all the way to the end of the pond, and then turn until they were entirely lost to her sight. Only then did she feel far less happy with her freedom, feeling all at once as if she were only endless circling to no purpose but to keep her blood moving. As her thoughts were, for now, too, she began to wonder if that were not analogous to her whole life here in London.

"I'd a music box once, with a little Dutch maid who skated around and around the mirrored lake of it when I touched a lever. Tell me, do you hum a tinkly little tune, too?" a familiar voice asked, startling her from her reveries. "For you look very like her, without the long blond braids and the wooden shoes, of course," Beau said as he skated up beside her.

He took her gloved hands in his, as a matter of course, and skated alongside her. He skated effortlessly, as he did everything else, she thought, and was glad of her hood, for from the side he could see little of her embarrassment but her red-tipped nose, and that could be from the cold. And luckily, she, of course, couldn't see him, though it seemed she could feel every atom of his presence beside her.

They skated in silence, until she saw Livvy wave to her as she glided by with the dashing Harry Fabian, with Creighton following, arm in arm with young Elizabeth Trundell.

"Why are you not skating with your fiancée?" Marjorie asked, without realizing she would, and then wished she could gather up her words as they hung in the frosty puff of air they'd been born in, and reswallow them.

"She's well occupied," he said, after a pause in which she was gratified to note, by the way his hands tightened on hers, he'd slipped.

"But she is your fianceé," Marjorie persisted, hating herself for showing what she'd been thinking, as he never did, and no person of fashion would. "I don't see Neville skating with anyone else but his Felicia."

"She's been my fiancée since I could toddle, much less skate," he said quietly. Then raising his head and voice, added more merrily, "As to that, I don't see Rake Neville and your cousin Felicia. Where have they got to, do you think? Ought we to look? A trifling thing like snow and cold is no bar to mischief, after all, else there wouldn't be so many Laplanders, would there?"

"*Lord* Neville and my cousin are likely someplace where they can be alone, I don't doubt," Marjorie said as coldly as she felt everywhere now, "since I've observed that engaged persons usually cannot wait to be alone together."

She braced herself for his rejoinder, but all he said was a soft, "Yes, that's often so," before he skated on, silently, with her.

"We're going around in circles," he eventually said. "Large circles, but definitely rings. It's ornamental, no doubt, but accomplishes nothing."

She turned her head to gaze at him in surprise and sudden foolish hope.

"The pond is larger than this," he went on, "else where did Neville and Felicia disappear to? Shall we go search? And move like the wind as we do? Or," he asked, showing his white teeth in a teasing smile, "have you become so coated with town bronze by now that you cannot move quickly?"

She grinned back at him.

"The wind," she promised him, "cannot go so fast as I can. I only wonder if a tulip of the *ton* can keep up with me without wilting."

He tucked her arm in his, and they fairly flew through the crowd of slowly circling skaters as they made for the far reaches of the pond, the place that in summer was little frequented because of its heavily wooded shores. It was even less so now since there were few spectators there, and most of the skaters had come to be seen, after all.

When they reached the farthest frozen shores, they were both winded, red-faced, and laboring for breath, for the icy air didn't seem to fill their lungs completely no matter how deeply they drew it in. But neither wished the other to see or to know that the reason they linked arms so tightly now was so they could remain standing upright. And so both were surprised and delighted to see that when they stopped and turned to look, the other was just as stricken. Marjorie laughed outright, though she could scarcely afford the breath, when she saw the elegant gentleman blowing like a tired cart horse, as she told him between her own gasps. He laughed to see the lovely fashionable lady with a nose red as a sot's, as he was only too pleased to inform her it was, when he could.

But her nose and cheeks seemed redder because her skin was so white and clear. Her hood was thrown back, for cold as she was, she was overheated from her exercise now, and he saw that her hair was clean and shining in the sunlight, pale and fine, lovelier than the swansdown that had framed it, and he wondered how it would feel, streaming like silken floss through his hands. That was before he saw her ruddily blushed and parted lips, and could not look elsewhere again.

She saw the sun glinting in his eyes, blue as a summer sky in all the cold, and for once, totally clear and filled only with delight. Too bemused to be comfortable, she looked up—only to see strands of his tousled hair, escaped from beneath his hat, fluttering, glowing like ripe wheat blown in the wind. Gazing down again, she saw his parting lips, and then, in sudden delight and fear, she hastily looked away to the horizon, so that she could not stop herself from not stopping what she knew was to come.

But she didn't have to. When she looked over his shoulder, she saw Felicia and her lord. They were standing on the ice, not far away in distance, but leagues removed in every other sense. They were closed in an embrace, oblivious to all else: cold, wind, ice, as well as time and place. Marjorie stared, and then closed her eyes tightly, before she hung her head in guilty shame for spying—and for forgetting the reason for what she'd seen: what a promise of love and marriage meant, or was supposed to mean, and that the man she'd wanted to kiss her had made just such a promise . . . to someone else.

He knew immediately, from her mouth, not her eyes. For it tensed and thinned, and he was forced to look up into her eyes to see what had happened to blight the sweet promise that had been there. Then he saw what she was staring at. From the moment her eyes closed, he knew what she was thinking. That was the damnable thing, he thought in fury, he knew very well. And could not, despite all his vast past experience and best efforts, quite manage to ever forget it.

"I think they're safe," he was able to say calmly a moment later, "save for the fact that if they stand there too long, they might very well melt the ice. Then wouldn't we have a time hauling them out? But even love can grow cold on such a day, and I believe they'll eventually remember where they are," he said lightly, for it was remarkable, he thought with bitter pleasure, how he always could say something light, no matter what he was feeling or thinking.

"In the meanwhile," he said, "it is extraordinarily cold. Shall we make icy tracks whilst the sun shines?"

She nodded. And they skated away. He was right. The only constant in English weather being its variable nature, it wasn't long until the clouds drifted across the sun, and even the illusion of warmth was gone. By then they were back where they'd begun, silently making circles in the perpetually circling crowd of skating fashionables.

"I am not so young as you, alas," Beau said eventually. "Should you like to suffer an old man's crochets and warm yourself at the edge of a fire and sip something hot with me?" he asked.

Her nod sent swansdown flurrying about her face, and they skated off the ice. He helped her remove her skates with quick, sure hands, not making an elaborate flirtation of it as so many other gentlemen were doing with their escorts. Then he led her to warm her hands at the edge of a fire while he went to get her a cup of hot punch or sweetened tea from the cart of one of London's many opportunistic vendors clustered at the fringes of the pond.

"I daresay you are used to such weather," Livvy said as she approached Marjorie, speaking as though she were only continuing an ongoing discussion, as she so often did, "but I can tell you I'm half frozen. Oh, do go get me a cup of something steaming, as Beauford's doing for Miss Makepeace," she remarked absently to her escort from over her shoulder as she came up to the fire. He hastened to do her bidding without a murmur.

"Do you like it at Chesham's?" she asked as soon as she was alone with Marjorie.

"Yes, very well," Marjorie said.

"I cannot see why," Livvy said coolly.

"She is my cousin," Marjorie said, but Livvy cut her off by saying, impatiently. "I know, I know. But so are Creighton and Beauford mine, and I scarcely have to live with them. She has no need of you," she went on before Marjorie could remind her that she would, indeed, someday have to live with one of them at least. "I wonder that you don't feel like her mother-in-law and not her cousin. Why, see, here they come. He looks as if he could devour her on the spot, as ever. And she, as if she wished him to. How singular," she said as she eyed the lanky nobleman as he walked arm in arm with Felicia. "You could have stayed on with me," she continued. "You still can, if you wish," she added, turning to see Marjorie's reaction. As she did, she lost her usual calm demeanor. She gazed over Marjorie's shoulder, her eyes widening and her lips turning up into a delighted, curling grin.

"Oh I say!" she said, brimming with merriment, in that moment looking younger and prettier than Marjorie had ever seen her. "He's in a pickle now, isn't he? Whatever shall he do, do you think? Of course, he can't be vexed with her. The park is free territory, after all, and yet, still, she ought to know better," she tittered. "Perhaps she does. He *is* in a fine muddle, isn't he?"

Marjorie looked to see what Livvy was staring at. Beau was paused, halfway to them, bearing two cups of some steaming liquid. But the clouds that rose from what he held didn't entirely conceal his face, and it seemed he was suddenly at a loss, for his expression was arrested, still, and cold. An extremely pretty dark-haired young woman was standing before him, smiling at him as she sipped at her own cup. He glanced up to see Livvy and Marjorie watching, and his face grew graver. Marjorie saw nothing wrong with the scene before her, and couldn't imagine why Beau was so nonplussed, and Livvy so enchanted.

"Who is she?" Marjorie breathed.

"His familiar. His lightskirts," Livvy giggled.

"His leg of mutton?" Marjorie asked, shocked.

Livvy laughed outright, "Bit o' mutton, not leg of mutton, my dear," she corrected Marjorie, her eyes sparkling. "Yes."

Marjorie stared at the girl, who kept smiling sweetly at Beau as he said a few words to her.

"Oh poor Livvy!" Marjorie gasped, wondering how she could get her away from the dreadful scene before them.

"I beg your pardon!" Livvy said, caught between astonishment and anger, her good spirits evaporating as she noted Marjorie's tearful, sympathetic expression. "Why are you looking at me that way? Whatever is there to be sorry for?"

"Well, that Beau has his . . . you know, his lady friend here, and now, and you have to see her, you know . . ." Marjorie babbled, all the while wondering why she was apologizing for feeling sorry for Livvy.

"His whore?" Livvy asked, as Marjorie gasped. "Well, that is what she is, with no bark on it. Only she's not exclusively his, by any means, at least not for very long. She was the Duke of Torquay's familiar once, and when he wed, she went to the Marquess Bessacar, and now she's begun the rounds. I daresay Beau will tire of her rapidly, I imagine he's already done, actually, which is why she played him such a trick. Revenge for his inattention, I suspect. Much good it will do her, when Beau is done with a female, it is over."

"But don't you care?" Marjorie blurted.

"About what? That Beau's been paid back? I'll have a fine time roasting him over it, that's true, and doubtless Creighton will tease him to shreds about it. Just look over there, he's seen, too," Livvy said on a light laugh, before she looked to Marjorie and was struck silent by her expression.

"My dear," Livvy said a bit defensively, for the first time in their acquaintance unsure of Marjorie's good opinion, and so aggressive toward her for it, as was her way, "I don't know how it is in the provinces, but that's the way of the adult world. Beau's not wed, nor is he dead, so he seeks company for his bed . . . I believe that's how the little rhyme goes, does it not?"

"No, no it does not in the provinces," Marjorie said angrily. She was enraged, and didn't know who was most deserving of her scorn: Beau, Livvy, or herself, for being such a nodcock as to ever think these jaded, heartless people had a thing in common with her at all. "In the provinces," she said steadily, though her eyes burned with light, "we care for the feelings of our loved ones, and expect fidelity from the moment a declaration is given. If we discovered a promised husband didn't have an empty bed before we wed, why . . . why, I think we'd think it correct to strike the malefactor dead! Were I you, I'd be in tears, or pulling hair by now, Livvy—his or hers. Or something like. I truly would. But not to care, and worse, to jest at it? And with him? Why, that is to be almost as bad as they are. I cannot understand you at all. And do you know," she said, for once absolutely sure of her ground with her sophisticated friend, "I believe I am very glad I don't!"

She turned on her heel, slipping a bit on the packed snow as she did, and then with all the dignity that a woman can muster whilst striding across snow and ice, made her way to her cousin Felicia's side. After a few words, Lord Neville, after one startled glance back to Livvy, took Marjorie on one arm and Felicia on the other, and led them from the park. Livvy was still staring after their receding figures when Beau returned.

"Where's Marjorie got to?" he asked.

"She marched off with her cousin after handing me my head on a platter," Livvy said in shocked accents.

"Indeed? What did you say to her?" Beau asked, a hint of tension in his soft voice.

"I only pointed out your *cher ami* to her," Livvy said, turning to see that the woman, after shrugging one shoulder, was sauntering away.

"Ah," Beau said, "and she was enraged at me?"

"Devil a bit!" Livvy said with more spirit, "she was furious with me! Imagine that. I'd never realized what an utter rustic she was. Why, she thought I should rage, shout, and clean your platter," Livvy laughed bitterly. "And said a man who was promised in marriage ought to be faithful even before he wed! And then actually announced that I was as bad as you and your little doxy for not carrying on about the fact that you so obviously were not."

"Did she?" Beau asked, with a sad smile playing about his lips, before he took her hand. "Liv," he said suddenly, "About that—I'm sorry, I really am. I didn't know she'd be here."

"Oh, don't apologize to me for that," Livvy said abruptly, fluttering a hand as though she were brushing away his comment. "It's Miss Makepeace who ought to be tendering me an apology now!"

"Should she?" he asked slowly and thoughtfully.

The late Earl of Chesham's men-at-law were pleased to announce that they found Miss Marjorie Makepeace's claim on the estate valid, and sorry to say that it didn't matter very much. Because the legacy the old fellow had left to her was a pittance, a mere remembrance, and a sop to his conscience, the biggest surprise being that he seemed to have had

one, however tiny it was. But the heiress was
strangely satisfied with it, and thanked them kindly.

"For in truth," she told her cousin Felicia later,
"I'd be uncomfortable with the thought that he val-
ued me highly, or held me in any regard at all,
because then the legacy would be a burden, and a
constant reminder that I never made a move to see
him while he lived. This way I know for a certainty,
you see, that he thought of me as I did him—infre-
quently, and with more of a sense of nagging duty
than love or esteem."

It was nicely said, even though Felicia didn't
believe a word of it. Marjorie's face belied her words,
as did the tiny quaver in her voice as she said it. Oh,
she never regretted the amount of money, not that
she couldn't have used it. But the lack of love, even
from beyond the grave, mattered far more. For who
else did she have? her cousin wondered. And so Felicia, a girl who'd always had all of her parents' love
and now was wrapped in all of her promised husband's, and yet now knew there could never be a
surfeit of it, grieved for her.

"But you will stay on here with me until I wed,
will you not?" she asked immediately.

"I'd thought to leave with the old year," Marjorie
said, with an attempt at a smile, wondering how she
could avoid Beau, Livvy, and Creighton until then,
even as she wondered if she could bear to.

"Oh please," Felicia pleaded, "I need you."

Even though Marjorie knew she was needed as
much as the sun needed a candle, she relented. For
surely, she thought confusedly, seeing him would
eventually cure the ache she felt each time she saw
him. Seeing him would be all she'd do, she vowed.
She could scarcely avoid it, anyway. The Christmas

season was upon them, which meant parties, balls, routs, and all sorts of gala entertainments, and as the three cousins never missed any in less festive times, they'd scarcely miss any now.

So Marjorie wasn't at all surprised to discover they'd accepted her cousin's invitation to a Christmas ball. The evening was planned as a neat way for the new earl and his countess to introduce themselves to the *ton*, prepare them for Felicia's coming wedding, and warm the town house with the company of acceptable persons for the first time in many years.

It was certainly the first time so many fires had been lit in the house all at the same time, in decades. The place was wreathed in holly, hung with evergreens, plentiful food and drink were set out, even for the servants, and according to their oldest customs, the earl and his lady had set candles at the windows and lanterns in the trees in front and in back of the town house, to greet the glad new season. If there'd been any trace of the old earl's spirit lingering, it must have fled in confusion at seeing his old house consumed by such high and good spirits.

Marjorie wore green velvet and she danced with a dozen gentlemen who complimented her on everything they could think of, and nothing she put much importance to. She nodded at Livvy most civilly, gave her hand to Creighton for a country dance, and avoided Beau at every turn. And never stopped looking at him from across the room, beyond her partners' shoulders and behind her fan. Yet no matter how discreet and clever her actions, she never failed to find him gazing back to her with great sadness deep in his laughing eyes.

It was toward the end of the evening, when everyone had eaten too much and drunk far more, and yearned for their beds, yet refused to face them, that she found herself face-to-face with him at last. She'd gone to the lady's withdrawing room to bathe her face so as to refresh herself, and found it so crowded with gossiping ladies that she'd taken a quick turn in the frozen back garden instead, so that when she came in from the night, she was cold to the touch and scented with pine. And yet still her lips, Beau thought confusedly, were like fire beneath snow, they warmed so quickly to his own.

He'd meant to pass it off as a jest: a quick kiss under the mistletoe. Or at least, he thought dazedly, he thought he'd meant to. He'd watched her all night and when he saw her disappear into the back garden, he'd waited in the shadows for her to return. When he realized she'd have to walk through the hall and pass beneath the hanging mistletoe, it seemed a perfect excuse. To talk, nothing more. Just a quick buss on the lips, then a rueful smile, and then perhaps he'd have a chance to talk to her without seeing that quick hurt spring into her eyes. Just talk, for after all, as he knew only too well, he couldn't ask for more—could not in all decency and honor, which he was shocked to find he still possessed, for all he'd sat up all these past nights searching for a way to deny it.

But then he touched her lips. And found they sprang to life beneath his as his arms automatically enfolded her, as hers, after a moment of denial, clung to him. But neither of them were in a position to claim passion had swept away all reason, even if it did banish most. Because after a long moment, when he paused and drew back to look into her eyes, as he had to do for pleasure as much as for pain, they saw each other clear.

When they stepped away from their embrace, in confusion and regret, they couldn't say anything. Not the facile Lord Beauford, or the virtuous Miss Makepeace. He couldn't say a seductive, easy thing, as was his wont, nor could she accuse him of perfidy or misbehavior, as he almost wished she'd do. They could only stare at each other until they heard Livvy's cool, dry voice.

"Good heavens, Beau," she said in exasperation, "I understand but I doubt Marjorie will. These rogues," Livvy went on, gesturing to a silent Creighton at her side, as well as to Beau, "once had a wager as to which of them could kiss more ladies beneath the mistletoe, and they were only sixteen at the time. I thought the downstairs maid would have a fit. She was a Methodist, you see. Do you never grow up?" she asked Beau with a rueful shake of her head. "Pray excuse him, my dear Marjorie," she went on, as Beau stood silently gazing at Marjorie, his face shadowed by more than shadows now, "as I do."

The hall was deserted except for the four of them. Even the footman had somehow melted into the shadows, or was gone on another task. Their words had a cool resonance in the marble hall, and Marjorie's came clear and cold to them, even if she was still shaking in reaction to Beau's touch, as well as with suppressed rage.

"No," she said clearly, "No."

Her pale hair was like a small light in the dim hall, and tousled as it was from the wind's touch and Beau's hand, it shone about her like a nimbus, as if she were some bright Christmas spirit. But her words were not of forgiveness and goodwill.

"No," she said again, "I do not. Nor should you. Nor do I forgive you. But how should you know better, after all? This house, this street, this city—this world of yours, Livvy, Beau, Creighton, has not taught you any better . . . but I doubt that's it. No. For there are good people here, as everywhere. I think it's in the blood—in your cold blood.

'Please," she said holding up one shaking hand as Livvy began to speak, "Let me go on until I'm finished. When I met you," she said, her head to the side as the words came, as well as the sudden wisdom through inspiration born of need, "I was shocked that you didn't grieve for your uncle, remember? You were amused with me, and assured me he wouldn't expect it, for he felt no great love for you, or anyone. But you claimed, even so, he was superior to my grandfather, who loved not even books, as your uncle did, but only his pleasures. That wasn't so. I came to the wrong funeral and was abashed, but now I think there wasn't so much difference between them after all. They died, as they lived, only a matter of yards apart in space as well as temperament. For neither loved any living thing so well as themselves. Two cold old men," she said musingly, and her words vibrated as though the very walls of the house were listening and murmuring them over again to themselves.

"I've only just discovered I inherited very little from my grandfather, but I was glad of it," she went on. "I'm gladder now, for I think I inherited even less. While you—why, all of you inherited a great deal from your uncle, without ever knowing it. I suppose Livvy, you think I'm quaint and amusing, even now. And you Creighton, you look at me with no expression, perhaps you feel nothing at all. You, Beau, feel too many things, and none of them have anything to do with the heart. You three are like curious, inhuman children, for all your sophistication. You're frozen fast, in the grip of a winter even harder than this one. God help you," she said sadly, "as I hope He helps me for caring so much.

"There, I'm finished," she said. "Altogether. Good night."

As they stood seeking words, she went up the long stair to her chamber, seeking solitude and escape from the inescapable truths she'd said.

Livvy paced her drawing room, and rounded on her visitors at last.

"It is not a matter of having the last word. If I'd wanted that, I could have written her a devastating letter. Then, if she replied, I could tear up the answer without reading it. That is the only way to have the last word, short of shooting someone dead before they can answer—or fleeing up the stairs before they have a chance to," she said with a sour smile.

"At least it proved she was all too human," Creighton remarked. "I'd begun to wonder. Bad enough to have one's heart read clearer than a gypsy reads a hand, it was only bearable because she took fright, and flight at the last."

"You," Beau said quietly from the depths of a chair where he sat cradling a glass of amber liquid, "are blameless."

"Yes. Always. That's the point, isn't it?" Creighton said, his handsome face serious, for once. "The eternal amused observer, I," he said softly.

"No need to hold a wake," Livvy said curtly. "She handed us some home truths, and I, for one, am angry at it. But not at her. We did treat her abominably. Beau ought not to have flirted, ought never to have kissed her, for such a chit doesn't know flirtation from a true tendre, and he knew it. And I," she said, cutting off what Beau began to say, "ought never to have countenanced it, at least, not in front of her. We owe her an apology, I think. A formal one."

She took another paced turn about the carpet and then faced them.

"I discovered, through my various sources, that she's changed her plans. She leaves London this week. She's decided to return home with the new year. If we announce our coming, she'll doubtless find a way to avoid us. So I thought we'd pay a surprise call tomorrow, in the afternoon. I spoke with Neville at the Talwin's the other night, and he mentioned he's taking Felicia to his aunt's then, and scarcely had to mention that Miss Makepeace won't be accompanying them. She goes nowhere anymore, that's why they're letting her go home. They assume she's pining for it," she said, looking away and down at the carpet, just as she'd done when Lord Neville's eyes had told her exactly what Marjorie had been pining for.

"I'd rather not," Beau said with quiet reason. "I think we've done enough harm."

"Afraid?" she asked pointedly, and saw his hand shake once, before he brought the glass to his mouth and downed the contents at a gulp, as he'd been doing of late. "I am not," she continued. "And if you gentlemen can suppress your smiles whatever you think of her bourgeois attitudes and country manners, I believe we'll get through it respectably enough. Simply say you're sorry, appear to mean it, and have done. It's only fair to her, as well as to ourselves. I find I don't care for being cast as a villain," she said coldly. "Do you?"

"I don't care about the casting," Creighton said. "I don't want to be one anymore. What time shall I be here tomorrow?" he asked as he walked to the door.

"Two," she said absently.

He nodded, said, "Servant, Liv, Beau," and left them alone.

There were some moments of silence when he'd gone.

"Shall you come?" Livvy asked at last.

"I suppose I must," Beau answered. "Although I sent a gracious note—I'm very good at that—days ago."

"It is not the same," she said.

"No, no, it's not," he agreed, and with a show of boredom and languor, finally arose from the depths of his chair, and after a sketch of a stretch, faced her.

"Well, then," he said with perfect calm, "I'll leave you to your other good works now. And shall see you tomorrow. At two."

"Beau," she said with sudden command, stopping him in his steps to the door, "father was much struck by the celebration at Cheshams' that fateful night. He suddenly remembered my age, it seems. He wants to know if we've set the date. We haven't. Shall we?"

He didn't turn to face her as he accepted his hat from a footman, and then waved him away.

"Ah well," he said once they were alone again, as he gazed at his hat, "I did want to speak with you about that, Liv. It seems my man-at-law discovered some problems with my sugar plantation in the West Indian islands. You remember, the one I bought into with my old friend, Brightwood, years ago. I'd hoped to go and see for myself, this very spring. I know you detest the heat, and believe you'll despair of the sea. And so, as it's a long journey, and as I don't know when I can honestly say I'll return, not being familiar with the problems or the tides, I thought we'd let it go for this season. What matter, after all? We've been promised for eternity for an eternity, haven't we?"

"At least that," she agreed, "but isn't that dangerous? There's a war on, isn't there?"

"Another reason I cannot in all conscience ask you to accompany me," he said, as though the idea had just struck him, and looked up at her as though to congratulate her for her cleverness. What she saw in his eyes made her look away to the window and drag in a deep breath. They were blue as the winter sky, and as dead and cold. She hadn't seen him look so since he'd been very young, and had broken his ankle, and yet refused to cry while it was being set.

"I see," she said. "Well, it shall take some convincing arguments, it appears Father likes the smell of orange blossoms since he's gotten a whiff of them. But as he likes the smell of gold far more, I think I can persuade him to postpone his yearning for a grandchild until next winter."

He grew still at the mention of the purpose for their union, and then remained so, as though waiting for her to release him to go about his errands.

"Tomorrow, at two, then," she said.

He nodded, bowed, and left her.

Marjorie had been repacking her cases, as she'd been doing all week, when the maid came to tell her she'd visitors. When she heard who they were, she'd the instant desire to leap into bed, pull the covers up to her nose, and plead the headache or the plague, so that they'd let her alone. Then she recalled that she'd be alone in a matter of days, and for the rest of her life after that, and that only a coward would hide. Even if she were a coward, she could scarcely act as she'd accused them of doing. She'd said some hard things, some absolutely unforgivable things, and she had to reap what she'd sown. And even if she never wanted to see him again, she couldn't bear the thought of not seeing him again when he was directly downstairs.

She put on a pretty rose-colored frock pied with tiny flowers, and pinched her cheeks mercilessly so she looked as healthy and unconcerned as a milkmaid on a May morning. She arranged her hair in artless curls, and put on a sweet expression that she resolved not to put off until they'd gone. They wanted a country girl, a bucolic little rustic, and they'd have one. She only wished she'd a bit of straw to put in her hair or between her lips as she went downstairs to meet them and let them have at her, as she doubtless deserved. And to let him ignore her, or pity her, or be condescending to her, as she needed him to do so she could die a little and then go on with a new life.

She saw Livvy first, standing dead center in the drawing room, waiting. Livvy looked cold, collected, and very attractive in a dark green military-style walking dress. If she hadn't tried to resemble a simpleton from the outskirts of the countryside, Marjorie would have felt dreadful for being so outdressed by her erstwhile friend. Creighton looked very unlike himself, although he was dressed top-of-the-trees as usual. But he wore no smile, and that was so singu-

lar, she almost didn't recognize him. And she refused
to look at the third person in the room.

"Marjorie," Livvy said, coming forward and taking
her hand, "how enchanting you look. You needn't
quake," she said on a grudging ghost of a smile as
she felt that small hand tremble in hers. "We're not
here to eat you. In fact, we're here to tender our
apologies. We behaved dreadfully to you, every one
of us. Please forgive us."

"Yes," Creighton said, "please do."

And the third visitor said nothing..

"But I am the one who ought to offer my apologies," Marjorie said in a small voice. "I said some
ghastly things."

"With every good reason," Beau finally said.

"But I ought not to have," she said, looking at him,
and then, as unable to look away as she was to judge
what was in those bleak blue eyes, she went on. "I
didn't know your uncle. So I shouldn't have made
any judgments of him. Nor do I know how you
behave to those you consider your equals, so I
ought not to have insulted you as I did. Pray accept
my apologies."

"After you've just done it again, and with equally
good reason?" Beau asked with a small, sad smile.

Livvy looked at him. "Speak for yourself," she
said. "I consider the matter closed, with all apologies
made and accepted. I wish you well, my dear. And
do not wish to make this a protracted visit, as I hope
you can understand. So I shall take my leave now,
good day, Miss Makepeace," she said. "Come along,
Creighton."

Creighton joined her, and took Marjorie's hand in
his turn. But as Beau came up to Marjorie and looked
down at her downcast eyes, Livvy spoke again.

"Not you, Beau. I do not think it advisable. I believe we've caused enough gossip as it is, and if you were seen walking about with me this morning, it would give rise to more than even I could cope with."

He left off gazing at Marjorie to stare at Livvy in puzzlement.

"I sent in the announcement ending our engagement yesterday," she said. "It will be in the *Times* tomorrow, with London's morning toast. I don't wish to end the way Uncle did, you see. Nor do I wish that sort of life on you, Beau. For I have some affection for you—if not, admittedly, the kind required for marriage. Do not argue with me on this, it is done. Even Father understands, and so doubtless he will approve, in time. Give me that time, please. Good day, Marjorie. Good-bye, Beau, make good use of my New Year's gift to you."

She walked to the door, and then turned around once, with what appeared to be a real smile at last.

"I remembered," she said to Beau as he stared at her, "that you detest the heat as much as I do, you see."

Marjorie scarcely believed what she'd heard and seen, and when Livvy had left with Creighton, couldn't find words she could say, much less the ones she knew she should. She didn't need them. He simply pulled her close in his arms, and held her so tightly she couldn't have protested even if she wanted to, or had breath to. When he released her, his eyes were brilliant, and she couldn't tell if it were tears or joy that made them so.

"Marjorie Makepeace," he said hoarsely, before she could summon the protest he knew she felt obligated to, "marry me. Oh my," he said on a boyish laugh, "so many 'm's. But you must," he said, altogether serious now. "I hadn't hoped, I hadn't dreamed of achieving my freedom so soon—but I would have gained it, I vowed it. To myself, of course," he added, "because I'd not shame you again by my attentions until I was free to do so." He laughed again when he heard what he'd said. "Not well phrased," he said. "But you know what I mean. At least I pray you do. As I could only hope you'd remain free until then, as well. Because I was not, not from the moment we met at that ghastly, wonderful funeral, no, nor do I ever wish to be again. Bless Livvy," he said, before he forgot his benefactress and instead kissed the girl he held in his arms.

"No, not a word, unless it is 'I will,' but that's two—oh, Lord, what a simpleton I'm being, and isn't that delightful," he said when he spoke to her again. "You must," he said, shaking her gently. "You cannot leave me now. I don't detest all heat, I need human warmth so very much. Please, don't leave me here to freeze to death for life. Save me from the cursedfamily ice—or the icy-family curse, I cannot stop laughing," he said in delighted amazement with himself, before he did stop abruptly.

He stared down at her with stark entreaty and said quietly, "Oh, God, warm me, love, please. I have been so cold."

"Yes," she said, as she would continue to say for some time, until they recollected themselves and were able to be composed enough to share their happiness with others. "Yes, Beau, be sure, I will."

Livvy strolled down the street with Creighton, having waved away the carriage they'd arrived at the Chesham town house in.

"It's a lovely day, though cold, of course," she remarked, as Creighton tipped his hat to an acquaintance, "and we don't need a closed carriage now. There's no need for subterfuge any longer."

"No?" Creighton asked, carefully.

She almost stumbled, and then turned her face to his, "You romanticize," she said coldly.

"Do I?" he asked. "It was a noble thing. A thing only someone who loved him very much could do. I *am* the eternal observer. And a good one, too. You see, I know you very well. It was a good thing to do, Liv," he said as they strolled on.

"I simply did not wish to end as Uncle did," she said in a steady voice.

"You will not," he assured her. "Uncle never loved anything but his own ease. Uncle could never sacrifice for anything, indeed, for all his tomes, I doubt he knew the meaning of the word. Nor would he," he added, "ever have felt enough for anyone to be able to give away what he most wanted for another person's sake."

"I did not give it away," Livvy disagreed, "for it was not mine to give. Oh, see—there's Talwin. And with a girl young enough to be his daughter. Oh! How disappointing, I believe it *is* his daughter."

She laughed, as did he. But she, because she felt enormous relief in knowing what she'd done was right, and what she'd said so lightly was nevertheless true. For her love for Beau would always be with her, as it had always been: hidden, burning steadily, and true. Except that perhaps now that she'd renounced it to the world, it would continue to burn on within her, thawing her enough so that one day she'd be able to admit love to the one she loved, should she ever love again someday. Now, as she strolled through London's iciest winter, she thought that she might, just might.

Because for all the cold and fear of more, she none-theless felt a warm glow within. And that was enough to keep her from freezing, as she suspected she'd begun to do, just as Marjorie had said, and so that was enough for her, for now.

"Sometimes hath the brightest day a cloud;
And after summer evermore succeeds
Barren winter, with his wrathful nipping cold;
So cares and joys abound, as seasons fleet . . ."
—William Shakespeare

A LOVE FOR
ALL SEASONS

It felt most peculiar to move from one home to another without bringing so much as a stick of furniture along, as if one were merely a goldfish being moved from one bowl to another. But inheritance laws being what they were, and the London home of a belted earl being what it must be, there was little sense in moving furnishings from a country manor to the city. Or so her husband said, and so Rachel agreed was sensible. Still, a small, defiant, nonsensical part of her heart wished she could have brought something familiar along with her, aside from her husband and daughter. For he, too, was recently changed, if only by his new title, and their daughter's name and residence was due to be changed by her new husband in a matter of months. And for all these glorious changes, there was something about them all that made Rachel uneasy and afraid.

But then, doubtless she was a country mouse. Or so she was teased, and so she agreed—when not being teased—she surely must be.

She hadn't brought many servants along either, only two to ensure safe passage to the city, for the house was well staffed, they said. And as she knew that she'd need new clothing to fit her new position, the contours of her traveling cases were decidedly flat. She was, she realized, light in all but spirit as the coach finally stopped before her new home. *Temporary home*, she promised herself as she drew in her breath and put on her gloves. She might be a countess now, and this might be her new London address, but her heart was at home, and home would never be this tall, cold stone slab of a house in the middle of a street of stone. Only the dead ought to reside in avenues of silent stone, she thought, and shuddered.

"Cold? This is a damnably cold winter," her husband said, noticing her trembling. "Told you to wear your heavy pelisse. But no, 'it isn't in fashion,' " he mimicked in a squeaky high voice. "Women," he muttered.

"But it isn't, Papa," his daughter said, laughing. "And you know very well a female would rather freeze to death than be a dowd—as would the gentlemen here in London, or so Nigel says."

At that, both Rachel and husband forgot their private thoughts and glanced at each other, grinning. "Nigel says" was their daughter's favorite phrase these days, and they found it both amusing and sad. Because her independence of spirit had been their delight as well as their despair, and because she was their constant delight, and it meant that she was already gone from them to her fiancé, Nigel, Lord Neville, in many ways.

"Chin up, Mama," Felicia said softly as they mounted the stair, correctly reading her mother's mood, as ever. "You won't step wrong. Manners are manners, country or city. Besides, now you're a countess, and so now you can do no wrong. Nigel says that if you take to plucking chickens in the parlor, they'll think it's the newest rage."

"Where else would I pluck them?" Rachel asked in great amazement, as Felicia laughed.

And then the door swung open.

The butler was impeccably polite, the staff conscientious to the point of embarrassment. Their anxiety to make a good impression on the new Earl and Countess of Chesham—and by so doing, retain their posts in these difficult times—went a long way to making their new employers more confident. Which was all to the good. Neither Hugh nor Rachel Carstairs had been brought up in a barn; they came from the countryside, it was true, but they came from old families and good stock. Still, the sudden elevation from country squire to an earl was dizzying. And their new house boggled them.

It had lofty ceilings and long windows, beautifully inlaid floors made from exotic woods; the staircases twisted and turned to the upper regions of the house with a grace that could only have been born of a true master of architecture, as did each well-proportioned room and tiled fireplace. The furnishings were old, that was true, and doubtless might be considered old-fashioned by those whose lives were ruled by style and who didn't realize true art had nothing to do with fashion. It was a solid, rich, and handsome interior, and paradoxically the very quality of it made the weight of her new position lay heavily on Rachel's heart.

What upset her most was the fact that she and Hugh had been given separate bedchambers. She knew many persons of quality lived that way, but she and Hugh had shared a room and a bed since the night they'd first wed, nineteen years before. Now he was expected to share only a dressing room with her, and she was ashamed to ask his opinion about the matter, or to ask for a change while servants were still hovering about them. But Felicia was delighted with her room and her new home, and her joy, as ever, made everything seem much better.

They saw to the unpacking, and tried to remember the new servants many names and their purposes. When they came downstairs to enjoy a light repast, they found Felicia's fiancé, Nigel, Lord Neville, awaiting them. He'd come to welcome them to London, but only stayed a little while, because, he said, it was lowering to a fellow's feelings to find his every remark, and not only his jests, answered with a yawn. But they'd been on the road since dawn, and when he left, they all eagerly sought their new beds.

When the earl's new valet had left him and Rachel's new maid had left her, Hugh Carstairs, Earl of Chesham, appeared in the doorway between his wife's and his connecting rooms.

"Want me to stay here with you tonight?" he asked.

"I was going to ask you if we should tell them we want to share a room," she murmured, trying to fight sleep so she could answer him.

"Which room should it be?" he asked on a yawn.

"I dunno," Rachel answered groggily, as he approached her bed.

"Hugh," she said, coming wide-awake as she felt his weight on the bed, "you didn't tell your valet you were changing rooms for tonight, did you? But won't he look for you in the morning? My maid will cer-

tainly come in here. I don't want her seeing you, or
him seeing me—in bed."

He remained still, his knee on her bed. They were
as unaccustomed to the many servants they now had
as they were to the rules pertaining to their duties.

"Aye," he said consideringly, the thought of his
elegant valet seeing so much as one of his wife's
round and lace-draped white shoulders, much less
that part of her anatomy that usually greeted the
morning—because she slept on her stomach toward
dawn—making him frown. "Then I'll be off to my
own bed this night. Too tired for anything else anyway," he said, yawning again, and left, listening to
her chuckle trail off in sleep.

She scarcely saw him the next day. He was up and
off after breakfast to meet with his lawyers and fac-
tors to discuss matters to do with his new estate.
And so soon as she'd swallowed the last of her morning coffee, finding London's more fashionable morning chocolate too heavy for such an early hour—
before she discovered that no female but a servant
was supposed to be up and about before noon anyway—Felicia and Lord Neville carried her off to see
a "modiste." Where Nigel left them. The fact that
Rachel had heretofore only patronized dressmakers
was enough to make her follow in silence. But the
first garment she was shown moved her to volatile
speech.

"Heavens no!" she said, appalled. "I thought this
was for my daughter. A pink frock? A skimpy pink
frock with a flowery design, for me? My dear
woman," she said to the modiste, who looked nothing
like any dressmaker she'd ever seen, being thin and
superior, and not at all comfortable-looking, "I am
eight and thirty, far too old for such."

"Woman twice your age, my lady, wear half so much, I assure you," the modiste answered. "The color suits you, and you've still a good form. This is how I believe you ought to look. However, if you disagree and want garments suitable to an aged female, I cannot help you, I'm afraid."

"Mama," Felicia said softly, drawing her mother aside, "Nigel said she's all the crack, the very thing. Everyone uses her, and it is a lovely frock."

"Nigel," Rachel retorted, "knows far too much about females, I think."

"Rather say, 'he did,' that's true," Felicia said, only blushing a little, "for he didn't get that horrid name 'Rake Neville' for nothing. But never say he doesn't know the correct thing to do."

"Of course he does," Rachel said, relenting. "He's marrying you, isn't he? But that frock—I'm eight and thirty, my love. And that frock is simply too, too . . ."

". . . Too beautiful not to get, Mama. At least try it on," her daughter pleaded.

It was lovely, Rachel had to admit. And she still did have a figure, it appeared, or so the frock made it seem, she thought, smiling at her reflection. There was certainly more of her than there had been when she'd last looked so closely, but the extra weight made her rounder in all the salient places, as the modiste delicately put it. The pink hue brought color to her cheeks and made her masses of wavy light brown hair seem to shine. She looked more like her daughter now than ever, except that she was smaller and stouter, as she observed, to much protest. And as she always complained, Felicia had got Hugh's warm brown eyes, not her own boring gray ones. But she still did have long lashes, she noted, and the line of her chin was still firm, as were, remarkably enough, her breasts and her bottom. At least, so they seemed in her new frock. Her new fascination with her body and her foolish giddiness at seeing how well she looked made her feel even younger than her daughter.

The blue gown made her eyes glow, the brown one was elegant, the ribbon-striped one was a work of art, and the several others each had their own charm. She purchased a hat, and then another; they went from shop to shop and with Felicia and the shopkeepers urging her on, she gathered up stockings and fans, shoes and linens, shawls and fichus, all manner of accessories, and at last, that rarest of good things: a warm coat that was both fashionable and flattering.

That night they dined *en famille* with Nigel, and his teasing flattery made Hugh stop and stare at his wife. He noticed the first of her new frocks then, and said, "Oh, yes. Nice, very nice, my dear." Which, while lacking much, pleased her, because she knew it was high praise from him.

The highest praise came later, when all were abed, and he tiptoed into hers.

"You looked beautifully tonight," he said, before he kissed her.

And since he never said more after that first kiss, she only sighed and relaxed in his arms as they made love. It was as comforting and comfortable as always, and warmed and pleased her as it reassured her, as ever. But when he was done, and had complimented her on the pleasure he'd had, as he always did, he sighed deeply, fished at the side of the bed for his nightshirt, pulled it over his head again, and arose from the bed.

"Forgot to tell that blasted Perkins that I was

going to spend the night here," he explained, as she stared up at him. "Didn't think of it, didn't plan to, actually, but you looked so good tonight. If I stay a moment longer, I'll fall asleep, you know that. Good night, sweet," he said, and after kissing her lightly, the same fond kiss that usually ended their nights, he went off to his own room.

She'd never slept alone after love, and when he'd gone, she felt lonely and oddly abandoned—in a new and not altogether unpleasant way. It made her feel less married, she realized sleepily, and that was new enough to be amusing, and amusing enough to chase away the loneliness. She wondered if it were an entirely bad thing, after all, and wondering, fell sleep.

Much teasing, a little taunting, and the good offices of his prospective son-in-law finally got the new Earl of Chesham to Weston for some fine tailoring. A strong sense of duty got him to don his new clothes and pay the social calls he knew he must, just as a love of peace in his family moved him along the many social rounds that a father to a lady who was to be marrying a nobleman must travel. He'd arrived in London with the coldest winter in years, dreading the duties he must shoulder, but shoulder them he did. The best thing about them, he confided to his wife a week after they'd arrived, was that they kept him so busy, he'd little time to think about how tedious it was, and how he yearned to be done with the show, have his daughter wed and accepted, so he could return to the countryside again.

"Which countryside?" she asked worriedly. "The manor is our home. But so now, too, is Four Chimneys, for that's the Earl of Chesham's traditional seat. And we've not so much as seen it above twice in our lives. Where shall we go when we're done here?" she asked, staring out into the dark of her bedchamber as they lay side by side late one night after love, before his departure for his own chamber.

"Aye, well, I've been thinking," he said, crossing his arms behind his head. "You've your friends at home, don't you? And you'd miss them. As I'd miss mine, I'll confess. We've both got ties there—ties? Huh. Say our whole lives and it would be truth. Friends of a lifetime are hard to leave. But Four Chimneys . . . it's hard to leave a great manor house like that to the tender mercies of estate managers. Foolish, too. They can rob a man blind, cheat his tenants, and there's a lot of them depending on us now. Ah, how I wish that old reprobate had lived forever," he said, thinking of his predecessor, "as doubtless the owner of his new manse, the Devil, does now, too."

Rachel couldn't bring herself to say "don't speak ill of the dead," as she ordinarily would, because she couldn't think of a good thing to say about the selfish old fellow who'd been her husband's cousin. Not only hadn't she known him well, she'd been glad of it. A cold old man, devoted to his pleasures, and most of them unseemly for a man of his age—as they'd been since he'd been young.

"Where shall we go then, after Felicia weds Nigel and there's no real need for us to stay on in London? Unless you wish to remain and become a figure of fashion," she teased.

He was glad of a chance to laugh, it helped him delay his answer. Because he didn't know what to say, duty and desire warred within him.

And she, who so often gave him excellent advice,

had none to spare, for she'd the same conflicts. He ought to go to Four Chimneys, and as his wife, she thought, she ought to urge him to. But oh, how she'd miss the last of her family, and those friends who'd become family over all the years. She'd been born and raised near to his home, they'd shared their youth, and courted in their backyards, quite literally. They'd married and had expected someday to be buried not far from where they were baptized and wed, in the southernmost corner of the old churchyard, where their two infant sons were already awaiting Judgment Day. But now this . . . she didn't know what to tell him anymore than he knew what to do.

"We've weeks, months yet, to decide," he finally said, and she sighed with relief as he arose and bent to kiss her, for not thinking about a thing was sometimes the most comfortable, if not the smartest thing to do. But one grew weary of being clever, she thought sleepily.

For example, she remembered as he passed through the dressing room on his way to his own bedchamber, she ought to have asked why they didn't just share a room now instead of just a bed now and then, now that they'd realized the servants would accept anything they were pleased to do. But she hesitated to, for now there was a new niggling doubt in her mind, since he'd not said another word on the subject. And so she found that not thinking about that, too, was a far better thing to do. Just exactly as he did, when he reached his own cold bed.

They hadn't been in London for over a week when they received an unexpected visitor. A lovely girl, fair and fragile-looking but well-spoken and with a light of intelligence in her eyes that struck a corres-

ponding chord in Felicia, both of her parents could
see that. Miss Marjorie Makepeace was almost
exactly Felicia's age, as well. The old scoundrel
who'd been the last earl had been her grandfather,
although in his anger at his son, who'd been brave
enough to defy him, he'd kept her existence a secret
from the rest of the family. She was cousin to them,
an orphan, and had inherited little more than a token
bequest and the knowledge of their existence. Yet if
she were to be believed, and Hugh Carstairs thought
he knew enough of people to judge that she was, she
wanted nothing from them but that, for she'd pre-
cious little other family in the world.

But she needed more, that was clear to see. She
was from the countryside of Worcester, in London
for the first time, too, and staying with the Honorable Miss Peckingham, a redoubtable young woman
of such high fashion and sangfroid, that she made
even the earl's impeccable butler a trifle unsure of
himself. She and her two handsome male cousins,
who accompanied her everywhere, were top-of-the-
trees, ornaments of the *ton*, and fashionables par
excellence. It was clear to the new Earl of Chesham
that the poor girl was misplaced, a violet that had
somehow found itself in a hothouse full of orchids.

As Rachel sat in the drawing room with her husband, their newfound cousin, Felicia and Nigel, as
well as Miss Peckingham and her two constant
escorts, all this became clear to her, too. It was
equally evident that the girl had much in common
with Felicia, and that, moreover, the girls liked each
other on sight. Naturally then, Felicia would want
her to stay on with them. Indeed, she deserved to,
she was family. Yet Rachel wished she would not,
even as she prepared to ask her to.

Not that there was anything wrong with her. Nor, for a moment, did Rachel worry that her reformed rake of a prospective son-in-law might be enticed by her beauty. Not only did she think Felicia handsomer, and Miss Makepeace not at all the sort of girl who'd cast sheep's eyes at another girl's beloved, but she knew Nigel to be so far in love with Felicia that all other women became little more than background to the one ornament in his besotted eye. In any event, she'd seen an unguarded look Miss Makepeace cast at one of Miss Peckingham's exquisite cousins, and knew there was an altogether different sort of heartbreak waiting to happen there. Yes, clearly the girl badly needed friends and family. But so, Rachel thought guiltily, did she.

Felicia had been as much friend as daughter to her. Since she'd met Nigel, of course, she'd had less time and inclination to sit with her mama and gossip and thrash out all the problems of their immediate world. This was good and natural, and though Rachel might miss her daughter's undivided love, she'd never want it otherwise. Then, too, she was worldly wise enough to know that even if things would never be the same again between mother and daughter, they'd eventually return somewhat more to normal, in time, when the novelty of marital love wore off, or rather, wore on for Felicia.

But she missed her now, and knew that if Miss Makepeace came to stay, it would be only natural for Felicia to have more in common with her, and so there'd be even less left for her mother. And how she needed someone to confide in, chat with, and laugh with these trying days. Because Hugh was so often away now and the world was suddenly all as new to her as if she'd been a young girl, too, again.

And, she thought, before she immediately suppressed the thought, as her daughter had been born nine months to the night she'd been wed, she'd never been completely alone with him for over nine months, all told, in all of their nineteen years together.

But the girl smiled bravely now as Hugh invited her to stay on with them. She shook her fair head in the beginning of a denial, although all her desire to agree was clear to read in her young, defenseless eyes. Rachel was used to being mother, and couldn't have stopped what she found herself saying next even if she had wanted to.

"Do come stay with us, dear," Rachel said. "This place has dozens of rooms. Stay at least until Felicia weds this spring, and then," she said with dawning pleasure as a new and happy inspiration came to her, proving that further good comes from good deeds, "after, as well, if you can remain single yourself. For when she leaves us, we'll likely be dreadfully lonely."

"Oh piffle!" Felicia jested. "What a bouncer! They can't wait to hand me off to this dreadful fellow. But please, Cousin, come stay with me, at least until I wed."

They made jests, and then discussed it, and in the end, just as Rachel hoped and feared, Miss Makepeace breathed a heavy sigh, and smiling as though the weight of the world was off her slender shoulders at last, agreed to be their guest.

And just as Rachel had suspected, the addition of one to their small family soon led to a subtraction of two. For Felicia and Marjorie went everywhere together, and Rachel was wise enough to know when she was not needed.

The house seemed very still. It was not, of course. A dozen servants were busy within it, clearing up after dinner, readying beds for the night. But the thick oriental carpets absorbed the sounds of footfalls, and the bare wooden floors between were so well waxed that no one dared hurry without risking a broken limb or neck. Soft, considered steps were safest, as well as most correct for the servants who silently glided about their many errands while the master and the mistress of the house sat in the drawing room, sipping after-dinner drinks and trying to make conversation to defeat the deafening stillness in the house.

They never said so in so many words, of course.

"You look very well, tonight," the Earl of Chesham informed his wife.

She did, and she knew it, and the compliment made her feel bad. The ribbon-striped frock cried out to be seen by more than a husband of nearly nineteen years. At least tonight it did. It seemed youth was contagious. Dangerously so. Felicia and Marjorie had dressed in her bedchamber so that they could all laugh, gossip, and compliment each other while they were doing so—Marjorie had turned out to be the most charming girl—and then Felicia and Marjorie had gone out for an evening at the opera, on the arms of Nigel and one of his friends. And Rachel, who'd known she looked well, as well as having been told so by her maid, both girls, Nigel, and his friend, had stayed home to dine with Hugh. And now sat looking at him in the drawing room, listening to the mantel clock tick the night away.

She was here because Hugh detested the opera, the young people ought to have time alone together, and Nigel's elderly widowed aunt was a perfect chaperon . . . and perhaps, as Nigel had jested, Rachel thought with a sudden surge of unfamiliar despair, she really was too young to be a chaperon. But tonight she envied one.

"You look very well yourself tonight," she told her husband.

So he did. His new dark blue velvet jacket was fashionably tight, but not strained at the shoulder, despite the fact that his shoulders were very wide; and his buff pantaloons showed a trim waist and shapely, muscular leg. Hugh was only of average height, but he'd always been a bruising rider and a hearty outdoorsman, so although he was heavier than he'd been as a youth, the weight had gone to bulk and width, his naturally muscular body was still agile and strong. He'd a constant tan from all his outdoor activities; even in London, he'd found time to walk and ride. His hair was cropped short, but he still had all of it, and it was a rich brown, as was his handsomest feature, his clear brown eyes. He'd regular features and strong white teeth—save for a fretful molar he'd sacrificed the previous summer. In sum, Rachel thought, he looked very well for his years. For he was two years older than she was, and so if she suddenly felt eight and thirty wasn't as ancient as she'd felt of late, why then, forty wasn't either.

"Everything's in order for the party, I've even ordered up some mistletoe, as Felicia demanded. What harm, after all? She's engaged," Rachel reported.

"Hmm. What harm, indeed?" he asked. "Perhaps it will even give little Marjorie a chance to be soundly bussed by someone so she can forget that rogue she keeps her eye on. I'm surprised at her. Sensible chit, and yet she's obviously pining for that ice princess's fiancé."

"Oh, Miss Peckingham's cousin? Ah well, Hugh,

when is love ever sensible? Or don't you remember?"
Rachel teased.

"Why, we were, to be sure," he said offhandedly.
"We knew each other since infancy. I might have
been the first thing you saw when you opened your
eyes, poor mite. As for me, I don't recall a time when
you weren't there. Our marrying was as sensible as
could be."

She sat up straight, feeling as though she'd been
insulted. But it was only true. Now she looked back
on it, she couldn't remember any heartburnings,
tears, and fears, such as Felicia had suffered before
she'd brought the clever Lord Neville to his knees.
Nor could she recall looking at Hugh as though her
heart were in her eyes, and then looking away before
anyone else could guess that it was, as poor Marjorie
did whenever she saw the cold and heartless Lord
Beauford, Miss Peckingham's icy blond cousin. No,
she and Hugh had gone from hand in hand at childhood games to hand in hand at the altar, without a
serious doubt as to the course they were taking or
each other's feelings about it. Her parents had
approved as heartily as his had done, and with good
cause. They suited and had always done.

But now, for the first time, Rachel wondered if
she'd not missed something along the way, for all the
happiness she'd had and the good sense in what she'd
done. It was beyond foolish to regret missing pain
and doubt, and she knew it. And so she told herself
again.

"Good thing Marjorie came to stay with us," he
said.

"Yes, very," she agreed, and looked at the clock.

It was only ten o'clock. She wouldn't get a wink of
sleep until Felicia came home. She knew Felicia was

safe with Nigel. But still, this was London, there were footpads and theater fires, and carriages lost wheels as often as horses ran mad anywhere on earth. No, she wouldn't sleep until Felicia came safely home, though doubtless Hugh would. He was already yawning.

He'd go up to bed soon, he thought. Not that he was tired, but there wasn't anything else to do, and he didn't want to be found sitting at the doorstep like an old watchdog when the young people came home. Young people . . . he smiled to himself at that. He didn't think he'd ever been as young as Nigel, for Nigel was perhaps the worldliest young fellow he'd ever known. But he'd never been so young as to be so obviously madly in love. Nigel stared at Felicia as though he were afraid she was going to be snatched away from him if he took his eyes off her. It would be embarrassing if it weren't so humorous, although the naked hunger for her that flashed in Nigel's eyes now and again was definitely embarrassing for her father to see.

You'd think the lad could conceal it better, Hugh mused, since the fellow's reputation would guarantee he'd had dozens of women . . . Hugh squirmed in his chair, as though it had got too hard for him. For here he was, about to be a father-in-law, and perhaps soon after—from the look in the lad's eyes—a grandfather, and yet he'd had only two women in his whole life. And as for the 'lad,' he realized with a sudden jolt, why, Nigel, Lord Neville, was nigh on to eight and twenty, and he himself was only forty. Only a little over a decade separated them and yet here he was, a prospective grandfather, and Nigel, who'd had vastly more sexual experiences, was going to marry an eighteen-year-old. His daughter. It boggled the mind

and distressed him unduly now. But not because of
any fears for Felicia.

Nigel had bedded so many women that he'd likely
forgotten half of them. Hugh himself had bedded
two, and where he'd hardly forget his own wife, he
never would forget that other either. He'd paid for
her, and it had been a sorry business, lasting only
long enough to prove to him that he could do it. But
she'd had long dark hair, little pear-shaped breasts,
a dark mole on her belly near to her navel, and a
crooked front tooth. She kissed hot and wet, and she
was nothing like Rachel in skin, hair, scent, or tex-
ture, and because of that he never forgot a moment
of it.

He looked over to Rachel, feeling oddly guilty for
that unforgettable moment, over twenty years ago.
But he'd not been promised to her then. Still, he
ought not to think of the two in the same day, much
less moment, he told himself. Rachel was his friend
and lover, and mother of his children. There'd been
three, only the one had lived, and that was still their
only great grief. They'd been very well suited, and
had been smart enough to know it.

But still, he couldn't help but wonder how many
women Nigel had had. And what harm had it done
him? And why was he himself yawning and longing
for bed, when he knew Rachel wouldn't make love to
him until Felicia had come home and told her everything that had happened this night, and by then, he'd
be too far gone in sleep to care anymore. And so then
he was yawning and longing for bed, he thought with
a sudden chill, because he was getting old. He found
himself hating the ticking of the mantel clock.

But there were safer, respectable, honest ways to

stave off boredom and the passing of time, he remembered, and relaxed.

"I've been asked to join Whites. And Boodles and Brooks, and several other clubs of all political and intellectual stripes," he found himself saying. "Well, the title gives me entrée, and Nigel says . . . aye, laugh, but sometimes one must say 'Nigel says,' for he knows a thing or two about London. There are some good chaps that belong there. Would you mind?" he asked, for he never did anything without discussing it with her. Although now it sounded odd to his own ears for a grown man, and an earl, no less, to be asking his wife's permission to do what every other gent in London did as a matter of course.

"I mean to say," he said in some embarrassment for his shame at what had always been a foundation to their relationship, as well as for it, "I'd likely be passing some time there, but you're so busy with Felicia and Marjorie, and wedding plans, and spending all our money these days, I thought you'd not mind if I found a sanctuary for every now and then."

"I thought you'd rather join a coaching club, like the Four-In-Hand that Nigel spoke about, or pass your time at Tattersall's looking at livestock to ride in the park," she said, her head to the side, watching him curiously.

"Ah, well, that too, perhaps. What do you think?" he asked.

"But what about my time, when I'm not with Felicia? Which is more and more these days," she said sadly in return.

"What about the other mothers?" he asked.

"Oh yes," she said in some annoyance, "the very thing. I've so much in common with London matrons.

Most have dozens of children, it seems, who take up all their thoughts."

He sensed her pain and began to speak, to change the subject if he could, even if it meant he must put off the idea of gentlemen's clubs for a space, but she went on before he could interrupt her.

"And those who do not have hordes of children are not interested in a lady in for the Season from the countryside. Ah, but the days are no problem, women are accustomed to being alone then. But the evenings . . . Shall I ask Lady Leith to dine with me, Mrs. Merriman to the opera, and then ask a dowager duchess to a ball? Do be serious. A lady needs an escort, and I will not sink to stealing Felicia's or Marjorie's. Or sit in the corner like a good chaperon. Shall we compromise? You take me to the sort of *ton* parties we've passed up because you detest 'doing the pretty,' as you always say, as well as to the theater and opera, and I shan't make a peep of protest about your clubs."

"Bother," he said crossly, "I will, when I can. The other times—why, why don't you go with the children, eh? I'm sure you'll find good company once you're there."

"Oh surely, for dancing and dining? Not that I couldn't find any. You wouldn't mind if I took an occasional twirl with a tall, dark, interesting stranger?" she asked slyly, "as so many fashionable ladies of London do, as Nigel says." She grinned like a girl and added mischievously, "Or shared my pâté and champagne with one or two?"

"Rachel, my love," he said, laughing, "I've known you forever. You'd not play me false. So what if you twirl and sup with fascinating gents? I'd not mind if it made you happy . . . and spared me the effort of capering and clucking at all those parties. But only at the parties, mind," he added with mock threat when he saw how still she'd grown, for he didn't mean to hurt her, only to save himself from the miseries of the fashionable life. And the new and dangerous thoughts of age and missed opportunities that plagued him.

"Well, very well," she replied, "and mind you don't game the house out from under us, or drink it away."

They both laughed, for he'd a hard head, and had no use for games of chance.

"I do think," she said after another moment, "you're quite right. We ought to go out more. We're not that old, are we?"

"Decidedly not!" he said bracingly.

And then they sat and listened to the mantel clock.

It was not only amusing, it was delightful, and there was nothing to fear after all, Rachel discovered. London never minded a respectable titled lady, matron or not, going unescorted to a *ton* party. In fact, London approved! At home, she'd be expected to give her host and hostess a dozen pardons and a firm excuse if Hugh didn't accompany her. If he didn't two times in a row, the gossip would be flying. Here, Rachel thought, as she moved through another country dance, the talk began when a lady came to two parties in a row with her own husband! She smiled to herself, and her partner, an earnest, balding bachelor who loved to dance as much as he hated to speak, smiled back at her. Delightful lady, he thought, as had all of her partners tonight. Or so they'd said.

The elderly Mr. Greeley had thought her a pretty lady with a sweet smile, and so he'd told her; the handsome, if effeminate Lord Skyler, though years her junior, made her feel very young again with his fulsome compliments on her gown and her hair. Lord Dearborne, who was only a boy and yet far too rackety to be let near Felicia, nevertheless flirted outrageously with her, and the widowed Mr. Billings, just Hugh's age, and very like to him in many ways, told her she was the nicest thing that had happened to him all evening. Heady stuff, even if none of it were true, she thought, curtsying to her partner and beaming at his pleasure.

And then Lord Wycoff bore her off to the waltz she'd promised him. He was Hugh's age or older, but London born and London bred, and polished to a high and unnatural sheen on the Continent. Taller than Hugh, and more classically handsome, too, he'd fine light brown hair and a cool smile. He was witty, attentive, and an excellent dancer. But for all his smiles and grace, he made her feel awkward and countrified, because he seemed to be amused, and she couldn't be sure it wasn't with her.

"Now what could I have said to make you crease that fair forehead in a frown?" he asked, as they danced.

"Nothing," she said.

"Ah, then what is it that you think I ought to have said?" he asked, "and I shall."

Too much for her, she thought, looking up into his amused eyes, she'd heard of such gentlemen, and for all she was a mature matron and far beyond the age of silliness, he made her pulses race and her tongue feel thick. She'd heard of such gentlemen and was thrilled to have met one, but oh, he was far, far too much for her. And because she was what she was, she told him so.

"You, my lord, are far too much for me," she confessed, laughing, to take the tension from the moment. "I'm a countrywoman, and cannot hope to match wits with you. I think that's why I was frowning. You're a new breed entirely to me, sir."

"As you are to me, perhaps that's why I find you enchanting," he replied. "Apart from your lovely complexion, speaking eyes, and your abundant charms, that is to say."

"Oh my!" she said, laughing honestly now, looking far younger than she knew. "That's just what I mean! My husband would be shocked," she added, so as to let him know, if he were not joking, which he surely was, that she was wed and never forgot it for a moment. "But not perhaps, as shocked as I am. We don't say such things in the country, you see—unless we're very young and free."

"But you make me feel young, and I am free," he said, as he continued to dance, not missing a step. "And my wife wouldn't be at all shocked, except perhaps, if I were slow-top enough not to tell you how I felt. For we are not, I remind you, in the country now."

She couldn't say a thing more, and they danced the dance through to the end in silence. He held her no closer than necessary, but it seemed very close to her now. Ludicrous really, she scolded herself, keeping her eyes from his knowing ones, for she was eight and thirty and had a beautiful daughter about to be wedded. She decided that her wits had been overset by chivalry, and hoped she wouldn't become like one of those foolish matrons at home: seeing compliments in common courtesies, flustered at a butcher's sally, flattered by a schoolboy's glance. But there was that in the way he moved, and that in his lazy eyes when he caught her trying to steal a guarded glance at him, that stirred feelings long forgotten, ones no one but Hugh had a right to, and she'd all she could do to keep her mind on the dance.

When the music stopped, he bowed. When he straightened and looked down at her again, his smile became a fraction warmer and almost human.

"Don't fret, my lovely country lady," he said softly. "It is London, and it is a game here. Only a game."

"Oh," she said with relief, "thank you."

And then not knowing why she'd thanked him, she blushed, and he paused and said, "Enchanting," before he left her, smiling his usual cool smile again.

But then she left off dancing for a space, and sought Felicia and Nigel. Dancing with strange men was innocent enough, and there was no harm in it— or so she'd believed before she'd danced with Lord Wycoff. But he'd made her wonder at how odd it was to feel a different-sized man in her arms, to breathe in the scent of oriental spices, not soap and bay rum while in a man's close embrace; he'd made her see how different it was to look up into a pair of blue, not brown, eyes when she wished to know how she made a man feel. And to have to look so far up, at that, and seem to see something he ought not feel, or at least, reveal. She sought Felicia and Nigel because she didn't want to risk another dance. Or see him dancing with another. Or see him looking at her. Or think about the dance they'd had anymore at all.

Although she did, of course, that night alone in her bed, because even though she'd come home late, Hugh came home long after that. She heard him and noted the hour, because she couldn't get to sleep. He didn't make much noise, but she heard him nevertheless, although he only paused at the door to their connecting rooms before he went to his own chamber, thinking she was just as sound asleep as she wanted him to be.

He'd been to his favorite new club. And then to a gaming hell, where he'd watched a few fools lose more than they could afford, but then, he realized, he'd think that even if they were Midas's, because he was not a gamester. Then he'd gone with a few new friends to a convivial tavern, and laughed immoderately at some outrageous jests. Late in the night, as the other fellows had begun to leave, one by one, to go to their beds or those of their mistresses, he'd left them, surprised to find the night had fled so fast. It never passed so quickly at home, he'd have been abed for hours by now, at home.

But London never slept, and he felt pleasantly tired, not weary, and excited by the fact that he didn't seem to need to sleep as much anymore. He hadn't done more in the day than ride in the morning and walk to his club, and at night he'd done nothing more than drink, laugh, and tell stories, listen to better ones, and then, when he decided he'd had enough, go home. But that had made him feel young and free. Because, he realized, as he finally laid his head upon his pillow, he suddenly was. Everything he'd done all day and night had been for his own amusement and done at his own pace. And it was delightful, because, he realized, he'd never been his own man before.

They met in the morning, at the breakfast table.

"Where's Felicia?" Hugh asked.

"Still abed, as is Marjorie. Poor children. The young need their sleep," Rachel said as she buttered her toast.

"Ah, and you're so ancient, you don't? I think I see a few shadows beneath your eyes, old woman," Hugh said, jesting, and then looked closer to see he'd spoken the truth. She'd such fragile skin, he could always know how she'd slept at a glance, and now he saw telltale shadows under her eyes.

"I was up late last night," she said, lowering her lashes and her head, as if to avoid his gaze. "I'm a country mouse, remember? Speaking of rodents, you, my good old man, must have come in with the bats, for I never heard you at all."

"Well, you know how it is," he said, picking up his newspaper.

"No, I don't," she said softly. "Did you have a good time?" He must have, she thought. For all that he'd gotten to bed so late, his tan skin glowed and his eyes were clear. When he was out of sorts in any way, he grew sallow and his eyes dimmed. But now he looked rested, and pleased with himself and his world.

"I did," he said, putting his paper down and smiling at her. "What can I tell you? Nothing. That's just it. Do you know, I did absolutely nothing of any merit or import to speak of, but I did have a good time at it. There are some lovely chaps here in town; I must introduce you to them when they come to the Christmas party we've planned."

"Good," she said absently. "Be sure to look over my list to see that I've included them."

They'd planned a party to formally introduce themselves to the *ton* so Felicia would be established in her own right when she wed her infamous Nigel. It was also a way to firmly establish his new, good name. He was more aware of the importance of that than they'd been. For it was he who'd insisted on a few months wait, instead of marrying Felicia at once, as he'd longed to do after he'd declared himself. But he wanted no one able to so much as hint that there'd been a need for hasty nuptials.

"And you?" he asked. "Did you have a good time? Or need I ask?"

She glanced up at him and hesitated. What was there to say? That she'd badly frightened herself because she'd unexpectedly found herself drawn to another man? Yes, of course, she thought, smiling at the very idea of saying that to him. He saw the little burgeoning grin and prepared to smile himself, and when she looked at him, she saw it.

"I had a lovely time," she said, and added defiantly, almost hoping he might see beneath her words. "And I might just have a few lovely gentlemen to introduce you to, too."

He saw nothing but teasing in her comment. He trusted her entirely, the idea of her infidelity in thought or deed never so much as occurred to him. He laughed.

"I don't doubt it," he said. "I'd best brush up on my dancing skills so that I can at least compare to them. So then, sweet, not in such a lather to run home now anymore, eh?"

She sighed and hesitated, taking advantage of the morsel of toast in her mouth that prevented her from answering immediately. For she'd thought a great deal during her restless night, and had decided London had only done what it had done to generations of innocents in the past. It had presented her with opportunity. In her case, the opportunity to see that she couldn't trust herself as implictly as she'd thought; to see that temptation was not beyond her, however content she'd thought she was. But the long dark hours had also shown her that opportunity was not the same as destiny. She'd really only herself to fear. And although, being sane, she always fled what truly frightened her, it simply wasn't possible to escape herself.

Of course, if Hugh had wished to leave, she'd have been grateful. Removing the source of temptation was an excellent way of handling it. After all, when Felicia had been an infant, it had been far simpler to remove a sharp object from her view than to continually tell her no and no again. She'd learned over the years that it wasn't always possible, or even sensible, to face all challenges. Sometimes flight was right. In the countryside, Lord Wycoff could become a memory—in time, perhaps, even a pleasantly titillating one to dream about as she sat by the fire. Here, in London, he was real, near, and dangerous as the fire itself. If Hugh had been so much as bored, or unimpressed with London as he'd been before, she'd have urged him to go.

But he looked so very happy now. She couldn't insist on leaving if he wanted to stay. That would be craven. And how should she explain it? No, she could, she reasoned, simply avoid Lord Wycoff. Ask him to the party, of course, and then avoid him. She had to learn how to do that, after all, if she were going to stay on here. There well might be others like him, however impossible that seemed just now.

"No," she finally said on a sigh, "no, I'm not about to rush home. Are you?"

"No," he said in all honesty. "No, of course I'm not."

Felicia looked beautiful. Her gown was white, as befit a young girl, but it was draped with silver net and festooned with sparkling brilliants, and her white neck glistened with icy-faceted diamonds, to show that she was a wealthy, privileged young lady as well. Her tall, thin fiancé was her perfect accessory tonight, because he looked elegantly slim in his evening clothes, and indeed, the consummate sophisticate, he moved as gracefully as he spoke. And as ever, sophisticate or not, he couldn't take his eyes from her, and those intent eyes, as one wit murmured, clearly showed everything else he wished to take off her.

Marjorie Makepeace stood near the happy couple, dressed in flowing green velvet, her fair hair dressed high, with a borrowed necklace of silver, and wreathed with shy smiles, she resembled a dainty Christmas spirit visiting earth for one joyous night.

Hugh, in the receiving line next to Felicia, looked handsome, proud, as at home in his evening clothes as though he'd been born to the purple, and not merely succeeded to an earldom by the laws of inheritance and the hand of chance. Rachel stood next to him, and wore a close-fitting gown of dark silver silk, with a series of narrow silver satin panels at the hem. Opals glowed at her breast, and her hair had been swept up to show more opals shifting light at the lobes of her ears. She'd thought to compliment Felicia, to echo her beauty in a restrained manner. But the silver made her dark gray eyes shine and dance with light, and the opals discovered all the hidden tones in her brown hair and made them gleam, and the sinuous material showed her form to perfection. She looked regal and lovely; a ripened rose to her daughter's budding beauty. Or so, at least, Nigel said, before he added how grateful he was to see what Felicia would become in time.

He could scarcely be more grateful than his many friends and relatives, who finding their rake restored to respectability and discovered to joy, were in such high spirits that their gladness lightened the entire atmosphere. And so, as ever where there are genuinely happy guests, all the company became infected, since high spirits are—after alcoholic ones—the most contagious of human creation. Everything added to the mirthful atmosphere.

The house was hung with evergreens for the Christmas season, as well as all manner of exquisite red and white flowers, all blooming deliciously out of season. The fireplaces roared out welcomes, the tunes the musicians played were all popular pieces, interspersed with carols, not the more usual classical pieces generally performed at *ton* parties. Because, as Nigel said, the best music was the music one wanted to sing along with, not merely admire.

But for a moment, Rachel found her spirits flattened. Because in that moment, when Hugh turned to talk with a new acquaintance and Felicia, Neville and Marjorie chatted with their friends, she found herself alone, staring at the Christmas greens and suddenly wondering what they were all doing at home now.

The Amberlys were probably entertaining, as usual. Which meant Sally Hanscomb was likely three sheets to the wind by now, after three cups of John Amberly's punch, which he always vowed was made only from juices and spices, and which always reeked of rum. They'd be telling the same jokes and reviewing the same stories, and soon they'd go outside to welcome the wassailers in for a cup of cheer. She'd have been singing again, Rachel thought, seeing far beyond the swag of pine she was staring at. Then she'd be laughing as she came in from the cold, removed her shawl, and heard John Amberly telling the vicar's wife it was only fruit juices and spices, and hearing the vicar say dryly, as he always did as he accepted a cup, "Yes, yes, entirely true, sugarcane's a spice, to be sure, and even spicier when it ferments for a spell, isn't it? Thank you, most kind."

"What? Tears in those magnificent eyes on this magnificent night?" Lord Wycoff asked. "No, I was mistaken," he said as Rachel returned to her time and place with a start. "It must have been a trick of the light, for see, she smiles, the sun comes out from behind thunderclouds—or does it? My lady, your misty gray eyes grow solemn and gay by turns, like an unsettled day. But it's lovely to see. Allow me to present my wife: Harriet, this is the Countess of Chesham. Is she not as charming as I said? Countess: my wife, the Lady Harriet."

Rachel smiled and curtsied, and did all she knew she must as Hugh greeted the couple in his turn. Lady Wycoff was slim, attractive in an unspectacular fashion, and seemed as bored as was proper to be at a social event in London, for she smiled her thin smile and yet all the while her clever eyes kept scanning the crowd beyond her hosts as though looking for more interesting persons. But Lord Wycoff, for all he dutifully greeted everyone in the receiving line and said all that was correct, nevertheless seemed only to gaze at his hostess, and did it with such easy charm that it was impossible to say there was anything irregular about it.

Rachel's thoughts never wandered again after he'd arrived, although she used every mental trick she knew to keep her eyes from following her present thoughts.

In time, the music struck up a lilting waltz, and Hugh took to the dance floor with Felicia as Nigel made his bows to Rachel, and with the assembled guests loudly commenting on how charming it was, they opened the ball. When Hugh relinquished Felicia to Nigel, he came to Rachel, bowed as though he were a stranger, and smiling, took her into his arms to finish the first waltz. In that moment, Rachel felt her heart quiet and her pulses return to their usual tranquil pace. She gazed up at Hugh as if she really were about to dance with him for the first time, and saw such admiration and pleasure in his dark eyes that she felt all her wrought-up tensions evaporate.

His face, his arms, his scent, all was familiar, and yet tonight unfamiliar because he was dressed so grandly, because of late they'd been living separately for the first time in such a very long time, and because this was a new circumstance and new milieu for both of them. It was bittersweet and curious, as exciting as it was commonplace, like coming home to a beloved stranger.

Rachel moved into his arms as they stepped lightly into the dance, and waited to hear him say healing words so that her night would be saved, her tranquility spared, and her joy complete.

"Devilishly fine do," he said happily. "You've done us proud, old woman."

It was a jest. It was their oldest one. He'd called her that since the first day they'd wed. It was only a jest, she reminded herself.

"Thank you," she said. Then, shaking off the jest

and seeking more in his words and eyes, she asked, "Do you like the way I look?"

"Certainly," he said, astonished. "Didn't I say so? Well, and if I didn't, be sure I should have. You're looking very fine."

"Do you like this gown?" she persisted, even as she began to wonder what it was exactly that she was waiting to hear him say.

"Oh yes. Very nice, very nice. Is it new?" he asked.

"Yes," she said, growing vexed, wanting to step on his toes, and not entirely sure why, "I just wondered if you liked it."

"Why, of course, I do." he said warmly. "I'd have sent you right upstairs to change if I didn't think so."

She thought it fortunate for him as well as herself that the music stopped then.

But as she surveyed her guests when the next dance began, she thought it very dangerous. Because she saw Lord Wycoff smiling at her as if he knew precisely what had been said, as he made his way through the throng toward her.

A hostess has a thousand things to do, Rachel told herself, smiling back at him as absently as she could, as though he were only another one of all her invited guests, before she beat a retreat into the crowd, off the dance floor, to chat with the wallflowers, dowagers, chaperons, and generally decrepit who sat in a line at the outskirts of the dancing. And then there were the shy guests to see to, and the young ones to introduce to each other, and the old ones to compliment on how well they looked. A ball in London was not so different from one in the country, she thought as the night went on, save for the fact that the persons here were sometimes famous, often fabulously

wealthy, frequently capable of destroying one's reputation, and one in particular, who continually smiled
as he watched her at all her hostessing chores,
lethally dangerous in more ways than she dared
count.

Dinner was served buffet style, and though she sat
at a table with Hugh, Felicia, Neville, and Marjorie,
she scarcely had time to speak with them, for there
were so many other things to see to, thank heavens,
she thought. She never left off directing the servants, though she seemed to be chatting with her
family and never left her seat. But a raised brow
brought hot prawns to replace the cold ones, a nod
refilled glasses, and an inclined head could send a
footman scurrying to replace napery. A good hostess
never ate so much as tasted, never chatted so much
as listened, never drank so much as watched to see
how much her guests were drinking.

When dinner was done, the dancing began again,
as did her other duties. She seldom saw Hugh, for
he was busy at his chores, as well, but when the
night was almost done, she caught sight of Marjorie
and the sight halted her in her tracks. For the girl
was ashen, and seemed on the verge of tears. Rachel
hadn't far to look to seek for the cause. Lord Beauford, icily handsome and clever young Lord Beauford, cousin, constant companion, and fiancé to Miss
Peckingham, was staring at Marjorie bleakly, with a
strained white look about his handsome mouth. Marjorie fled the room, and Rachel followed swiftly.

The blond girl hesitated at the entrance to the
lady's withdrawing room, and then spun about and
flew down the long hall, seeking the door that led to
the small back garden. Rachel paused. No harm
would come to the child outside, but it was icy cold

tonight, and she wondered if she should follow, if only to talk her into the warm house again. As she wondered what to do, Marjorie reappeared, her pale cheeks stung by the cold to a semblance of health. The cold must have restored her in other ways, because her step was firm and she no longer seemed distressed.

But then she passed beneath a sprig of mistletoe on her way back to the ballroom, and Lord Beauford stepped out of a shadow, enfolded her in his arms, and kissed her. Deeply and thoroughly. And moreover, Rachel thought in dismay, Marjorie made no attempt to break free.

Rachel wondered if, as hostess, relative, and experienced older female, it was her place to act, and hoped it was not. Before she could decide, the couple sprang apart, and it was difficult, not merely because of the shadows, to see which of them was more moved, shamed, and overset. They stood staring at each other, and Rachel had the happy notion to step forward and appear to have just happened upon them, in order to end the moment. As she took that first step, Miss Peckingham and her other cousin, Lord Creighton, moved out into the light and confronted the dazed couple.

"Good heavens, Beau, I understand, but I doubt Marjorie will," Miss Peckingham informed her fiancé in a voice that sounded more peevish than outraged.

Rachel closed her eyes. It wasn't merely that a scandal at her ball would be dreadful for Felicia, she felt dreadful for all the parties concerned.

"Very sad, true," Lord Wycoff said softly at her ear, and as she literally jumped and turned around to see him gazing down at her, he went on in a low voice, which nevertheless overrode all sense of what

Miss Peckingham continued to say, "but never fear. Lavinia Peckingham is up to all the rigs. She knows how to quash scandal, the gentlemen are not likely to come to blows, and they're all too bright to make a fuss over this. Come, come away, there's nothing you can do here but intrigue your guests should they come in search of you. And we don't want that, do we?"

She shook her head dumbly, let him take her hand, and they walked off down the hall toward the ballroom once again.

"Now, don't I deserve a dance with you for that?" he asked when he'd gotten her into the light once more.

He did, and her thanks, but as she looked up into his searching eyes, Rachel knew no power on earth could move her into his arms in front of everyone at this ball.

"I have offended you?" he asked softly.

"No, not in the least," she said, biting her lower lip.

His eyes watched her mouth as he asked, with something very like laughter in his voice, despite how somber he sounded, "Then I wonder why you've avoided me all night? A very busy hostess is our Countess Chesham, but busiest of all whenever I happen by. Why is that, do you think?"

She could not play his game, and was wise enough to know it. All she knew was honesty, and she gave him that.

"What is it you want?" she asked in a small voice, trying to surprise some reciprocal honesty from his eyes, if not his lips.

But his eyes remained fond and amused, as he answered.

"A dance?" he asked as reply.

She shook her head in the negative, like an abashed schoolgirl, hating the fact that she couldn't accuse him as answer.

"You're right," he said, and her eyes flew wide.

"What I want is exactly what you think I want. Delight. Mutual delight. Come, my dear, you and I are grown people. I know you feel this delicious yearning, as I do, it's in your eyes, if not your actions," he said softly.

They stood on the side of the ballroom, in plain sight of everyone, as music played, and her own husband danced by in the arms of a wallflower he'd taken a host's pity on. Lord Wycoff smiled tenderly, as though he were discussing what a delightful time he'd had, while he told his hostess truths about her secret nighttime desires, and his intent to fulfill them. That wasn't the only thing that made her shake her head in disbelief.

"No," she said sadly, not seeking to deny what she could not, but determined to tell him precisely why she could not act upon such wishes. "No. I am married, and so are you, but it's obviously different for me than it is for you. I could not. I could not."

He smiled tenderly, looking very human and very kind.

"Of course, you could," he said gently. "And you know it, which is why you're so very frightened, isn't it? Because there's nothing else to fear. It would change nothing, but only bring pleasure. I ask for, and give, nothing more. Nor would I ever disclose it, if it were to ever come to pass, anymore than I'd plague you with my earnest desire to make it come to pass. Have you ever heard different of me?"

She shook her head again. She'd made it a point to listen when his name came up, and he was known as a polished, intelligent, decent fellow, very au courant, and very much his own man, despite his popularity. She'd never heard otherwise. For if he made it a habit to stray from his marriage, it was no matter to those of his circle, so long as he did it circumspectly. And he did. She couldn't fault him on that. This was London, and the rules were very different here for man and wife, she was beginning to accept that much at least.

"So I shall only tell you of my admiration and my desire," he went on. "I could make you very happy, my dear. I think you know that. But I see you're not ready. Very well. I'm not going anywhere, and whatever my future entanglements may be, be sure I'll always be ready should you ever decide in my favor. It will only take a look and a nod—or less," he laughed. "You're very lovely, very bright, yet very vulnerable, and that I find very exciting. For I think you'd not hurt me, anymore than I would harm you. And be sure, I can be hurt, incredible as that may seem to you. Oh, Chesham," he said, without a pause, without so much as a blink, as Hugh approached them, "I was just telling your magnificent countess how lovely I find her, and how glad I am that you brought her up out of the wilderness to delight us."

"Hardly the wilderness," Hugh said, "although I understand you London chaps think anyone who lives an hour in any direction from St. James is a farmer. Well, and so I suppose we are," he said on a laugh.

They stood and laughed together, and Rachel looked from one man to the other. In that moment she felt sick with shame and surprise at her shameful

desire, as well as at Hugh, for seeming a fool for not
knowing he was speaking with a man who planned
to cuckhold him, and a wife who suddenly did not
know if she should.

It was hours before she was ready for bed, but the
family stayed up with her for those hours after the
ball. Marjorie was determinedly bright, though her
eyes were too bright, and Felicia and Nigel discussed
every bit of gossip, as Hugh and she sat listening
and laughing. Rachel was never more eager to get
to her bed.

When Nigel had left, and the last servant had put
out the last candle, and dawn stained the sky outside
her bedchamber window, Rachel, beyond exhaustion,
lay wakeful, worrying. And then Hugh came to her,
moving from the darkness of the dressing room like
a partially materialized shadow in the half-dawn
light. He slipped into her bed, took her into his arms,
and kissed her, without a word said. Perhaps that
was why she let herself imagine, for a moment, how
it might be if his hair was longer and silkier beneath
her hands. And how it would be if he were taller, so
that when they embraced, his shoulders were higher
above hers; and how it would feel if he were entirely
different: if he, for example, were not certain to
move his lips from the nipple of her right breast to
her left one for once, as he was now doing, but
rather, from her left to her right instead . . . or . . .
some such.

It was when she realized exactly what the "some
such" she was looking for was, that she froze. He
felt it and stopped. And rolled back from her with
something between a chuckle and a sigh.

"You're right," he said, giving her a kiss on the
forehead before he got up from the bed, smiling

patiently, familiar to her now as her own face in the growing dawn light. "It's a poor time for lovemaking, after all the work you did tonight. Tonight? Rather say, this morning. Lord, look at the day rising! It's Saturday already. And you and I doubtless will have guests calling to congratulate us on our hospitality not hours from now. Get some sleep, sweet. Good night. Or rather, good morning," he said on a chuckle, and left her to her guilt and despair.

Until she realized he was right. It was already Saturday morning. That explained much; it meant that he'd come to her on what he'd thought of as a Friday night. Which made terrible, perfect sense. Because he always liked to make love on a Friday night. And that made her cry until she laughed.

Four days later, when Rachel had finally memorized every word she wanted to say to Marjorie, and several more she knew she ought to say, as well, she came home from an errand to find her entertaining Lord Beauford in the drawing room, by being locked fast in his arms. Before she could catch her breath to say a word, they'd separated and looked at her with open, happy countenances, and not a bit of shame in their eyes. She knew, before they spoke, and rejoiced.

"Ma'am," Lord Beauford said, with no trace of ice in his eyes or voice, "Miss Makepeace has just agreed to marry me, and so although I know I've taken liberties with your hospitality, please don't believe I've taken any with her person, or her honor. Oh," he added as gracelessly as a boy, and looking all the better to her for it, "and yes, my engagement with Miss Peckingham has been severed, this very day. I'm not a rogue, not even fickle, my lady, not anymore, that is to say," he said, smiling at Marjorie, who smiled dazedly back at him, "for my previous engagement was one of long standing, contracted when I was a boy, and I am a man now."

Rachel's delighted smile began to fade and misunderstanding her reaction, Lord Beauford added quickly, "Not that youth excuses any man from folly, but though a lad may know his own mind from an early age, I doubt any but the most extraordinarily mature can know his own heart so soon in life. Now I do. Please believe me, I shall never betray it, or Miss Makepeace—Lady Beauford," he corrected himself, smiling again, looking to Marjorie and forgetting his audience again, more like a boy now that he'd declared his manhood than she'd ever seen him.

Rachel was as happy for them as they'd wish her to be. But though she stayed on with them to bear them company, as chaperon, until Hugh came home, and Felicia and Nigel returned from a visit to his family, she couldn't wait to be away from them. It wasn't so much their radiance, the very aura of love and promise that surrounded them and locked everyone else out, which discomforted her, so much as it was his words about youth and love that she couldn't forget, and couldn't wait to be alone to dissect and remember. For they seemed to her, as she sat nodding and listening to them laughing and planning their future, to be the very essence of truth.

The footman brought two glasses and a bottle of champagne, and then left them. Hugh uncorked the bottle with solemn ceremony, poured out two glasses, and handed one to Rachel. He glanced at the mantel clock, and then, to be certain, took his watch from his fob pocket and studied it. He needn't have bothered. In a moment they heard the first of London's many church bells begin to chime, and soon the night seemed filled with far-off music.

"Ah, a new year," he said, and raised his glass, "Happy New Year, my dear."

"And to you, as well," Rachel said, and raised her glass before she drank her toast down at a swallow, like bitter medicine, as though it were a sovereign remedy for the loss of another year.

"Well, then," he said, and putting down his glass, Hugh bent and kissed her.

Then he sighed and sat in a chair near the fire, as she took an adjoining one. The children had gone out to a gala party, all four of them; the two girls now related in matters of new love as well as family, the two young men, now reconciled and newly friends, bound by mutual expectations.

"You could have gone to your club," Rachel said as she gazed into the fire.

"And leave you? Nonsense, a married fellow stays with his wife on such a night. But you, you could have gone to any number of parties, it seemed to me you were invited to a hundred," he said.

"But I know you don't care for any. Oh, you'd have gone, for you're a good fellow, but you wouldn't have had any pleasure in it," she said. "And I'm . . ." she was about to say "content," but that was not true, or "happy," but neither was that, so after a pause she said only, ". . . better off here at home tonight, I assure you." For that, she thought, was certainly truth.

"Well, yes, it is comfortable here, isn't it?" he said.

They sat by the fire until the clock struck one into the new year. By then, Hugh had taken another two glasses of what he proclaimed to be excellent champagne, and then by mutual agreement, they went to bed. For she was obviously weary, and he couldn't stop yawning. Each went to their separate bed and remained there, for the first time in all the years of their marriage not beginning a new year with lovemaking, their own especial New Year's rite.

They lay awake, each half hoping the other wouldn't remember that singular lapse, each distraught because they couldn't forget it, separated by a dressing room, a new year, and their own thoughts, until the night was finally, blessedly, over.

It was to be a party for Nigel, given by his friends, and only gentlemen had been invited to attend. As he was slated to be wed in a matter of weeks, it was to be a farewell to his bachelorhood, a good-bye to his light fancies, and the sort of ribald commentary he'd be the butt of was not intended for tender, female ears . . . or at least, certain female ears. For some, obviously, were not tender. Nor were those ears their most calloused parts. That could be discerned at a glance.

Not that the females in attendance were not lovely. They were, in fact, far more attractive than the general run of women to be seen in London. But then, too, most women didn't wear so many cosmetics and so little of anything else. Still these women could dress as scantily as they pleased; they didn't have to venture into London's freezing streets in order to get to the party, because it was held in the very house where they lived and worked.

Hugh had never seen the like, though he'd have bitten off his tongue rather than say so. He said very little, in fact, from the moment that the footman accepted his coat, and the proprietress of the house greeted him and showed him to the grand salon where the party was already in full spate. Because he was as shocked as he was surprised, and even more titillated than that.

The house was a grand one, on a decent-looking street. The furnishings weren't in ghastly taste, as he'd been told was the case with the interiors of such houses—indeed, as the interior of the one house he'd patronized, a generation before, had been. Everything in that house had been a poor gaudy display of execrable taste, including the females within it. But it had been stimulating for all that.

This house was as elegant as a duke's, and if the females hadn't been dressed for the stage or a bed, and hadn't been clearly exhibiting the fact that they'd the talents for one and were ready for the other, he'd never have guessed their trade. For old Jeffries, for example: portly, spotty, bald old Jeffries could never have moved that dashing young dark-haired female to take such liberties with his person unless she were a superior actress. And the fact that she was dressed—or rather—almost dressed enough to carry out what she was clearly enticing him to, left no room for doubt in Hugh's mind as to her occupation, despite her beauty and the elegance of the room. And that made the place he found himself within beyond merely stimulating. He was fascinated.

He'd expected Nigel's dinner party to be held in high state, someplace traditional and proper, and had expected to feel out of place among Nigel's merry young friends. He'd anticipated eating overmuch, but had vowed to himself that he'd stay awake during the speeches, and had memorized a brief one to present to the bridegroom in his turn. He'd never anticipated that he'd be asked to a brothel. Or that Nigel would actually countenance such goings-on. But there he stood, at his ease, in the midst of a crowd of well-wishers and jolly young friends, with a glass of champagne in his hand and doubtless, a quip on his lips, to judge from the way his friends were laughing.

There were more than merry young men in this house tonight, Hugh noted, as he looked away from Nigel's party and gazed around the room. He recognized several older gents from his clubs: married, titled, respectable fellows, every one of them. When they saw him, they nodded or smiled, as if they saw nothing untoward in being recognized, or in recognizing him here.

Hugh realized he had to stay, at least for a space. Leaving at once would be rude and might make Nigel uncomfortable, and moreover, he wondered if such a puritan reaction might well not be hypocritical. He frankly didn't know. It would require thought and further study, he decided. Staying overlong, however, he realized, as he saw some of the girls he was eyeing beginning to eye him in turn, would be far more embarrassing. Still, he thought, as he accepted a glass of champagne from a passing footman, still and all . . . it was intriguing.

He watched a pretty little brown-haired creature, as she saw him noting her. She left off twining her fingers around a lock of the gentleman's hair in whose lap she perched, and turned her head to give Hugh a saucy smirk. Petite and shapely, she grinned like a boy, but her brief negligee showed how unlike one she was. He'd a hard time removing his gaze from her upturned breasts with their carmined and pursed nipples that could so clearly be seen beneath the thin

fabric scarcely covering them, but when he succeeded, he looked higher to see she was openly grinning at him. She fancies me, fancy that, he thought,
stirred by the vagrant thought as much as everything
else about her and the situation.

Then he realized, with shockingly sudden clarity,
how simple it all was and could be. To simply glance
across a room, as so many other men were doing,
until one saw a female one wanted. A nod or a smile,
and she'd approach. Then all one had to do was follow
her. To bed. To delight. To a new body, a different
flesh, a woman's body that would offer anything a
man might want, or want to have done to him. Without courting or commitment or a word of denial from
her. An opportunity to be completely intimate and
yet entirely detached. Then one merely paid and left.
No worries as to what she'd thought or felt. And one
never had to see her again. A simple business of
simple pleasures, rare and fine rutting with no
excuses needed, without fuss and doubt. Without
worrying about her rejecting him, or being disappointed, or wondering whether she preferred a different fellow since she didn't want him anymore . . .

Simple, he thought, willing other less simple
thoughts away.

The girl continued to smile, and then whispering
something in the gentleman's ear, she arose from his
lap in one sinuous motion, and began to walk toward
Hugh. And then he realized conjecture might become
reality. And knew it was time to leave.

Because of Nigel, of course, he thought as he
turned and went to find him so he could bid him good
night. It would never do to stay and disport himself
before his son-in-law, like Noah being naked before
his daughters or . . . some such. It was a disastrously

distasteful thought, and killed all his newly sprung guilty desire. But now he knew where the house was, a small voice sniggered in his mind, and so now he'd know where a man could return alone someday, if he wanted to.

As for Nigel—he thought, frowning as he looked about the room and didn't see him, only a hypocrite would condemn him for staying for sport. But he was a father, and so he did. It might be all in the spirit of a groomsman's games, and might be high fashion in Nigel's circles for all he knew, but it was poorly done of him. It was entirely wrong for a man entering a marriage he'd claimed he'd contracted in the spirit of love and trust, he thought, as he went to get his hat and cloak. And refused to think, as another small voice urged him to, of what the difference was between a marriage about to be entered into, and one that had been so contracted years before—aside from those years.

Hugh breathed deep of the iced air as he stood on the steps in front of the house, despite how it chilled all the way down into his chest, feeling cleansed by the cold. Yet he shivered, terribly afraid now for Felicia as well as for himself.

"Good to see you, sir!" Nigel said with relief, as he detached himself from a shadow behind the stair and came to his side, rubbing his gloved hands together. "I thought you'd be here soon, and am glad I was right, another five minutes and I'd have had to hold my mouth to the gaslight to thaw it enough to open it to speak."

But what if I hadn't come for an hour? Hugh thought with a panicky relief for his good sense, should you ever have been able to speak to me again, at all?

"Some of my friends are fools," Nigel said, falling into step with his prospective father-in-law as they went down the street in search of a hackney, it being too cold to wait for one. "Although, I'll grant, a few years past—nay, only so far past as before I'd met Felicia, I'd have thought it good sport. I suppose it was, until I realized the act was merely physical exercise without that spark of mutual concern to make it something of mind and heart, as well as body. Not that I've experienced anything like it yet, sir," he said hastily. "Only that so I see it now, and so I expect it should be."

When he noted how silent Hugh was as they trudged along against the wind—for every direction seemed against the wind this bitter night—he added quietly, "I hope I'm not speaking too broad, sir, but I do, if only because you know my history very well—alas, the world does, does it not? And I want you to be sure it is all history. I'd no idea of what the surprise was in store for me tonight when my companions came to call for me. When I realized where we were bound, and for what purposes, and that the idiots had sent out invitations, and one to you as well, I went, only to say thank you, like a good boy. And to find you, and discover myself to you. I'd no desire to stay. That's all behind me now. I want more of life: I want love, for I perceive that what fools call the act of love is nothing like, without actual love.

"Mind," he added as they walked on, laughter in his voice, as Hugh remembered he never could remain serious very long, "I'm not saying it was ever boring, precisely. But lonely, oh yes," he said in a suddenly sad voice. "Yes, for all it was anything else, it was always lonely, at the heart of it. For it had none, do you see?"

"I do," Hugh said at last, for he did. And yet he wondered if that was really entirely necessary—for some men, in some circumstances. And because of that, he spoke up at once, so as not to think about it.

"I never doubted you, lad. Well, I suppose I did. You gave me a hard moment there. Felicia's our life, you know, and I wouldn't want to hand her over to anyone who thought less. You made me happy tonight, and so I suppose it was all worthwhile, else how would I have known the truth, unless I saw it in action? Or inaction," he said, with a sidewise glance to Nigel, making him laugh.

"The other thing it showed me," he went on, "is that I'm far too rustic for all the rigs and runs of the *ton* in London town. I'm provincial, lad, and no disguising it. I think it best that I be off on my way home—my new home in the country—as soon as I see you tie the knot. I've things to do there, a great deal of work, yes, yes a great deal, to be sure, what with learning the new land and managing the place," he said, realizing it was so, and realizing with enormous relief that moreover, he'd enough work to keep him out of mischief there.

"I think that's the right decision, sir," Nigel said.

There was something in his voice that made Hugh stare at him. But the night was so dark, and his eyes watering so from the cold that he could see nothing in Nigel's face but politeness. He was, in that moment, both glad and shamed for his temporary blindness.

*   *   *

There was no longer any sense to it. There was no more joy than point to any of it, she thought. This Season, this introduction to the *ton*, was causing far more pain than pleasure. And the thought of the pleasure it might yet bring only brought more pain. The new Countess of Chesham sat high in her box at the theater as the play went on—or was it the farce?—she no longer knew or cared. Because the continuing play in her own mind was far more absorbing, and she feared for the outcome of it. She couldn't see how it could be more than a farce or less than a tragedy, for she could see no happy ending to it, however much she might enjoy it in due course.

She sat with her family, in a box in the first tier. And he, of course, with the same persistent irony that had marked this adventure from the start, sat in the next box, faced toward the stage and her. So that she knew his eyes were always upon her, as they'd been all these past weeks wherever and whenever they'd met, while all the rest in the theater thought him absorbed in the play. If they'd watched more closely, they'd have known better. For the play that was being presented tonight could never be responsible for the expressions she'd caught on his face whenever she'd dared to look. No, this poor offering tonight couldn't account for the solemn awareness, the sympathetic smile, the acute longing, and then the sadness that crossed over his usually calm and amused countenance when he saw her gazing at him.

Hathaway, Lord Wycoff. She'd learned his Christian name was Hathaway. Too formal for her, it suited him exactly, she thought, but she couldn't bring herself to call him that even in the intimacy of her own thoughts. She'd tried a shortened version of it in the night, in her bed, alone with the dark exciting thoughts of him she harbored. She'd said it soft, intoning it to the empty night, as a young girl with her first infatuation might do so as to conjure the image of her first love there before her. It came out as a sigh: "Hath." Silly, really. But the whole of it was more than madness. "Hath-." Not so different from "Hugh." Entirely different from Hugh.

How handsome Hugh looked tonight, she thought. His hair was a bit longer than it had been at home, in deference to the London fashion. His new clothes fit to perfection, he no longer looked so much the hearty country squire as he did a tanned and healthy sportsman: a noble gentleman given to pursuits of the turf, the chase and the road, as they were pleased to call men of his cut. She'd noted other women glancing at him as they'd entered the theater, and could scarcely blame them. How very handsome he looked tonight, Rachel thought admiringly, even as she felt another man's eyes upon her. And realizing that, she couldn't look at him any longer.

She longed for someone to talk to about it as much as she longed for the man of her infatuation, and to be free of the thought of him. Discussing a thing, the very shaping of it into words, would bring it to its proper shape and size. If she could speak of this, she knew she could see it clear. But she was alone here in this great city—she could scarcely talk to Felicia about such a thing, nor could she write about it to her friends at home—and she knew that even were she at home, she couldn't bring herself to say such things to them. And she'd lost her best friend sometime past. There was only one person she could discuss it with, and she had to steel herself to do it. She must.

Hugh sat and watched the play. It was as amusing as it was dreadful. He scarcely knew whether to laugh or cry. It seemed each time she looked to the gentleman, she flushed, bit her lip, or glanced away. And it seemed she couldn't keep her eyes from him for more than a moment or two together all night. Nor could he keep his gaze from her. The most amusing thing of it was that they didn't seem to know he could see it, had seen it from the first, though he'd not admitted it to himself then. The most tragic thing was that he couldn't stop watching. He never noticed a moment of the play on stage.

It wasn't the first time a woman had desired a man who wasn't her husband. Wasn't that what this very farce tonight was about? And indeed, the way she looked these days—the way she'd always looked, he realized—it was scarcely surprising that even the jaded Lord Wycoff couldn't keep his eyes from her. It was, in a sense, a form of divine retribution that she should seek something in another man's glance now, so soon after he himself had imagined seeking far more in far less of a woman's arms. But "imagined," that was the key, Hugh thought, how much was she imagining and how much would she seek to make reality? If she hadn't already? And how could he bear it if she did, no matter how he deserved it?

He doubted she'd betray him. But that was then. He didn't know her any more than he knew himself these days. Should he challenge the fellow? He was good with a pistol as well as his fists, and didn't mind even death if it would preserve his honor—or hers. But what should he challenge the fellow for—

longing? Or having acted upon that longing? Ought he to accuse him? How could he? How could he not? It was more than his pride. His whole soul hurt, and he didn't know how to heal it, or if it could be healed.

He no longer knew what to do. That was unlike him, but he'd never been in such a situation before. If he could discuss it with someone he trusted, someone whose advice he respected . . . but who could he speak with about such things? It had taken him this long to admit it even to himself. He couldn't voice it to another soul, not even the vicar at home—he'd his pride. Nor any gent at his club, nor man at home, nor any woman he knew. But one he'd known—yes, certainly. Ah, but she was never further from him than she was tonight. He sighed.

"You're right," Felicia said in a low voice, hearing him, "it's a dreadful play. But see, it has Mama close to tears."

"Very sentimental is your mama," Hugh said.

"Mama? Weeping for this foolish play?" Felicia scoffed, and giggled.

"Hush," Nigel cautioned softly, warningly, "and watch the stage."

Rachel had never been in such an aggressively masculine room before. It was dark, heavy, and bold. The furniture was thick and wooden, the draperies dense and velvet, the bed itself a massive thing ornamented with spires. It didn't seem to suit its occupant, not at least, what she'd thought he was. But how should she know the secrets of a man's heart? Recent experience had taught her she knew little of her own. And some men, she'd begun to fear might have hearts that peeled away in layers like onion skins, to reveal nothing at the heart at all.

It was an unrelentingly male room, nothing alleviated the stress it put on gender, except for herself. And she felt alien as well as insubstantial, threatened, and out of place here. But she forced herself to walk further into the bedchamber, although she dreaded the outcome. Still, she went on, she knew what she must do if she were ever to know an end to this longing, or a semblance of peace with herself again.

"Rachel?" he asked from the dark, his voice raw, but alert, no trace of sleep in it.

"Yes," she said and stopped, made unsure by that strange note in his voice, no longer so sure of what to do or say.

"Come," he said simply, patting the bed as he raised himself and putting a pillow behind his back as he sat up, "come, sit, and talk awhile with me."

He slept without a nightshirt, and she was glad of the darkness, unbroken save for firelight. But nevertheless, she looked away from him as she stepped up to the bed and sat beside him. For he was never more of a stranger to her than he was tonight.

"You're troubled," he said.

"Yes," she said, no longer able to deny him anything.

"As am I," he said on a sigh and took her hand. Only that.

"You?" she asked, amazed, staring at him, trying to see his expression.

"You think I don't know?" he said sadly, and held her hand as she turned her head. "I knew from the first, I can feel your feelings by now," he said quietly. "I know what delights you as well as what frightens you. And you feel both of these things now, don't you?"

She couldn't answer.

"Well, and what are we to do now, do you think?" Hugh asked on a sigh.

"I don't want to do anything," she protested.

"Oh Rachel, Rachel," he said, "please, I know what you want."

"Do you?" she asked bitterly, the words torn from her by anger and guilt. "Once, perhaps. But now? We came to London, and we came apart, didn't we? Almost at once. First separate rooms, then separate thoughts, separate beds: separate lives come naturally after. You've your clubs and your new friends. Perhaps even your mistresses, how should I know?"

"You should know," he said sadly. "*That* you should know. I'd never betray you."

"Would you not? Never?" she asked, and he grew still, for he knew she knew him very well, too.

"I have not betrayed you," she said.

"Shall you?" he asked, and his hand tightened on hers, though his voice didn't change. "A foolish question to ask some wives, I know. But I think one I can ask you. One I must ask you, as well as another— Do you want me to leave you here in London? I've decided to go, you see," he said, "after the wedding. Four Chimneys needs me. It's a new life, there are new responsibilities I should not shirk. And temptations, I will grant you, that I should. For my own honor, if not yours. But I'll not have an unwilling wife. Or an unhappy one. But mind," he said in a toneless voice, "neither will I have an unfaithful one. If you wish to remain, you may. As you may leave me, if you wish. But understand, please, you may not come back to me if you do. There are some things

I cannot forgive. I'm not a Londoner, nor am I sophisticated, nor can I share you, no. There would be some things I could not forget."

"Ah," she said in a choked voice, "I see. Honor. Possessiveness. Tradition. How would it look? 'What I have, I hold.' I understand. You're quite right."

"Do you love him?" he asked dully.

"No," she said. "Not at all."

"I think," he said, "you had better go now. Now. Because if you do not," he said quietly, "I may well kill you. Please leave me."

She rose slowly, pausing only when she heard his voice again.

"How did it happen, do you think?" he asked, as if asking himself.

"I don't know," she said, shrugging her shoulders, although she knew he couldn't see her or her tears in the dark. "Perhaps, when we went our separate ways. For me, I think, when you took to your new room as though it were a gift from Heaven, being free of me except for lovemaking. I thought it amusing, maybe even exciting, freedom always is at first. But not for very long after."

She could almost hear his stillness.

"You never asked me to remain," he said.

"You ought to have known," she answered, and began to move away, only to find that he still held her hand, hard.

"How?" he asked. "You never had time to speak to me. You seemed pleased with the arrangement. I'll admit I was, too, at first, because it was a novelty. An almost stealthy thing. Odd, how stealth enhances such things as the marriage bed, even after a lifetime of openness there. But then, when I grew weary of it, I thought perhaps you'd grown weary of me as well, because you never asked me to stay. And you would have if you'd wanted me enough. That much, I know. For I know you very well, Rachel, and not at all, either. I don't know how that came about, but there it is.

"Rachel," he said when she didn't answer, and he heard the gulping sobs that she made when she tried to stop her tears; remembering how she'd always hated to cry, even when she'd been tiny, perhaps because he'd grown disgusted with her for it then: refusing to play with a 'bawling baby.'

"Rachel," he said, remembering all those years, those thwarted tears that came only when her control was worn down by utmost extremities, "I have loved you. Faithfully, but perhaps not too well, for I'm not a smooth fellow and never was. Perhaps too steadfastly, too. Because I see now that a lifetime with one lover makes one careless of love. But always, that I vow. I still do," he said, and fell still, dismayed with himself because he'd said too much and too little, and could not go on.

She didn't answer him. She only turned and stumbled back to him, as his hand pulled her, and she fell into his arms where he held her fast. She lay against his chest and wept, and he stroked her hair, and now and then, reached up a hand to wipe his own tears as stealthily as possible, for a man never cried, and it would shame him if she saw what she knew.

"Hugh," she finally said, drawing away from him so that he could hear her clear, though her voice was glutted with tears. "Hugh," she said, and sniffled, "I don't want to leave you. What you said is true of me, too. I love you. But I want to be desired, I need to be needed, and I thought you were tired of me . . .

perhaps, I wanted to think so. What an odd thing to say to one's husband," she mused as she surreptitiously wiped her nose on the back of her hand as she'd done when she was a little girl, and he was glad of a chance to grin in the dark. "But there you are," she went on, "I speak to you as I would to myself. You are myself now. Hugh," she said with an air of great discovery, "perhaps that's why I wandered—if only in my thoughts—because it's very frightening."

"To be with someone so long?" he asked, knowing the feeling very well, "so long that it makes one feel old, when all the world seems young?"

"No," she said, frowning, trying to frame the enormous new notion that had come to her in words so she herself could understand it better. "No, not just that. Because . . . because I think, of realizing what a loss it would be if I lost you—like losing part of myself, I think. And perhaps," she said, pinning an even more elusive thought, her eyes widening, "perhaps that's why I tried to lose you now, by my own doings, or exaggerating yours, so that I wouldn't be destroyed if I lost you later . . . here, to London, or eventually even—to life. It takes more than love, I think, after a while, it takes great courage to love someone that much. Do you see?"

"Yes. That's so," he said after a long moment. "I see. As always, as you do, Rachel, my love. I won't ask if you've that courage, I know you do. Only, do you think I deserve it? I pray you do," he said, hoping he knew her answer.

"I will not leave you," she said fiercely. "It's only that I was frightened and lonely, whoever it was who made me so. And I will kill you if you leave me again, or let me leave you," she vowed.

"Please do," he said against her lips, "for it would mean I'd lost my mind, not my heart. I've been a foolish old man, young woman."

"Idiot, idiot, idiot," she murmured against his mouth. Which was a foolish way to begin lovemaking. But since it led to such rapturous conclusions, neither mentioned it. Or anything else but their oldest pleasure made new now by how nearly they'd come to losing it forever. They touched, clung, and tasted in every way they knew the other loved, and by so doing loved expertly, with new passion, in all the old ways. But even so, he discovered something new: that novelty stirred the appetite, but nothing but love could feed his deepest desires. And she: that he needed her fully as much as she did him, which was to say, as much as a woman could be needed. And that was enough, as always, for her.

The wedding would be the talk of the town for at least a week, which was considerable in the rarified circles the talk would be wafted in. Everyone was there. And those who were not would pretend they had been, since there were so many at the church, and so many more at the house afterward for the wedding breakfast that those that hadn't been invited could say they'd been there in the certain knowledge that no one would be able to prove them wrong.

The bride was radiantly beautiful, young, titled, and rich, such an appealing and unusual combination as to make the company sigh with pleasure at its own excellent standards. The groom was titled, attractive, wealthy, and wise, and as anxious as he was nervous, which made the company smile with wicked delight to see the table so turned upon him. The

bride's parents were uncommonly handsome and
even more uncommonly, evidently as in love with
each other as the young couple were—and if a certain
person in the company wanted to weep to see it, he
was too honestly astonished at such a strange new
emotion, as well as far too facile, to ever reveal it to
anyone but himself.

It was only as the guests were busily stuffing
themselves with breakfast and gossip, and the bride
was changing to her traveling clothes, that her mama
had a moment alone with her. The maid of honor,
Miss Marjorie Makepeace, was already in the
deserted library, closed in an embrace with her
fiancé, Lord Beauford, as they were whenever they
could manage a minute alone together, for their own
wedding was more than a month away. The matron
of honor, the svelte Viscountess Clifford, was in
another chamber, nursing her new son, while her
doting husband, Euan, looked on adoringly. The
groomsman, his old schoolmate, Nicodemus Brand,
Earl of Fairlie, newly come from a long respite in
some distant land, was, with his new wife Bronwen,
saying farewell to Nigel. He'd some excuse of an
urgent appointment, although no doubt, as his eyes
had revealed all through the ceremony, he was only
desirous of keeping that appointment with his new
wife, alone, and as soon as possible. To be sure, they
were all interesting persons and delightful guests,
but Rachel was glad of the opportunity for a last
minute conference with her daughter.

After sending the maid away, Rachel helped Felicia with the last of the buttons on her dress.

"There are a few things I think I ought to say,"
Rachel said. And watching Felicia's reflection beginning to grin in the glass she was looking into, she

said hurriedly, "No, nothing to do with the marriage bed, I assure you. We covered that fairly completely years ago, I believe."

"Oh you did!" Felicia said merrily. "A most enlightened Mama, even Nigel says so. But do you remember the look on Mrs. Carroll's face when she told you what Elizabeth said after I'd set her straight? 'Mrs. Carstairs!' " Felicia repeated in high, aggrieved tones. " 'Imagine my horr-roar when *my* innocent Elizabeth said *your* daughter told her that the only way a gel could get babies from cabbage leaves was if she lay atop them with a fellow whilst begetting them!' "

Felicia laughed as Rachel colored, and said, "Well, how was I to know you'd start a ministry of truth? At any rate, I shouldn't presume to talk about that now, and not only for that reason. For what Nigel doesn't know about that sort of thing is something I'm not sure I'd want to know! All you have to remember," she said gently, as Felicia giggled, "is to love him before, during, and after anything you do together, and as I know you do and will, I've no fears on that head.

"Still, love is the very thing I want to discuss with you," Rachel said seriously. "Come, sit a moment with me. For this is important, so important, I wish someone had said such things to me on my wedding day."

Felicia looked at her mother curiously, then obediently came to sit beside her, and held her hand.

"Love isn't just all those admittedly marvelous goings-on in the marriage bed," Rachel said. "—and let me assure you again, it is marvelous for ladies as well as gentlemen, no matter what Nice Nellies are implying these days. But as I'm sure you've heard, it can also be marvelous for a great many people without love, too. No, love isn't just blanket doings. It would be far simpler if it were. And I'm sorry to say, on this your happiest day, that love isn't always very wonderful either. Sometimes," Rachel said sadly, as she gazed at her daughter, "it's about the worst thing I can think of. That's the best, and the worst part of it."

Felicia looked at her mother apprehensively, and held her hand tight.

"The thing of it is," Rachel said, stumbling over the words that had come so smoothly to her in the night as she'd lain half-asleep, warm and comfortable against Hugh's side, "that you'll never again be as happy as you are today. But . . ." she said quickly as she saw Felicia grow pale, "you may well be happier, sometimes. Only it will never be quite the same— never—not two months in a row. But that will mean that it's precisely right.

"No, don't look at me so," she laughed, "as if I'd lost my wits. Bear with me, for I've only just found them. Love's a living thing, if it's right, and so like all living things, it must change. The only things that do not, are dead. Even—even the living year," she said with sudden inspiration, "is a thing of constant change. And so it must be. Spring's delightful, but it must become summer. And summer winter, and then on again, do you see?

"So it follows," she said carefully, "that like the changing seasons of the year, sometimes you'll find love is unpleasant: oppressive, hot, and tedious. Bear with it, it will change. Sometimes it's so cold, you'll think you'll freeze to death in his arms—stay with him, it will change, if your love is still alive. And you must try to keep it so, in all weathers, despite the storms and dry seasons. As he must. It's easy to always seek new love, nothing's simpler: everyone loves first love. Anyone may enjoy it, too, that is why so many repeatedly do, I suspect. But few know the joys of old love, of one that has turned with the seasons and lasted a lifetime.

"I wish you that sort of love with your Nigel," Rachel said gently, smiling at her daughter. "The sort I've had, and hope to continue to have, with your father. Although, I'll confess, not very long since, I'd have wished you a love that was eternally spring. But I've changed, too," she said on a growing smile, "and now know I cannot wish you any such thing, for it doesn't exist. And should not."

Felicia smiled, though there were tears in her eyes, "Oh Mama," she said impulsively, "I'm so glad. Nigel said I oughtn't to worry . . . and I'd hopes when I saw you two these last days . . . but it's all worked out, hasn't it? I mean, with you and Papa?"

"Nigel," Rachel said a bit tersely, both embarrassed and pleased that her son-in-law had had the wit to see the problem, and the faith to predict its outcome, "is too clever by half. But it's true. That's why I wanted to talk to you. For no one ever told me that, I had to discover it for myself."

"But it doesn't matter," Felicia said happily. "Dear goose. Don't you see? You had to learn it for yourself. As I shall. Or so I do hope," she said, kissing her mama on the cheek.

"Nigel," Rachel said mistily, "is lucky beyond his desserts."

"Oh never, Mama," Felicia said earnestly. "It is I who am the lucky one."

"Good," Rachel said, rising and helping her daughter into her pelisse, for though it was early spring, it was a chilly day, "that will do for a start, my love."

The newlywed couple were snug in their coach, in each other's arms, on their way to their manor house, giggling because all the world thought they were bound for someplace far more distant and exotic.

"As if I'd have eyes for anything except you this coming fortnight," Nigel, Lord Neville, told his bride. "In fact, I wonder if I'll ever be able to see anything else but you wherever I go, so I wonder if there's any point to my ever traveling again," he said musingly.

"Ah, how unhandsome of you, to use flattery to cheat me out of all your fine promises," his bride said with spirit, before she added more seriously, "Of course, you will, Mama said . . ."

She was interrupted by a groan.

"I adore your mama," Nigel said with mock despair, "but shall I have a life filled with 'Mama said'?"

"Of course," she answered, "for that's precisely what she and Papa say about 'Nigel says . . .' At any rate, Mama said—hush, lout—Mama says that there'll be times when we'll positively detest each other, and that will be quite all right."

"I doubt that's what she said," he laughed. "Likely she said very much the same as your father told me before we left. Things to do with expecting change and accepting it, for however bad it looks, it will bring good, as change always does if you ride with it. It does seem that they have mended fences, and I'm happy for them, but love of mine, we've our own discoveries to make, and I cannot wait to get on with them so that we, too, can be founts of wisdom on our unfortunate childrens' wedding days. What's this?"

he asked languorously, against her lips, as he felt a bit of paper crackle beneath his hand, and drew it from a pocket at her breast.

"Something Mama gave me as we left," she sighed.

"More advice," he said as he dispensed with her coat utterly, "since I doubt it's a shopping list. We'll get to it later."

"Nigel," she said breathlessly, "if we keep up with this, we may get to a great many things sooner than I thought."

"Oh, you've a great deal to learn, thank heavens," he said with a wicked leer. "The first being that anticipation can in itself be an act of love. Never fear, I'll be a traditional husband tonight, and you a most traditional bride, due to my enormous sensitivity— and a lively fear of your father—and now, when it's entirely legal and moral, a distaste for initiating such a delightful thing in a jouncing coach—for who knows what things can go awry with all this joggling about? Well, I do, even if you don't—or at least, aren't supposed to," he said, grinning. "Ah, but let me teach you something further along the lines of anticipation . . . if I can manage to control myself better than the coachman's managing his team—and that wouldn't be difficult—or would it? . . . Stop that, or rather, don't stop that, you delicious wretch," he said, and she laughed, before she sighed again, and he let the bit of paper flutter from his hand, which was far more pleasantly occupied.

When he retrieved the paper later, he was puzzled, but Felicia only smiled. For it was only a few lines of a verse by an obscure Elizabethan poet that her mama had scratched out for her. But it pleased her very much. So much so, that she copied it over in a neat hand, and eventually did it over again in needlepoint for a pillow for the nursery as she awaited their third child. Because it was as simple as a nursery rhyme, and yet the years that had passed since she'd gotten it had taught her it was very wise, withal:

"There is no season such delight can bring,
As summer, autumn, winter, and the spring."